Fetching Captain Henry

Also by Robert J. Shade

The Forbes Road Series:

Forbes Road

Conestoga Winter

The Camp Follower Affair

Lord Dunmore's Folly

The Rebellion Road Series:

Pursuit Through Chaos

Flight From Bonniecrest Manor

Freedom At Gwynn's Island

Fetching Captain Henry

A Rebellion Road Novel

Robert J. Shade

Sunshine Hill Press

Sunshine Hill Press, LLC
2937 Novum Road
Reva, VA 22735

ISBN: 979-8-218-36418-2

Artwork with specific permission:
Front cover: *First Honors: Order of the Purple Heart* by
Pamela Patrick White
(www.whitehistoricart.com)

Major Characters

Historical

George Washington	Lieutenant general commanding Continental Army
Martha Washington	Wife of George Washington
Alexander Hamilton	Lieutenant colonel, Continental Army general staff
Patrick Henry	Governor of Virginia
Dorothea Dandridge Henry	Patrick's wife, first lady of Virginia
John Henry	Captain, Continental Army Artillery, eldest son of Patrick
William Howe	General commanding British Army in America
Henry Clinton	Lieutenant general relieving Howe
John Andre	Major on British general staff
Thomas Stirling	Colonel commandant of 42nd Foot (Black Watch)
Banastre Tarleton	Captain, 16th Light Dragoons
Elizabeth Loring	"Friend" of William Howe

Fictional

Wend Eckert	Major commandant of the Legion of Continental Guides
Warren Bradley	Captain, Anne Arundell Light Horse Troop
Geoffrey Fairfield	Captain, 1st Troop Palmetto Light Horse
Reese Newkirk	Captain, Frederick County (Virginia) Light Foot Company
Shay O'beirne	First Lieutenant, Frederick County Light Foot Company
Edward Childers	Third Lieutenant, Frederick County Light Foot Company, adjutant of the Continental Guides
Simon Donegal	Sergeant major of the Continental Guides
"Quinn"	Senior sergeant, 1st Troop Palmetto Light Horse
Colleen Allison McGraw	Proprietor of Red Vixen Sutler Company
Mary Fraser	Matron of the hospital, 42nd Foot (Black Watch), seconded to British Army general hospital
Charles McDonald	Major, 42nd Foot (Black Watch)
Barrett Penfold Northcutt	Colonel, Kings Loyal Virginia Legion, seconded to British general staff
George Markwood	Captain, Kings Loyal Virginia Legion, seconded to British general staff
Emma Wilbourne	Daughter of prominent Tidewater family
Samuel Crowder	Spymaster in Washington's espionage web in New Jersey
Nell Porter	Tavern maid, agent working for Crowder
"Harkness"	Loyalist spymaster working for Barrett Northcutt

Contents

Major Characters v

Chapter One	The Governor's Letter	1
Chapter Two	Jersey Country	35
Chapter Three	The Lodger	71
Chapter Four	Blood in the Night	103
Chapter Five	The Response	135
Chapter Six	Millstone River	163
Chapter Seven	Duel at the Ford	195
Chapter Eight	Washington's Order	229
Chapter Nine	Complications on the Road	259
Chapter Ten	Decisions	287
Chapter Eleven	Difficult Transitions	309
Chapter Twelve	A Time for Campaigning	337
Chapter Thirteen	On the Move	365

Author's Historical Notes 391

Acknowledgments 411

Chapter One
The Governor's Letter

The senior officers of the Legion of Continental Guides, which most people in the army simply called "Washington's Guides," or just "the Guides," left their camp near the army headquarters in a group and strode eastward along the road that ran through the encampment of Valley Forge. The April sun warmed them as they walked, and signs of spring were all around them.

Major Wend Eckert, commandant of the Guides, a stone-faced man in his early thirties of medium height, dark hair, and lean build, led the way. He wore a blue-coated uniform with red facings, which denoted that he was of the Virginia Line. Beside him, dressed in a similar uniform, walked Captain Reese Newkirk, commandant of the company known as the Frederick County Light Foot, which made up the core of the legion. Newkirk was tall and as lean as Eckert, with a horse face and a perpetually serious countenance. Behind the two Virginia officers walked a pair of men in cavalry uniforms. The taller of the two, gray-coated Captain Geoffrey Fairfield, was leader of the First Troop of the Palmetto Light Horse from South Carolina. He was a youthful-looking man, tall and razor thin, with nary an extra pound on his body and with a handsome face and beguiling smile that attracted the eyes of virtually every lady in a room when he entered. Only lines around his eyes betrayed that he was older than his looks. The other cavalryman, Captain Warren Bradley of Maryland's Anne Arundel Troop of Light Dragoons, was in his mid-thirties, with startling blue eyes, high cheekbones and blond hair. He had the look of gentry all over him and was elegantly uniformed in an impeccably tailored light-blue shell jacket, white breeches, and highly polished black leather riding boots.

The four were headed toward the headquarters of the army's quartermaster, General Nathaniel Greene, located in a stone house at the eastward perimeter of the encampment. On either side of the dirt road were rows of huts sheltering the men of various regiments, many with smoke wafting out of the chimneys. En route they came to a wide parade ground, where a Pennsylvania battalion was at drill. At the moment, the unit, to the cadence of drums, was carrying out the essential and difficult evolution of deploying into a two-man-deep line of battle from marching in a column of fours. Wend halted his group, and they stood watching with critical eyes as the unit performed the drill.

After a moment, Bradley said, "Amazing how far the army has come since January. Look at how they march. Von Steuben has done wonders." He motioned toward the German volunteer officer, who stood observing the drill at the side of the parade ground with a cluster of staff officers surrounding him.

Reese Newkirk spoke up. "Donegal says our line battalions can now march and maneuver in the field as well as any he's seen in the British Army." He thought a second. "Maybe now Von Steuben will release him from his temporary role as a drillmaster, so that he can resume his duties as our own sergeant major."

Wend nodded. "Pray you are right. We've missed him. And with the new campaign about to begin, it's essential he returns to us. It will be our duty to be the first into the field." He mused a moment. "I'll stop by Von Steuben's headquarters and pose the question to him."

Fairfield laughed. "Anyway, you are always welcome there. You're one of the few officers in the army who can converse with him in his own language."

Wend uttered a small laugh. "That's true enough, but actually, on one occasion after a few drinks, he confided to me that he thinks my German is rather coarse." Wend shrugged. "I replied, 'General, my family were Jaegers and mechanics, not gentry. What do you expect?' and he just laughed and offered me another drink." Wend shrugged. "He calls me his American Hessian."

Bradley, the Marylander, said, "Well, I'd say that's quite accurate. As you've mentioned to me, your family *is* from Hesse-Cassel." Then he pointed to the drilling battalion, which by now was in line of battle. "They not only drill well; they look very military in those new uniforms."

"Indeed," responded Wend. "We've come a long way since December, when most of the regiments were in rags and desperate for food." He pointed eastward toward a stone house in the distance. "We can thank Greene for the food we eat and the clothing and other supplies that have been flowing in since January. Washington made a brilliant move by putting him in charge of quartermaster matters." He made a tight smile. "He was a businessman before the war and stands for no nonsense in procuring and moving material. And no one thinks he's lining his pockets from the job. If anything, he's using his own money when the necessity arises."

Fairfield smiled broadly. "And I'll attest that his planning for foraging raids has been excellent. We've cleaned the farmers out over a broad area in eastern Pennsylvania and Southern New Jersey."

Bradley agreed. "Yes, we've become quite adept at official thievery."

Wend shrugged. "Well, the local farmers may hate us, but at least the army became well fed after Greene took over."

Newkirk spoke up. "Speaking of foraging, is that what this meeting is going to be about? Are we going out again for another sweep?"

Wend shook his head in puzzlement. "I have no idea why he called us to his headquarters. I was of the understanding that Greene had gotten the supply lines from central and western Pennsylvania working well enough to preclude the need for any more local foraging. And in any case, the farms hereabout are quite picked out." He shrugged and added, "We'll just have to see what's on his mind." He turned and resumed walking toward the general's headquarters, and the others followed.

Presently they arrived at the stone house that served as Greene's headquarters. It was surrounded by tents and temporary huts used by his staff. Wend led his officers up the front stairs and into the hall, where Captain Goodwin, the general's military secretary sat at a table.

Goodwin looked up and said, "Good, you're here! Go ahead and take seats in the dining room, and I'll tell the general of your arrival."

The four went into the dining room, which doubled as a meeting room, and took seats at the table, just as they had done many times before. Maps of eastern Pennsylvania and New Jersey were tacked to the walls. They were just in their chairs when there was the sound of a female descending the stairs, and then, with a bustling of skirts and petticoats, Caty Greene swept into the room in her usual dramatic fashion. Wend was reminded how her style was reminiscent of Peggy, his own wife. In her midtwenties, with a handsome countenance, flashing eyes, and petite figure, Caty was coquettish and fun loving. She had been the spark of the officers' social circuit in Valley Forge over the winter. All the officers rose to their feet.

With a broad smile on her face, Caty greeted each of them by name.

Then she exclaimed, "Well, gentlemen, sadly, I've come to say *goodbye.* The general has dictated that it's time for me to leave, in view of the impending campaign." She swept her hand in a manner taking in all the officers and continued, "I have so enjoyed my time here in this camp. And I shall miss no one more than the officers of the Guides." She raised a finger and looked at Wend. "Major Eckert, you must promise to say goodbye for me to that dashing Lieutenant O'beirne and tell him how much I have enjoyed dancing with him at entertainments. And also to speak for me to your adjutant, young Lieutenant Childers."

Fairfield spoke up, feigning disappointment, but with a smile on his face. "Why Mrs. Greene, I thought it was me who was your favorite partner?"

"Geoffrey, you are my *other* favorite." She made a coy smile. "It is quite possible to have more than one favorite."

The officers laughed, and Wend said, "It will be my pleasure to convey your compliments to Lieutenants O'beirne and Childers. Are you leaving very soon?"

"I'm nearly all packed, and the general is arranging transportation for me."

Bradley said solemnly, "You're not going back to Rhode Island, are you? The British and loyalist parties are all over New York and the country along the way."

"Oh, no, Warren! I wouldn't think of it. And be assured, I wouldn't go that far from the general in any case. No, I'm just going as far as York, where Congress is meeting. I have many acquaintances among the representatives, and I'll be staying with friends."

Fairfield said, "Well, rest assured, Mrs. Greene, we shall all miss your lovely and bright presence and all the parties that you have so graciously hosted for the officers."

Caty laughed. "Geoffrey, you southerners are so gallant! Well, in truth, I shan't desert you for long. The general will be less than delighted, but if there are any lulls in the campaign, as there always are, I intend to jump into my carriage and rejoin the army in the field. I am of the opinion that a general's wife should be with him as much as possible." She grinned mischievously. "And I confide, I do so enjoy being with the army!"

At that moment, Greene's adjutant general, Colonel Jared Holcomb, entered the room and announced, "Gentlemen, the general!"

All the officers turned toward the door, and Greene appeared momentarily. Wend, not for the first time, was taken by the striking contrast between the general and Mrs. Greene. He was more than a decade older than Caty and tended toward baldness and corpulence, with a quite visible double chin and a permanent limp from an accident early in life. By far the greatest contrast was in their personalities, for while Caty was gregarious and flirty, her husband invariably presented a thoughtful countenance and displayed a definite reticence on social occasions.

Greene smiled at his wife. "I see that Mrs. Greene is entertaining the officers of the Guides."

Caty responded cheerfully, "We've been having a nice chat, Nathaniel." She turned to Wend. "But I can see from his eyes that the general has serious matters on his mind. So I'll take my leave now." She turned to go. "But I will see you all after the campaign, if not before!" And with that she left the room, and momentarily they could hear her ascending the stairs.

Without preamble Greene waved to the table and said, "Take your seats, gentlemen." Greene remained standing, and once the Guides officers and Holcomb had done so, he continued, "Without a doubt, I am sure you are wondering why we are here." He motioned toward a map of the area around Valley Forge. "Well, we're going to mount another, and most likely our final, forage sweep. Starting tomorrow."

Wend was puzzled. "Sir, may I speak?"

Greene raised an eyebrow but nodded.

Clearing his throat, Wend said, "Sir, I was of the impression that the wagon convoys from the west were providing adequate supplies and that our foraging ventures were no longer required." He pointed toward the map. "And in any case, we have pretty much scoured the farms for anything useful. In addition, of course, to raising the ire of the farmers themselves."

Greene nodded. "You are absolutely correct, Major Eckert. We have drained them of cattle, hogs, vegetables, grain, and fodder for horses. But this time we are going for something different. This time we're going after the horses."

All the officers stiffened. Wend said, "With respect, sir, the anger of the farmers will be beyond anything we have yet seen. The horses are their livelihood."

Greene nodded. "You are absolutely correct. But the army has a critical problem. The cavalry brigade has an urgent need for horses. They have never had enough mounts, and this winter has been particularly hard on them. Many of the troopers are on foot. So Washington has ordered for us to requisition all the suitable horses we can find." He raised a finger. "That means all the horses suitable for riding. We'll leave the farmers their draft horses. This will be careful work. Each farm must be left with at least enough animals for plowing and hauling wagons."

Holcomb spoke up. "You will also be accompanied by wagons and teamsters. You are to take as much hay and oats as you can find."

Wend shrugged. "This is pretty drastic."

Greene responded, "Indeed, but it must be done if the cavalry is to be of any use in the upcoming campaign." He turned to Holcomb. "Show them the area we plan for the expedition to cover."

The colonel rose to his feet and stepped over to the map of the countryside. He was just about to speak when there was a tap on the door, and it swung open to reveal one of Greene's aides. Another man was looking over his shoulder, and Wend realized it was a junior aide to Washington himself. Holcomb walked over to Greene and spoke quietly to him. The general raised his eyebrows as the aide whispered to him, then looked over at Wend.

"Eckert, General Washington wants to see you. *Immediately*. Lieutenant Wellings is here to escort you."

Wend rose and looked over at Bradley. "Warren, you can brief me when I get back to our camp." Then he turned to Greene. "With your leave, General."

Greene nodded. "Of course."

Wend followed Wellings out of the headquarters house. To his surprise, two horses were waiting. "You brought a horse just to go over to Washington's headquarters?"

The lieutenant looked at Wend. "He was quite adamant that you be brought posthaste."

Wend said nothing, and in silence the two mounted and turned their mounts westward to traverse the road to the army's headquarters.

Wend and his escort soon arrived at Washington's headquarters, a large stone house near the western edge of the encampment, known as the Potts House after the family that owned it, and sited close by the Schuylkill River. Wend dismounted, handed the reins to the other man, and ascended the stone steps to the front door. Once inside, the first person he encountered was young Alex Hamilton, one of Washington's aides-de-camp.

"What's toward, Alex? Why did the general call for me?"

Hamilton shrugged. "It's a mystery to me. All I know is that one of Talmadge's men came in about a half hour ago, and within a few minutes, the general summoned you." He motioned his head down the hall. "Maybe Colonel Scammell can give you some idea of what it's all about."

Wend walked down the hall to what had been Mrs. Potts' sewing room and stepped into the open doorway. Colonel Alexander Scammell, Washington's adjutant general, looked up from the papers on his desk.

Wend was about to speak when Scammell held up a hand and said, "Don't ask me, Eckert. He hasn't told me what it's all about. It seems to be something personal." He waved in the general direction of Washington's office. "Just go in; he's expecting you, and no one else is with him."

Nodding, Wend turned and walked to the parlor, which had been converted to serve as the commanding general's office. He tapped on the closed door, then eased it open. He could see Washington at his desk, quill in hand, writing something.

The general looked up briefly and without speaking motioned Wend to enter and then pointed to a chair located in front of the desk. Wend took his seat, and Washington went back to his writing. After a long minute, he signed his name, then dusted the letter, placed the quill back into the ink stand, and moved the paper to one side. Still without speaking, he reached into a drawer at his right side, extracted a folded piece of paper, and handed it to Wend.

"Eckert, read that. Take your time and make sure you understand it completely. And then we'll talk."

The general took a document from a basket on the desk and resumed his work. Wend unfolded the paper. It was a letter addressed to Washington personally, and he quickly looked at the bottom. He was startled to see the signature—*Patrick Henry*. His interest now aroused, he returned to the top and began reading the words closely. Within a few lines, the content had astonished him, and his mind became completely engrossed. After finishing, he returned to the top and read the entire missive again. Finally he believed he had it all and looked up at Washington. "Sir, I've finished."

"Good, Eckert. Now throw it into the fire."

"*Sir?*"

"You heard me, Eckert. Do it."

Wend rose, walked slowly to the hearth, and tossed the letter into the crackling fire. The paper flamed up and disintegrated in a few moments. Then he returned to his chair.

Washington looked at Wend. "Well, Major, what do you think?"

"It leaves me speechless, General."

"Do you know Mrs. Henry? Dorothea Dandridge Henry?"

"I met her once, at an Independence Ball, in 1776 at Williamsburg. It was just after she had been betrothed to Patrick. A beautiful young lady. I only spoke to her for a few moments, but she seemed mature for her age, which I was informed to be nineteen, and quite socially adept."

"I myself met her when she was still a child. But even then she was showing the promise of great attractiveness and intelligence. But more pertinent, do you perchance know Captain John Henry, Patrick's son?"

"I've never had the opportunity to meet him, sir. And I had no idea that before Patrick asked for the lady's hand from her father, young John had been courting her."

"Nor I. It is indeed an extraordinarily awkward situation." Washington paused a moment, a reflective look in his eyes. "Not something I would have expected from a man of Henry's position."

Wend sighed. "May I speak my mind directly, General?"

"Please do."

"I've never been a particular admirer of our governor, Patrick Henry. I have, by chance, several times been under his orders, and it was not to my pleasure. I find him with a penchant for being manipulative and devious." Wend cleared his throat. "So while I am surprised reading the train of events described in the letter, I don't find it outside the realm of what I would believe possible of Henry in the pursuit of his own desires."

Washington lifted an eyebrow. Then he said, "Well, did you miss the anguish that permeated Henry's words in the letter?"

"No, sir, that was evident. But rather *late*. Henry should have thought about the consequences of his actions before making a decision to seek Dorothea's hand from her father."

Washington looked down at his desk for a long moment. "Well, Wend, Patrick and I have not always seen eye to eye. We have certainly disagreed about certain matters of policy as this quest for independence developed. However, in this matter, I prefer to assume that he was not aware of his son's emotional involvement with Miss Dandridge."

"Of course, I respect your judgment, sir."

Washington nodded, then said, "In any case, after reading the letter, I decided there was no choice but to accede to his request that I use my resources to attempt to find his son." Washington rose from his seat and slowly walked over to the hearth, obviously in deep thought. "As you read, young Henry did not know about his father's marriage to Dorothea until just after the Battle of Saratoga, where he served quite admirably in command of his artillery company. Then he received a letter from his father announcing the wedding. And it was immediately afterward that he disappeared."

Wend responded, "I should think he became despondent. It seems obvious that he expected to ask for Miss Dandridge's hand after he returned from army service." Wend though a moment. "But I don't understand desertion. In a matter like that, focusing on his duties to take his mind off his loss would be more mature and ultimately more responsible."

Washington turned to Wend, and the merest of smiles crossed his lips. "Now, Major Eckert, I should think you—particularly you—would have a little more sympathy for the lad's reaction. I should believe you would understand the irrational effect that the power of first love has over young men."

Wend was puzzled. "I'm not sure what you mean. Why do you think that would particularly refer to me?"

"Well, sir, our mutual friend William Crawford told me a story about you that he heard from your own lips. It was something you mentioned to him beside a campfire during Dunmore's campaign against the Shawnee back in '74. The story of an elegant, golden-haired young lady from Philadelphia, with whom you were enamored and who was abducted by the Mingo during a massacre on Forbes Road in 1759. It seems in Pontiac's Rebellion of 1763 you left your prosperous trade in a Pennsylvania village to scout for Bouquet on the march to relieve Fort Pitt, all in the hope of finding the lass." Washington paused for a moment and smiled again. "Many men would think that was not a rational move to pursue her after she had been five years living among the Indians. Not rational at all."

Wend thought a moment, then quietly said, "I take your point. You are saying it is hard to judge the acts of a young man who loses his first love unexpectedly."

"Quite, Major." Then Washington clasped his hands behind his back and stared into the flames of the hearth. A prolonged silence ensued and he seemed lost in deep reverie. Presently, still looking into the fire, he took a deep breath and said in a very soft voice, "Wend, I will confide in you that as a young man I once was besotted with an extraordinary woman of the gentry who lived near my home. For reasons which are not important now, she was beyond my reach, but that did not prevent me from having passionate thoughts and in fact, in some measure to act foolishly with regard to her. So I am not wont to overly condemn young Henry for rashly abandoning his duty."

Wend was startled by Washington's confession. But he simply responded, "I understand your position, General."

Washington turned to face Wend and nodded. "Let us now get to the immediate matter. After considerable thought, it is my intent to do what Patrick so beseechingly requested in the letter you just read: to find Captain Henry and return him to his family with the hope of reconciliation. I realize there might be some criticism of this by members of the Congress, or others. I might be accused of favoritism toward a fellow Virginian. I always try to avoid any appearance of that. But in this matter, I believe I am on solid ground for two reasons. First, I would do the same for any son of a governor or member of Congress. Second, and even more important, because John is the son of a man who is known by the British to be one of the important figures behind the drive for independence, it would be inopportune to let him fall into British hands."

Wend said, "Yes, I can see that. They would find ways to use the news of his capture, and particularly his departure from the army, to their favor."

"Precisely, Eckert." Washington walked back over to his desk and resumed his seat. "Soon after receiving Patrick's letter, I requested Major Tallmadge to use his web of informants to attempt to locate John. A short while ago, a courier informed me that there is a report of a man fitting his description lodging in a tavern in New Jersey near New York City. Tallmadge is working to confirm the location and that it is Henry." Washington stopped speaking and looked at Wend. "I think you can guess why I have called you here."

"I presume you want me to go fetch Captain Henry."

"Yes. You are to take a small detachment of the Guides and march northward through New Jersey to a plantation owned by a sympathizer to our cause just south of the town of Spanktown." He handed Wend a folded sheet of paper. "Here is the name of the gentleman and the location of his estate. Once there you will bivouac and wait for one of Tallmadge's people to contact you with a confirmation that the man in question is John Henry and details as to where he is lodging."

Wend nodded. "How many men do you think I should take? New Jersey is dangerous ground, particularly in the area between New York and Philadelphia. There are numerous loyalist bands patrolling, and I have heard of partisan bands raiding plantations and small villages."

"You are quite correct, Eckert. I get reports of burned-out plantations, their owners murdered at the hands of these brigand bands. Tallmadge's spy network has identified several groups, the largest and most vicious of which is led by a former slave going by the name of *Captain Tigh*." His face tightened. "I frequently receive pleas for assistance by county militia in Jersey." He reflected a moment and then said, "In fact, that will be the announced purpose of your foray—helping the militia fight the partisans. A show of force, if you will."

Wend thought a moment. "I see what you are getting at, general. You don't want it known that we are after Captain Henry."

Washington nodded. "Precisely, Major. There are British spies all over the Jersey area. If they get wind of your real mission, the British from New York or Philadelphia may get to Henry before you. On the other hand, if you can assist local militia without detracting from your main objective, that will be all to the better and will get us some credit with the people of New Jersey." Then he looked directly into Wend's eyes and continued, "But remember this: your main duty is to retrieve young Henry."

Wend contemplated what Washington had said. Then he asked, "What if perchance Captain Henry refuses to return with us?"

The commanding general leaned forward, a grim look on his face, and said, "Then you will apprehend him as a deserter and bring him back. Freely or as a prisoner, he will be returned."

"It will be done, sir."

Washington sat silent for a moment, then continued, "As far as the strength and organization of your detachment, I will leave that up to your judgment." He raised a finger. "Except for this—you must be able to move fast, in case you encounter a large British formation, with which you will make every effort to avoid contact, and you will do your utmost to refrain from serious combat. I cannot countenance a significant loss of our Guides, for they will be invaluable in scouting during the forthcoming campaign. Our cavalry brigade is in such a wretched state."

"I understand, General. And when do you desire for us to depart?"

"Tomorrow will not be too early. But of course, take the time you need to properly form your detachment."

"We will leave early on the morrow." Wend rose and asked, "Is there anything else, sir?"

"No. Godspeed to you, and bring John back so I can restore him to his father."

—ɱ—

The officers of the Guides sat around the dining table placed just outside the mess hut. It had been moved outside at the end of April, and a canvas canopy had been rigged in order for them to take advantage of the spring weather. All nine were present to enjoy the supper. Service was provided by Corporal Billy Wood, an African who had been a free servant in Wend's home, and his wife, Melinda, a light-skinned former slave who was the cook for the mess.

The Guides officers, and for that matter, the entire legion, ate rather better than the line battalions of the army. Naturally, that was a factor of their role as one of the main elements of the foraging force under Greene. There was no serious objection from the main body of the army, for most of the soldiers appreciated that their food supply had been greatly enhanced by the work of the Guides. And they also realized that the Guides' work had been carried out through the depth of winter, amid freezing rain and vicious snowstorms.

As commandant, Wend sat at the head of the table with the other officers seated along the sides in order of seniority. Young lieutenant Edward Childers, the adjutant, sat at the foot of the table as befitted his duty as the mess manager. As usual, supper was accompanied by jocular banter about news and happenings of the day. During a pause, Reese Newkirk, a sly expression on his face, looked over at Childers, then turned to Wend and winking conspiratorially, said, "Our adjutant has been busy reading and rereading a letter he received today from that young lady in Williamsburg."

Shay O'beirne grinned and said, "I believe that's the second letter in a fortnight. It appears the wench is getting serious about things."

Edward raised his eyes from his plate, a look of irritation on his face, and said, "I would hardly call Miss Emma Wilbourne a *wench*. Her family has one of the largest land holdings in the Tidewater, including an elegant home plantation on the York River with numerous outlying farms around it. And not to mention a substantial house in Williamsburg."

O'beirne laughed. "Now, lad, be all that as may be, I would caution you against *disdain* for wenches. A lad of your years could greatly benefit from some time with an experienced tavern wench." He raised an eyebrow and looked around the table, then back at Childers. "She could teach you some *stimulating* and very useful lessons."

Grins and nods appeared on the officers' faces around the table. Childers sat silent for a moment, a thoughtful look on his face. Then he smiled and said, in mock seriousness, "I appreciate that advice, Mr. O'beirne, since I am quite aware that no one at the table has spent more time with tavern wenches than you, and none are as much as an expert on the subject as yourself."

Bradley exclaimed "Hear, hear!" to Childers's words, then looked at the Irishman and said, "I dare say the lad gave as good as he got on that exchange."

There was laughter around the table, and finally Wend said, "Well, Edward, it's a shame we haven't been able to meet the young lady. Perhaps then we'd better understand why she has so charmed you."

Childers raised his hand. "But sir, you *have* seen Emma. It was at the Independence Ball at the Governor's Palace in Williamsburg, back in '76, sir. She was that young lady who greeted me as we entered the ballroom and then asked you if she could steal me away to join old friends. Afterward, you remarked on her beauty."

Wend thought a moment. "Ah, yes! I remember. A petite young lady with golden hair and rather beguiling eyes."

"Indeed, sir! That's *my* Emma."

"Well, Edward, you do seem to know a lot of the young people of the capital from your time at William and Mary."

"Yes, Major, and also a lot of the young crowd came in from plantations for the social season. That's how I met Emma—at a ball in the Governor's mansion in '74."

Reese Newkirk said, "I recall you met that French artillery officer—I believe his name was Arundel—who had the idea of a wooden mortar and was killed by the explosion when he fired it."

Shay interjected, "Yes, and what that fellow actually invented was a complex way of committing suicide."

Childers stared into the distance for a moment, sighed, and said, "He was a very personable man. Many of us spent hours together with him in taverns." He thought a moment. "He convinced my friend John Henry to go into the artillery instead of joining a cavalry regiment."

Wend stiffened upon hearing his words. "Did you say John *Henry*?"

"Yes, sir. John Henry, Governor Henry's son. He and I are close friends. He's twenty-one, just like me. I believe he's with Gates' army up north presently."

Wend thought, *Childers knowing Henry will be helpful—he must go with the detachment.*

At that moment, Melinda approached the table. "Now you gentlemens, if you are finished, Billy and I will bring your sweets. We got for you a nice cake I baked this very afternoon."

The two picked up the officers' dinner plates and replaced them with ones holding the cake. The men enjoyed the course in near silence.

When they had finished, some of the men pulled out cigars or pipes. Billy came around with a taper to help them light the tobacco.

As they were doing so, Wend spoke up. "Gentlemen, I'm going to declare supper finished and convene a meeting about some important business."

Bradley looked over and asked, "Does this mean you are finally going to tell us why you suddenly got called to Washington's headquarters?"

Wend nodded. "Indeed, Warren." He looked around the table. "Washington wants us to make a show of force against the British and Royalists who are raiding through the New Jersey countryside." Wend looked around the table. "He's particularly concerned with the bands of partisans who often burn plantations and murder the owners. Some of them consist of mixed-race groups, including former slaves." Wend paused, then continued, "One group that is particularly feared is led by an African who is called Captain Tigh."

Bradley's brow furrowed. "When is this to happen?"

Wend responded, "Immediately."

Reese Newkirk stiffened. "What about Greene's horse foraging expedition?"

Wend raised a hand. "I'm to take a small detachment to New Jersey, to depart tomorrow. The rest of the legion will continue on Greene's forage, under Bradley."

Warren Bradley raised his eyebrows. "How big will your detachment be? And who will go?"

"That's what is important and the reason I'm bringing it up this evening." He looked around the room. "It will be twenty-five men to consist of the following: ten cavalry, one field squad of ten from Reese's company serving as mounted infantry. Then Childers and myself plus a cavalry trumpeter and two men to drive a wagon with supplies."

Fairfield stiffened. "Which troop will be supplying the cavalry?"

Wend responded, "You'll both share the misery. One set of four and a sergeant from your troop, another four and a corporal from Warren's."

Geoffrey nodded. "That's all well and good. But where do the horses come from for the field squad? Some of our horses are weak after the winter, and we're already having trouble mounting all our dragoons. We should have as many mounted men for the forage as possible."

Wend grinned. "Oh ye of little faith. I've already talked with Gibbs of the Life Guards. They'll supply the extra horses. Have Sergeant Quinn take some men over there this evening and get them." Wend motioned toward the lieutenant. "And by the way, I want Quinn to be the sergeant who accompanies the detachment."

Fairfield shot Eckert a scowl. "Damnation, Wend! Quinn's my top sergeant! He's my right hand!"

Wend grinned back at the Carolinian. "Geoffrey, I need a good sergeant to manage the dragoons and horses on this trip. And just as important, Quinn is the best mounted scout in the legion. In any case, you've got Sergeant McCrae, who can serve you as well as Quinn. They were both in the Irish Dragoons together."

Newkirk asked, "Do you have any preference for the field squad, or should I pick one?"

Wend thought a moment. "Make it Schreiber's squad. They are quite well trained and we've used them as mounted infantry before."

Bradley looked over at Wend. "Is that it?"

"Yes, except that we plan to leave as early as possible consistent with loading provisions into the wagon. So get the orders out to the affected people right after you leave here."

Just as he had finished, Wend looked up into the evening dusk to see a diminutive female figure, escorted by an officer of the Life Guards, coming from the direction of the Potts House. He quickly realized the woman was Martha Washington. "Gentlemen, to your feet!" Wend motioned toward the approaching lady. All the officers took one look, then sprang up, extinguishing their tobacco.

In near unison, the men said, "Good evening, Mrs. Washington!"

Martha Washington smiled and returned the greeting. Then with all eyes on her, she smiled and said, "You know, I believe I've met all of you at the entertainments over the last few months. But as I was walking over here, it occurred to me that while I have visited the messes of most of the brigades, I have never been to the mess of the Guides. I've thought about it before, but you gentlemen have been so busy with General Greene that the proper opportunity never presented itself. And now I must soon take carriage to return to Virginia for the summer." She shrugged. "And tonight I can't spend time visiting with you, for I have come to discuss something with Major Eckert."

Bradley, ever the gentleman, took the cue immediately. "Well, Mrs. Washington, we all have business we must attend to—evening rounds and all that. And we are preparing for another forage on behalf of General Greene. So we will take our leave, ma'am."

The other officers in turn said good evening to the lady and then departed. Wend assisted Mrs. Washington to a chair beside the fire and then offered her a libation, which she accepted. The officer who had accompanied her stood out of earshot, waiting patiently.

After Melinda had brought the refreshment and then withdrawn to the cook house, Mrs. Washington looked over at Wend and said, "I have come to talk to you about something that is most personal and which I consider very serious."

Wend looked at the woman he had first met in the previous year's winter encampment at Morristown. But until now, his interaction with Martha Washington had always been as part of a group at social events. This was the first time he had talked with her individually. Now he watched her as she stared into the flickering light of the fire and took her first sip of the drink. She was in her midforties, and Wend reflected it would not be accurate to call her *beautiful*, but the word *handsome* would be entirely appropriate. She had a round face with delicate features. Wend thought her mouth seemed a little too small for her face, which was nicely framed by her dark-brown hair. She was actually quite tiny, and he had often noted how her husband towered over her, but then, the general towered over most men, let alone women with their smaller stature.

After a few more moments, Mrs. Washington took another sip and then looked over at Wend. "Major, I am aware of the mission you are embarking on tomorrow. George showed me the letter from Patrick on the day it arrived. He felt he could have done nothing else, considering my family relationship to Dorothea."

Wend replied, "I'm aware your maiden name is Dandridge."

"Yes, according to the rules of genealogy, Dorothea and I are distant cousins. But I've always been close to that branch of the family, and I've known her since childhood. I also know Nathaniel, her father, quite well. He and his wife attended my first wedding, to Daniel Custis, in 1750, and also in 1759, when George and I were married."

Wend furrowed his brow. "So your first marriage only lasted a few years?"

"Daniel died of heart failure in 1757." She smiled. "But in that time we did have four lovely children, two of whom survive."

Wend nodded his understanding.

Mrs. Washington resumed speaking. "The reason I came here tonight was to talk to you about marriage—marriage among the gentry. I believe it will help you understand the importance of your mission."

"Mrs. Washington, I believe I fully understand the gravity of the duty. The general made it quite clear."

"Yes, I'm sure you understand the political and military importance of retrieving young Henry. But I want to explain it from a woman's point of view. And what finding John and restoring him to his father and facilitating a reconciliation between the two means to the Henry family *and* to the Dandridge family."

Wend said, "Yes, I see. I would appreciate that."

"Major Eckert, I know you are married. Colonel Morgan, who I understand is your neighbor, once told me that your wife is a true beauty, unrivaled in Frederick County and Winchester."

Wend felt himself flushing. "You will find no argument from me."

"Now let me ask you a delicate question: Were you in romantic love with her when you wed?"

Startled by the question, Wend blurted out, "Of course, Mrs. Washington!'"

She looked at him sharply. "And how did you know that, Major?"

Wend thought back to that night in 1764. The events came back in vivid memory. He said, "It's a bit of a story."

"I have the time; please relate it to me."

"Well, the moment I knew of my love for her was on a frigid night on the crest of North Mountain, about ten miles above Carlisle in Pennsylvania. Peggy McCartie and I were transporting her younger sister, Ellen, from where we lived in Sherman Valley to a doctor in Carlisle. Ellen had been wounded in the explosion of a gristmill; she was unconscious and had a huge splinter impaled in her back."

A look of shock came over Martha Washington's face. "Good God, Wend, how horrible."

"We knew her time was short, and I was hurrying, with my team racing. As we started downhill from the mountain crest, I let the wagon roll too fast, and I couldn't make a sharp turn. We ran off the wagon track, nearly upset, and a wheel spoke was cracked. We couldn't go further unless we could fix it. I had a coil of strong cord in my wagon, which I kept for such emergencies; we would wind it around the spoke, closing the crack and holding it together. Sailors do that on ship's broken spars; it's a technique called 'fishing.' But to be successful, the cord must be wound very tight around the spoke, so it takes two people to be done correctly—one to do the wrapping, and one to hold the cord tight."

Martha nodded thoughtfully. "Yes, I see how it would be done." She thought a second. "So Peggy had to help you?"

"Exactly, ma'am. We had to work as a team." He reflected a moment. "It took about half an hour. Peggy and I had to be very close together. She had only a light cloak on, and by the time we were finished, she was shivering uncontrollably. I had a heavy army overcoat, and I shed it, took the cloak off her, and helped her into the coat. Our faces were very close, my eyes right in front of hers, and suddenly I knew I loved her. Without thinking, I took her into my arms, pulled her close, and embraced her. To my surprise, she returned it with the same enthusiasm. After that moment, there was no doubt we would wed."

"A wonderful story." Then a look of concern crossed Mrs. Washington's face. "Did the sister, Ellen, survive?"

"Yes, we got her to the doctor in Carlisle, and he immediately went to work removing the splinter and closing the wound. I was exhausted and immediately fell asleep in a chair. But Peggy, tired as she was, stayed with the doctor and acted as his assistant. When I awoke, she was standing beside my chair, to tell me Ellen would survive. Only then did she sleep."

"So, after you returned to your village, did you ask her father for her hand?"

Wend laughed. "Mrs. Washington, I never did. Things were a little complicated. First, Peggy went to a man whom she had been keeping company with and explained to him it was all over. Then *she* told her father, the town's tavern keeper, that she was going to wed me. And that was that."

Mrs. Washington smiled, then remarked, "A very romantic story. And besides being beautiful, it is obvious your Peggy is a very strong woman. You are indeed a very lucky man to be wed to such."

"I have always thought so."

"Indeed. But fortunately, your story leads to the main point that I wanted to discuss." She looked into the fire for a long moment, obviously choosing her words carefully. Then she turned back to Wend. "Your engagement and marriage was much different from how these things occur in the gentry."

"I'm quite aware that it is much more formal, Mrs. Washington."

"Please listen to my story. I have no intention of talking down to you, but there are some customs about marriage among the landed that I believe will help you understand the weightiness of your mission."

"Of course, ma'am."

"My first marriage, to Daniel Custis, like most such marriages, was negotiated between my father and Daniel's. Daniel and I had become familiar through church activities, and he began to visit with me. After a while we realized we had an affinity for each other. My father went to Daniel's father, to discuss a potential marriage." She hesitated a moment, then said, "Things did not go well between them. Daniel's father, John Custis IV, was not happy with the idea. He was a member of the powerful Governor's Council and felt his son would be marrying below himself, for our plantation and land holdings were considerably less extensive and valuable than those of the Custis family."

Wend was puzzled. "Mrs. Washington, I had the perception that the Dandridge family was quite wealthy and influential."

Martha's lips formed into a small, tight smile. "There are several branches, and ours was the least prosperous." She sighed. "John wanted a union more advantageous to his family. However, Daniel pleaded with his father and mother, and we were allowed to continue seeing each other. Eventually John conceded, and we were married in 1750."

"I always felt it my duty to fit in well with Daniel's family while upholding the traditions of my own—in other words, to help the families blend amicably. I think I succeeded in this, even in the few years before Daniel passed on, for after a brief period of awkwardness with the Custises, I always felt welcome and part of the family."

Wend nodded his understanding.

"Then, about a year after Daniel's passing in 1757, when I had just finished formal mourning, the then colonel Washington and I met. Then he visited me twice on my plantation. When he left at the end of the second visit, we had reached a tentative agreement to wed." She made a small laugh. "There was little romance; it was more like a merger, with families instead of businesses. He felt it was time to wed and begin a family, and frankly I needed someone to deal with my properties and financial situation. Since Daniel died with no will, I had received my dower inheritance from him, which was one third of his wealth, and the children received the rest. But it was my responsibility to control it all until they reached maturity. Upon our marriage, George, who of course had very substantial holdings, took over the management of the entire amount, and I focused my attention on ensuring that the three families—Custis, Dandridge, and Washington—lived in harmony. And along the way, a strong bond of affection grew between George and me. That is often how things develop in such marriages." She shrugged. "I have gone on and on, but I feel this background was important to what I'm going to say about Dorothea and Henry."

Wend said, "I think I see where your words are leading. You believe it is Dorothea's duty to promote good feeling throughout the combined Henry-Dandridge family?"

Martha Washington gave Wend the broadest smile he had seen from her. "That is precisely correct. And from what I have learned from correspondence with friends, Dorothea is taking that task very seriously. Besides having the need to cement her bond with Patrick, she has taken over the job of shepherding the Henry children who are still at home—there are five from his previous marriage. And I have heard that she is also performing the role of the governor's lady in an admirable fashion."

Wend said, "That is a lot of responsibility for a woman who has, I believe, just turned twenty and who is nearly two decades younger than her husband."

Martha Washington cocked her head and smiled at Wend with a twinkle in her eye. "Major Eckert, it may surprise you to learn that I was exactly nineteen years younger than my first husband."

In his surprise, Wend blurted, "I had no idea, ma'am!"

"Well, it is quite true, and given that experience, I have much sympathy for Dorothea's situation. With all she has to do, the anger and despair of young John, if left to burn within him, will be like an open sore that will serve to sunder the family and obstruct all her efforts." She looked directly into Wend's eyes. "John must be recovered and restored to his family, so that Patrick can effect some sort of accommodation that will allow peace to prevail and will permit Dorothea to bind the family together." She leaned forward slightly in her seat and said in a low but emphatic tone, "*That* is why your expedition is so important."

Wend smiled and nodded slowly. "I truly understand your concern, Mrs. Washington. I pledge to do everything in my power to bring back Henry."

Martha leaned back, and a look of satisfaction spread over her face. "That is all I can ask. To be frank, sir, you *must* accept that the fate of the Henry-Dandridge family rides on your shoulders."

With that, she stood up and put down her cup. "Thank you for your hospitality, Major, and for your patience in hearing out the words of a very worried lady. I shall be leaving for Virginia in a few days and likely will not be here when you return. But at Mount Vernon I shall be waiting and hoping for news that bespeaks of your success."

With that she signaled to her escort and bade Wend good night, and the two of them started back toward the Potts House, leaving Eckert staring after them.

—ꟾꟾꟾ—

Following Mrs. Washington's departure, Wend sat in front of the fire, thinking over what she had told him. But his thoughts were interrupted by the voice of Billy Wood.

"Mr. Eckert, Meli and me got something to tell you."

Wend looked up to see the couple standing together. They had been cleaning up the cook house after supper while Martha and he had been talking. "What is it, Billy?"

"We heard you talkin' with the officers about this trip you are going to make, up into New Jersey. About how there was these bands of partisans, sir." He stopped and looked over at his wife. "Well, it turns out we might know somethin' about that man you talked about, that Captain Tigh."

"Captain Tigh? How could you know him? Neither of you are from New Jersey."

Meli answered, "That's it, Major Eckert; it were down in Virginia that I met him. It was on Gwynn's Island right after I ran away from the plantation. He was part of Lord Dunmore's African regiment, them Ethiopians. The man I'm thinkin' of was named Sergeant Tigh then. Thing is, Tigh was from New Jersey. He ran away from his master up here in Jersey, and made his way south, 'cause he wanted to get his freedom from Governor Dunmore after that proclamation, right at the beginning of the war."

Wend thought a moment. "But can it actually be the same man? Most of the Ethiopians died from smallpox. And we know that those that survived and came north with the British Army are used for labor, helping to build fortifications around New York."

"Sir," responded Meli, "this Tigh fellow had been inoculated, just like me and Billy, against the smallpox, and he did go with the British when they left Gwynn's Island. And he could read and write. The officers made him a sergeant 'cause of that and the fact that he was a great talker and quick to learn soldiering. All the men in the regiment looked up to him."

Wend considered all that for a long moment. "Well, it *could* be the same man." Then he looked up at Melinda. "Meli, how do you know so much about him?"

It was Billy who answered. "Mr. Eckert, truth be, he took a real shine to Meli." He looked over at his wife, grinned broadly, and continued, "With her good looks, there was a lot of them men who was payin' attention to her. So Sergeant Tigh used to visit her every chance he could get, comin' over to the officers' mess of Colonel Northcutt's regiment, where Meli was doin' the cookin'."

Meli shrugged. "I didn't do much to encourage him, leastways after Billy arrived on that mission to spy on the British, but Tigh wasn't no man to accept no for an answer. He was fixin' to fight Billy over me, but that never happened 'cause Billy got off the island to tell you about Dunmore's plans."

Wend put his hand to his chin, looked into the fire, and contemplated what Meli and Billy had said. He thought, *It's actually possible. If Tigh was the man who came north with the remnants of Dunmore's loyalist forces, he could actually be this leader of partisans.* And then another thing hit him: Barrett Penfold Northcutt, who had been the colonel of the King's Loyal Virginia Legion, had come north with Dunmore and was now known to be an advisor concerning loyalist matters on General Howe's staff. He would have known about Tigh and his abilities as a leader, perhaps to arrange for him to command this band of renegades.

And then another idea occurred to Wend. He looked over at the African couple. "Since you two may know this Captain Tigh, I want you to come along on this trip. Billy, you won't march with the company tomorrow on the horse forage, you'll drive the wagon with my detachment. And you, Meli, will come along to take care of supplies and cook for the men and ride in the wagon with Billy." He motioned toward them. "You can identify Tigh from the Ethiopian Regiment, and it may be useful if we actually encounter this partisan band. So get ready; we'll march early on the morrow."

—∞—

Wend was still sitting at the fire when Shay O'beirne strode out of the dusk. "Newkirk told me to advise you that Schreiber's squad is informed about the detachment and getting ready to ride. And the horses are here from Washington's Life Guard."

Wend nodded.

O'beirne continued, "And just as I was arriving here, I thought I heard you saying that Billy and Meli are going along with your detachment."

Wend shrugged. "That's correct."

"I must protest in the strongest terms. That means that Sergeant Flannagan's wife will be doing the cooking for the officer's mess. Ah, now, my darling Major, that's a cruel thing indeed to which you are sentencing us."

Wend laughed. "I expect you'll be in the field for most of the time we're gone. You won't have to suffer her cooking for long."

O'beirne called out to Billy. "Can a man have a wee cup of Donegal's whiskey on a chilly night?"

It was Meli who came out, cup in hand, and handed it to O'beirne. "Now thank you, lass. I was just telling the good major here how much I'll be missing your lovely touch with our rations."

"Mr. O'beirne, you never do miss a chance to make a compliment. But I'll be back soon enough. And I'm looking forward to a nice ride through the country after bein' holed up in this camp all winter."

O'beirne gave Meli a serious look. "Careful what you wish for, Mrs. Wood. This little ride may be more than you count on."

"Now lieutenant, whatever happens, it will not be dull, and I am ready for some excitement." She turned and walked back into the mess hut.

The Irishman sat down, took a deep pull on the whiskey, then looked over at Wend with a sly smile on his face. "Can we be droppin' all the army formality for a wee bit, Major?"

Wend shrugged. "Speak your mind, Shay. You'll do it anyway."

"Well, the truth is I'm finding this little trip you are planning to be a very curious thing."

Wend raised his eyebrows. "It seems very straightforward to me."

"Ah, now Wend, some things about it have my Irish intuition ringing like a fire bell." He grinned broadly at Eckert. "Let me just make a few little points."

Wend nodded. "Give it your best, Shay."

"Now, first of all our esteemed commanding general sends an aide to pull you right out of Greene's little meeting, no delay allowed. Then he wants you to go off posthaste on this trip into New Jersey, to encourage the militia up there, as it were. Now, this little war in Jersey has been going on for a couple of years; it seems it could have waited a few days until this forage for cavalry horses, which Greene stressed was very important to the army, was finished." He paused and then raised his hand with two fingers showing. "Second, Major Gibbs, with no argument, happily loans you ten of his Life Guard horses, which everyone knows are in the best shape of any in the army, undoubtedly at the behest of Washington himself." He pointed a finger at Wend. "And why is this a mounted expedition anyway? Seems to me that a company or two from Daniel Morgan's light foot brigade would be a better force to encourage the militia. Horses means there's a need to travel fast." He showed three fingers. "Then, the good and lovely Mrs. Washington suddenly decides she has to have a little heart-to-heart talk with Major Eckert on the very same day all this is going on."

"I suppose I should ask you to state the specific point you are trying to make."

"Easy, my most esteemed major: It seems clear to me that this little expedition is about more than encouraging the Jersey militia. It's something personal with the Washingtons—and obviously very urgent." O'beirne's eyes lit up. "And it has just occurred to me that there is a fourth point." He grinned mischievously. "At supper just now, you suddenly showed a lot of interest when young Childers started talking about his friendship with that crowd of youngsters in Williamsburg, and particularly one *John Henry*, scion of the governor's family. And right after that, you announced that Edward would be accompanying your little party." He rolled his eyes. "It would have made more sense to take one of the cavalry subalterns, seeing as it's a mounted expedition."

There was a long period of silence, then Wend replied, "Shay, that suspicious Irish mind of yours is running wild like a berserk stallion. Rein it in. You are way off the mark. And I caution you, don't go planting ideas in the minds of the other officers."

O'beirne raised his eyebrows and smiled conspiratorially. "Now, my darling Major, you could keep me silent by taking me along. Whatever you are really up to in Jersey, it seems likely to be more fun than this organized horse thievery we're about to perform. And you know I'm very good in these nasty little jobs, which I have no doubt it is going to be."

Wend felt his face flushing. He leaned forward in his chair. "Damn it, Shay, now listen well: You *will* be quiet about your ideas, and you *will* march with the Guides on Greene's forage expedition. You are first lieutenant of the Frederick County Light Foot, and Newkirk needs your assistance. I'm telling you, let that be an end to it."

The Irishman pushed himself up out of the chair, grinning from ear to ear. "Now my dear Wend, we've been together since the beginning of the Light Foot those many months ago in Winchester, and it's certain I'll follow your order." Then he reached into his pocket and pulled out a coin and held it up so it shined in the firelight. "But this says when you return, and the real story comes out, I'll be proved right, and this little piece will stay right in my pocket."

And with that, he turned and strode off toward the company area.

Chapter Two
Jersey Country

With the sun well above the horizon and a clear sky above, Wend Eckert led the Legion of Continental Guides from their camp. The morning muster said the legion itself consisted of 153 officers and men and one farm wagon, with two occupants. Attached were eight Conestogas, each with six horse teams and a contract driver, along to carry grain, hay, and other items to be confiscated from the local farms. With the two cavalry troops leading, the column forded the Schuylkill River and followed a road heading northeasterly.

About an hour into the march, they came to a fork in the road, and Eckert held up his hand to halt the column. One branch swung westward while the other continued in a northerly direction. He ordered the special detachment to fall out from their places and form along the side of the road.

Wend motioned for Bradley to join him where he sat his horse, Sonny. "Well, Warren, you've got command." He looked at the Marylander. "And I don't envy you the job of taking horses from their owners."

Bradley shrugged. "It's going to be grim work, I'll vow. There will be weeping and gnashing of teeth. Most of them will never see their animals again." He cocked his head. "How long do you expect to be gone?"

"No telling, Warren. It will just depend on how involved we get with the various militias. But I can tell you, Washington wants me back in time for the start of the campaign. So it will not be much more than a week or ten days. Certainly less than a fortnight."

Bradley extended a hand. "Well, good luck, Wend."

Wend shook the hand and said, "And the same to you."

Bradley took his place at the head of the column and ordered the advance, leading the column along the westward branch. Wend waved for the detachment to move, and they continued along the road to the north.

Wend set a moderate but steady pace as they traveled through mixed farm and forest land. Frequently they dismounted and led the horses, for not knowing what the future held, he wanted to conserve their strength. As they marched, they encountered travelers of every stripe—freight wagoners, farmers in wagons, people on horseback and on foot. All looked at them in curiosity, obviously wondering what business the mounted column was about. In the late afternoon, Sergeant Quinn hurried ahead to find an appropriate bivouac for the night. With dusk settling, the Irishman waved them into a campsite amid a pleasant stand of trees with a creek flowing near the edge.

Quinn and Harley, the corporal from the Maryland troop, supervised setting up the picket lines for the horses, feeding and watering them at the stream. Additionally, they spent some time ensuring that Schreiber's squad knew how to care for their animals. Meanwhile, Billy and Meli laid and lit the cook fire and began organizing supper for the detachment. Wend had specified that they would be traveling in light order, so everyone would be sleeping in the open around fires without tents. Billy had laid out the blankets for him and his wife under the wagon bed. Meli immediately addressed herself to preparing the evening meal, and soon the aroma of a beef stew was permeating the camp.

After the meal, Childers and Quinn made the rounds of the campfires and horse lines and then reported to Wend, where they briefly discussed the posting of sentries and the routine for reveille, morning meal, and departure on the morrow. Then Quinn left to return to his own fire, and Wend motioned to the lieutenant to take a seat. Reaching into his saddle bags, Wend pulled out a bottle of Donegal's whiskey. He said, "Get a cup if you'd like some of this."

"I would greatly appreciate it, Major." Childers produced his own cup, and Wend filled it, then did the same to his own.

Wend raised his cup, as did Childers. Childers looked over his cup. "You know, sir, after the war I'm going to take over one of father's farms. It's four thousand acres, with access to more forested land for clearing."

"That will be quite an estate, Edward."

"Well, the reason I brought it up is because I'm trying to decide what I'll grow on it."

"I would assume it would be tobacco, as on your father's plantation and on most of the plantations in the county."

"I'm not sure, Major. I'm thinking of concentrating on producing grain, as you do, sir, and setting up a distillery for whiskey and a brewery for ale. You are doing well selling the whiskey that Donegal makes, and I'm thinking it would be more advantageous for me than being just another tobacco grower."

Wend nodded. "There is definitely money there. And growing grain is easier and cheaper than tobacco. But you have to have a man who knows how to produce the whiskey or ale. I was lucky that Donegal had the knowledge and a fine recipe. You'll have to find a man to help construct your distillery and work out a blend that will have good appeal. It's not an easy process to get started."

"I've talked at some length with Donegal about it. And I plan to make a study of the financial aspects of whiskey production."

"Well, lad, I wish you luck and good fortune." Wend grinned. "But I can assure you neither Donegal nor I will give you any hint of our recipe. You'll have to work that out yourself!"

"I'm keen to do that, sir." He smiled broadly. "Perhaps someday Childers whiskey will be your major competitor in the valley!"

Wend raised his cup. "Well, I accept your challenge, Edward." Then Wend cleared his throat and said, "Edward, it's time we had a talk about the details of this job we've been sent on."

The lieutenant grinned. "Yes, sir. I've been wondering how we were going to work with the militia."

Wend looked into his lieutenant's eyes. "Edward, this mission is not about helping the militia, unless we happen to run into a situation in which it is expedient for us to do so."

Childers looked up from his cup, puzzlement spreading across his face. "Sir, I don't understand."

"The truth is, we're riding to find your friend, John Henry."

A look of shock came over the Childers's face. "But he's with the Northern Army! With General Gates!"

"No, it appears he's in an inn near New York City, having taken unauthorized leave from the army right after Saratoga."

"You mean he deserted? John deserted?"

"Washington chooses not to characterize it as that, at least for the present. The details of why he left, and the specific circumstances, are not known."

"But, sir—why? Why would he do that?"

"It appears because he found out that his father married Dorothea

Dandridge. Apparently he was in love with her and expected to ask for her hand after his service in the war. And it appears he had reason to believe she was amenable to that when he left with his artillery company last year."

Edward said nothing, simply staring into the fire over his cup.

"Do you know Dorothea? Was she among your group of friends in Williamsburg?"

Edward nodded slowly. "Yes, she was indeed. She was beautiful, vivacious, and quite popular. We were all of about the same age and in her company at many social occasions."

"Were you aware John was infatuated with her? That he planned to court her and ask for her hand?"

"No, I was not." He shook his head. "Everyone liked Dorothea. But now that I think on it, John was with her more than others. But he didn't say anything about it to me." Childers put his hand to his chin. "In reflection, Dorothea did seem to favor him above others."

"So you weren't surprised when her betrothal to Patrick Henry became known?"

"I was only surprised, to some extent, by the difference in age between her and the governor." He shrugged. "But it wasn't all that unusual. I've known of many marriages with similar differences of age." He looked up at Wend. "I'm familiar with her father, Nathaniel West Dandridge. What I'm not surprised about is that he would favor a marriage of his daughter to Patrick, given his influence and power. Obviously he saw it to his advantage to choose the governor over a young artillery captain. He would want her to marry a man which would add to the status of his own family."

"And if Dorothea were in love with someone else, do you think she would have objected?

Edward stared into the fire for a prolonged moment. Then he looked at Wend and shook his head. "No, sir, I believe she would obey her father, even if it were against her wishes. Dorothea was dutiful to her family and to her father." He raised a finger. "There was a story I heard that she had been courted by a sailor—a merchant captain—while in Fredericksburg, a dashing man whom she was quite taken with. But Nathaniel thought the man wasn't suitable and forbade him to see her. Dorothea acquiesced to her father's wishes."

Wend nodded. "Yes, I've also heard that story. I got it from James Wood. By the way, I understand that merchant officer happened to be a certain John Paul Jones."

"The captain in our navy? The one who was captain of the *Providence* and the *Alfred*?"

"The very same, Edward. And I understand he is now in command of a ship called the *Ranger*." Wend paused for a moment to gather his thoughts. "But back to Dorothea and John. It seems to me that given that precedent, Dorothea would also follow her father's guidance even if she were in love with young Henry."

Edward slowly nodded. "Yes, as I said, Dorothea was an obedient daughter. I believe she would obey her father in that case. She's very traditional: it's the way she was raised, sir."

Wend replied, "Well, the result is that John left the army and apparently has become a wandering drunkard. Major Tallmadge informs Washington that they have located a man who could be him at an inn in Elizabeth Town, essentially just across the harbor from New York. Tallmadge's people are trying to confirm that. In the meantime, we're to proceed to a plantation named Wallen Farm near a village called Spanktown and wait for further information."

"So we're to retrieve him from that inn?"

"Exactly. And that's why you are along. You'll be able to recognize John. And moreover, he may need some convincing to come with us. I believe he'll listen to a friend more than myself, a stranger."

A frown came over Edward's face. "What will happen to John when we bring him back to Washington?"

"The general plans to send him home, by some means. Mrs. Washington made it clear to me that there must be some attempt to make a reconciliation between John and his father." Wend pondered for a second. "And I presume with Dorothea. Mrs. Washington thinks it is necessary to unify both the Henry and Dandridge families, and further to allow Dorothea to properly function as the governor's lady."

Childers took a deep breath. "How can such be accomplished? How do you repair such a deep fracture within a family?"

"I have no idea, Edward. And I thank God my job is simply to find and return John. The only person who can effect a reconciliation is Patrick Henry himself, for he is the one who caused the rift."

Edward had been staring into the fire as he listened. Now he looked up and said, "No, there is another person who will have to help with the reconciliation." He paused, then continued, "And that is Dorothea. She must convince John to accept *his* father's actions." He reflected a moment. "And to accept *her* father's decision. She must act as the intermediary between them."

The two men remained silent for a long minute. Then Edward spoke up. "Sir, can I ask a question?"

"Of course."

"When are you going to tell the rest of the detachment about our real mission? They're going to have to know sometime."

"Yes, Edward, I've been considering that. Once we get to Wallen Farm, we're to wait for word from one of Tallmadge's spy ring to tell us when and where to find John. That's when I'll have to tell the men what we are actually about."

—m—

The detachment was back on the road just after dawn. In midmorning, they halted at a stream to rest and water the horses, and Wend sent Quinn out to scout the road ahead. They were just preparing to move out when they heard the noise of pounding hooves, and everyone looked up to see the sergeant appear over a small rise, his horse racing at full tilt.

Wend held up his hand to stop the column, and Quinn arrived, pulling up his mount in a flurry of dust. He saluted and called out, "There be British ahead, Major: a loyalist troop of about thirty light dragoons coming our way!"

"How far ahead, Quinn?"

"A little over a mile when I spotted them. Coming at the walk, sir!"

"Did they see you?"

"Not a chance, sir. I topped a rise and saw them, and then I darted into a grove of trees, so to get a count of them. Then I rode back down the hill through wooded country a'fore I took back to the road. No, sir, they didn't catch sight of me."

Childers had come up to join them. "What are we going to do, Major?"

"I want no contact with them. We'll have to take cover somewhere."

Quinn said, "I figured that's what you'd be wantin' to do. So I looked for a likely spot, and there be a small wagon track branching off the road just a quarter mile ahead. It goes into heavy woods. If we hurry, we'll get there in time to hide before they pass."

Wend raised his arm and shouted to the troop, "Forward at the gallop!" The column hurried up the rise, led by Quinn. It took only a few minutes to reach the small track, and Quinn waved them into it. Wend slowed the column as they rode into the woods, and in very short order the forest opened into a hay field. He turned to Childers. "Edward, dismount the column; have the men lead their horses into the wood at the edge of the field. Have them stay with their horses to keep them quiet." He turned to Billy Wood. "Corporal, find a place to hide your wagon along the tree line and tend your horses." He stood up in his stirrups and shouted so that all could hear: "It's essential we keep silent! No talking and no noise from your horses!"

Wend dismounted and turned to Quinn. "Come with me, sergeant, we need to find a place to spy on the main road." He looked over at Childers. "Edward, stay with the detachment and make sure it makes no noise to betray us."

With Wend leading, the two ran back along the trail toward the road.

Quinn called, "I see a spot there, about fifty feet from the road, behind that fallen tree. We can stay hidden and still be able to watch the road."

They ran to the tree and crouched down behind it. Wend saw that they did indeed have a good view of the road. And it was none too soon, for in just a minute the head of the dragoon troop came into sight.

The mounted men were in a column of twos, proceeding at the walk. Wend saw that they were dressed in green coats and breeches and wore tall round, black caps.

Quinn whispered, "Mounted hussars from the Queen's American Rangers. I'd know them anywhere from their caps."

Wend thought a moment. "The Queen's Rangers consist of both mounted and foot troops. I wonder if this troop is alone on patrol or if it's the vanguard for a larger force?"

"I didn't see any foot behind them when I first spied them from that ridge. But there's no telling without scouting back up the road once this lot is gone."

Wend said, "Damn, you are right. We're going to have to send out a patrol to check before we resume our march."

They then remained silent until the column had passed and disappeared around a curve in the road. Wend had a thought. "Sergeant, you spent years in the Irish dragoons and fought in Europe during the French War. What is the difference between Light Dragoons and Hussars? They seem to be armed and used in the same way."

The veteran cavalry sergeant laughed and shook his head. "The name Hussar comes from the Hungarian army. It means the same thing as light dragoons. Some regiments just want a damn way to be different from the others. So they dress in the Hungarian-style uniform and call themselves Hussars but do the same thing as any other light horse regiment."

Wend shrugged. "Sometimes all this military custom is beyond the understanding of a back-country gunsmith."

Quinn was quiet for a moment, and a scowl came over his face. He reached up and touched the left side of his face, where a long thick scar stretched up from the jaw to the ear, the lower half of which was missing. "It was a damned French Hussar who did this to me, back in the Seven Years War."

"Well, at least you recovered from it."

"That's a fact. I was lucky to get to a surgeon, right after I killed the bastard who did it with a slash of my saber." He smiled. "Nearly took his head off, I did." He shrugged. "The doctor stopped the bleeding, trimmed my ear neat-like, and then sewed up my cheek. Couldn't do anything about the scar." Quinn looked toward where the troop had departed. "And I ain't had a woman what I didn't have to pay for ever since that day."

Wend responded, "You have my sympathies, Sergeant." Then he motioned to Quinn and the two walked down the trail to where the men held their horses.

He called out, "It's safe for now. Gather around me!"

When they had done so, Wend told them that they would remain in place while Quinn and another man scouted the road ahead to make sure no other British were on the march. He concluded by saying, "Now listen close: This is a warning that we are on dangerous ground. Jersey is disputed country, with militia and partisans from both parties on the move. And the British have sent out regular troops like the cavalry that has just ridden past us to support those on their side. We are alone, with no support, and shall have to be very cautious as we travel, and you must attend to your weapons to ensure they are always ready, for we could find a fight waiting for us around every bend."

The late-afternoon sun still had enough strength to warm Mary Fraser's shoulders as she walked along Walnut Street, encountering many pedestrians along the sidewalk and considerable vehicle traffic on the paved roadway. Soon enough she came to her destination, a pleasant, good-sized red-brick house. She turned into the entrance walkway, went up the steps to the door, and used the hinged knocker to make her presence known. Almost immediately the door was swung open by a very young, dark-haired maid.

"Miss Fraser! Come right in. Mistress Loring is waiting for you!"

Mary smiled at the maid and walked past her into the foyer. The house had been the residence of a patriot family that had chosen to flee

Philadelphia after its occupation by the British and had been subsequently requisitioned as a suitable residence for the family of Joshua Loring, commissioner of prisoners of war for the British Army. It mattered little that the esteemed commissioner was seldom present, as his duties mostly kept him in New York City. This meant that his wife, twenty-six-year-old Elizabeth Loring, was quite free to engage in her *very close* relationship with General William Howe, commander in chief of the British Army in America.

"The mistress is upstairs, packing, Miss Fraser. She said for you to come right up." The maid pointed to the stairway. "Shall I show you the way?"

"No, Theodora, I know the way quite well. And thank you." Mary picked up her skirts and ascended the stairway, and then turned right to proceed to Elizabeth's room. The door was open, and she could see Elizabeth, or Betsy, as close friends called her, bending over a trunk.

Betsy looked up, and a broad smile came over her face. She brushed a loose strand of her golden hair away from her eyes and said, "You're here! I'm so glad you could come this afternoon!"

Mary responded, "It is very nice to get some time away from the hospital." Then, even as she said it, a look of concern came over her face. "But it is saddening to see so many families preparing to leave their property. I passed many wagons being loaded with possessions and others already rolling along the streets on their way to leave town or down to the waterfront."

The muscles in Betsy's face tightened. "This is such a disgrace. After all the trouble of last year's campaign to capture Philadelphia, so many men injured or killed, and our new General Clinton decides to abandon it and concentrate around New York City." She shook her head. "Confidentially, I can tell you William is incensed about it." She sighed. "But in a short time, Clinton will have succeeded him in command, and William will be on a ship bound for England. So etiquette demands he must remain silent and cannot do anything to change the decision."

Mary said, "But all these loyal subjects of the crown will lose nearly everything. They must leave Philadelphia before the rebels enter the city."

"Yes, how well do I know. Joshua and I went through this when the army was forced out of Boston. We left behind almost everything to board a ship for Halifax. And now these people of Philadelphia, who cheered the army's arrival, and have supported William so strongly for many months, face the same thing."

"When will the army leave? There are all sorts of rumors flying around the city."

"That is up to General Clinton to decide, after he assumes command from William. I am told it will probably be in June." She grimaced. "As I said, William is quite upset about Clinton's plans. So much blood and treasure was spent in the campaign of 1777 to occupy this city."

"But Betsy, why? Philadelphia is the largest and most prosperous city in the colonies."

Elizabeth shrugged. "Clinton says his force is too small to hold both cities and carry out the strategy he has in mind, particularly after the loss of Burgoyne's army at Saratoga." She motioned in the general direction of the waterfront and continued, "And then there's the harbor. New York's is larger and more easily accessible from the sea—you don't have to go through the Delaware Bay and up a long river."

Mary pondered that for a long moment. Then she asked, "Where are the loyalists to go? There are so many families who fear the rebels and want to leave."

"Yes, you can't imagine how many. It is thousands. The general told me that there are so many that Clinton has had to change his plans. He was going to ship everyone—both troops and refugees—to New York by sea. But the number of refugee families is so great, there are not enough ships. So he has made the decision to ship the loyalist families by sea, along with some of the soldiers, but the rest of the army will have to march overland from here to Perth Amboy, where they will be ferried across the harbor to the city." Elizabeth walked over to a window and looked out on the street. "And the loyalists will be transported to New York, Canada, and England itself, just like myself. They will have to make their preferences known."

"My God, Betsy, that will be a gigantic undertaking." And then a thought hit Mary. "And with the army marching overland, the rebels will have an opportunity to attack, or at least harass the troops as they travel."

Elizabeth smiled. "You are absolutely correct, Mary. General Howe has confided to me that his spies tell him that Washington has been drilling his men hard over the winter and is spoiling for a fight." A look of satisfaction came over face. "The fact is, our esteemed General Clinton may get considerably more than he bargains for in this movement."

At that moment, Theodora entered, carrying a tray with a tea service. She set it down on a table and made ready to pour. But Elizabeth waved her off. "That will do, Theodora, we'll serve ourselves."

The maid nodded and left the room, and soon her steps were heard descending the stairs. After she had gone, Elizabeth served the tea, and after each had had a sip, she motioned toward the trunks around the room. "I've nearly finished packing myself. Then I'll have to do the children. It has been arranged for us to sail to England on a large, comfortable ship as soon as the evacuation begins. Everything is in the trunks except the clothing I need for the next few days and, of course, the Mischianza." She looked over at Mary. "Major Andre is in charge of planning the festival, and he has told me that Captain Marley of the staff is to escort me for all the events." Then she grinned mischievously. "And I have it on the highest authority that Colonel Northcutt will shortly ask for you to accompany him to the great banquet and ball on the final night."

Mary had feared that would be the case. She sighed and bit her lip but said nothing.

"My dear girl, you look very distressed. Don't you want to come to the ball? It is to be the most glittering affair ever seen in Philadelphia!" She waved a finger. "And Barrett Northcutt, besides being rather attractive and distinguished looking, is such an influential man on the general staff—not to mention his wealth and landholdings in New York. And he has been so gallant to you over the last two years since Halifax. Why would you not be delighted at such an invitation?"

Thinking quickly, Mary said, "Of course, I should be very flattered if the colonel formally invited me. He has already spoken to me, but I deflected the question, protesting that I might have duties at the hospital. But my hesitancy was because I really have nothing appropriate to wear to such an affair. I have but one evening dress, which I bought two years ago in Glasgow before sailing with the regiment. Now it is showing its age. I fear I shall have to make my excuses."

"You will do no such thing, Mary Fraser!" Elizabeth got up and went to a trunk and opened the lid. She searched around for a while, and then pulled out an elegant pale blue gown. Turning to Mary, she held up the garment and said, "Here is your gown! We are of nearly the same size, and you can make the few adjustments which may be necessary. Take it! It's yours."

Astonished, Mary exclaimed, "Oh, Betsy, I couldn't! That's such a beautiful thing. I can't allow you to give it up."

"Nonsense! You must. Think of it as a farewell present from me."

Suddenly tears appeared in Elizabeth's eyes, and she went over to Mary and hugged her tightly. "Oh Mary! These past two years, ever since that night in Halifax when you helped me get through the miscarriage, we have become so close. You are my dearest friend. And you must come, or I shall be so alone. All the women are turning on me. They used to treat me with respect and deference, because they knew of my relationship with Howe. But now that his authority is waning, they are beginning to show disdain for what I have done and to shun me. Please come to help give me the courage to get through it!"

Mary sighed deeply. "Betsy, you have done so much for me. So many kindnesses. And you arranged for me to be temporarily transferred from the 42nd hospital to become the matron of the army general hospital here in the city, where I have learned so much."

Elizabeth looked into Mary's eyes. "And Director Morris tells me you have found many ways to improve the performance of the orderlies and nurses and to make the hospital more efficient."

Mary squeezed her friend. "How can I turn you down? Of course I'll accept Barrett's invitation, if indeed he tenders it."

"Good! I can say there is no doubt he will ask you. And I'll make sure you are seated at my table for the banquet." She laughed and said, "Fie on those straight-laced ladies of Philadelphia. We shall defy them and have a marvelous time!"

Wend led the detachment through generally flat Jersey country which was a mixture of woodland and the cleared fields of plantations. It was the third day since leaving Valley Forge, and evening was in prospect when Childers, riding beside Wend, pointed to the road ahead and said, "There's Quinn sitting his horse in the road about a quarter mile ahead."

"Yes, Edward, I see him."

As Wend spoke, Quinn, who had been scouting for the column, stood up in his stirrups and waved for them to come on and then pointed to the side of the road with his right hand.

Childers said, "It looks like we have arrived."

Wend nodded. "Indeed."

They picked up the pace, crossed a sturdy bridge over a swift-flowing creek, and then rode through woods on both sides of the track. As they approached Quinn, they could see what he had been pointing toward. A drive led northward, and a sign was posted near the road that announced, "Wallen Farm. Joseph Wallen, Master."

Wend halted the detachment and rode up beside Quinn. He looked up the drive and could see that, perhaps two hundred yards away, the trees gave way to a wide yard with a substantial two-story stone house.

Quinn said, "Well, sir, we be here. I saw what looked like some blacks driving a wagon past the house a few minutes ago."

Wend responded, "Come with me, Sergeant; we'll go see the master." He turned to Childers. "Bring the detachment up the drive, just off the road, and wait for my return or the signal to come on in. I don't want to antagonize the owner by having the whole troop ride right into the yard without discussing matters with him."

The two rode up the drive and dismounted before the house, tying the animals to a hitching post near the steps. Wend looked around. To the west was an expanse of green fields, where he could see the early growth of what he presumed to be wheat and hay. They were bordered on the far side by a band of forest. Looking to the east, he saw the working buildings of the farm, a substantial stable, storage sheds for crops and hay, two fenced pastures with horses and cattle, and beyond that more fields. Some distance behind the main house, he saw small cabins that he took to be the quarters for the Africans and other hands.

Wend motioned for Quinn to accompany him and climbed the steps to the porch and knocked on the door. Presently an African butler, dressed in a coat and breeches, appeared in the doorway, and Wend gave his name and rank, and asked to see the owner.

"Yes, sir, Mr. Major Eckert. Please step inside, and I'll inform Mr. Wallen you are here."

Eckert and Quinn entered into a center hall. Wend took off his cap, and Quinn removed his helmet and tucked it under his left arm.

A tall, dark-haired, balding, somewhat corpulent man entered the hall. He was dressed in a short jacket, breaches, and riding boots. He walked toward the pair of soldiers, hand extended. "Well, Major Eckert, I'm Joseph Wallen. And we've been expecting you."

Wend returned the greeting, then said, "So I assume you understand that I've been led to believe my detachment can camp here on your farm for a few days."

"Indeed, sir. I have been briefed on your mission. And we are very glad that General Washington has finally acceded to our request for a military presence here in the area. Perhaps this show of force will help keep these scurrilous bands of partisans at bay."

"Yes, that was the general's hope. I regret that only twenty-five men could be spared, but that is a useful number if some of these partisans do intrude in the area. We intend to work with the local militia if possible."

"Major Eckert, there have been partisans operating not far from here. We have an active but rather small militia in the county. They do what they can, but there is a strong contingent of loyalists who have organized their own force and often support the actions of the partisans."

A feminine voice interrupted. "I fear my husband is understating the problem. There are partisans marauding quite near here. It is by mere chance we have not been attacked."

Wend looked along the hall to see that an attractive, petite, slim-waisted woman with brown hair had entered the hall from a room near the back of the house. She was dressed in a green everyday gown with an apron over the front. She seemed a few years younger than Wallen himself.

Wallen motioned toward her. "Major Eckert, this is my wife, Rachel."

Wend bowed his head and said, "It is my pleasure, ma'am."

"And mine also," responded Rachel Wallen. "But I have no hesitation to say that we live in daily fear of these ruffians. Just two nights ago, they raided Deep Creek Farm, not four miles from here, and hanged the master, Jebediah Rouse. Then they stole everything of use and burned most of the buildings and took the Africans with them, probably back to New York."

Joseph nodded agreement. "Yes, we could see the flames reflected in the sky from here."

Rachel sighed. "They spared Melissa Rouse and her young ones, but there is no way they can survive on what is left of the farm. I am told she took her children and fled to her parents' estate. well to the north of here."

Wend replied, "I am sorry to hear that. You can rest assured that we will do everything in our power to keep you safe, Mrs. Wallen."

Rachel shot Wend an exasperated look. "Yes, I'm sure you will. But you will only be here for a short time. There is nothing to protect us after you leave. I fear I may find myself and my children in the same plight as Melissa any time now."

"But surely the county militia can do something to protect the farms."

The mistress of Wallen Farm gave Wend a look of disgust. "The militia? Mr. Eckert, they are too few in number and ill prepared at best. And when they do attempt to catch these rascals, they are always too late." She stamped her feet and then said in a voice of desperation. "Why can't the army keep troops here and defend us! That is what the army is for! Instead they sit at Valley Forge and drill all day. Surely Washington could spare some soldiers for New Jersey."

Wend felt obligated to reply. "Mrs. Wallen, the army's purpose is to win our freedom from the king and parliament. It must stay together and be in position to confront the British force now occupying Philadelphia. We must be ready to campaign when they come out, as indeed they shall any time now."

Rachel looked at Wend with smoldering eyes. "Freedom will be of little use to this family if the partisans put us in the grave, a situation which is clearly likely. I fear our only resort is to flee to some place of safety and abandon all we have worked for to their clutches."

Joseph Wallen moved to intervene. He put his arm around his wife and said, "Now, Rachel, you know we have organized and armed some of the hands here on the farm to help defend it. And it is unfair and impolite to take your anger out on Major Eckert. He can only obey his instructions and cannot speak for the army's command or Congress." He paused and stared meaningfully at his wife.

Rachel took a deep breath, and some of the ire drained from her face. "Yes, yes, Joseph. We must remember our manners and hospitality." She looked over at Wend. "Please forgive my outburst. I meant no disrespect for you or your men, Major." She took a few more breaths, then said, "You must accept our hospitality tonight and join us for supper. We set a good table here, and I would be most pleased if you would partake of it with us this evening. And please bring your officers."

Wend made a slight bow from the waist. "It will be our pleasure, Mrs. Wallen. And I have only one other officer with me, a young lieutenant named Edward Childers. We shall both look forward to your hospitality."

Rachel's eyes lit up. "A young lieutenant? Well of course he would be most welcome."

Joseph made haste to change the subject. "Now, Major Eckert, come with me, and I will show you the best site for your camp, which is just to the west of the yard here, and your horses will go to the fenced paddock, which is just to the east of the house." He headed to the door and motioned for Wend and Quinn to follow.

Once outside, he showed them the places he had mentioned. Wend told Quinn to mount and bring the troop up to the yard.

Once he had left, Wallen turned to Wend and said, "Now I have some confidential information for you. It is from the man who told me to expect you and convinced me to allow you to camp here on the farm."

Wend was immediately at full attention. "Yes, and who is this man?"

Wallen laughed. "I don't know who or what he really is. I am of the opinion that he leads the army's web of spies in this area, but I cannot be precisely confident of that. And he goes by many names. However, right now he is calling himself *Crowder*. And he told me to let you know that name and that he will come to you to provide information that you need to accomplish your mission."

"Did he say when?"

"He never says when. He never says when he will come around or where he will be at other times. You should just wait here, and he will come when it suits him. But I suspect that will not be long."

—ꟽ—

In preparation for dinner with the Wallens, Wend had changed into his blue uniform from the hunting shirt he had been wearing since the departure from Valley Forge. He was standing in front of the fire that he and Childers shared when Sergeant Quinn approached.

"All right, sir, camp is nearly set up, and Mrs. Wood has started preparing rations. And I've got the picket up at the road as you ordered. Found them a good spot in the woods where they can see the road, both ways, without bein' seen. All our horses are in Wallen's small pasture; they'll be easy to get in a hurry, if'n somethin' comes up. And I hope they can stay there for a couple of days feeding on his good spring grass; we pushed pretty hard on the ride up." He looked over at the fire where Meli had started the evening meal. "If you got no more for me now, I'll get ready for supper."

"That will be fine, Quinn. If you need me tonight, you'll know where I'll be. And I don't intend to tarry long at the Wallens'." He thought a moment, then added, "After supper, check on the picket. Keep them alert. I'm told a band of partisans is operating in this area."

Quinn frowned. "I'd do that in any case." And without another word, he turned and hurried off.

Momentarily, Edward, also now attired in his dress uniform, joined Wend. He looked over at his commander. "Well, sir. I'm ready to visit with the Wallens. But I have to say, I'd rather spend the evening sitting comfortably by the fire, after the ride of the last few days."

"Edward, it's our obligation to accept the hospitality of our hosts. We must ensure that cordiality reigns because the Wallens are putting much effort into supporting our detachment. And to be honest, if the loyalist faction learns they are providing us support, they may become a target after we have departed. They are being rather brave given the circumstances."

Childers smiled. "I understand, but I'm still tired. However, wearisome though it might be, I shall do my duty tonight."

Wend laughed. "Stout fellow. Now let's go see the Wallens. At least we'll probably have better food than the field rations the rest of the detachment will eat tonight."

They were greeted by the same butler who had met Wend in the afternoon, who showed them into the Wallens' parlor. Wallen himself was standing beside the hearth, cup in hand, while Rachel was seated on a settee. Wend introduced Edward, who greeted the farm owners with the ease and impeccable manners of one raised in the gentry. Joseph offered the two officers a libation, which was eagerly accepted. While he was pouring the drinks, Rachel called the butler and asked him to call for the children to join them.

Wend heard footsteps on the stairs, and then two young boys entered. He guessed one was about twelve and the other perhaps ten. They were introduced as Richard and Harry, and they behaved with suitable manners.

Then Rachel turned toward the door, announcing, "And here is our May."

Wend looked toward the entrance and saw a young girl he judged to be perhaps sixteen, who was obviously her mother's daughter. She was petite, brown haired, and just about the same height as Rachel, with brown eyes and a nicely shaped mouth—all in all, most attractive to Wend's eyes. He quickly looked over at Edward and saw the youth's eyes light up and a broad smile of appreciation spread across his face.

Wend saw Rachel closely watching the young officer, and satisfaction appeared in her countenance as he looked at the girl. She said, "Major Eckert and Lieutenant Childers, may I present our daughter May Anne?"

Wend made a slight bow and said, "My pleasure, Mistress Wallen."

Edward made a much deeper bow from the waist and gave her his most gracious smile. "Miss May Anne, it is indeed a pleasure. And may I say, that is a most lovely gown you are wearing."

The young woman cocked her head and asked, "Oh, Mr. Childers, do you think it flatters my figure?"

Edward drew himself up and responded, "Miss Wallen, in truth it is *you* who flatters the gown."

Wend observed that May Anne flushed and smiled at his words while her mother absolutely beamed.

The girl said, "Mr. Childers, you are such a gentleman. I find southern manners are so lovely."

"I would not say it, Miss May Anne, if it were not true."

Wend was wondering how long this would all go on when the butler appeared and announced that supper was on the table.

Rachel turned to the company and said, "Shall we go into the dining room?" She offered Wend her arm. "Major, won't you escort me to the table?"

Wend took her arm and led her to the foot of the table. Edward did the same for May Anne. The master of Wallen Farm took the head chair and motioned Wend to his right hand and Edward to his left. May Anne eagerly took a place beside Childers, and the young boys took the other two seats on either side of their mother.

The centerpiece of the meal was a great roast of beef, which a servant brought in on a tray, and Wallen stood to carve the meat. While he was doing so, vegetables, potatoes, and gravy were served. It was altogether the best meal Wend had partaken since the army had gone into camp at Valley Forge. He looked over at Childers to see that the food was not nearly as much on the youth's mind as the charms of May Anne. The two were exchanging smiles and whispers, seemingly unaware of the others at the table. Rachel Wallen was observing them with thinly disguised satisfaction.

As they were just finishing, the butler came in and quietly whispered in Joseph's ear. Wallen looked over at Wend. "Your sergeant is at the front door. Apparently someone has come into the camp who says he has urgent business with you." He raised an eyebrow meaningfully. "I am informed his name is *Crowder*."

Wend picked up his napkin and folded it. "Ah, yes, I've been expecting him." He turned to Rachel. "Mrs. Wallen, please accept my gratitude for this fine meal, but business calls."

Rachel nodded and said, "We are sorry you have to leave so peremptorily, Major. I have so enjoyed your company."

Edward looked up. "Shall I come also, sir?"

Wend grinned. "That won't be necessary, Mr. Childers. Enjoy the rest of the meal and the Wallens' hospitality."

Edward smiled and replied, "That would be my pleasure, sir."

Wend smiled back, thinking, *Undoubtedly the charms of young Miss Wallen have made him forget all about the weariness he complained of earlier.*

Quinn was waiting on the porch. "Major, there's a man, calls himself Crowder, came into camp and says it was important to see you. I told him you was in havin' supper with the owner, but he insisted I get you straightaway. Said both you and Wallen would understand when I mentioned his name." The sergeant made a face. "You tell me you don't want to see him, I'll put him in his place right away, put him back on his horse, and enjoy doin' it."

"It's all right, Quinn. He's the man I came here to meet. And his name is about as valid as Fairfield's."

Quinn guffawed. "I take your meaning Eckert. Geoffrey has used at least three names since I met him."

"I'm sure Crowder will be using something else next week."

Eckert and Quinn walked over to the officers' fire. The man calling himself Crowder was sitting on a camp chair, a cup in his hand, staring into the flames. Crowder heard the pair approaching and rose to his feet and turned toward them.

Wend looked over the man, who appeared to be on the far side of forty. He was below average height, visibly corpulent—particularly around the waist—with a belly stretching the material of his waistcoat. He had a round face, with a prominent double chin, topped by a hairline that had receded halfway to the rear of his head. Wend decided he looked like a small-town shopkeeper.

"I assume you are Eckert?"

Wend replied, "Yes, I am *Major* Eckert."

"Ah, yes, *Major* Eckert. My name is Samuel Crowder." He held up the cup. "I took the liberty of drawing some of the whiskey from the jug sitting here. Rather good stuff, actually."

"Most people think so, Mr. Crowder." Wend turned to Quinn. "Thank you, sergeant; that will be all."

"Aye, sir. I'll be at my fire. Give me a call if you need me."

Once the sergeant had departed, Wend turned back to the little man. "If you are the man I've been waiting for, there should be a word you will give me, a word told to me by the man who is ultimately directing this mission."

Crowder grinned. "Ah, yes, indeed, sir!" He leaned closer, close enough for Wend to smell the whiskey on his breath, and said in a whisper, "*Jumonville.*" He paused, then laughed. "Does that prove my bona fides, Major?"

"I'm satisfied." Wend motioned toward the camp chair. "Please be seated."

Wend sat down. "Do you have information about my primary assignment?"

Crowder drained his cup and looked over at Wend. "Pray, may I have some more of this?"

Pointing at the jug, Wend said, "Help yourself."

Crowder poured another cup, took a long sip, then sighed.

Wend said, "Now, sir, what is your information?"

"It seems likely we have found the man you are looking for. He has traveled from the north. And he's taken a room at an inn in Elizabeth Town."

"But you are not sure it is Captain Henry?"

"No, he's using another name. And of course, we have no one who knows him by sight. But he fits the description."

"How long has he been at this inn?"

"Just a few days. But I can tell you he is in desperate shape: drinking heavily and selling his possessions to obtain money. I have it on direct authority that he sold his horse and saddle two days ago. My source tells me he keeps to his room constantly, just ordering drink and meager meals."

A worrisome thought occurred to Wend. "He sold his horse? How does he plan to continue his journey?"

Crowder looked directly at Wend. "Now you have hit on an important point. Perchance he doesn't plan to travel any further. He may feel he is at the end of his string."

"Then it is crucial that we get to him posthaste."

"The thought *had* occurred to me. That's why I made haste to get here now."

"Then we will ride out to find him tomorrow."

Crowder took another gulp. "That will not be too soon." He pulled on his drink and continued, "All right, here's information you will need: The name of the inn is the Good Queen Bess." He handed Wend a folded piece of paper. "Here are directions to get there. If you leave early, you can arrive just after the noon hour."

Wend took the paper and opened it. It was a hand-drawn map and written instructions. Then he leaned closer to the fire to make out the details. After a few moments, he frowned and looked at the little man. "That's just over the harbor from Manhattan."

"Indeed, sir. It will be dangerous ground for you. It is loyalist territory, and the proprietor of the inn is of the king's party—not to mention there are British patrols."

"I'll take enough men to overpower any resistance he may have."

"Yes, but there is also a well-organized royalist militia that can muster at short notice."

Wend nodded. "So we must be quick about our business. In and out rapidly."

"Yes, whatever happens, don't tarry long at the inn." He held up a finger. "One other thing: I have an associate placed at the inn—a serving girl, and she knows the man's room. She will contrive to contact you after you arrive and let you know where he is. But let her arrange the manner of doing so. I want to keep her role in my organization unknown to the proprietor."

Wend nodded. "I understand." Then he thought of something. "What is the proprietor's name?"

"Thomas Grimsby. Take care to watch him, for he is crafty."

"All right, Crowder. Will you stay the night here?"

Crowder sighed deeply. "No, Major, I have miles to ride tonight for I must consult with another of my informants. There are many things afoot besides your business." He drained the cup in his hand and set it down, then rose to his feet. "In fact, I must leave now. He pointed to the moon, which was well above the eastern horizon. "I must ride while the light is good enough to be of some use."

Wend escorted Crowder to his horse, which was hitched to a rail of the paddock fence. Wend noted that the horse was as nondescript as its owner.

Crowder pulled himself up into the saddle, looked down at Wend, and said, "I wish you luck in your endeavor tomorrow and godspeed on your way back to the army." And with that, he was on his way out the drive. Wend watched until horse and rider reached the main road and saw that he turned northward.

Wend momentarily wondered what mission the man was now undertaking, but soon his thoughts turned to making plans for the morrow.

—᯾—

Wend stood before the crackling flames of the detachment's cook fire in the morning dusk. At his back was the parked supply wagon. The entire troop was gathered in front of him. Some were standing, others sitting on the ground. Many still were working on their breakfasts, tin plates in hand. Others nursed mugs of coffee. Meli was working over a tub of water, cleaning up her cooking utensils, often making a clinking noise. He looked around at the assemblage and said, "All right. Give me your attention. I'm going to talk about our mission and, in particular, what is going to happen today."

Every eye was on him now, and Wend searched for the right words. "Men, you have been told that our task here is to support the patriotic militia in their fight against loyalist partisans. That is true." He paused for effect. "True as far as it goes." He swept the silent men with his eyes and continued, "But we have an overriding mission, one given to me personally by our commander in chief."

Even Meli stopped working at her cleaning and looked over at him. Wend glanced over at Childers, who knew what was coming, and saw that he was looking closely at the men to see their reaction.

"Men, at an inn a few hours' ride north of here is a man who is an officer in our army, a man who has fought valiantly in many battles, and particularly at Saratoga. However, for certain reasons, he has gone astray and is now in danger of falling into the hands of the British. Because his father is an important and famous leader of our cause, we cannot let that happen, for our enemies might use him to embarrass his father and ultimately our great movement. The mission that Washington has given us is to find and carry to safety this young officer."

Wend swept his eyes around the gathering to see how the men were reacting.

Before he could resume speaking, Quinn called out. "So who the hell is this person? Sounds to me like that wayward son in the Bible, that *prodigal* or whatever you call him."

Wend grinned. "Quinn, of all the men here, you are the last one I would have suspected of being a reader of the Bible."

A wave of laughter rippled around the troop, and one private called out, "You got that right, Major! He'd more likely be a disciple of Lucifer!"

Quinn glared at the private, then turned back to Wend. "Shit, sir, I'm *Irish*. And *every* Irishman grows up with the Bible close at hand. My sainted mother used to sit me down and read it to me every day." He grinned. "Not that it did much good."

Laughter erupted around the campfire.

But Quinn was not finished. When the laughter died out, he asked, "Now if you don't mind, Major, who is this wayward son we are going to rescue?"

There were nods around the circle of faces, and another private repeated the question. "Yes, who is it?" Immediately others joined in the questioning.

Wend had not intended to reveal the precise name, but now it became clear that was impossible to avoid doing so. The men would not be satisfied, and he realized that when young Henry was brought back, it would soon be evident who the important leader was. He held up a hand. "All right, men, I will say the name. But hear me clear: We must hold this information close. We must not reveal it to the local people lest the word get out. There are loyalist forces who, learning the name, would spare no effort to attack us with the purpose of capturing him."

There was silence around the ring of soldiers. Wend cleared his throat, then said, "The man we are seeking is Captain John Henry, son of Patrick Henry, governor of Virginia."

There was an audible gasping that ran through the ranks.

Wend continued speaking. "I think you can now grasp the importance of our mission. The British would like nothing better than to possess the son of the governor of our largest state and the man who is famous throughout America for one of the most important speeches calling for rebellion against the crown and parliament. The phrase 'Give me liberty, or give me death' rang through the colonies two years ago, and no one has forgotten who said those words. Think what the British could do with young Henry."

There were many nods.

Quinn, standing with hands on hips, said, "All right, Major, so where is Henry's son, and how do you propose we get him?"

Wend nodded. "That's the proper question to ask, Sergeant. Now all of you listen sharp. Here is the plan." He took a moment to organize his thoughts.

"Captain Henry is staying at an inn in Elizabeth Town. It is about nine or ten miles from this farm and is across the harbor from Manhattan itself. I am informed that it is a nest of loyalists, and British patrols frequent the area. Obviously, it is most dangerous territory for us. So we must be able to move fast."

Wend looked over at Quinn. "To that end, Sergeant, we will take only the squad of light dragoons to Elizabeth Town. Both Lieutenant Childers and I will go with the squad. We will take one extra horse for Captain Henry. I expect to leave as soon as the horses can be made ready, and with luck we will be back by the evening dusk."

Sergeant Schreiber, who had been sitting on the ground, stiffened, then rose up to one knee, a frown on his face. "Major Eckert! Why not my squad instead? We are all Virginians, and it is only right that we go to find our governor's son!"

Quinn laughed. "You're welcome to make this trip, Dutchman! We dragoons welcome the opportunity to lie about all day."

Schreiber shot back, "Ja, that's what dragoons are good for anyway!"

"Quiet, the both of you!" Wend shook his head. "I understand your feelings, Schreiber, but your men are mounted *foot,* not actual cavalry. We must be ready to fight from the saddle as well as dismounted. It's a job for *true* cavalry. The role of your squad will be to watch over, and if need be, defend our camp and the farm. And I'm leaving you in charge, since Lieutenant Childers will be coming with us. Keep a sharp watch on the road, in case partisans approach. The owner of the farm has armed a group of his men, and they will be able to help if it comes to a fight."

Schreiber nodded. "All right, Major. But we're not happy about it."

There were nods of agreement from men in his squad.

Wend admonished, "Now look here, the lot of you! We're all soldiers." He motioned toward the men of Schreiber's squad. "In the time since we left Winchester, two years ago, we've all had to carry out orders we didn't like. So I know you will do what is necessary." Then he turned to Quinn. "Let's get saddled and on our way." He pointed toward the east. "The sun will soon be above the horizon, and we'll need every bit of sunlight we can get this day."

—∞—

The column, two officers, Trumpeter Bloom, Sergeant Quinn, Corporal Harley, and eight troopers, was making its way northward, and the sun was now high in the sky. Wend figured they were about halfway to Elizabethtown. Quinn had moved up to ride beside Wend.

"Major, I got a question."

Wend looked over at the Irishman, whose face was screwed up in thought. "What's on your mind, Sergeant?"

"I'm thinkin' there was something missing in what you said this morning. Somethin' important."

"And what do you think that is, Quinn?"

"Just why the *hell* this young Henry left the army and is in need of rescue. And why he's in a dangerous place amid royalists and British." He looked over at Wend and raised his eyebrows. "I'm wantin' to know that, Eckert. I think we got a right to know it."

They rode on in silence for a few long moments, as Wend calculated how to respond. Finally he said, "All right, Quinn. I'll give you the full story."

"Damn well time, Eckert."

"It's a matter of love, Sergeant. John Henry was enamored with a certain young girl named Dorothea Dandridge. He went off to the army thinking she harbored the same feeling and expecting to ask for her hand when he returned. While he was away, his father met Dorothea and decided she was his cup of tea, and secured her father's agreement to marry her, which occurred at the end of last year. When young Henry, a captain in Gate's army, got a letter announcing what had happened, he bolted. Obviously he was nursing a broken heart and feeling betrayed by both the lass and his father. And he has been on the run ever since, probably not thinking about where he's going or what he's going to do about himself. Now he's out of money, stranded in a dangerous place."

Quinn's face wrinkled up in anger. "Shit, Eckert! That's what this is all about? So now we're supposed to put our lives on the line because some brat of the bloody gentry was besotted by a pretty little wench, and his father decided to take her for his own bed? I'm nearly of a mind to turn around and head back to the farm." He looked at Wend and pointed down toward his mount's legs. "Maybe some of our horses will come up lame, sudden like. That will put an end to this foolishness!"

"No, Quinn, you and I know that's not going to happen."

"And just why?"

Wend looked over at the Irishman with the broadest smile he could muster. "Quinn, we both know that you're a thief, a highwayman, and no doubt a murderer."

"I make no secret that there's not a mortal sin I haven't committed somewhere along the way. What's your point, Major?"

"But beyond all that, there's one more, very important thing you are. And that's a *soldier*. You're a damned good one and prouder of that than anything else—proud you were a sergeant in the British Army's Eleventh Dragoons. You've boasted about it many a time."

"What of it?"

Wend ignored the question and continued. "I remember last year you and McCrae goaded Fairfield into that charge against a troop of the 16th Light Dragoons. And you smashed them. Afterward you wildly celebrated the triumph of your South Carolina troop over Burgoyne's Beauties, shouting you had taught them a lesson. But what you were really excited about was the sheer joy of beating the enemy in a good fight. You weren't worried about your life then."

"McCrae and I had been wantin' to show them dandies they couldn't stand up to Irish dragoons."

"But my point is, Quinn, you fight because you like a good fight, and you aren't afraid to put your life on the line. And so you are very good at it, probably better than anyone else in the Guides." He fixed his eyes on the sergeant and said, "That's precisely why I brought you along—you're the perfect man for desperate action in a tight place. And now you are going to fulfill that promise by helping me get young Henry out of trouble."

Quinn stared at him for a long time. Finally he said, "All right, Eckert. We'll go get the young captain and damned well won't let anything stand in our way. But if there's trouble and I take a ball, mark my words, I'll go to eternity wishing the hell Fairfield had let me blow your brains out back there that night in '75 beside the Shenandoah."

"I can live with that, Sergeant Quinn. Besides, you made that clear long ago. And if it happens, you and Fairfield can fight it out in hell with the devil as the judge because we know sooner or later he's going to join you there." He grinned at Quinn. "Now let's go get the wayward son."

Chapter Three
The Lodger

The dragoon party arrived at Elizabeth Town on schedule and rapidly rode through town until they reached the street where sat the Good Queen Bess. Samuel Crowder's instructions had been precise and accurate. Wend halted the detachment and, glancing up at the sun, saw that it was slightly past noon. He looked at the inn, perhaps 150 yards in front of them, and realized it was quite substantial. The main building was constructed of red brick and had two stories. On either side of the brick structure were wooden additions, also of two stories. The main door was up three steps and in the very center of the inn. On the far side of the building, Wend could see an alleyway with a sign that said, "Stable."

Childers, sitting his horse beside Wend, spoke up. "I don't know if you noticed, sir, but we've been attracting quite a bit of attention as we rode through town." He pointed back to the street corner thirty yards behind them. Wend looked where he pointed, and a group of five men were standing there, watching them closely.

Wend nodded. "Yes, I doubt they often see Continental dragoons in this part of New Jersey."

Edward responded, "They may be trying to figure out who we are. There are loyalist dragoons who have uniforms of similar color as ours."

"I hope you are right, Edward. The longer they puzzle over who we are, the better."

Wend turned to Quinn. "Sergeant, we'll dismount and leave the horses in front of the inn. Place Corporal Harley at that door with one other trooper, to watch the horses and to warn us if any kind of gathering appears on the street. The rest of the men will come in with us, since we don't know what we'll encounter."

Quinn nodded. "Right, Major."

Wend waved for the column to move forward at the trot. They pulled up before the inn and dismounted. He looked back along the street and saw that the group of men on the corner were watching, talking heatedly among themselves, and pointing at the squad.

A thought struck Wend, and he turned to Quinn. "I'm making a change in our plans, Sergeant. Before we go in, have the men take all our horses around to the inn's stable yard. They will attract too much attention out here on the street." He pointed to the alleyway and sign. "Then come back here. I'll wait for your return before we enter."

The troopers gathered the reins of the horses and started to lead them to the stable area. Wend called out, "Bring all your firearms back with you—pistols and carbines. We must be ready for anything we encounter."

When they returned, and the corporal and his man had been posted near the steps, Wend led Childers, Quinn, Bloom, and the seven troopers up the stairs and into the tavern. He had expected to find the common room right inside the door, but instead there was just a small reception room with a hall ahead of them. He looked to the left and saw a wide entrance-way and walked over to see that the common room occupied the bottom floor of the wooden addition on that side of the inn. In fact, the common room was a great open space with a high ceiling instead of a second floor.

There was a wooden loft above the rear half of the room, where he could see additional tables and chairs. He looked around and saw that there were perhaps twenty patrons at tables. Several servers were moving around the room or in and out of the cook room, which looked to be inside the rear of the original part of the building.

Wend strode into the common room and motioned the rest to follow. He turned to Quinn. "Place your men in positions so they can cover all in the room with their pistols."

Every face, patron and staff, turned to look at the men entering the room. Silence suddenly dropped over the room, except for the noise of the soldiers taking their positions. Wend felt all eyes on him.

Then one server, a young lad, went to the door of the cook room and called excitedly, "Sir, sir! Come out here!"

Then the boy turned to watch the soldiers and was soon joined by a heavyset, middle-aged, balding man with a face red from the heat of cook fires. He was wearing a white apron over his clothing, and it was stained with grease in several places. A cloth was draped over his shoulder.

The man in the apron looked at Wend, then around the room at the soldiers with pistols in hand, and then back to Wend. He took a step forward and said in a loud voice, "Who, sir, are you? And what is toward that you so boldly invade this establishment with armed soldiers?"

Wend did not directly answer. "I'm looking for Grimsby, the proprietor of this inn."

The balding man took the cloth from his shoulder and wiped his face, then threw it down on a table in front of him. "I am Thomas Grimsby, and I say again, who wants to know?"

"I'm Major Eckert of the Continental Guides. And we're looking for a man who may be staying at this inn."

At the word "Guides," a man at one of the tables leaned forward and called out to Grimsby, "Thomas, I ran into the Guides at Princeton last year." He held up a crutch which had been leaning up against his table. "They ruined my leg forever and left me needing this. They work for Washington himself. Don't get crossed with them!"

"All right, Hallam, I hear you. But I'll not be bullied by anyone, let alone a rebel, in my own place." He turned back to Wend. "By what right do you have to enter here and make such a demand? Do you have some warrant? My lodgers have a right to privacy."

Wend motioned to the armed men and tapped the butt of one of the pistols in his belt. "This is my warrant. Now, will you show me which rooms are occupied?"

"You'll have to find out yourself, for I will *not* assist you. Most particularly under the threat of rebel firelocks."

Wend was thinking on how to respond when Childers, who stood next to him, nudged him with his elbow. The lieutenant motioned with his eyes up to the loft above, and Wend followed his stare. There, almost obscured by darkness in a corner, was a young serving maid. She was motioning with a finger and pointing toward a door from the loft into the second floor of the inn.

Edward said, "Sir, we're wasting time by bandying words with the man. It seems there's nothing for it but to search the inn ourselves. I suggest we start with the second floor and work down." He pointed to the stairway that led up to the loft and the door into the older portion of the inn.

Wend nodded. "That is precisely what we shall do." He looked over to Quinn. "Leave all but one of your men here. Then you and your trooper, Childers, and I shall inspect the rooms." Wend swept his hand around the room and said, "All of you, continue as you were. We shall not harm you if you remain at your tables."

Having finished, he led the way up the stairs. When he reached the top, the young girl, keeping out of sight of the men below, quickly opened the door and entered. Wend and the others followed, to find themselves in a hall with doors on either side.

The girl faced Wend and said, "I know where the man is; I'll show you the door."

She was of above average height, with a willowy figure, raven hair, and a pretty round face with penetrating blue eyes. Wend asked, "Who are you? And why are you helping us?"

"My name is Nell Porter." She grinned, and the smile made her look even prettier, and then she continued, "And I have a word for you: *Jumonville*."

Wend nodded. "That satisfies my question, Nell. So where is the man we are looking for?"

"He is in room five, right down there on the left. It looks out over the yard."

"All right, Nell, lead on."

Quickly they arrived at Number Five. Wend pounded on the door. There was no answer.

Nell said, "He's in there. I just delivered him a jug an hour ago, and I've not seen him leave."

Wend pounded again and said, "Open up, sir!"

There was silence for a long moment, then an unsteady voice called, "G-G-Go away. I am busy."

Wend shouted, "I'm an officer of the Continental Army. We have business with you!"

There was no further sound from inside the room. Wend looked over at Quinn. "Is it within your power to open the door, Sergeant?"

"Shit, sir. Nothing would be easier." Quinn lifted his boot high and smashed its sole into the door, which immediately popped open and slammed back against the wall.

Wend saw a young man with red hair sitting on the bed, staring straight ahead. In front of him was a jug with a cup beside it.

From beside Eckert, Childers said, "That's him!" then called, "John, it's Edward Childers! We're here to help you!"

John Henry turned his face toward the door and scowled. Then he reached down with his hand and raised a large horse pistol, which had been lying on the bed beside him, quickly cocked it, and put the muzzle to his forehead.

Edward screamed, "John! No! No!"

Acting on instinct, Wend snatched a pistol from his belt and in one swift movement raised it until it was in line with Henry and pulled the trigger. There was a loud bang, and the horse pistol flew from Henry's hand and smacked up against the far wall before falling to the floor.

There was a shocked silence. Quinn looked over at Wend and said in a nonchalant voice, "Now that was a hell of a shot, Eckert. Sometime you'll have to tell me how you did it."

Wend replied, "A compliment from you, Quinn? Something I never thought to hear."

"Yes, sir. But don't get used to it."

Wend walked into the room. Henry was staring at his right hand, which was covered in blood. All the fingers were intact, but the ball had grazed the side of his hand between the thumb and wrist.

John looked up at Wend and said in slurred, indignant words, "For God's sake, you might have killed me!" As he spoke, the powerful smell of liquor nearly overwhelmed Eckert.

Wend responded,. "Then I'd have only done for you what you intended to do yourself."

Henry raised his eyebrows and stared at Wend. Then he broke into shrill, insane sounding laughter. In a moment it ended, and he giggled out, "You are so right!"

Childers went over to his friend and took hold of his injured hand. "It's not that bad, but we've got to get a dressing on it."

Nell Porter said, "I know what to do." She went over to a wardrobe and opened it. Inside was a white shirt. She took it off the hanger and quickly ripped the rear tail off it. Then she wrapped it around John's hand and tied it off. "It's not a proper dressing, but it will hold the blood until it can be treated."

Wend said, "Let's get all his belongings together. We need to get out of here fast."

Nell said, "There won't be much, he's traded most of his clothing to Grimsby to pay for food and lodging. That was days ago, and Grimsby was going to kick him out soon."

Childers had been looking over his friend, and he turned to Wend. "Sir, he's besotted. He can't ride like this."

Quinn lifted the jug. Then he said, "The damn thing is almost empty. He's done a lot of drinking in an hour. Must have been pourin' it down his throat."

Wend nodded. "He was working up courage to use the pistol." He grimaced. "We've got to sober him up enough so he can ride. Somebody find some water—we'll douse him and see what that does."

Quinn looked around. Then he called out, "Here's a bucket." He grabbed it and dumped it over Henry's head.

Nell looked over at him. "Sergeant, you just poured the night soil all over him."

Edward made a face. "Oh, my God!"

Nell smiled mischievously. "The smell alone may sober him up."

Quinn said defensively, "Damn, I thought it was just water."

The tavern maid appeared to be right. Henry, who had been sitting on the bed with a drowsy look on his face, opened his eyes wide, stiffened, and proclaimed, "What have you done to me?"

Wend grabbed Henry by the collar of his shirt and started to shake him. "Get yourself together, John. You have to ride soon."

Suddenly a loud voice emanating from the doorway interrupted the proceedings. "Now what the *devil* are you doing! I heard a shot. What in the *hell* is this about?"

Wend looked back to the door to see Grimsby standing there. "We're taking this man with us, Grimsby. That's all you need to know."

The inn keeper's face screwed up into a snarl. "No one invades my place, fires a pistol, and seizes one of my guests. You won't get away with it."

Quinn said in an evil tone, "You bastard—who's going to stop us?" He tapped the butt of one of the pistols in his belt. "Go back to your common room and tend to your business."

Grimsby backed off into the hall but said belligerently, "Don't tell me my business. You think you can do what you want because of all your bloody firelocks. Well, when you leave, you will find yourself confronted by armed men who outnumber you." He waved toward the front of the inn. "I suggest you look out on the street."

Wend motioned to Quinn. "Check it out."

The sergeant pushed his way past Grimsby to look out a front window.

Meanwhile, the inn keeper snarled at Nell. "And you—you little bitch—you've been helping these damned rebels. I'll deal with you when they're in the hands of our militia." He thought a moment. "In fact, I may let the militia take you with them. That will teach you to help traitors to the king!"

Quinn came back in a rush and, standing in the doorway, said, "Major, the bastard's right. There's twenty armed men out front, and more comin' up the street. We got a big problem."

Grimsby grinned. "That's right. I sent a runner to call out our local militia. We support His Majesty here, and you'll all be on your way to the prison ships soon enough." He pointed at Nell. "And you with them, you traitorous wench."

Wend, with more certainty than he felt, said, "Your damned militia won't stop us." He turned to Edward. "Get him ready to move. Forget his stuff, we have to move now." He turned to Quinn and the trooper, whose name was Trillby, and, pointing at Grimsby, said, "Take hold of him. We may be able to use him for trading purposes."

Quinn pulled a pistol and motioned to Trillby to do the same. Then he grabbed the inn keeper and slammed him against the wall of the hallway. "All right, you ass, don't try anything, or it'll be my pleasure to put a hole in you."

Grimsby laughed. "It matters naught. You'll be the prisoners soon enough, and I'll be back tending the inn."

Quinn laughed. "Not if you've got a ball in your head."

Nell, with fear written on her face, cried, "Major, you've got to take me with you. They'll have no mercy on me."

Wend nodded. "I don't know at the moment how much protection I can afford you, but if we leave on our own terms, you'll be with us. Now stay with Lieutenant Childers and help him with Henry."

Wend hurried out of the room and went to a window and looked down on the street. He estimated there were now twenty-five armed men, mostly with muskets, in a group, confronting Corporal Harley and his compatriot, Private Sanders, who stood on the small porch at the front door. Wend's heart seemed to leap. It would be only through great luck that they got away clean. And he would have to act fast, before more loyalist militia showed up.

He went back to the room. Childers and Nell had Henry on his feet, one on each side holding him steady. "All right, Edward and Quinn, get him down to the ground floor and out a back door to the stable yard. Then get him on a horse."

Quinn looked at Henry and scowled. "He still ain't in much condition to sit a horse."

"I don't care how you do it. Lash him to the stirrups if you have to or throw him over the saddle and tie him there, but get him on a horse." He pointed to Nell. "She's light as a feather; she'll have to ride behind someone."

Quinn said, "Right enough. But what about you—and how are we getting out of this damned trap?"

Wend said, "Now, listen close. Get all our men out of the common room to the stable yard and mount up. Form a tight group in that alleyway, weapons ready, and listen for the sound of a pistol shot. When you hear it, come out of the alley fast and lay into the mob in front of the inn with sabers and pistols. You can't hesitate to use force."

Quinn laughed. "As if I would."

"And have someone leading the horses for Harley, Sanders, and myself." He motioned toward the door. "Get going now. I'll take Grimsby with me and try to stall that mob out front."

Quinn said,. "All right, let's get out of here." He led off toward the stairs. Edward and Nell half lifted, half dragged Henry. And Trillby drew his pistol and followed.

Grimsby watched them go, then turned to Wend and said, "It's all folly. You'll never get out of here. Our boys will stop you."

Wend pulled a pistol and whipped the barrel across the inn keeper's face. Grimsby's nose was smashed, and blood flowed out of the nose and mouth. He leaned over and spit out a front tooth. "You bastard!"

Wend held the pistol up as if ready to strike again. "Now listen close. That was to show you I mean business. You are going to come with me and do as I say, or someone else will be running this inn after today. Understand clearly—I'm a desperate man, and I'll put a ball in you unless you do as I say."

Grimsby was holding a hand over his mouth and blood was oozing out between his fingers. There was terror in his eyes as he nodded he would cooperate. Wend grabbed the man's arm and said, "Now let's get down to the front door."

When they arrived on the front steps, Corporal Farley and the other trooper, Sanders, had pistols in hand, staring at the armed militia, who were grouped in the middle of the street, no more than ten yards away. Some of the men were shouting epithets at the two soldiers.

Farley asked, "Major, I sure am glad to see you. When are we getting out of here?

Sanders interjected, "I don't mean to be disrespectful, sir. But my question is, '*How* the hell do we get out of here?'"

Wend didn't answer directly. Instead, he released his grasp on Grimsby, who sank to his knees. Pulling his pistols from his belt, Wend shouted out to the mob, "Who is your leader?"

A tall, powerful-looking man, dressed in working clothes, took a step forward. "I am Captain Howard Todd, of the Elizabeth Town Loyal Militia Company."

Wend responded in a loud voice, "In the name of the Continental Army, I order you to disburse. We are on official business and will be departing instantly!"

Todd laughed out loud and looked around at his compatriots, some of whom joined him in laughter or at least grinned. The militia captain said, "You are telling *us* to disburse?" There was more laughter. Todd pointed at Wend. "I see three of you," and quickly looked around at his men, "And near thirty of us. And *you* are ordering *us* to disburse?"

Wend said in a loud voice, "I'm telling you for the last time, disburse! Disburse, or there will be consequences for you."

More laughter from the armed loyalists. And they actually bunched closer together, as if to defy his words.

Farley whispered, "Major, things ain't looking so good. Pretty soon they're going to come for us."

Wend forced a smile and said with considerably more confidence than he felt, "Naw, Farley, we got them just about where we want them."

The corporal shot a surprised look at Wend. "Sir?"

Wend's answer was to raise the pistol in his right hand and fire a shot aimed to fly just over Todd's head. The militia captain and several others instinctively ducked as it smashed into a window on the far side of the street, followed by the tinkle of falling glass. There was silence over the group of militia and in fact all over the street.

In just a few seconds, the silence was broken by the loud, brassy sound of a hunting horn playing the "chase" call of a foxhunt, emanating from the alleyway. It was immediately followed by the sound of many horses, their hooves clattering on cobblestones. In seconds the squad of dragoons appeared on the street and quickly formed a loose grouping that ranged across the street, Childers and Quinn at the front.

Then Quinn called simply, "Sabers!" Immediately the men pulled their blades from the scabbards and shouldered them.

Wend looked over at the militia. Every head had turned to look at the cavalry. He was about to again order them to disburse, but Quinn upstaged him. The sergeant shouted at the top of his voice, "Forward at the gallop! A bloodcurdling shout came from all the troopers, and at the same time, the trumpeter resumed his call. The horsemen dug in their spurs, causing several of the animals to whinny, but they surged forward as one, sabers held high.

There are events that become frozen in your mind forever, like a painting in full color. And the first moment of that dragoon charge was one such that Wend knew would stay with him until the day he died. There were the dragoons, some in the gray of South Carolina, others in the light blue of Maryland, the sun flashing off their high-held sabers, ready to strike. There was Edward Childers, his own sword drawn, with Nell Porter hunkered down behind him, her arms around his waist, a look of trepidation on her face. There were the flying hooves of the horses. And most of all, well out front of them all, like the centerpiece of the painting, there was Quinn, mounted on a great hunter, his countenance screwed up into a fierce snarl, swinging his saber in a menacing circle above his head as he bore down on the startled militiamen.

For a brief moment, the militiamen stood staring at the approaching horsemen and the raised sabers. Then there was movement in the closely packed group. First the men closest to the advancing cavalry started pushing their way back, then the whole mob turned and ran away down the street as fast as they could manage. Several muskets lay abandoned on the cobblestones.

One man tripped or was pushed to the ground by his fleeing comrades, and he abandoned his firelock and hastened to scramble on all fours off the road to shelter by the steps of a store. Wend looked back at the fleeing men and saw they were disbursing, each seeking shelter between buildings or actually running inside.

The dragoons swept past Wend, not pulling up until they were nearly at the first street corner. Meanwhile, trooper Trillby, leading three horses, stopped in front of the inn's porch, and Wend and the other two quickly mounted, leaving Grimsby crumpled before the door.

The three quickly joined the rest of the squad where they sat their horses. Quinn looked over at Wend and said in a calm voice, "Now my darling Major, I suggest we get the hell out of here before some of that mob finds a shred of courage and starts firing muskets at us from their shelter."

"My thought precisely, Quinn." Wend turned to Childers. "How have you got Henry secured to the horse?"

"We've got his legs tied to the stirrups. I think he can hang on! And I'll ride beside him to make sure he stays seated."

Wend held his arm up and then waved it forward. "At the trot, column of twos!"

Lieutenant Colonel Barrett Penfold Northcutt, dressed in the uniform of the King's Loyal Virginia Legion, strode up to the front door of the Darragh House and entered without knocking. The house was still in private hands, but the upper floor had been rented from the owner, and several rooms upstairs had been converted to serve as an improvised annex to the army's main headquarters building, which was just across the street in the large Penn House. There were several offices and a conference room.

Northcutt's loyalist regiment had largely been destroyed during Lord Dunmore's unsuccessful 1776 campaign to hold Virginia for the crown, and the remaining men, formed into a single troop of light horse, were attached to the Queen's American Rangers. General Howe had maintained the regiment on the army rolls as an artifice to enable Northcutt, who was serving as an advisor on the general staff, to retain his rank and pay.

After climbing the stairs, Northcutt walked down the hall and entered his office. His assistant, Captain George Markwood, was already at his desk, a cup of tea in hand, looking down at some paperwork. Markwood pulled out a pocket watch and noted the time was nearly ten in the morning. He raised his eyebrows, replaced the watch, and remarked, "A late and busy night, sir?"

"Damn your eyes, George. You know I was at the card table with the general last night. He and Mrs. Loring were in no mood for an early evening. Colonel Rogers and I had no choice but to continue playing until they were ready to retire, which was well after midnight." He looked at the captain and smiled. "But my compensation was in the form of winnings. I took a respectable purse from Howe. Damn, I'm going to miss that man when he sails for England!" He sighed, "The other thing I won was a nasty headache, which shows no sign of abating."

Markwood got up and went over to a small table by the single window in the room, where a tea set was laid. He poured a cup and fixed it the way Northcutt preferred. "Here, sir, it's lukewarm at best, but it may help your head."

Northcutt accepted the cup and saucer and sat down at his desk. There were some papers laid in front of him, but he found he had no appetite to look them over.

Meanwhile, Markwood said, "Sir, I have something here that may make you forget the pain." He reached into a drawer and pulled out a folded piece of paper. "This came in by one of our disguised couriers. I went ahead and decoded it while awaiting your arrival."

Northcutt put his hand to his forehead and closed his eyes. That helped mitigate the ache behind his eyes. "You tell me about it."

Markwood grinned at his superior and then said, "One of our spies reports that the Guides have left their camp in Valley Forge. There were six Conestogas and a small farm wagon with them."

"That's it? They're obviously off on another of those foraging expeditions." He shook his head as if to shake off the pain. "Nothing to be excited about."

"Yes, that part of it. But there's more."

Barrett looked over at the captain. "So what *is* the rest of it?'

"At a crossroads several miles to the north of the Forge, the force split. Most of the legion and the Conestogas headed westward into Pennsylvania. A small troop, all cavalry and the small wagon, took a northward road."

Northcutt raised his eyebrows in curiosity. Even that small movement increased the pain. "How small?"

"Our observer thought about twenty-five or thirty mounted men in addition to the wagon."

Barrett pondered that a moment. "The small wagon only? If they had taken a couple of the Conestogas with them, it would look like they were just splitting up to cover more territory in their foraging." He put his hand to his chin. "But with only the small wagon, that doesn't seem to be the answer."

Markwood said, "There's more, sir. Something I think you'll find very interesting."

The colonel shrugged. "Interesting? Don't keep me in suspense. What is it?"

"The small detachment was led by a major."

Northcutt stiffened. "A major? There's only one major in the Guides—Eckert."

"Yes, sir. And to me that's why it is all quite interesting. Why is Major Eckert leading a small detachment northward into New Jersey?"

Northcutt sat for a long moment, pondering his assistant's words. Then he said, "You are absolutely right, Markwood. They are up to something out of the ordinary."

"But what, sir? Not much could be accomplished with a small detachment like that."

Barrett sighed. "I have no idea." He thought some more. "George, we need more information. Get a messenger—an undercover messenger—off to our man Harkness in northern Jersey. Give him the details of what we know and tell him to alert his net of watchers to look out for Eckert and his column, then keep tabs on it and attempt to find out the object of its mission."

Markwood nodded and turned to his desk, picking up a quill to write.

"And George, make sure he sends dispatches daily, even if he has nothing he thinks is important. We must be the ones to evaluate what he finds out."

Northcutt rose from his chair. "I'm going over to see Andre. He ought to know about this."

Markwood looked up from the desk. "Right, sir. I'll have this finished and coded in no time. Then I'll take it personally to someone who can carry it northward and make sure they have no trouble getting through the road guards."

"Excellent, George. I may be gone for a while. I have some personal business to attend to after seeing Andre."

Northcutt picked up his cap, reached down and finished the dregs of his tea, and left the office.

—m—

Northcutt quickly walked across the street and entered the main headquarters building, which like the Darragh House, was a former residence. In fact, it was known as the Penn House, for it had been the home of Richard Penn, grandson of William, and lieutenant governor of Pennsylvania until the outbreak of the insurrection. The house was of red brick and quite substantial—three full stories with an attic above. Northcutt climbed the stairs and went to the second-floor office of Major John Andre, Howe's closest aide-de-camp. Andre, like Northcutt, managed a web of spies throughout the New Jersey–New York area, and the two worked closely together on providing Howe with information on the activities of the rebels.

Andre's door was open, and Barrett stood looking at him. Andre had a handsome face and a lean physique and dressed in exquisitely tailored uniforms. He was a favorite of the unattached ladies of Philadelphia, and some of the *not* so unattached. Northcutt knew that at the moment, he was intimately involved with Miss Peggy Chew, the exceptionally attractive eighteen-year-old scion of one of the most important families in Pennsylvania. Papers were scattered all over the major's desk, and he was so engrossed in them that he remained unaware of Northcutt's presence in the door.

After a nearly a minute, Northcutt finally interrupted Andre. He cleared his throat and said, "Good morning, John."

Andre quickly looked over at him, surprise registering on his face. It was followed by a look of irritation. Then he spoke up in a partially serious, partially jocular tone. "Go away, Barrett! Can't you see I am desperately busy? The Mischianza is fast approaching, and I have so much to do. It is essential that I get all the appropriate invitations out *today*. *Absolutely* essential." Then he thought of something else. "By the way, where is Howe? He was supposed to come in today to meet with Clinton. He hasn't shown up yet. Clinton is not amused. You wouldn't happen to know where he might be?"

"If you are asking me officially, I have no idea. But if that is a strictly personal inquiry, I would confidentially venture to suggest that he is at Mrs. Loring's place, seeking solace in her charms for all the money he lost to me last night, or more accurately, I should say in the early hours of this morning."

Andre raised his eyes toward the ceiling. "Ah, yes, I might have guessed it was something like that." He shrugged and turned back to the desk.

Northcutt said, "John, I have a matter to discuss with you, of some importance. A matter of the operational kind."

"Barrett don't be boorish. The only matter of operational importance at the moment is preparing for the Mischianza. Come back when it is over."

"John, I have word that something is afoot in New Jersey."

"Something is *always* afoot in New Jersey. For the moment, just let the good people up there amuse themselves."

"You may be interested to know that the Guides are out."

Without looking up from his work, Andre responded, "Undoubtedly another one of their foraging expeditions, which have the effect of raising the ire of the farmers, which is good for us."

"Yes, except for one thing, John. A small detachment broke off from the main body and is heading northward, deep into New Jersey. About twenty-five dragoons, and Eckert is leading it."

Andre stopped writing and sat staring at the wall in front of his desk for half a minute. Then he turned to Northcutt, his countenance focused in concentration. Finally he spoke. "That *is* singular. Eckert wouldn't be leading a routine patrol. What could he be up to?"

"My question exactly." Barrett looked directly at Andre. "Now, John, I have ordered my web of informants to keep an eye on Eckert's column. And the reason I'm here is to suggest that, if you can make the effort to steal a moment from the *bloody* Mischianza, you might want to do the same with your people. The more eyes the better until we find out what is toward."

Andre slowly nodded. "It will be done posthaste." Then he held up a finger. "And now that I think of it, I have an important errand for you to do."

Barrett cocked his head. "And what would that be?"

"I and Miss Chew, along with Mrs. Loring and her escort, Captain Marley, will be seated at the general's table during the banquet and ball on the final day of the Mischianza." He paused and pointed his finger at Northcutt. "And Betsy, in her own inimitable way, has insisted to me that you and Miss Fraser are also to be seated there. She wants the Scotswoman to keep her company. And she is concerned that you have not yet invited her."

"That is not *precisely* true, John. I asked Mary some time ago, but she was noncommittal, saying she might have duties at the hospital."

"Well, Betsy has told me that she has it on authority that Miss Fraser no longer has anything preventing her from attending and will be quite receptive of your request. And she further made it clear that I was to communicate that to you. So to keep me from being the subject of her wrath, I most respectfully suggest that you wait upon the auburn-haired lady and finalize arrangements with her."

Barrett grinned. "As a matter of fact, I was planning to do just that right after talking with you."

Andre smiled and turned back to his desk. "Excellent. Now, pray honor me by leaving me to my labors."

—ꝏ—

Wend led the dragoons at a fast pace on the road out of town and, about two miles south of Elizabeth Town, came upon a rise with a grove of trees at the top. He raised his hand to signal the halt. "Dismount and ease the girths on your horses. We'll rest here for an hour." He looked over at Quinn. "Post a lookout to watch the road and notify us if there is a pursuit. We must be ready to move if they are able to mount a chase."

"Aye, that'll be done."

Wend looked over to Childers, who was helping Nell Porter descend from his horse. "Mr. Childers, get Henry off the horse, then find someone who is carrying dressing material and look into cleaning and bandaging his hand."

Trumpeter Bloom called out, "I've got some medical things in my saddlebags, sir."

Wend motioned to Edward. "Go ahead and attend to him."

Quinn called, "Permission to start a fire? The lads can do with some coffee while we rest the horses!"

"Yes, Sergeant, but be quick about it! And make a lot of it." He called over to Edward, "After you get a dressing on Henry's hand, pour coffee down him to see if that will sober him up enough to know what he's doing. We have a hard ride to get back to Wallen Farm this day."

As the troop bustled about their duties, Wend felt the excitement that had buoyed him during the episode at the Queen Bess draining out of him. Suddenly he felt exceedingly weary. Looking around, he sighted a large tree and went to sit down with his back against the trunk. He called out to Quinn, "Sergeant, have someone fetch me a cup of coffee when you've got it boiled."

Quinn looked over and said, "Aye, sir."

The next thing Wend knew, the sergeant himself was bending over him, a cup in his hand. Wend shook off the sleep. "How long have I been here?"

"I should say a little over an hour." He handed the cup to Wend. "That's the dregs of the pot, since you was sleepin' so long, but the bitterness of it may help you rouse yourself."

"Damn, sergeant, you shouldn't have let me sleep—not here where danger could arise in short order."

"Now, Major, after all these months of war, you should be knowin' that the sergeant will take care of things when you ease your eyes for a wee bit." He waved his arm to take in the surroundings. "And as you can see, there be nothing nasty what has happened."

Wend said nothing, instead taking a deep gulp of the coffee. "Damn, Quinn, you were right. This stuff is foul." Wend sighed. "Tea was better, when we had it. Even the dregs of the pot were palatable."

"Foul bottom of the pot or not, it will get you movin'. And I'm thinkin' it's time for us all to be gettin' on."

Wend finished the coffee in one long pull, shivered at the bitterness of it, and then got to his feet. "How is young Henry?"

"Lieutenant Childers and the serving wench have been working on him. They used a lot of the coffee." A sly smile formed on Quinn's lips. "And if I do say so, the two of them have been gettin' along rather famously as they was soberin' Henry up."

"Getting on famously? Childers and the maid?"

"Have you looked closely at the girl, sir? She's a real tidy piece and quite well equipped in all the places a woman should be. I'd say our lieutenant is a bit taken by her." He grinned. "If they were here, Fairfield or O'beirne would be after her in a second."

Wend grinned at Quinn's words, then looked over to where Edward and Nell were getting coffee into Henry. The wayward son was sitting on the ground, holding his hands to his head, the right one heavily bandaged. Childers was on one knee beside him, holding a pot, and Nell was kneeling in front of Henry, cup in hand. As he watched, she made him take another gulp of the liquid. Then both Nell and Edward broke into laughter at some comment she made while John was drinking.

Wend looked at Quinn. "Yes, I see what you mean. She is a *very* pretty lass. And Childers obviously is enjoying her company."

"Hell, sir, they're of an age. Be funny if they didn't notice each other. Fact is, I wouldn't be surprised if they found a way to be snuggling up under blankets one of these nights."

"Now, Sergeant, I dare say Mr. and Mrs. Childers, of Greenfields Plantation in Frederick County, might have something to say about that. I trust they have a very proper lady of an influential family in mind for their Edward."

"Wouldn't be the first time a pretty tavern girl got under the skin of a son of the gentry."

"True enough, Sergeant. But now I'd better go over there and see how ready Henry is to travel." He waved at the fire and the picketed horses. "In the meantime, put out the fire and have the men get ready to ride."

Wend strode over to the three young people, looked down at Henry, and asked Childers, "Is he alert enough to ride?"

"If we watch him carefully, sir."

Wend nodded acknowledgment. Wend addressed Henry. "How do you feel. Can you sit a horse on your own?"

Henry didn't respond. Instead he continued to hold his head and stare at the ground.

Wend grabbed the young man's collar and shook him.

Finally, Henry dropped his hands and looked up at Eckert with angry, bloodshot eyes. "Damn you, sir! Why are you doing this?"

"It should be obvious. We're trying to get you ready to ride back to our camp."

"No, I don't mean *that*. Why did you come after me in the first place? And what do you intend to do with me?"

"We came for you on the orders of the commander in chief."

Henry's eyes opened wide. "Washington? George Washington himself?"

"Direct orders to me from him personally."

John's face screwed up in puzzlement. "But why? Why would Washington send dragoons to find me?"

"At the behest of your father. He is determined that you be restored to your family."

The young man laughed, not of amusement, but of disgust. "Why would *my* father care? Why should *I* care? My father has shown the utmost contempt for me and my feelings."

"Regardless of what you think, your father is most desirous of you returning home."

"What if *I* have *no desire* to return to him?"

"Your desire means little in this matter, at least for the present. I have my orders, and I *will* carry them out. You'll either come willingly, or I'll bind you to your horse. But I *shall* deliver you to General Washington. Then you can discuss your future with him." Wend paused and stared into Henry's eyes. "But there's a second reason the general ordered me to get you out of New Jersey."

Henry shook his head back and forth as if trying clear himself of the intoxication. "A *second* reason? What could that possibly be?"

"Put that alcohol addled brain to work. You are the oldest son of one of the earliest, most vocal, and best-known advocates for rebellion and independence, who now happens to be the governor of Virginia, the largest state. The British would love to have you in their custody and trumpet how Patrick Henry's own kin had deserted the army and the patriot cause. Or on the other hand, maybe put you in chains and publicly show how they deal with members of the rebellion once in their possession. They have many options on how to use you to their benefit, and Washington is determined they will not get the opportunity."

Nell spoke up. "Pardon me, Major; let me speak."

Wend nodded approval.

"John, you have trusted and confided with me during the time you were at the Queen Bess. Listen to me now: Getting you back to the army has taken many people, not just these dragoons. A web of watchers and agents worked for days to locate you, sometimes at great personal danger, so that you could be protected and then transported back to the army and to the arms of your family. You owe it to them to at least see General Washington."

As he listened, it occurred to Wend that Nell Porter was much more well spoken and thoughtful than any tavern maid he had known. He guessed that Crowder, or whoever was her actual master in Talmadge's spy service, had recruited her from a higher station in life to play the role of a serving girl. But dismissing the thought for the present, he put his hands to his hips and said, "So, Mr. Henry, now's the time to get up and get mounted, or by God I'll tie your hands and then lash your legs to the stirrups. If that doesn't work, I'll lash you over your saddle like a sack of flour. It's your choice, but one way or the other, you ride with us."

John stared up at Wend, anger burning in his eyes. Then, finally, he looked over to Childers. "I seem to have no actual choice in the matter. Edward, help me get to my feet."

Childers helped him to rise, then held his arm until he was steady. "All right, Major, I'll ride on my own."

Wend nodded. "Good." Then he turned to Nell. "Miss Porter, what about you? We're going to our camp near Spanktown. Then we're heading back to Valley Forge. Where will you go?"

"Clearly, Major, my usefulness here in northern New Jersey is over. I have relatives near the Pennsylvania border. If possible, sir, I would be most obliged to be able to accompany you nearly to the Valley Forge encampment."

Wend said, "Certainly we can accommodate your wishes." Wend glanced over at Childers to see the lad was clearly pleased at the prospect. Then he turned and headed toward where the men of the squad stood to their horses. "Quinn, let's get mounted and on our way."

—~~—

The general hospital of the British Army in Philadelphia was not in a single location but instead spread across the city in numerous buildings. Several churches, drafted into service by proclamation, and a large warehouse served as patient wards. The main offices were located a short distance from Howe's headquarters in the confiscated house of a rebel who had fled the city in advance of the British occupation. It was to this house that Northcutt repaired after his discussion with Andre.

Barrett ascended the front steps and entered though the open door. A medical orderly was seated at a reception desk in the hall. He looked up and said brightly, "Ah, good day, Colonel Northcutt." Then he smiled knowingly and said, "Can I assume, sir, that you are here to speak to Miss Fraser?"

"You know I wouldn't have any other business here. Is she in her office?"

"Aye, sir, that she is. She's working on her list of apothecary items, getting ready for the march up to New York. Been at it for hours."

"Then she should be ready for a few moments of diversion. Would you please announce me?"

The orderly went down the hall, tapped on the frame of an open door, then entered Mary's office. As he was waiting, Northcutt became aware of the loud voices of two men, seemingly in contentious discussion. He couldn't make out the words clearly, although the men were in a room somewhere nearby.

The orderly emerged in few instants and returned to his desk. "The matron says she would be delighted to see you, sir."

Northcutt nodded to the orderly and walked to the open office door.

The room was furnished with cabinets and tables containing neatly stacked papers and ledger books. There was one window, through which poured bright midday sunlight. Mary Fraser was seated at a desk in the middle, a ledger before her, pen in hand. She was looking back and forth between the ledger and a set of papers also on the desk. She made entries in the ledger with quick strokes of the quill. Meanwhile, the light from the window silhouetted her profile and reflected off of her auburn hair, seeming to make it shine like bright copper. Then Northcutt thought, *No, not copper, it is much richer looking than that—it's more like burnished bronze.*

Barrett's heart seemed to miss a beat, for, even in work clothing and at labor, she was to his eyes as beautiful as the first time he had seen her at that ball in Halifax, two years ago. In those moments, and during the ensuing hours that night when she had nursed Elizabeth Loring through a miscarriage, he had come to the certainty that she would be the only woman to whom he would willingly give his heart. Since that time, he had discretely and cautiously campaigned for her favors. Then a wave of frustration flowed over him. For the truth was, despite his best efforts, that campaign seemed of little avail. For though she was polite to him and in fact warm, engaging company on those occasions when she had accepted his invitation to dine or to attend parties thrown by officers, he had achieved no emotional breakthrough. It was a source of jealousy that he had seen her escorted by young officers on other occasions, and she seemed to be equally good company when with them. But this Mischianza would be a special occasion, and they would be seated at the most important table, with the outgoing commander in chief. It would be a memorable event, and he hoped that the elegance of it would impress her and raise him in her estimation.

Mary, so engrossed in her work, had not realized he had arrived. He said in a quiet voice, "I wish I could attack the papers on my desk with as much disciplined attention. I admire your perseverance in the face of such a daunting amount of work."

Mary raised her green eyes from the desk and turned to look at him, a beguiling smile on her face. "Why Barrett, what a pleasure to see you! Please come in." She waved toward a chair beside the desk, and continued, "My dedication to this paperwork is not by desire, but by necessity. I absolutely must get the inventory of medications in order before we load the wagons for the trip to New York. Then when we do load the wagons, I can properly note what is in each wagon."

Northcutt took a seat and put his hat in his lap. "I've come to remind you of your promise to answer my invitation to accompany me to the Mischianza. You delayed your response because you were not sure if your duties would keep you at the hospital."

"Of course I remember my promise." She smiled and was about to say more when the voices of the two men Northcutt had heard earlier suddenly erupted in even louder tones, echoing through the house.

Barrett looked in the general direction of the voices, and then said, "For God's sake, I wonder what that is about."

Mary shot him a perplexed look. "Unfortunately, the subject is me."

"I beg your pardon?"

"That's Michael Morris, the director of the general hospital, and Alex Potts, the surgeon of the 42nd. Potts wants me to return to the regimental hospital in time for the departure from Philadelphia. I am here, supposedly temporarily. Morris wants me to stay permanently."

Northcutt grinned. "I'm not surprised."

"Well, I've enjoyed my time here. It has been interesting being in the middle of Philadelphia. And in truth, when we're in garrison, there's not much to do at a regimental hospital. But I do feel my place should be with the regiment when we march, for it is likely Washington's army will come out to fight when that happens. And that would mean serious casualties."

As she was speaking, the arguing voices reached a crescendo and became more heated. The muscles of Mary's face tightened in irritation, and she rose to her feet. "Excuse me, Barrett, this cannot go on." Then she marched out of the room and strode off down the hall. In a few moments, the shouting abruptly subsided.

Northcutt sat there, feeling extremely frustrated and with anger rising. He crossed his arms in front of himself. The meeting with Mary was not going in any way as he had envisioned. He had prepared himself emotionally to renew his invitation to her and had carefully thought of the words he would use, and now the mood had been broken.

He was still sitting that way when Mary returned. She literally stalked into the room, her face flushed red, and dropped unceremoniously into her chair. Sighing deeply, she looked over at Northcutt. "Well, *that's* settled. I quieted them and then made them listen to reason. I told them I'd rejoin the regiment for the march up to New York and then go back to the general hospital, at least temporarily, to help them get established in the city. After that, we'll see. They seemed satisfied with that, because it's clear that the general hospital will not be treating patients during the march, whereas if there's fighting, regimental hospitals will bear the load."

"But then the question will again arise once you are in New York."

"Yes, but who can tell what will happen between now and then? And there's speculation about various expeditions Clinton will be planning once we are settled in New York. Perhaps the 42nd will be ordered on field service away from the city. In that case, I shall insist on returning to the regiment."

Northcutt smiled. "One thing is clear, and you should be flattered: your services are much desired and in demand."

Mary looked upward as if toward the heavens. "That is a mixed blessing, as you can see."

He was about to change the subject back to the Mischianza, when Mary took the initiative.

"Now, Barrett, let us return to our conversation." She smiled pleasantly. "Morris has made clear that my services can be spared during the Mischianza, so it will be my great pleasure to attend the festivities with you."

Northcutt couldn't help but laugh. "Well, one must admire your directness and brevity. I didn't have the opportunity to make a ceremonious reiteration of my request, which I was prepared to do."

Mary laughed. "Barrett, you asked me before. No need to repeat the entire process." A thoughtful look came over her face. "I hear that it will be most extravagant and quite costly."

"Indeed, Mary. Major John Andre and Captain John Montresor, the army's chief engineer, are planning it, and nothing of this magnitude has ever been seen on this side of the Atlantic. As for expense, Andre tells me the total cost will be near 3,300 guineas."

"Good God, Barrett! That's a fortune! Where is it coming from?"

"The officers of the army have contributed the money as their farewell tribute to General Howe. They believe he has been a good and beneficial commander."

Mary shook her head and sighed. "You know I grew up as an orphan in the 77th and 42nd. I lived on a child's ration and wore discarded clothing, often from people who had died or been killed on the battlefield. The only money I had was pennies from laundering men's clothing and mending their uniforms. I hardly had any money to myself until I became a governess in Scotland." She took a deep breath. "Three thousand guineas. I cannot even imagine that amount."

Barrett smiled. "It will be quite an affair, Mary. First, there will be a procession of barges along the waterfront carrying Generals Howe and Clinton and all the important guests. The naval fleet will make a massed gun salute, seventeen guns per ship, as the barge flotilla moves along the harbor. Then there will be a parade through the city, from the waterfront to Joseph Wharton's estate—Walnut Grove—where the rest of the events will take place. There will be a jousting tournament as in the days of knights, a fireworks display, and finally a great banquet and ball." He looked at Mary. "I assure you, it will be an event neither of us will ever forget." He looked at her directly. "And you and I will dine at General Howe's table at the banquet. That will be something you can tell your children about someday, Mary."

Mary Fraser sat silently staring into the distance for a few moments. Then she said in a quiet tone, almost a whisper, "Yes, Barrett, if in fact I ever have children of my own. But certainly I could never have imagined that the daughter of Sergeant Fraser of the 77th Highlanders would wear an elegant gown and dine in the company of generals."

Northcutt saw an opening. He said, "Mary, you are endowed with beauty, intelligence, and talent in the arts. I remember your magnificent singing performance at the ball in Halifax. And with admirable discipline, you have educated yourself far above the station of your birth. And I daresay this will not be last time you find yourself socially in the company of influential people. It is something to which you should accustom yourself. Beyond that, I am quite aware that you are in high demand by many young officers of the Royal Highland Regiment who seek your favors." He paused and smiled directly into her mesmerizing eyes. "And it is my great honor that you allow me to serve as your escort on this singular occasion. I shall be the object of much envy."

Chapter Four
Blood in the Night

Wend sat before the campfire under the bright stars of a clear night. Around him were the fires of the detachment in their bivouac at Wallen Farm. The party of dragoons had arrived back from Spanktown after darkness. After a hearty supper prepared by Meli, Wend was feeling drowsy and ready to sleep in the wake of an arduous and often tense day. He was alone at the fire, except for a sleeping John Henry, who, still feeling the effects of the voluminous amount of spirits he had consumed, was under blankets across from Wend. Edward Childers and Nell Porter were sitting on the front porch of the Wallen house with May Anne, all three of the young people talking and laughing, seemingly free of any care and weariness after the events of the recent hours.

Wend, on the other hand, had serious matters weighing on his mind. He shook off the desire to sleep and made himself concentrate on plans for the return march to Valley Forge. He was doing so when Henry stirred, groaned softly, and then pushed himself up on one arm. He looked around as if unsure where he was. Then his eyes fixed on Wend, whom he stared at for a long minute, then he raised himself into a sitting position.

"Well, Mr. Henry, welcome back to the world."

The young man nodded slowly, then he spoke up. "It occurs to me that I've never heard your name. Who are you?"

"Well, in all the hurry and confusion back at the inn, there wasn't time for introductions. I'm Major Wend Eckert, commandant of the Legion of Continental Guides."

"The Guides? He looked around at the people at their fires. These are the Guides?

"Well, a small detachment of them."

"Everyone's heard of the Guides, even in Gates's Northern Army. Men tell stories about how you held off the Hessian Jaegers at the Delaware River, so the last of the army could cross during the retreat from New York back in '76. And all the work you did in the campaigns of last year, locating the British forces and leading Washington's army into battle. In Gates's army we heard about it from Morgan's men when they joined us for Saratoga. But I thought your legion was for scouting, skirmishing, and guiding the army."

Wend grinned. "That's right. But we work directly for Washington, so we also get sent on all the nasty little jobs that come up between battles."

Henry sat up more erect and scowled. "So taking me out of that inn was a *nasty* little job?"

"Actually, John, it could have gotten *very* nasty if things hadn't worked out as they did. I mean lots of blood flowing back at the Queen Bess. As it happened, we didn't have to actually shoot anyone, and we took no casualties ourselves. So it's gone smoothly, at least so far."

John replied in bitter tones, "The fact is, Major, your mission was unnecessary. If you had arrived a few minutes later, I would have solved everyone's problem. I would have been in hell. Father and *dear* little Dorothea would have been free to live their life without me. Washington wouldn't have had to worry about the oldest son of Patrick Henry falling into British hands. Everyone happy ever after."

"You're wrong, John. Your father is desolate about how things have turned out. I saw the letter he wrote to Washington; it was extraordinarily emotional. Washington believes Patrick didn't understand the relationship between you and Dorothea. I've thought about it, and speaking confidentially, I believe the real problem is the lust for influence on the part of Dorothea's father—he probably knew about you and Dorothea but was more interested in seeing his daughter married to the governor, more desirous of the prestige and power it would bring to his family."

"But Dorothea went along with it."

"True enough. She obeyed her father, which I understand many in the gentry believe is the duty of a daughter."

"And *you* are not of the gentry?"

Wend laughed. "Not likely! I'm a gunsmith. I work with my hands and my head for a living."

Henry did not respond. Instead he simply sat for a lengthy time, staring expressionlessly into the night, making no effort to speak.

Wend said, "John, I've no more time to discuss the rights or wrong of this matter tonight. But you know what my orders are from the commanding general. I need your word, on your honor as a gentleman, that you will not try to slip away from the detachment while we are traveling back to Valley Forge. Nor that you will grab a firelock and try to finish what you were attempting at the inn. Otherwise, I shall have to have you watched continuously or bind you when that is not possible. What is your decision?"

John Henry glared at Wend. Then after a few moments, he shrugged and said, "You have it. I might as well be comfortable if there's no choice but to go with you."

Wend was about to say more, but he was stopped by the shout of the sentry near the drive. "Sergeant Schreiber! Sergeant Schreiber! Rider coming in! Galloping up the drive!"

Wend saw Schreiber jump up from his fire and run toward the sentry. Quinn also left his fire and joined the other two. Wend rose to his feet, and walked to where he could look up the drive. There he saw a man pushing his horse hard at the gallop, frantically applying the whip, the sound of the flying hooves now audible throughout the camp. And then he saw something else: mounted behind the man was a smaller figure. Wend strained to see through the darkness and finally discerned that it was a small child—a young girl with her arms around the rider and skirts flying as the horse galloped.

In a few seconds, the animal arrived in the yard of the farm, and the man pulled up the horse. Wend could see that the horse was almost finished, covered with sweat and frothing at the mouth. The man looked around, an expression of surprise on his face at seeing the soldiers. Then he slid down from his mount, turned, and gently lifted the child down. Wend could see he was of middling age, dressed in dark clothing. And the girl looked to be no more than nine or ten years old. Her face was dirty, and her skirts were torn. Once on the ground, she threw her arms around the man and held on tight. Then she began to sob, streams of tears rolling down her cheeks.

Looking at the soldiers, the stranger asked Schreiber, "Who are you? Where are the Wallens?"

Schreiber looked over at Wend, who responded, "I am Major Eckert of the Continental Guides. Who, sir, are you, and what has driven you to ride like the devil himself is in pursuit?"

"The Continental Army? Oh, praise the Lord! He has answered my most desperate supplication!" The man clasped his hands together and gazed up toward the heavens, his mouth moving in prayer.

Wend responded, "Damn it, man, you can pray later. I must repeat, what has you in such a state of alarm?"

The man stared into the night to the west for a long moment. Then he unclasped his hands and raised the right one, pointing in the direction of his eyes. "*That* is what has me alarmed! You said I was riding to escape the devil, and there is where Satan is doing his work!"

Wend and the others turned to look where the man was pointing.

Quinn said it first. "Damn! Something's burning, way in the distance. I can see the red glow in the sky!"

Wend answered, "You're right, Sergeant, and it looks like a damn big fire!"

At that moment, Joseph Wallen came running from the house, the three young people with him. Rachel came out on the porch, then followed her husband. Wallen called out, "Reverend! Reverend Banbury! What is it? What is the matter?" Then he saw the girl. "That's Lizzie Dawson! What's she doing here?"

"It's the partisans! A band of murderous ruffians! I was riding back to my church from visiting with some parishioners and was astonished to see the Dawson place on fire! I rode into their yard to find the main house consumed by flames. Dawson himself was hanging, dead, from that big oak near the house. There were other bodies lying on the ground. And everyone else was gone—run off or taken by the rabble." He shivered as if cold. "Then I rode back out to the road intending to head east to the Graham farm, to warn them. And suddenly I heard a voice crying out, calling my name." He looked down and put his hand on the girl's shoulder. "It was Lizzie. When the partisans were approaching, her mother sent her out of the back of the house to hide in the woods. She saw what happened and was trying to get away from the farm when she saw me." He looked down at the girl. "So I got her up behind me, and we headed eastward along the road."

Banbury stopped talking a moment to catch his breath. Then he continued, "I came in sight of the partisan band, marching with their wagons and booty along the road, just as they were going into Graham's place. My God, there were at least a hundred of the swine!"

Rachel arrived and threw her arms around the girl. "Oh, Lizzie, are you all right?"

The girl answered through her sobs. "Yes, Mrs. Wallen, I'm not hurt." Then she wailed, "They killed my father! And Mother was in the house. And it was burning all over, and I couldn't find her when the bad men left!"

Meanwhile Wallen quickly asked, "Reverend, you say they're at Graham's?" He looked at Wend. "They are our neighbors just to the west."

Banbury nodded. "Yes, that was just a few minutes ago. I held back so the ruffians wouldn't see me, and then when they were all going down the drive toward the Grahams' house, I got off the road and led my horse through the woods to keep out of sight, and then I remounted and rode for here to warn you."

Wallen said, "We're glad you and Lizzie are safe, Hiram."

Banbury replied, "Thank you, Joseph; praise the Lord." He paused and then said, "But it is the safety of you and your family I was worried about. I was going to tell you to flee with your family and your people, because without doubt they will be here next." He looked over at Wend. "But now that the Lord has placed you and your men here, Major, that won't be necessary." He pointed toward the west where the Graham farm lay. "If you hurry, you can catch the murderers unaware and save Graham and his family before more harm comes to them. But you must go posthaste."

Wend said nothing but turned and stared in the direction of the Graham farm, his thoughts racing. As he watched, a column of flames suddenly shot up, reaching high in the sky, much closer than the other fire.

Reverend Banbury gasped. "The Graham farm! They've fired it!" He grabbed Wend's arm and leaned close to his face. "Sir, you must march instantly! People will soon be dying there, if not already! You must stop the slaughter!"

Rachel turned to Wend and exclaimed. "The Reverend is right, Major! You must go strike the rabble over there at the Graham place! Or they will soon be here! Unless you destroy them, they will serve us the same way!" Horror was reflected in her face. "What I have long feared is upon us!"

Wend looked around at the people who had gathered: Quinn, Schreiber, Childress, Wallen, Rachel, May Anne and the young girl. Now all were staring at him, waiting for his response. May Anne was shaking and crying softly, tears running down her cheeks, hands clasped in front of her face. Rachel, one arm around Lizzie, had now also put a consoling arm around her daughter.

Nell Porter stood, hand on hips, a defiant look on her face, watching the flames rising from the bordering farm and frequently glancing over at Wend. She said, "Something must be done! Will you march to the rescue of those people, Major?"

Wend took a deep breath and then spoke out, loudly enough so that all would hear. "Now listen! We are *not* marching to the Graham farm. That would be foolish and probably too late to help. We are going to prepare to defend this farm." He saw a small smile form on Quinn's face, and the sergeant nodded slowly. Turning to face Banbury and Wallen, he said, "I don't have enough men to attack. They are a hundred, and I only have twenty-five. And I don't know the land. We can't just march up into the Graham place; they hold the ground, and they'll have all the advantage. They could easily prepare an ambush for us. In any case, they could easily cut us down. But with twenty-five men I can—with luck—defend this place, if they come here. And I do think that's likely—the night is still young."

There was a profound silence, everyone staring at Wend.

Then the Reverend exploded. "God above, you can't abandon those people!" He stretched his arm out, pointing in the direction of the fires. "I told you what occurred at the Dawson farm! The master dead, God only knows what has happened to all the family and the servants!" Banbury stepped forward and grabbed Wend by his shirt. "What do we have an army for if not to defend the people! You must march to the Grahams' rescue. It is your duty!"

Wend snatched the minister's hands off his shirt. "Banbury, don't tell me my duty. And if you keep this up, I shall order you bound to a fence post."

The minister's face curled up into a scowl. "You are a *coward*, Eckert! A coward, do you hear me? If I survive this night, the Continental Congress shall hear of your refusal to aid innocent people from these murderous rogues! I know our representatives to Congress, and they shall hear what has happened here."

Wend was about to order Quinn to take Banbury into custody when Rachel interceded. She said in firm tones, "Come, Hiram, let us go to the house. You need some spirits to calm yourself. I need to tend to Lizzie." She looked over at Wend with angry eyes and said with an accusatory tone in her voice, "Clearly, Major Eckert has made his decision, and you won't be able to change his mind. We must leave him to his work and hope his men will keep us from harm." She gave Wend a final disdainful glance, then led the still-fuming minister away.

Wend called Childers and the two sergeants to him. "Quinn, get all your dragoon horses saddled and your men fully equipped." He pointed down the drive. "Meanwhile, go out to the end of the drive near the road and find a place to conceal your entire squad and horses where they won't be seen."

Quinn looked up the drive and grinned. "Aye, sir, and I'm beginning to see what you have in mind."

Wend looked at Schreiber. "Send out two men to the road, and have them stand picket in the woods about halfway to the Graham's drive. When they see the partisans coming this way, they are to come back fast and inform us, moving through the woods, not along the road so they won't be observed. Do you understand?"

"Right, sir."

"Meanwhile, Schreiber, find a place where your men can hide here in the yard so they won't be seen by the partisans coming up the drive, but close enough so you can get across the end of the drive fast."

The sergeant nodded. "I take your meaning, sir."

Wend nodded and then addressed Childers. "Edward, get a couple of men and put out all the campfires. Then do everything you can to make sure nothing out of the ordinary is visible from the drive."

"Yes, sir."

Wend looked around and saw that Wallen was still standing nearby. "Joseph, before supper last night you said that you have a number of firelocks and have trained some of your servants and farmhands to use them. Are you ready to help us repel this mob?"

"Do you need to ask, Eckert? Tell me what we are to do."

"Get your men together and armed. Then come back here, and join with Sergeant Schreiber's men for now."

Wallen turned to go, but Wend said, "Wait, Joseph. One more thing."

"Yes, Major?"

"Whatever happens here tonight, we're going to need a place to treat the wounded and nurses to do it. Will you ask your wife to suggest a place and then make preparations to receive injured men?"

"Of course. Major, Rachel is upset right now. In a moment she will calm herself and will be willing to help. She treats the servants and hands frequently. But she'll need to know what is needed for battle wounds."

Wend responded, "I'll send Meli Wood, our cook, to show her what's needed and to help with preparations. She's an experienced nurse."

"Right, Major. I'll talk to Rachel and then get my men ready."

As Wallen strode off, Wend felt a hand touch his arm and turned around to see Nell Porter.

"Major, you forgot about me. I want to play my part. I know something about medical work. A relative is a physician, and I have often assisted him. Should I go help Mrs. Wallen?"

Wend nodded. "I should appreciate that very much. And thank you for your offer."

The girl walked off toward the house. Wend thought, *More evidence that the young woman comes from a family of some substance.* He wondered how she had become mixed up in the world of spying, and who had induced her to take up such a dangerous role.

Then he looked around to see that the campfires had been extinguished, and the yard and stable area of the farm were a hive of activity. The dragoons were saddling their mounts, Schreiber's men were looking to their weapons, and Billy Wood and Trumpeter Bloom were gathering up men's personal gear from around the dead campfires and depositing them in a pile beside the paddock fence.

That left Wend alone to contemplate the likely train of events that might soon ensue. And the more he thought, the more he didn't like the odds: one hundred to twenty-five or thirty. Even if the plan that he had worked out in his mind went in their favor, it could still be a deadly night for his men. He watched as they went about their work confidently, some cracking jokes, trusting his judgment to bring victory. He wished he could be as confident of the outcome as they were. As he stood there, now that the fires were out and the cold of the spring night had settled in, he felt himself shivering. But he knew the source of his chill had little to do with the temperature.

—m—

The detachment's wagon had been pulled up beside the farm's paddock, where it would be out of the way. Quinn's squad had their horses saddled and ready, and the men were standing by, talking quietly next to the fence. Wend climbed up into the wagon and stood on the seat, which afforded him a better view of the fires burning at the Graham farm. And as time had passed, more fires were visible. It seemed clear that the partisans were taking their time, stealing whatever they considered of value in each building and then setting it afire. Wend envisioned the scene: Massive destruction in progress, the master captured and maybe already dead. Other people killed or doomed to die at the hands of the ruffians. His stomach turned at the thought of it and that he could do nothing about it.

As he watched, Joseph Wallen and five others approached Wend. "Here are my men, all armed and ready to fight. They're all reasonably proficient with their firelocks. Two have militia muskets, and three have fowlers."

Wend looked them over, then said, "They'll do. And the shot of the fowlers will actually be effective in the night. We're looking for a volume of flying lead, not necessarily accuracy tonight."

Wallen waved his men over to join with Schreiber's squad, and stood by the wagon, joining Wend in watching the fires. "Damn, they are doing a thorough job."

"Well, Joseph, the longer it takes, the better for us." Wend climbed down from the wagon. "I've thought of something that might help us, but I want your agreement." He pointed to a large tree right where the drive began. "You see that tall, narrow pine?"

Wallen looked and then nodded. "Yes, what about it?"

"I'm thinking we can use it to even the odds for us."

"How so, Major?"

"With your permission, I propose we chop into the trunk, but not all the way through it. Then we station one of your men by it, with an ax. We also tie a rope as high as we can manage and lead the rope across the drive."

Wallen began nodding vigorously. "Yes, yes, I see your idea! Then when the partisans approach, the axe man can finish the cut, and men across the drive can haul on the rope to make sure the tree falls so as to make an obstacle."

"Exactly, it will slow them down, cause them to bunch up and make them better targets."

"I'll get it all arranged, Eckert." Wallen was about to leave, when suddenly there was a shout from a sentinel. *"Armed men comin' down the drive! Looks to be about fifteen or twenty."*

Wend scrambled back up onto the wagon to get a better view. *His mind was racing. Had the partisans sent an advance guard? And if so, why hadn't the pickets out on the road given warning?*

Schreiber hurried his squad out into the drive and formed line. He called out, "Look to your firelocks!"

Wallen had also climbed up to the wagon seat and stared at the approaching men, mostly shadowy silhouettes in the dark. He looked at Wend. "I've seen partisans before, and those don't look like them to me."

Just at that moment, the men in the drive stopped, and a voice called out, "Wallen! Joseph Wallen, are you there? It's Richard Dowling! I've got sixteen men with me! We're coming in!"

Wallen shouted back, "I'm here, Richard! There are Continentals here on the farm. We won't fire!" Still looking down the drive, he said to Wend, "That's our county patriot militia. Dowling is one of the lieutenants who lives nearby."

Wend called out, "Schreiber! Stand down! They're ours!"

Schreiber replied, "Aye, sir!" and then waved his men back to their hiding place.

Dowling led his men into the yard, where they grounded their arms and looked around, staring curiously at the soldiers. The lieutenant walked over to where Eckert and Wallen were standing by the wagon.

Wallen said, "Richard, I'm sure glad to see you tonight." He pointed toward the fires in the west. "The renegades are out—they've hit the Dawson and Graham places. Reverend Banbury says Dawson is dead, and all his family and hands have disappeared." He shook his head. "Don't know the situation with Graham, but the place is all afire, so we fear the worst."

"I know where one of the hands from Dawson's farm is—he's at my place, exhausted from running all the way. Dawson sent him for help as soon as the partisans came in sight. He got to my place, and we turned out everyone we could. Sixteen is all I could round up." He shrugged. "More may straggle in later. My boy is riding to put out the word to gather here."

"Good, we need all the men we can get tonight." Wallen motioned toward Wend. "This is Major Eckert, of the Continental Guides. He's here with twenty-five men."

"I've heard of the Guides! There are stories of what you did at the Delaware River in "76 and at Princeton. What brings you to Spanktown?"

"Washington wanted to show the people of New Jersey support in their struggle against the British loyalists and partisans." Wend glanced back toward the fires in the west. "But we didn't expect to be confronted by a band of partisans amounting to one hundred." He motioned toward Dowling's men. "I hope we can count on you and your men to stand by us if the raiders come here."

"You *hope,* sir?" Dowling grinned. "It will be our honor to be able to say we stood in line with Washington's Guides. I most willingly place my half company under your command."

Wend said, "Thank you, Lieutenant. Before we can tell stories about this night we need to get through it alive. For now, find a good place for your men in the woods by the end of the drive here, across from where Schreiber's squad is covering."

Dowling nodded and went back to his men. Wallen headed off to get an ax and rope. As they left, Quinn walked over from his where his squad was assembled.

Wend said to the dragoon, "Well, Sergeant, the odds are getting a little better for us."

Quinn looked over at the militia. "Aye, if the damn militia will fight. They're farmers and shopkeepers. Many's the time I've seen the like of them turn and run the moment the enemy starts to get close."

"True enough, Quinn, but there's a couple of things which might give them courage tonight. First, they know these partisan scoundrels will be at their own doorstep sooner or later if we don't stop them now. And second, militia will often stand if they can shoot from cover. And I intend to make that happen." Wend pointed to the tall pine and explained his plan to the sergeant.

Quinn looked at the tree, thought a minute, and said, "It might work. But I ain't bettin' on it in advance."

Wend sighed. "Nor I, Sergeant, but it's the best I've got." Wend looked over at the flames to the west. "There's a chance the partisans will bed down for the night at Graham Farm. But if they are going to come, it will be soon. We're about an hour shy of midnight. Go ahead and get your men down to that hiding place in the woods you found and make sure they can't see or hear you when they turn down the drive."

"You don't need to tell me that."

"All right, Quinn. Then get it done. And you know what to do when you hear the hunting horn."

A murderous smile of anticipation spread over the former highwayman's face. "Damn right I know what to do."

And with that he turned and went back to his horsemen. In a few moments they were mounted and trotting down the drive toward the road. As he was watching them go, Edward Childers approached him.

"Major, I've been helping out at the house. The women have a hospital set up. Right now they're tearing up sheets to make dressing and bandages."

"Good, Edward." Then he pointed to the pine tree and explained his plan. "Now, I want you to take charge of the firing line—our squad, the militia, and Wallen's hands. When the time comes, I want Shreiber's squad in the middle, as the anchor, with the militia on the left of the line, and Wallen's men on the right. Make sure they have plenty of powder. And most important, no firing until I give you the order. Make that clear to all of them."

"I've got it, sir."

Wend thought of something. "Where's Henry? I haven't seen him since this started."

"He's on the porch of the house. Just sitting there, staring into the night."

"All right, Edward. Now get up to the where the men are and get things organized."

Wend walked to the house and saw Henry seated in a chair at one side of the porch. He had his arms crossed in front of himself and was staring down toward his feet, a sullen look on his face. Wend approached him and leaned up against one of the porch pillars. "John, there's going to be a fight here in a short time."

Henry looked up at Wend. "A statement of the obvious, Major Eckert." He cocked his head. "What's on your mind? You didn't come here to tell me what is perfectly clear to everyone on the farm."

"It's going to be a fight against heavy odds. Right now, between Guides, militia, and Wallen's farm hands, I've got less than fifty men. And we're facing over a hundred cutthroat partisans."

Henry looked over at the fires at Graham Farm and shrugged. "So why are you telling me all this?"

"I thought you *might* want to help."

The young man looked up at Wend with incredulity in his eyes. "You want my help? And what perchance do you expect me to do? What difference would one man make?"

"You are a trained soldier. I thought you might join us on the firing line. Every person who can shoot will be useful."

"I don't think I'm interested."

"I don't understand, John. You were a soldier and a good one in earlier days." Wend waved in the direction of the inside of the house, where the women were preparing for casualties. "Lots of people's lives are at stake here. Just because you lost a woman shouldn't prevent you from defending innocent people, and particularly women and children, from murderous men."

Henry looked at Wend with a wry smile on his face. "You think the whole reason I left the army was because of Father and Dorothea?"

"That's what I've been told. Why would I think anything else?"

"Well, Major, I'm going to tell you the rest. There's more to it. A rather important bit of more to it, at least in my mind."

"Well, then, go ahead and tell me. You obviously want me to know."

"I'll be short about it. The truth is, I joined the army in 1775 amid all the enthusiasm in Williamsburg about teaching the king a lesson and independence, and all of that. A French fellow named Arundel, *Dohickey Arundel*, convinced me that the only place to be was in the artillery. So I joined an artillery company and marched to New York City. I fought in the battles there and won praise for the effectiveness of my guns. We killed a lot of British. Then, soon enough the company was dispatched to Gates's Northern Army."

"Yes, I know that, John, and that you served quite honorably at Saratoga."

"Yes, *honorably*. I killed a lot of British men there, too. After the battle was over and we had won, I walked the field. There were the bodies of many men, mainly British, a goodly number who had been killed by my artillery, their bodies torn apart. But in truth the field was full of dead men from both sides."

"John, battles are about killing."

"Yes! Yes, indeed they *are* Major Eckert." Henry partially rose from his chair in anger. "They're *all* about killing. And soldiers fighting for their cherished cause." He dropped back into the seat. "And everyone on both sides is so sure of the righteousness of *their* cause." He took a deep breath. "Well, I suddenly realized how disgusting it all was."

"John, we all feel discouraged sometimes, particularly in the aftermath of a bloody battle. But it is our cause, independence and freedom, which keeps us going."

"Yes, I felt that way at the beginning. My father was so proud of me when

I joined the army. He lectured me about the righteousness of the cause of freedom. And I trusted him. I mean, this is the man celebrated throughout the colonies for defying the crown with the great 'Liberty or death' speech." He sat silent for a moment. "But that day at Saratoga I walked off the battlefield back to my tent, after two years of bloody war, disgusted with all the slaughter. Despite my feelings, I had every intention of carrying on with my duties. But then I found a letter there. The damned letter from Father, the man I loved and respected, telling me about his marriage to Dorothea." He took a deep breath. "The man who I believed stood for honor and justice had betrayed his own son. I felt like he had driven a spike into my heart. It was the final straw I needed to leave it all behind me. So that night I wrote a letter of resignation and laid it on my cot. Then I broke my sword blade in half, threw it into the bush, and rode away from the army and vowed never to lift a hand against another man again. As time passed, I began to feel intense shame for all the men I had killed."

"So when we found you at the Queen Bess, you were both full of shame at killing and distraught about your father's betrayal."

"*Now* you understand, Major. I don't expect you to agree with me, but at least you know the full story."

Wend sighed and was about to respond when he heard Childers's voice calling from the yard. "Major Eckert! The pickets have come in! The partisans are on the way!"

Wend called back, "I'm coming, Lieutenant!" He looked down at Henry for a moment. Then he pulled his pistols from his belt. "Here, take these. You may find them useful if the partisans break through our line." He took off his powder horn and pouch with balls for the pistols and gave them to Henry. Then he pointed to the house. "The least you can do is try to defend the women. That's not a cause; it's not war; it's simply the duty of a man."

Henry looked up and laughed. "You trust me with firelocks? How do you know I just won't finish what I started at the Queen Bess?"

"You gave me your word of honor, John. I've been led to believe that's important to you people of the gentry." And with that, Wend turned and ran to join Childers at the drive.

—~—

Wend arrived at where Edward Childers stood at the beginning of the drive. The lieutenant and Schreiber were standing with Schmidt and Woodruff, the pickets who had just come back. Both men were breathing heavily after dashing through the woods to report. Wend noted that two of Wallen's hands were taking turns chopping on the pine tree, the sound of the ax echoing through the darkness. A rope had already been looped around the trunk about fifteen feet above the ground and led across the drive.

Childers said to Wend, "Sir, the pickets stayed long enough to get a rough count. There really are at least a hundred of them. They got several wagons and some women walking behind them."

Wend asked Schmidt, "What kind of weapons are they carrying?"

"Well, sir, just about everything you could imagine. Looked like army muskets, fowlers, some just carrying swords and pistols." He waved his hand. "Even saw a halberd or two, like sergeants in the line battalions carry."

Woodruff added, "They wasn't in any kind of order. No, sir. They was just strolling along like a mob, as you might say."

Schmidt said, "We stayed till they was about halfway here from the other farm, sir. Took us a few minutes to push our way through the bush to here."

Wend looked up the drive. "So they could be making the turn into here any time now?"

"Sure 'nuff, sir. But they weren't travelin' that fast, seemed to be takin' their time about it."

Wend thought a second. "That means we may have a few minutes to finish our preparations." He nodded and said to Childers. "Get me the militia lieutenant and Wallen. And round up Billy Wood and Bloom. I want to talk to all of them and you."

Shortly the group was assembled.

Wallen pointed to the pine. "We're all ready to go. One of my men will be there with the ax to finish the final cuts on your signal."

"Good." Wend turned to Dowling. "Richard, station your men in the trees on the far side of the drive. Have a couple of your men ready to haul on the rope when the time comes and make sure it falls right across the drive."

"Right, sir."

Wend took a deep breath, then said, "All right, now we're going to organize ourselves for firing on the partisans when they approach." They were all looking at him closely. He continued, "We can't waste a single shot. First, the four riflemen in Schreiber's squad will form together." Suddenly he thought of something. "Mr. Dowling, do you have any rifles among your men?"

"As a matter of fact, yes. Taddy Pratt's got one. It's a funny one, though. Real short. He says it's an old German one."

"Have him bring it here."

Dowling shouted. "Hey, Pratt, come on over here."

A lean man of medium height came over.

"Taddy, show the major that rifle of yours."

Pratt held up the firelock.

Wend grinned when he saw it. "Where did you get that?"

"My pa bought it off an old Dutchman years ago. Ain't like them long rifles from Pennsylvania I've seen, but it works fine."

"Well, Pratt, it is German. It's what's called a *Jaeger* rifle. It's what our long rifles were developed from."

Pratt shrugged and looked down at the rifle. "All I know is it puts the ball where I aim."

"Well, I'm going to give you a chance to prove that point, Pratt. You stay with Schreiber's riflemen."

Wend looked around for a place for the riflemen to cover. He wanted them to be the first to fire. Then a thought came to him. "Schreiber, get your men to haul our wagon back over here from beside the paddock so that it's in front of the drive. It won't look that much out of place sitting in the front yard."

Schreiber looked puzzled. "Sir?"

Wend grinned. "We'll have the riflemen lay down under it, and maybe a couple inside the bed. They'll all have cover from the eyes of the partisans, and they'll also be able to brace their firelocks."

"Ja, sir! I've got it." He turned and shouted for his men to follow him.

Wend put his hand on Edward's shoulder and spoke to the group of men. "Now listen, here is how we will do our firing: On my signal, the riflemen at the wagon will fire at picked men in the front of the partisan column. Likely that will take out some of their leaders. Then when they've finished, Wallen's ax man will take the final cuts on the pine tree's trunk, and Dowling's men will haul on the rope to make sure it falls squarely across the drive." He pointed to where the tree would lie. "Then, all our men will take cover behind the pine: Schreiber's in the center, Wallen's men on the right, and Dowling's men on the left."

He looked to make sure they were all paying attention. "Lieutenant Childers will call out the order of firing." He paused for a moment. "Schreiber's squad will fire first, while the others are holding fire. Then Dowling's men will fire together. And finally, Wallen's hands will fire. Do you all understand?"

They nodded. Then he continued. "After that series of volleys, every man will reload and fire as fast as they can individually. Our objective is to get as much lead into the mob of partisans as possible." He held up a finger. "But remember, it is essential that no one fire until Childers gives the word. And equally important that everyone stop firing immediately when he calls cease fire. Is that understood?"

Another round of nods.

Wend turned to Trumpeter Bloom. "You make sure to stay near me and have your horn ready." Then he said to Billy Wood, "Get me my saddle rifle. Then form with Schreiber's squad. We'll need every musket we can muster tonight."

As he was talking to Billy, Schreiber and his men had hauled the wagon into place in front of the drive. Wallen signaled that the pine tree was ready and went to join his men.

Wend called out, "All right, everyone take your positions of concealment. The partisans should be turning into the drive any time now."

Schreiber and the other three riflemen of his squad crawled under the wagon. Wend motioned to Pratt, "Come on, Taddy, climb up into the wagon bed with me. We'll get a good view and be able to brace on the side of the bed."

"You going to be shooting a rifle, Major?"

"In the first volley. I want to get as many leaders as we can right away."

Billy came by, Wend's saddle rifle in one hand and his own musket in the other. Wend took the rifle and said, "You go take control of the musket men in the squad until Schreiber returns. Make sure they stay hidden until the pine falls."

"Aye, sir."

Wend climbed up into the wagon bed and prepared to brace the rifle on the side. Pratt looked over, a puzzled look on his face. "Major, I thought my rifle was short, but that's the shortest one I ever saw."

"I made it specially for gentlemen when traveling on horseback. It's about the size of a cavalry carbine but rifled instead of smooth bore. It fits nicely into a sheath on the horse saddle and handles easily when you're using it mounted." Wend checked the priming and then laid the firelock across the side of the box. Bloom huddled down behind the wagon, his horn at the ready.

Wend looked up at the sky. He said a prayer of thanks that the moon was out and shining brightly. Then he scanned the men waiting in their positions—Dowling's men hidden behind trees on the left side of the drive, Wood and the musket men of the Guides squad all on one knee behind bushes on the right side, and Wallen and his men close beside them. All were invisible to anyone approaching on the drive, and a profound silence prevailed in the yard of the farm. Wend turned around and saw that nothing unusual showed in the house, only candlelight from some windows. He could make out Henry sitting in the dark of the porch. Everything was as ready as they could make it.

Suddenly Pratt whispered, "Listen, Major! Here they come!" The excitement was clear even in the muffled sound of his voice.

Wend turned back to look up the drive but saw nothing. But then he heard them: loud voices in the night, talking, laughing, even shouting at each other. No discipline, no fear, no stealth in their approach. Obviously they were supremely confident after easily destroying two plantations in the last few hours and had no reason to expect trouble at a third. Then suddenly the first few of them came out from behind the trees that lined the road, paused momentarily at the head of the drive, and started to walk toward the farm. In the moonlight, Wend was able to see one of them stop, turn toward the road, beckon toward the unseen remainder of them with his hand, and shout something.

The lead group of partisans began striding swiftly up the drive toward the farmyard, and at that moment the main body began to appear, turning into the drive and following their compatriots, all still talking and laughing.

Wend whispered down to Schreiber, "Sergeant, get ready to take out that first group of men. I will fire on the rightmost man, Pratt will aim at the leftmost. You and your men select targets in between. Make sure everyone is aiming at a separate, distinct man. We can't have two people firing at the same person. And everyone, aim for your man's chest. We can't afford missing one because somebody wants to show us how good he is at a head shot. Everyone understand?"

Schreiber laughed and said, "Major, you're worrying too much. We got it."

"All right. And no one fires until I give the word."

"Sir, you already told us that."

Wend shut up and concentrated on watching the advance.

Then, suddenly, the lead group stopped. Wend's heart skipped a beat. *Did they see or hear something that has alerted them?* He fought a sense of panic as he watched. The group stood there for a long minute, and then one man turned around and waved rapidly at the rest of the column. Suddenly the man shouted out, "Come, come! Hurry and close up! Join us at the head of the drive!"

And then the small group started walking again. Wend sighed in relief—clearly they were the leaders of the entire band—and concentrated on judging their distance from the wagon and where the pine tree would fall. He wanted them no more than fifty yards from the wagon. Wend held his breath and waited as they continued to approach. He looked over at Taddy Pratt and saw that he was concentrating on his target, the Jaeger rifle balanced on the side of the wagon bed.

Wend turned back to his rifle and focused on the man on the right side of the group. He thanked God again for the clear sky and strong moonlight, which made accurate aim possible.

They were approaching the firing point he had selected. The long column of partisans was hurrying to catch up. Wend called out, "Fire!" Then amid the noise of the others shooting, he took a deep breath, aimed for the body of his man, and squeezed the trigger.

He was the last to fire. He looked up after pulling the trigger and saw that five of the men in the group were lying on the ground, and one was on his knees, hands to his chest. Then he slowly tumbled to the dirt. Two other men in the group stood looking down in shock.

Wend screamed out, "Cut the tree!" But he needn't have bothered, for as he shouted, the tree was already on its way down, the rope taught and pulling it across the drive.

At first the pine tipped slowly, as if consciously fighting to remain upright as it had lived for decades. But then there was a cracking sound, and it seemed to give up the ghost. It swiftly fell to earth, spanning the drive to the crashing noise of branches breaking and the sight of a dust cloud rising as it landed.

Then Wend heard Childers's voice shouting, "To the tree! All take your firing positions!"

There was a rush from the right as the Guides musket men, led by Wood, and Wallen and his men jumped up and found places to level their muskets through the foliage of the pine. Dowling's men came from the left and did the same. Meanwhile, Schreiber and his riflemen were furiously reloading and preparing to move up to the firing line. Pratt had jumped out of the wagon and was running to the tree.

Hardly had Wend noted all this when Childers called out, "Guides, fire!" His words were met by a resounding crash of muskets, seven firing almost as one. Then immediately Childers ordered, "Militia, fire!" followed by a ragged volley. And then Wallen's men fired, not waiting for an order.

Wend stood up in the wagon to be able to see over the pine and judge the effect of their fire. He was not disappointed. Numerous partisans were down, and most of the others were standing in shock. A few with quicker wits had dropped to the ground to obtain whatever protection that would afford. As he watched, one man was crawling toward the shelter of the trees along the drive.

By now individual musket fire had begun from the Guides, trained as they were for rapid reloading. Wend then heard the sharp crack of a couple of Schreiber's rifles who had managed to reload. And in a few seconds more, some of the militia and Wallen's hands had started to shoot. In another minute the firing along the fallen tree became general.

Wend again scanned the partisan column. Confusion reigned. Some men had turned and were trying to retreat back toward the road. Others were moving toward the trees. As he watched, one of those men was hit and stumbled to the ground. Many others were hugging the dirt of the drive. He could not make out any of the partisans trying to fire at the men at the pine tree. Wend called out, "Bloom, get up here and get your horn ready."

Wend looked back up the drive and was met with a surprise. Quinn had not waited for the sound of the horn to bring his dragoons out of their hiding place. The ten horsemen sat their horses in line abreast across the drive. There was a menacing stillness about them as they waited, sabers drawn and resting on their shoulders, moonlight reflecting off the shiny steel blades.

The partisans who were rushing back toward the road now saw the cavalry and sensed what was about to happen. Most turned and ran back toward the main body of their comrades, while a few headed for the trees on either side of the drive.

Meanwhile, the firing of Childers's line had continued. The question now was, *How long to keep firing to get maximum effect on the mob of partisans?* Then he noted that a few of the partisans, braver than the others, were starting to fire back toward the men behind the tree. He knew if he left it too long, more would start firing, and others would realize that safety lay in heading into the woods. Wend made a slow count to sixty. Then he shouted, "Mr. Childers! Cease firing!"

Childers heard him and echoed the command. A few more shots rang out, and then there was silence. Wend turned to the trumpeter. "Bloom, sound the hunting call. And keep blowing it until I tell you to stop."

Bloom stood up to his full height and sounded the horn, the brazen notes of the fox hunting chase call echoing over the yard and throughout the farm in the silence that had fallen after the cease-fire call.

Wend turned back to look at the dragoons as the hunting horn blared in his ear. He saw Quinn raise his saber straight in the air and then point it in the direction of the partisans. Wend had expected him to order the squad to immediately come to the gallop, but instead Quinn started at the walk. Then he brought them up to the trot, then to the cantor, and only as they approached the now-panicking mob did he order the gallop.

But it was extraordinarily effective, for the accelerating approach built up the realization of what was about to happen to the survivors of the musket fire and magnified their panic. They started running toward the fallen pine.

Wend called out, "Bayonets, Mr. Childers!"

The lieutenant gave the order, and the musket men of the Guides squad hurriedly drew their bayonets and locked them in place. Wend was gratified to see that the militiamen also did so.

Wend looked back to the drive just in time to witness the moment when the dragoons, now at full gallop, sabers raised to strike, drove into the rear of the fleeing partisans. The impact was fearsome, for the horses had been trained to run over the enemy, and the hindmost of the fleeing partisans were smashed to the ground and then trampled by the racing hooves. Those not overrun by the horses suffered the slice of swiftly swinging sabers—some losing arms or heads, others succumbing to uncontrollable bleeding of slashing wounds to their bodies. The drive echoed with bloodcurdling screams.

Wend turned his attention to the front of the partisan column and saw that it had advanced to just a few yards from the fallen pine. The partisans were bunching up, their retreat from the cavalry blocked by the tree. Hysteria was breaking out among them. Wend realized it was time for a counter charge. He jumped down from the wagon and ran toward the tree, intent on ordering the men forward. But he didn't have the chance, for young Childers took it upon himself.

Before Wend had covered half the distance, the lieutenant ordered, "Everyone forward! Charge—it's time for cold steel! With that, Childers and the entire Guides squad, Billy Wood included, jumped up and climbed through the branches of the pine, musket men pushing forward with their bayoneted muskets and riflemen with raised tomahawks.

Then Wend witnessed the militia do something he had never expected to see.

Dowling's men stood hesitating, watching the Guides charge but not possessing the fortitude to join them. Suddenly Dowling called out, "Are we just going to stand by and let the Continentals do all the work? This is our town! This is our county! We've got the chance to finish these murderous brigands for good!" And with that, he climbed up on top of the tree's trunk, looked down on his men and said, "Come on, for your homes, your women, your children, let's do it!" Then he jumped down and ran toward the enemy. The militia men looked at each other for a brief second, and then suddenly there was a rush, and every man of them went quickly over the tree and followed their lieutenant.

Now the partisans were caught between the bayonets and hatchets of the soldiers and the sabers of the dragoons, who were steadily slashing their way down the drive, leaving wounded and dead in their wake.

Wend crawled over the tree, pulled out his sword, and entered the fray. He swept his sword over the right shoulder of an African man who wore a cut-off version of a British regular's coat with ragged, dark-colored breeches. The man went down, left hand clutching his shoulder as blood oozed through his fingers. Wend finished him with a thrust to the middle of his chest, and the partisan lay still, lifeless eyes staring at the sky.

Suddenly he became aware that Joseph Wallen was near him, a hatchet in one hand and a dueling pistol in the other. Wallen fired at a partisan about ten feet away, and the man grunted and went down. Suddenly another partisan charged at the farm owner, swinging a halberd; Wallen dodged the blade but stumbled and went down on his knees. The partisan raised the halberd and was about to slash down on Wallen when suddenly a shot rang out, and the man dropped the weapon, clutched his chest, fell to the ground, and lay still.

Puzzled at where the shot had come from, Wend looked around to see John Henry straddling the trunk of the pine tree, smoking pistol in hand. As Wend watched, he put the empty pistol into his belt and pulled out the other. Then he jumped to the ground, steadied himself and fired the pistol at another partisan, who dropped to one knee, holding his shoulder.

Wend strode over to where Henry stood and looked him directly in the eye. "Welcome back to the fight, Mr. Henry. I'm glad you saw your duty clear."

Before John could answer, Wend turned to reenter the combat, only to find Quinn and his troopers just a few yards away and that the surviving partisans were surrendering en masse. Many were shouting, "Quarter! Quarter!" Others were throwing down their weapons and raising their hands.

Childers called out to the partisans, "Lay down your arms! Sit down on the ground and show us your hands with nothing in them! Anyone who doesn't surrender will be put to the bayonet!"

There was a mass movement to comply. Soon the living partisans were on the ground. All resistance was over. Wend looked back up the drive. There were literally dozens of men—and some women—lying dead or seriously wounded along the ground where the dragoons had charged. Many were writhing in pain and calling for help.

Wend walked over to where Childers stood and put his hand on the young officer's shoulder. "Well, Edward, you fought a damn good little fight here."

Childers shook his head. "Thank you, sir." He waved to where one man of the squad stood. "Look at his bayonet—covered with blood. They didn't hesitate to press the attack home." Then he pointed up the drive. "But my

God, sir. Look what the dragoons did. Look at the bloody havoc they have wrought. We could not have succeeded without their work."

Wend nodded. "Indeed, Edward, as we all know, the light dragoons are intended first and foremost for scouting. But as our good friend Shay O'beirne once told me, in actual combat their best use is to mercilessly destroy a broken and fleeing enemy. We saw that done to perfection tonight."

"Indeed, sir."

"Edward, what are our casualties?"

"Haven't checked in detail yet, but I suspect only very minor wounds, sir. As far as I can see, all our men, Guides and militia, are on their feet. A few may need attention from the nurses. The partisans were too shocked to offer much resistance, and those that did weren't very competent or determined."

"Yes, they are used to encountering terrified people who offer little resistance. I suspect few of them have any real training in their weapons or have used them in actual combat before tonight. They are brigands, not soldiers."

"Yes, sir. That seems to be the case."

Then Wend called out, "Officers and sergeants to me."

When all the leaders had gathered, Wend congratulated them on the success of the fight. There were smiles all around. But then Wend raised a hand. "But gentlemen, the night's work is far from done." He waved his arm in the general direction of the drive. "First, we have many prisoners to get organized and to ensure they can't escape. Mr. Dowling, I trust that job to you and your men. Second, I saw a number of the partisans escape into the woods on either side of the drive. We must hunt down as many as possible. Schreiber, use your squad to scour the woods to find anyone skulking there." Wend turned to Quinn. "Take your men out on the road and set up patrols to scoop up any of the partisans who make it that far."

Quinn grinned. "Aye, that will be our pleasure."

"And Quinn, give them the chance to surrender, and bring them back alive when they do."

The sergeant said in a disappointed tone, "*Yes,* Major."

Wallen was standing nearby, and Wend said to him, "Joseph, I complement you. Your farmhands behaved well. They did more than could have been expected."

"They were defending their home, Eckert. Jersey men are as determined to do that as Virginians."

"Indeed, Joseph. We certainly saw that tonight." Then Wend pointed to the men lying in the drive. "There are a lot of wounded and dying partisans out there. As a matter of humanity, we need to tend to them. The women were prepared to treat our wounded. Will they be willing to treat men who were coming to attack them?"

"Much as they hate the partisans, I'm confident the ladies will do so. I'll go talk to them."

Chapter Five
The Response

Barrett Northcutt, cup of tea in hand, stood at the window of his office in the Darragh House, looking out at the sunlit street below, which bustled with the commercial traffic of midafternoon. His assistant, Captain Markwood, sat at his desk, reading a newspaper that had recently arrived from London.

Suddenly the captain broke out in laughter. "Well, it seems our commander is going to face some serious questioning regarding his conduct of the war upon his return to Mother England."

Northcutt shrugged. "There has been considerable comment in earlier papers that he has not prosecuted the war with sufficient vigor. Is there more along that line in what you are reading?"

"Indeed, sir. But this piece goes well beyond that to a singularly personal aspect."

"Personal? How so, Markwood? Pray explain."

"The writer calls out Howe's relationship with Betsy Loring as the reason for his lack of aggressiveness in pursuing Washington's army in the aftermath of the battle of New York, back in '76. Listen to this: 'General Howe was at New York in the lap of Ease, or rather, amusing himself in the lap of a Mrs. Loring, who is the very Cleopatra to this Antony of ours.'"

"Good lord!"

"Yes, sir. And it goes on to call for a parliamentary inquiry of his actions in prosecuting the war."

"Damn, Markwood. I hope neither Howe nor Betsy read that drivel before the Mischianza. I'm going to be sitting with them at the banquet, and it will certainly put a damper on things."

A voice from the doorway said, "And just what is going to put a damper on the banquet? I will not hear of any such thing!"

Northcutt and Markwood turned to see Major John Andre standing in the doorway. Northcutt said, "Markwood, show him the newspaper."

The captain handed it to Andre, pointing out the article.

The major looked at the title. "Oh, another criticism of the general's conduct of the war? We see those all the time, gentlemen." He shrugged. "It comes with the territory."

Markwood said, "Major, I commend you to the third paragraph."

Andre looked down and read silently, his lips moving as he did so. Then he looked up at the other two officers. "Damnation! This *would* have to appear just before the Mischianza. It will be all over the town in no time. There will be whispering behind the general's back, and of course he will be aware of it."

Northcutt asked, "I don't suppose there is any good way from keeping Howe or Mrs. Loring from seeing it?"

Andre sighed and shook his head. "There's nothing for it. The general reads every journal from England as soon as they come off the ship." He looked around at the others. "The last time this happened was when that captured rebel general, Charles Lee, wrote a letter about all this that became public. He called Betsy the general's *'Little Whore,'* and Howe stormed around in a huff for a week. Everyone on the staff avoided him to keep from feeling his wrath."

Northcutt shot a wink at Markwood but said to Andre, "I don't recall that it caused Howe to pay any less attention to Betsy."

The major glared at Barrett and looked as if he was about to respond with anger but hesitated and then thought better of it. Instead he said in calm tones, "But as I said, what will happen will happen. In any case, in a few days the affair will be over, and both the general and Mrs. Loring will be making their separate ways back to England." He dropped the paper on Markwood's desk. "*Now,* gentlemen, back to business. Prithee, what is this urgent matter you have called me here for? The Mischianza is upon us, and I really have time for little else."

Northcutt pointed at the map table. "I have news concerning that detachment of the Guides, and we have the appropriate maps laid out and marked here. I thought it best for you to see the maps themselves to appreciate the situation."

"All right, tell me about this new information if you maintain it is so important."

The three men gathered around the map, which showed the whole of New Jersey. Markwood said, "We had another courier come in late last night. He bore a message that indicated where the detachment has gone."

Northcutt put his finger on a point of the map. "They have bivouacked here, at a plantation owned by a rebel sympathizer near Spanktown."

Andre looked closely at the map. "Spanktown? Why, that's damned close to New York City itself. A short day's ride at most. What business could they have way up there?"

Northcutt responded, "That, my dear John, is *precisely* the question.

They didn't march all that distance just to collect forage. And that's why I thought you should see it with your own eyes. I have no idea of why Washington would want so small a unit up there, where we have many loyalists, and our partisans frequently raid wealthy plantations. It's a dangerous place for Continentals."

Markwood added, "In fact, if our information is up to date, Captain Tigh's band is afield and raiding in that area."

Andre put his hand to his chin. "You don't suppose Eckert has been sent to stop Tigh? His raids have been very damaging and are causing an uproar among the plantation owners who support the rebellion."

Markwood shook his head. "Seems rather unlikely to me, sir. The detachment is only twenty-five men, and Tigh is known to have close to a one hundred, if not more. Washington would have sent a larger force if that was the objective."

Northcutt added, "Indeed—my sense is that they've got something else in mind. But dashed if I can fathom it. Nothing I can think of makes sense."

Andre put his hand to his chin and stood looking at the map for a long moment. "I have an idea. In fact, we should have thought of it rather sooner. Look, the rebels are aware that Clinton wants to evacuate Philadelphia and consolidate things in New York. And we fully expect they will try, in some way, to interfere with our movements as the army marches northward. I suspect that Eckert is up there simply as a scouting expedition and to prepare the local militias for cooperation with Washington's main army when we do move. He's on a patrol simply to gain knowledge. After all, that's the Guides' main function, and such a mission certainly would be consistent with that."

Northcutt looked down at the map and then at Andre. "Perhaps his objective is as innocuous as you say. But, even without knowing what Eckert is up to, I believe we should act. We have an opportunity here—whatever the detachment actually does, we can cut them off from returning to Valley Forge. If we can capture or destroy a significant part of the Guides, and perhaps their commander, it will be a newsworthy and useful action. I suggest we send a small force of cavalry and foot to march at once."

Andre thought a moment, and then a knowing smile spread over his face. "And it I imagine it would please you no end, Barrett, to capture or kill the man who destroyed your regiment and shot to death your friend Welford down in Tidewater, Virginia, two years ago. I suspect personal vengeance is why you are so eager to strike out at this rebel column."

Barrett suppressed his irritation at Andre's smug assertion. "John, my personal feelings aside, it just makes sense. A chance to damage Washington's prime scouting unit. I don't think we can pass it up."

Andre shook his head. "Look, Barrett, I'm not going to advocate sending out an expedition while the relief of command is in progress, and amid Howe's farewell celebration. However, I will take your proposition to Howe and suggest alerting a troop of dragoons and two companies of light foot. That should be more than enough to deal with the Guides column if in the event it is decided to intercept them. And I'll also advise him that we should wait for more definitive information that Eckert is still in northern Jersey and what he is up to. We're getting our information a day or more late. Eckert could have broken camp and already be nearly back to Valley Forge. Get me word that he's still around Spanktown, and I'll consider a recommendation of sending out troops."

Northcutt felt a flash of anger at Andre's words and nearly lashed out. But instantly he knew it would get him nowhere, and he didn't need to antagonize one of the staff's most influential officers. So he said, "All right, I understand your reticence. I know just how busy you and the generals are, what with the relief of command in progress and of course, the onset of the grand Mischianza."

"Indeed, Barrett, things are quite hectic. As I have said, it is hard for me to concentrate on anything else right now. And the two generals are intensely focused on details of the change of command."

Northcutt pointed to the map again. "One more thing, John. I'll get a message off to Tigh—to alert him of the presence of Eckert and his men nearby."

Andre said, "Good idea. He does a lot of beneficial work for us at little expense." Then he turned to leave. "Now, gentlemen, I must return to the important matters of the day, like final arrangements for the Mischianza." He looked to Northcutt. "I shall see you and the lovely Miss Fraser there if not before."

After the major had departed, Northcutt stood, hands on hips, looking at the door. Anger played across his face. Then he spoke out, to no one in particular, "Well, now, we can't let the bloody war interfere with something as important as the Mischianza, can we?"

Markwood ignored the colonel's words, simply clearing his throat and studiously concentrating on the newspaper.

Then Northcutt had a thought. He turned to his assistant. "Markwood, get on over to the cavalry headquarters. Give them advance notice of the possible expedition to New Jersey. And tell them when they are alerted to prepare a troop of cavalry to ride; it would please me greatly if it were Hargate's troop of the Queen's American Rangers."

Markwood looked up from the paper. "Why, that's our own men—the survivors of the Kings Loyal Virginia Legion."

"Exactly, George. I want our Virginians to be in at the kill when we finish Eckert. It will be perfect vengeance for his slaughter of the regiment at Mobjack Bay two years ago and for his murder of poor Welford."

Markwood stood up and reached for his hat. "I'll see to it immediately."

—∞—

Wend Eckert stood in the yard of Wallen Farm, steeling himself against the weariness which threatened to overpower him. It was at least two hours since the end of the fight against the partisans, and the effort to clean up the drive and care for the wounded was in full progress. He looked up at the moon in the clear sky and realized there were at least four hours until dawn, and no one on the farm save the dead was likely to have a minute's rest this night.

Meli, Trumpeter Bloom, Nell Porter, Rachel Wallen, and the other women of the farm were busily ministering to the wounded, both patriots and partisans. The militiamen had brought these to the yard just in front of the house.

Joseph Wallen's farmhands had used a horse team to drag the pine tree away from the drive to a place where they could chop it up at leisure. Then they had hitched up two wagons and were now in the process of loading the dead from the drive into them, where they would remain pending a decision on a burial location. Schreiber's and Quinn's squads had now rounded up all the escaped partisans who could be found and herded them to a spot near the stable where they sat under guard along with those who had surrendered during the skirmish, including several women. Wend was sure some of the partisans had made a clean escape, and that bothered him, for undoubtedly they would inform loyalist or British forces that might be in the area. He shrugged. There was nothing for it, but it meant that he should start his detachment back to Valley Forge as soon as possible to avoid any pursuit. But he was also aware that after this night's work, all the men would need rest. So he consoled himself to the need to remain another day and night at Wallen Farm before beginning their withdrawal.

Wend walked over to where Meli was bending over a wounded man and waited until she had finished applying a dressing. Wend looked at the rows of wounded partisans and noted there was about an even mix of white and black men. Presently, she stood up and prepared to move on to the next man. He asked, "How is it going, Meli?"

She wiped her hands on her apron and motioned toward the men lying on the ground. "We still got plenty of work to do." She shook her head. "I know how to deal with the men who been gunshot, but it's the ones who got bayonet or saber cuts that is really hard."

As she spoke, Rachel Wallen joined them. "She's right, Major Eckert. These sword injuries are terrible, deep cuts. No one here is experienced with closing and sewing those kinds of wounds. We need a real physician to treat them."

"Isn't there any kind of doctor nearby? Perhaps we could send a rider to summon him."

She nodded. "Indeed, there's Dr. Kirby, who lives in a village about three miles from here." She looked around. "If you could talk to my husband, he could send a man to the doctor's house to see if he will come. It would be a great help."

Wend said, "I'll go see him."

Eckert was about to leave when Nell Porter came up and stood beside Meli, a bemused look on her face. "Meli," she said, "there's a seriously injured African over there, a man who is drifting in and out of consciousness, and he's saying wild things."

Meli said, "What do you mean, Miss Porter?"

"None of his words are making much sense, but now and then he utters something that sounds like *your* name. He's talking to 'Mali' or 'Meli.' But it's very difficult to make out." She shrugged. "I know it sounds crazy; there's no way he would know you."

Wend and Meli exchanged looks. Wend said, "Nell, it's not as crazy as you think." He motioned to Meli. "Let's go see."

Nell led the way to a man lying on the ground. He wore a red jacket, and Wend quickly realized it was one of those that Dunmore's Ethiopian Regiment had worn. He looked over at Meli, who was staring at the wounded partisan. Then she said, "It's him, Major."

Nell looked between the other two. "Are you familiar with this man?"

"This is Captain Tigh, Nell. Meli knew him when he was a member of Lord Dunmore's regiment of Africans, back in Virginia. In those days, he was known as Sergeant Tigh." Then Wend asked, "How serious is it?"

Nell said, "He's got two wounds: a ball in his chest and what looks like a bayonet was driven into his stomach. I believe it would be possible to extract the ball, but the bayonet wound is oozing blood, and I can't staunch it. I think a doctor would say his wounds are mortal." She looked at Wend and Meli in turn.

Wend explained, "A bayonet blade is triangular in shape, and it's hard to make that kind of wound heal, even in less critical places, Nell. In the stomach, it's impossible. He'll die due to loss of blood, probably sooner rather than later."

At that moment Tigh moaned, his eyes closed, and he distinctly said, "Meli, oh, Meli. Where are you?"

She looked at Wend as if requesting permission to converse with Tigh.

"It's all right, Meli. Keep him company; comfort him."

Meli went to her knees. "Tigh, I'm here! It's me, Melinda. I'm here to take care of you."

The African exclaimed, "Meli, Meli, where are you?"

"Tigh, I'm right here. It's Melinda," she said again in a slightly louder voice.

The man's face wrinkled up, and then with a great effort, his eyes opened until a slit of his whites showed in the darkness. He asked softly, "Meli? Meli, is that really you? It be so hard to see."

"I'm here, Tigh. It's dark, and there's only firelight, but I'm right beside you." She gently put a hand on his face. "I'll stay with you."

"Oh, Meli, how can you be here? Are you a spirit who has come to beset me in my agony?"

She put her hand on his face. "No, Tigh, I'm real. Don't worry how I got here. The Lord has strange ways, and he put me here with the soldiers. I'm here to keep you company."

Tigh gasped for breath. "Yes, it's jes like back on the island. We had it so good, sharin' our blankets. The nights were so nice, I din't ever want the dawn to come, to have to leave you and start my soldier work."

Meli bit her lip and looked up at Wend, then back at her former lover.

A smile came over Tigh's lips. "Meli, do you remember the day I found you at that plantation? We landed from boats and came for foodstuffs and to free all the slave people. Then I saw you standin' on the front porch of the big house, and you looked so beautiful in your gown and that smile on your pretty face."

"Yes, Tigh, I can never forget that day. The day of my freedom."

A wave of pain came over Tigh, and it showed on his face. He closed his eyes and gritted his teeth. Then it seemed to pass, and he took a deep breath. "I walked right up to that porch and held out my hand and said to you, 'Come on, little Missy, I'll take you on a boat to an island where there won't be no master to you, and we'll take care of you."

"Yes, I remember."

"And I got you the job of cookin' for the officers of Colonel Northcutt's regiment, which made you happy." He smiled broadly. "And in a few days, we started sharin' blankets." He took another deep breath. "I remember those days so fondly. Dream about them at night ever since."

"Yes, Tigh, those were good days."

He shut his eyes and seemed to drop off for a few minutes. Wend was about to leave, when the partisan captain opened his eyes again, and a serious look came over his face. "And then it ended. Sudden like. That young stranger came to the island. That *Billy*. That Billy who was picked up on another raid. And then *he* was all you had eyes for."

He coughed up blood, and Meli cleaned his face with a damp cloth.

"And then the rebels attacked, and we pulled out of the island one night. And you didn't come with us. Why did you not come?"

"I stayed behind to take care of the sick people, the ones at the hospital with the pox."

Tigh coughed again. "I searched for you when the ships got us to New York. But you weren't there. Meli, you been in my mind all this time. I couldn't forget those days on the island. Don't leave me, now that you are with me again. I'll be gone soon enough."

"Tigh, it's all right. I'm here now, and I'll be with you till you leave to cross over the river."

A great smile came over his face, and he reached out and touched her face, and then he seemed to drop off into sleep.

Wend put his hand on Meli's shoulder and smiled. "You are a kind woman, Meli. Do what you can to smooth his way over the crossing."

Wend looked around and saw Wallen standing near the drive. He started to walk over to talk with him about getting the local doctor.

Just then Edward Childers called out, "Reverend Danbury is coming back!" Wend looked up the drive to see him riding in from the road. The Reverend had ridden out as soon as the fighting had stopped, intent on finding out what had occurred at the neighboring Graham farm.

Bunbury pulled up in the yard and, seeing Wallen, dismounted and walked to meet him. Wend joined them.

Wallen asked, "Well, Reverend, what did you find at Graham's?"

Danbury shot a look of sheer rage toward Wend, then said to Wallen, "I found what I expected. Graham and his overseer, Price, hanging from the limb of a tree. Everyone else run off to the Lord knows where. All the buildings in ashes. I should not be surprised if we don't find charred bodies in the debris."

Wend said, "After dawn, I'll send a detail to recover whatever bodies can be found."

"You will not, sir! *We* of Spanktown will take care of getting them and giving them proper burial." Danbury spit out the words, "You, sir, are as responsible as those devils over there," he pointed over at the prisoners sitting beside the paddock, "For the death and destruction at Graham Farm. I shall not forget, and I will correspond immediately with our representatives in the Continental Congress. You shall answer for the shirking of your duty this night. The reckoning will come, sure as night follows day."

Wend looked at Danbury and then at Wallen. He pointed to the two wagons of dead partisans, and then over at the porch of the house where lay the wounded. "I will stand by my actions tonight before Washington or Congress, if it comes to that. We have destroyed the largest band of partisans in New Jersey. Captain Tigh, their leader, lies dying over there. Not to mention we saved Wallen Farm and many others they would have sacked in the forthcoming days. I can live with my decisions, sir. So I invite you to do your damnedest in reporting me to whatever authority you choose." He turned and was about to walk off when Banbury called out his name.

"Eckert! Eckert, you listen to me! I know not what action Congress and General Washington may take, but I know one thing is certain: the Lord, in all his might, will in due course make you answer for your negligence and your wanton sacrifice of innocent people."

Wend turned around and stared at the fuming minister and laughed. "Reverend, I advise you that the Lord already has a rather prodigious list of things for which I must answer. So send him your appeal about this matter, and when he determines that my time has arrived, I will stand before him and settle all the sin on my account in one payment." He touched his hand to his forehead. "I bid you good night, Reverend."

—m—

Wend stared at the eastern sky. First light was coming, albeit more perceived than visual, simply a sense that the horizon was less dark than it had been a few minutes before. He sighed. What mattered was that the long, bloody night was coming to an end. Several of the wounded partisans had died in the darkness, and their bodies had been deposited in the wagons already holding many of their comrades. Another ten of the county militia, responding to Dowling's summons, had come to the farm and were assisting in the guarding of the prisoners and the completion of chores to clean up the drive. Wend had discussed the question of burial of the dead with Wallen, who was adamant that it not be done on his farm. Thinking for a minute, Wend suggested that the landowner discuss the question with Reverend Danbury, to see if he could propose a satisfactory site, a suggestion with which Wallen readily agreed.

Campfires had been lighted, and many of the soldiers, Guides and militia alike, had made coffee or had succumbed to weariness. Wend looked over at the improvised hospital. Unfortunately, the women who were treating the wounded could get little rest, for there were still many seriously injured who needed constant attention. At least they had received some relief in the form of a certain Dr. Kirby, who, summoned by a rider dispatched by Wallen, had arrived at the darkest hour of the night and had immediately set to work.

Wend had just decided to go in search of coffee when Meli came up to him. "Major Eckert, it's all finished with Captain Tigh. He has passed on. Just now." She looked over to the east, where there was now a definite sign of light. "He didn't quite make it to dawn."

Wend thought a moment and replied, "Meli, it's a curious thing, a real mystery. For some reason many dying people survive most of the night, fighting death with all their strength, then slip away just before a new day begins."

"Yes, sir, I've heard people say that myself."

They stood together for a prolonged time, looking east at the growing illumination on the horizon.

Presently Wend said, "I know you must be exhausted; this night must have been a terrible strain on you, but I've got to ask you to do something else now." He swept his arm around the yard, taking in all the campfires. "We need to have a meal for these men. They've fought hard and worked hard, and they want to sleep. But before that, we need to get some substantial sustenance in them. Something warm." He looked around for Billy. "I'll have your husband get a good cook fire started, and you get rations out of the wagon. And I'll talk to Wallen about any food that he can provide. We've got to feed all the soldiers, both Guides and militia, a morning meal. Are you up to it?"

"Sure enough, I can do it." She laughed. "I been up longer than this and gone to work." Then she sighed. "But right now I need to ask you somethin', Mr. Eckert. Somethin' important to me."

"What is it, Meli?"

"I got ask you not to tell Billy what Tigh said. What he said about me and him back on Gwynn's Island." She looked up at Wend, bit her lip, and continued, "About us sharing blankets and sleeping together." Meli thought a moment. "Mr. Eckert, I was just away from the plantation, and Tigh had taken good care of me. An' he was such a strong man that all the other soldiers looked up to him. And I admired him for that." She paused and looked down at the ground and said softly. "It was the first time I was with a man in that way."

Wend smiled. "I think I understand."

"Well, what I'm tryin' to say is, Billy knows Tigh was sweet on me, but he don't know I was spendin' nights with him. I never quite got around to tellin' him." She put her hand on Wend's arm. "Major, I got to ask you not to let Billy know about that part. He thinks he was my first man."

Wend smiled to himself. "Yes, that could be awkward, Meli. I will confess that my wife knows about some women whom I was with before we were married, and it has caused," he hesitated a moment looking for the right words, "some difficult moments."

"Yes, sir. That's it. Things might be *difficult*. And I wouldn't want Billy to think less of me 'cause I didn't tell him. There just wasn't any good time or any good way."

"Well, rest assured, Billy will never learn about it from me."

She sighed deeply and squeezed his arm. "Thank ye, Mr. Eckert. Thank ye!" She dropped her arm and said, "Now I'll start getting them rations ready."

—∿—

Mary Fraser looked around the glittering ballroom, lit by thousands of candles, unable to shed a feeling of sheer awe at the scene. The banquet and ball of the Mischianza was underway, and when the meal was complete, there would be dancing until dawn. More unbelievable to her, she sat beside Colonel Barrett Northcutt at General Howe's table, surrounded by the most senior members of his staff and their female consorts. Close by was General Clinton's table, with staff officers close to him. And then there were tables with most of the other generals of the army, with their staffs in attendance.

Mary reflected on the events of the celebration, which she found overwhelming. Never in her days as an orphan living in the camps of the 77th and 42nd, spending her time washing clothes, doing the sewing for soldiers, and nursing wounded and dying men, would she have ever have dared to dream of one day becoming a participant in such a glittering, fairy tale proceeding. She was grateful that her eight years as governess on the Highland estate of Bonniecrest had provided her with the social graces and manners necessary to function successfully in an event of this nature.

The Mischianza had begun with a "regatta" or waterborne parade of nearly a score of colorfully decorated galleys and rowed barges bearing the generals and their retinues along the waterfront. It seemed as if all of Philadelphia lined the waterfront to watch the spectacle. The ships of the Royal Navy, anchored offshore, were dressed with colorful flags, their crews manning the rails and the rigging. The large frigates *Roebuck* and *Vigilant* rendered seventeen-gun salutes for Howe and Clinton as their boats passed. Then the dignitaries were landed at the pier of an old waterfront fortification and formed in a procession that marched along streets lined with tall Grenadiers from the various battalions of the army to the site of the afternoon and evening events at Walnut Grove, the large estate of Joseph Wharton, scion of one of the most prestigious families in Pennsylvania.

The grounds of the Wharton estate provided the site for a mock jousting tournament, as between knights of medieval times. Two bands of officers had been designated as knights. One group was called the Knights of the Blended Roses and the other the Knights of the Burning Mountain. Each band consisted of an officer designated the leader, or chief knight, with six officers as knights and another six as their squires. They wore clothing which they supposed replicated that of the Middle Ages. Each knight rode in honor of a young lady and carried her colors. There was a marshal of the field, heralds and trumpeters who announced with brassy calls each pair of knights for their contest. After the individual jousts with lances, in which of course, no one was injured, the two chief knights played at fighting a sword duel on foot. After a few minutes of fencing, the marshal of the field halted the fighting and announced to the assembled crowd that the fair ladies of the Blended Roses and the Burning Mountain were satisfied that their honor had been defended. A rousing round of applause answered that announcement.

And with that, all the invited guests retired to the Wharton mansion to begin the evening festivities. Before entering the mansion itself for the banquet, the assemblage had been entertained by an extravagant fireworks display, the most thrilling Mary had ever seen. Now, with supper over, the men of the orchestra were taking their places and tuning their instruments.

Presently, the overall manager of the Mischianza, Colonel O'Hara, rose from his seat and walked to a place in front of the orchestra to address the assemblage.

"Ladies and gentlemen of the army and Philadelphia, we hope you have enjoyed the proceedings thus far. Now, for your pleasure, we are ready to commence the dancing." He smiled and looked around the room. "But first, let us all rise and pay tribute to our sovereign, King George, with the playing of 'God Save the King.'"

Everyone stood up, and the orchestra began the anthem. First a few people started to sing the words, and then virtually the entire party joined in. Mary looked around the room and saw that many of the Philadelphia loyalists were among the most enthusiastic singers—and few had dry eyes. She reflected that this must be an incredibly emotional time for them, for many would be leaving behind their homes, businesses, and relatives when the fleet sailed, and the army marched for New York. Others who were determined to remain in Philadelphia faced an uncertain future and might well face retribution when the rebels reoccupied the city. She sighed at the thought of how the war was wreaking havoc with families on both sides.

Her thoughts were interrupted by Northcutt's voice. "Now, Mary, shall we go to the floor? The orchestra is about to play the music for the first dance."

"Why of course, Barrett, that would be my pleasure," Mary responded with some trepidation. She had danced many times in camp to the violin and pipes, but formal dancing was her least accomplished of the social graces. The mistress of Bonniecrest had engaged a dancing master to teach the children, and Mary had also learned the steps of several dances from him. Now her hope was that she could keep from embarrassing herself out on the floor in front of these high-born and wealthy people. She took Northcutt's proffered hand. Once the music began, she realized she need not have worried, for the dance was indeed one she had learned from the instructor, and with concentration and an eye on other couples, she remembered all the steps.

When the dance finished, they stood waiting for the next to begin.

Then one of the servants came out of the crowd and inquired of Barrett, "Are you Colonel Northcutt?"

"Indeed I am. Why do you ask?"

"Sir, there is a Captain Markwood at the entrance, seeking you and Major Andre. He says there is a matter of the utmost urgency he must speak to you about."

Barrett made a face. "Tonight? Of all nights?"

The servant said, "He told me to say to you it's about New Jersey and can't wait."

The muscles in Northcutt's face tightened, and he nodded. "All right, I shall talk to him." He looked around the room and asked the man, "Do you know Major Andre?"

"Indeed I do, sir. I will find him and have him join you." And with that, he was off.

Barrett turned to Mary. "My dear, I regret I must leave you for what I will assure you will be a brief interval. Let me escort you back to the table."

They found the table deserted, all the others dancing or standing in conversational groups. Northcutt said, "My dear Mary, I am deeply sorry for leaving you unattended. But be assured I will be back momentarily, after I see what this is all about. I can imagine nothing that will make me tarry long." Then he was off.

Mary sat down and took a sip of her dinner wine. Then she occupied herself with watching the people dancing or standing along the edges of the dance floor. But after only a short time, she heard a voice over her shoulder, "Miss Fraser, how is it that such a lovely woman finds herself unattended?"

Mary looked around to see a man who looked vaguely familiar. He was quite youthful, slightly below medium height, razor lean but muscular, with a thin, high-cheek-boned face. But the most striking thing was his eyes—cold and penetrating. He was dressed in the clothing of one of the knights from the jousting. Her mind raced to try to place where and under what circumstances she knew him.

"It's been nearly two years since that evening in New York when I had the pleasure of your acquaintance, Miss Fraser. But I vow your face has stayed with me ever since."

Then it hit her. She remembered the introduction but struggled for a minute to get the name. Then came to her. "Ah, yes, Cornet Tarleton. Banastre, if I recall correctly. Am I not right?"

"Indeed, mostly so. However, it is now *Captain* Tarleton. I was promoted after a rather interesting action in late '76."

Then she recalled, "Oh, yes. I heard something about that. You captured a rebel general?"

"Yes, a man called Lee. I think of him as a turncoat, since he was once a lieutenant colonel in our army." He smiled broadly. "But I didn't come here to talk of the war or traitors. I came here to ask you to join me in the next minuet, which will be starting shortly."

"Banastre, I'm most honored, but I'm with Colonel Northcutt this evening, and I expect him back momentarily."

"I'm afraid you are going to be frustrated in that, Miss Fraser. Something is brewing. Northcutt and Andre left and then just a minute ago both Generals Howe and Clinton were also summoned. I should think they may be gone for some time." He smiled, but it only extended to the lips, for his eyes retained the same penetrating look.

Mary thought a second, then decided there was no reason not to acquiesce. Besides, she was feeling awkward sitting alone at the table. "Well, then, it would be my pleasure, Captain."

"Oh, please, Mary, call me *Ban*. That's what all my friends call me, and I certainly would like to count you in that number."

Tarleton gave her his hand, and they walked to where the dance was forming.

—⁂—

Andre, accompanied by Northcutt, led the two generals, both carrying wineglasses, to a small room off of the ballroom. Captain Markwood was waiting there, standing arms crossed, looking out a window into the night.

Clinton, irritated at being pulled away from the festivities, turned to Andre and said, "Now, sir, what is this business which requires our immediate attention, well after midnight on this of all nights?"

Howe, who had been given a quick summary by his aide, said, "Yes, John, please explain the situation to the general." And he motioned toward Clinton. "Henry, I think you will find the urgency of this matter *well* warrants our brief absence from the party."

Andre nodded and extended his hand toward the staff officer at the window. "Gentlemen, this is Captain Markwood, who works with Colonel Northcutt in the liaison with our loyalist units and the oversight of a network of colonial spies and watchers in Jersey and New York. One of their men has just come in with disturbing news."

Henry Clinton looked bemused and asked, "Disturbing news?"

Markwood looked from Howe to Clinton, then said without preamble, "The Guides have destroyed our largest and most successful partisan unit. The one lead by Captain Tigh."

Clinton's brows furrowed. "Just who the *devil* are the Guides?"

Andre answered, "Sir, they are a small legion of light foot and dragoons, who are under Washington's direct command. They perform scouting for the Continental Army and particularly help lead it into position for battle."

Northcutt added, "They are very much similar to the Hessian Jaegers of our German allies, sir." Then he continued, "And between field campaigns, Washington also uses them for special missions." He hesitated a moment, "Which this obviously was." Northcutt motioned to Markwood. "General, the captain will explain the background and the events that have occurred."

Markwood said, "General, a few days ago a small detachment of the Guides, amounting to no more than twenty-five effectives, left Valley Forge and traveled northward, deep into New Jersey, to encamp on the estate of a well-known rebel sympathizer near Spanktown. It is quite close to New York City." He shrugged. "We had no idea what their objective was, but it now appears, despite their small size, the intent was to disrupt the operations of our partisan bands, which have been quite active in that precise area."

Howe asked, "So what specifically occurred, Markwood?"

"Sir, Tigh and his band had been raiding plantations in the area of Spanktown. Two nights ago, they raided a couple of estates and then moved on to the third, called Wallen Farm, where the Guides were encamped, unknown to Tigh. When they approached the farm, they were ambushed on the drive. Their leadership, including Tigh, were cut down by rifle fire at the very beginning, and then the column was subjected to volleys of musket fire. But the real devastation was done by a dragoon saber charge emanating from their rear, which cut up their whole column, leaving many dead and wounded. The survivors, in demoralized condition, surrendered en masse."

Clinton, a look of shock on his face, thought a minute then asked, "And just how do we know so much detail about this incident?"

Markwood responded, "Our operative was informed by one of the few partisans who escaped into the bush. Although seriously wounded in the shoulder, he made his way to a local town and sought refuge and medical treatment in the home of a loyalist, which is where our informant interviewed him."

Clinton nodded. "All right, but I find it hard to believe that a detachment of twenty-five men destroyed a formation of one hundred armed partisans. How could that happen?"

Markwood raised a finger. "Sir, our man believes Eckert was joined by a half company of rebel militia. He says a call was made by a local officer after it became known the partisans were raiding. That would have at least doubled the size of the enemy force and their firepower. And of course, Eckert is a wily tactician, we believe one of the best they have."

Northcutt added, "And Eckert would have had the advantage of both surprise and being in an established defensive position."

Clinton glanced around at the others, a puzzled look on his face. "Eckert? Who is this Eckert?"

Northcutt said, "Major Wendelmar Johann Eckert, master gunsmith of Winchester, in Frederick County, Virginia. He recruited an independent company of light foot, which forms the core of the Guides."

Disdain spread across Henry Clinton's face. "You say a gunsmith is an expert tactician? A mechanic is a military paragon? How on earth did he learn military skills?"

Northcutt responded, "I'm afraid, sir, we taught him."

"What? What do you say? *We* taught him military field craft?"

Barrett said, "Eckert is actually descended from a line of German Jaegers who came to the colonies in the early part of the century. As a youth in 1763, he marched with Henry Bouquet against the Indians during the Pontiac

War. He fought at Bushy Run. Then he served under Colonel Stirling of the 42nd, when he was a captain, on an expedition into the Ohio Country. Sterling says he was the best scout he ever worked with. I happen to know Eckert personally—in 1772 Governor Dunmore gave him a contract to refurbish old muskets, and later we commissioned him a staff officer for the war against the Shawnee in 1774." He paused to gather his thoughts. "Eckert is smart, with more than average formal education for a tradesman, and extremely crafty. It is difficult for me to recount this, but his company nearly destroyed my regiment in a skirmish in the Virginia Tidewater while I was in Halifax on a mission for Lord Dunmore, and during the engagement he personally killed my second in command, Major Welford."

Andre said, "General Clinton, the Guides were formed by Washington just after the battles around New York in November '76, in part to compensate for their lack of cavalry. Eckert's legion guided the army in its retreat across New Jersey to Pennsylvania. They made a stand at the Delaware that drove back our Hesse-Cassel Jaeger Corps and thus allowed Washington's rear elements to escape a trap Cornwallis had set." He shrugged. "Then they performed most effectively in last year's campaign to take this city, making up to some degree for the enemy's lack of effective cavalry."

There was a moment of silence as Clinton took a sip on his wine glass. Then he looked around the room and said, "I presume you did not bring me into this room simply to tell me about a defeat in a skirmish and educate me on the history of Washington's Guides and the personal characteristics of Major Eckert. I suppose you are about to recommend some measure of action?"

Andre waved toward Barrett. "Indeed, sir. Colonel Northcutt has a proposal regarding a response."

"Yes, General," responded Barrett. "I believe we can cut off and destroy

Eckert's column. We know they must return to Valley Forge, and we can set up an ambush to effect that objective, if we act tonight. That's why we have called you here."

Howe interrupted. "Henry, we've known about this detachment of Guides for some time. Based on Andre and Northcutt's recommendation, I have already alerted two companies of light foot—Highlanders from Grey's Brigade, which has the duty—and a troop of the Queen's American Rangers, which are quite familiar with the Jersey country. They can march at dawn—just a few hours from now. It's a force that can move fast and is more than adequate for the task."

Clinton walked over to the window and looked out into the night for a long moment, obviously considering the proposal.

Andre spoke up. "Sir, Eckert's defeat of Tigh's partisans will be an embarrassment to us when news of it becomes known and will encourage the rebel militia in Jersey. God knows, they're active enough as it is. But if we can destroy the Guides detachment, it will to large extent ameliorate the situation and have a positive effect on our supporters. And it will be a victory in the first days of your command that will start things off with a favorable tone."

Clinton turned around, a thoughtful look on his face. Then he finished off his wine and said, "Yes, yes, I see what you mean and quite agree." He swept his hand around the room. "Gentlemen, with General Howe's concurrence, let's make it happen."

Howe nodded. "It's the right thing to do, Henry."

Barrett raised his hand. "Sir, one more thing. I recommend that I ride up to Jersey independently with Markwood and a small cavalry escort. That way I can be in immediate contact with my web of informers, to help provide timely information and guide our force into contact with Eckert. I think that may ensure success."

The two generals looked at each other, and both nodded. Howe said, "Make it so, Northcutt, and good luck with your mission." Then he turned to Clinton. "Shall we rejoin the ladies, Henry?"

Clinton smiled. "Indeed, William. We have been among the missing for too long already."

With that they departed, leaving the three other officers in the room. Andre walked to the door in preparation to follow the generals. Then he turned back to Northcutt with a sly smile on his face. "Can I assume your personal mission has the real intent of a tête-à-tête with Eckert? A bit of fatal revenge for his assassination of your friend Welford?"

"You can assume whatever you want, John. But I do see it as my duty to ensure we avenge the loss of Tigh's partisans."

Andre said nothing but merely grinned and then left the room.

Markwood looked at Northcutt. "Snide fellow, isn't he?"

Barrett stared after the departed major. "Someday, when the opportunity presents itself, I will take that example of British haughtiness down a few notches and grin with pleasure as I do it."

Markwood shrugged. "Well, sir, in the meantime, we must get ready to ride. Should I call for your carriage so that you can escort Miss Fraser back to her quarters?"

Northcutt stiffened. "You may not! I have no intention of leaving the ball early. I intend to finish the night and enjoy Miss Fraser's company for every minute available. Then we will leave tomorrow at a reasonable time and ride hard after we do. In the meantime, get the word to the Highlanders and cavalry troop to march at dawn and arrange for the Queen's Rangers to provide us with an escort. That should take at least until the early afternoon tomorrow."

"Actually, Colonel, given that it's well past midnight, that would be afternoon today."

Barrett waved his hand dismissively. "Tomorrow, today, call it what you will. Just get things ready for us to leave after I have somewhat recovered from the entertainment. In the meantime, I will enjoy the pleasure of dancing with Mary Fraser."

Markwood gave his senior a wry smile. "As you wish, Colonel."

Chapter Six
Millstone River

Wend watched as Sergeant Quinn and his squad of dragoons rode along the drive toward the yard of Wallen Farm. He had sent them out the morning after the skirmish to see if, in daylight, they would be able to round up more of the partisans who had escaped the ambush. Now, with evening coming on, he could see that their sweep had evidently had some success, for they were herding a small group of men ahead of them.

Quinn rode his horse up to where Wend stood and slipped to the ground. "Well, we got six of them, Major Eckert." He grinned. "And then there was the one who tried to run away when he saw us, and I regret to say we were forced to shoot him." He paused and shrugged. "Fatally."

Wend responded in irony, "Yes, I can see the regret written all over your face, Sergeant."

"Just doin' my duty, sir."

"All right, Quinn, put them with the other prisoners so Dowling and his men can watch them. We've got quite a batch there."

"Major, I got somethin' I want to talk about." He motioned over to the paddock where his squad was dismounting. "It's about the horses."

"All right, what about them?"

"They been used hard, sir. There was the march up here, and then the ride to Elizabeth Town and back, and then they was busy most all of last night, and now this patrol today." He looked Wend in the eyes. "Sir, they need rest. They need at least a day in the pasture a'fore we start our march back down to the army. And that's the truth, Major."

"That means we can't start back until the morning of the day after tomorrow."

"They need the time, sir. And plenty of good grass and grain."

Wend thought about it and knew Quinn was right. But it meant increased possibility of pursuit by the British. Their spies or sympathizers would soon have word to either New York or Philadelphia about what had happened at Wallen Farm. He thought of the troop of Hussars they had seen on the second day of the march. There were bound to be other British units on patrol. Wend sighed and made the decision. "All right, Quinn. We'll spend another day here. But come hell or high water, we're out of here early the day after tomorrow."

Quinn led his horse off toward the paddock, and shortly Meli announced that the evening meal was ready. She brought plates of food for Wend and the other three people who were now messing at the officers' fire—Childers, Henry, and Nell Porter. As they ate, Wend reflected that the girl had done yeoman's work helping treat the wounded and had also been helping Meli with meals. She and Edward sat close together, exchanging glances at each other while participating in the general talk as the meal progressed. Since the night of the attack, John had become more conversant and also took part in the talk around the fire. When they had finished, Wend laid out his plans for return to the army's camp.

Nell asked, "How long will it take to get to Valley Forge?"

Wend replied, "If we have no problems along the way, three days' march."

She frowned. "Problems? What might that be?"

Childers hurried to answer. "Nell, there are many British patrols. We had to hide from a troop of cavalry on the way up."

Wend added, "And I would be surprised if some British authority has not been advised of what happened here and at Elizabeth Town. It's possible they are organizing a pursuit or an interception. All of New Jersey is dangerous ground. We'll have to be alert as we march, and I plan to move fast once we leave here." He shrugged. "Would that we could leave early tomorrow, but the horse problem precludes it."

Nell said, "Well, my relatives—my aunt's family—are in lower New Jersey. I'll leave you after two days and make my way to their place."

Wend replied, "Whatever suits your needs. And you'll go with my appreciation for all you have done for us and the wounded."

"That's very generous of you, Major." She looked over at the house and rose to her feet. "I must go now. I promised the doctor I would help him after supper."

Edward jumped to his feet. "Major, with your permission, I'll go with her and bring you back a report on the remaining wounded partisans."

Wend worked to avoid grinning, instead saying in a serious tone, "Ah, yes, Mr. Childers. That would be most helpful." Then he watched as the two youngsters hurried off toward the Wallen house, laughing as they walked.

Henry looked up as they went and said in a deprecating tone, "I see Edward is becoming quite intrigued with that tavern maid."

Wend smiled. "John, it might interest you to know that my wife was a tavern maid when I married her."

Henry's eyes opened wide, and surprise registered on his face.

Wend continued, "And I can say she has been a fine wife to me and raised my children, one of which is not hers, in a most commendable matter. Not to mention that she is called upon by the ladies of the gentry in Frederick County and Winchester and considered most polite and esteemed company by them."

The young man looked at Wend for a long moment, and then shrugged and said, "I meant no deprecation of Nell or any serving girl. It's just that I happen to know that Edward was courting a young lady in the tidewater, a lady of some means and position."

"Can I assume you are referring to a certain Miss Wilbourne?"

Henry's face again showed surprise. "You know of his affection for Emma Wilbourne?"

"It's my business to know the affairs of my officers." Then he motioned toward Henry. "In any case, referring to Miss Porter, it cannot have escaped your attention that she is a very intelligent and well-spoken young woman. And more importantly, that she used her wits to help us find you."

Henry thought for a long moment, then shrugged his shoulders. "Yes, that's true."

"And it seems that she was, after a manner, looking after you while you were in your cups at the Good Queen Bess. Well, John, I am of the opinion that Nell Porter, if that is her real name, is of a middling background and educated beyond that of most young women."

"I hadn't particularly noticed."

"Well, John, aside from her intelligence, there is something else that I find makes her an admirable young lady. She was facing danger by acting as a spy for the Continental cause. I'd say she is as much of a soldier as any of the men around us." He swung his hand to take in all the men sitting around at fires in the camp.

Henry's eyes followed the sweep of Wend's arm, but he said nothing and sat silent, staring into the fire.

Wend watched the young man for a long moment, then said, "Incidentally, while on the subject of causes, what motivated you to join in the fight last night? Not to mention saving Joseph Wallen's life during the scuffle at the pine tree. When we spoke on the porch, you considered the fight against partisans no affair of yours."

John Henry stared into the fire for a moment. "I came to the conclusion that it was my duty as a gentleman to help preserve the lives of women and children, and the other civilian people on this plantation. It most decidedly wasn't for the patriot cause. I'd have done the same for my family if we were on the frontier and attacked by tribal warriors or renegades. It was a matter of saving innocent people who were threatened by a rabble, not fighting a war."

"Well, John, for whatever reason you did it, I will include it in my report to Washington. It may influence his mind on how to ultimately handle your case."

A scowl came across Henry's face. "With all due respect, you don't need to do me any favors."

Wend looked at the sullen young man. "It is not my intent to do you any *favors*. But I will make an *accurate* report to the general for his information."

A very tired Mary Fraser sat at her desk at the general hospital, trying to focus on her apothecary inventory. But she was struggling to concentrate. She thought, *I should have just stayed at quarters today to recover from the ball, for all the good I'm doing here. Nobody would have blamed me.*

Northcutt had escorted her back to her rooms just after four in the morning. Stimulated by the excitement of the night's entertainment, she had had trouble dropping off and had spent only a few restless hours in bed. So she had arisen, dressed, and walked the short distance to the hospital offices, arriving shortly after one in the afternoon. That had been two hours ago, and she had little to show for her time. She had just decided to give it up and return home when there was a tap at the doorway, and she looked up to see the tall, angular figure of Kathryn O'Hara standing in the doorway. Kathryn, the wife of Sergeant Archie O'Hara, was the senior nurse of the 42nd. She was ten years older than Mary and had been with her at Bushy Run and Bouquet's march into the Ohio Country in 1764.

Mary smiled at her old friend. "What are you doing here in town today? Never mind! For whatever reason, I'm certainly glad to see you!"

"I got Surgeon Potts's permission to come and talk to you. We all want to know when you are coming back to the regiment."

"In just a few days—as soon as I get all these records organized and packed for the trip to New York. Then I'll be marching with the regiment for the campaign."

"It will be good to have you back."

Mary put her papers aside. "I'm not making much progress here. Let's go have some tea. I know a comfortable little shop close by, and we can talk."

Kathryn's narrow, horse face broke into a look of pleasure. "That will be most pleasing, because what I really want to hear is all about the Mischianza. It must have been wonderful!"

The shop she spoke of was actually only a block from the hospital office, and Mary had visited often, so the proprietor recognized her when the two women entered. After greeting him, they took seats at a table next to the front window, where they could watch the traffic passing on the street.

Mary launched into a detailed description of the Mischianza, while her friend sat mesmerized.

After she had finished, Kathryn grinned and said, "You are so fortunate that Colonel Northcutt is taken by you. I know you *say* you are not interested in him, but you must admit there have been many benefits to his attentions."

"Yes, that is true. But I fear things are reaching the point where, at least in his mind, it is time to get more serious. I must figure a way to hold him at arm's length and make him understand I have no interest."

"Mary, there's nothing for it; you are making a spinster of yourself for no good reason." She raised an eyebrow. "And we both know why you are doing it."

Mary was silent, merely staring into the distance.

Kathryn, realizing Mary would say nothing further about the matter, asked, "So when do you actually think you'll rejoin the regiment for the march up to New York?"

Mary smiled. "I would like to be there today. However, there are two things holding me here instead of in the camp."

"Well, you said that you are supposed to get the hospital records ready for transport before you come back. But what is the other thing keeping you here?"

Mary looked around the shop, then leaned toward her friend to speak confidentially. "Now, I know you are aware of my friendship with Mrs. Loring."

"Of course."

"At the Mischianza ball last night, she told me she will be boarding ship in just a few days for the voyage to England. And she begged me to stay long enough to see her off. She has so few other friends, particularly now that

Howe is essentially out of power." Mary sighed. "Other women of society, who formerly professed friendship, have begun to shun her."

Kathryn frowned. "Yes, I can see how that would happen." She put her hand to her chin and thought a moment. "I wonder how she will be treated back in England. I'm not worried about *her*—she has made her own bed—but I understand there are two young children."

Mary said, "Yes, Betsy is worried about that. She plans to take a place in the country, away from London society until her husband joins her. That way there will be less likelihood that her reputation will be known and that the family will be treated with scorn."

Kathryn took a sip of her tea. "Well, I can't say that I agree with what she did, but I do hope the children can escape bad treatment." Then she changed the subject. "Well, things were busy this morning, what with the expedition marching out—right after dawn it was."

Mary was puzzled. "Expedition? What expedition?"

"Why, a column marching into New Jersey. She looked questioningly at Mary. "I would have thought you knew. The word is that Colonel Northcutt is behind it. I expected he would have told you since I have it from Sergeant Major Tim McGregor that the decision was made at the Mischianza last night."

Mary put her hand to her mouth. "So that's why the generals and Barrett and John Andre left the ball for a few minutes." She shook her head. "Northcutt didn't explain, and we danced when he returned. I never thought to ask him about the reason for their absence." She thought a moment. "So, since you know so much more about it, please tell me what is toward."

"On the orders of General Howe—probably his last—the light companies of the 42nd and the 71st marched out this morning. And Tim told me a troop of cavalry is going along."

"Why are they marching now—even though the army is soon going to leave for New York?"

"Mary, this is the part that concerns you. A detachment of Washington's Guides attacked and destroyed a band of loyalist partisans up in New Jersey near New York City itself."

Mary felt a tug at her heart. She blurted out "*The Guides*?"

"Yes, the Guides. And the mission of the expedition is to attempt to cut them off and destroy them before they can return to the rebel camp in Valley Forge."

Mary's hand went to her face. "I wonder if Wend is leading the detachment."

"Captain Markwood, who brought the order, told Colonel Stirling that they believe Wend was in command of the column. Tim said he heard Markwood laugh and say they expressly wanted to get Eckert, one way or the other. Apparently he was responsible for the destruction of Colonel Northcutt's regiment in Virginia and killed a personal friend of the colonel's. Markwood said that Northcutt will not rest until he has Eckert in his hands."

"My God!" Shock and fear registered on Mary's face.

"Oh, Mary, I'm so sorry to be the one to tell you. I thought you were already aware of what was happening."

Mary gritted her teeth. "And I spent the night dancing with Barrett Northcutt, who may be responsible for Wend's death. How shall I ever live with myself?"

Kathryn reached out and put her hand on Mary's. "Mary, do not despair. For God's sake, remember they are going up against *Wend Eckert*. You have known him for nearly twenty years, since you were a little girl, and you know he has no equal in wiliness or the use of weapons." She paused, then said, "And he is a hard man to kill. Think on all the dangers he survived on the march with Bouquet and then at Bushy Run. You must have faith that he will elude them."

"I have faith in him, but it won't keep me from living in fear until I know he is safe."

Kathryn took a deep breath. "There is one more thing you should know."

"I have heard too much already. What more can you say to increase my anxiety?"

"It is this: the commander of our column is Major McDonald."

Mary gasped. "Charles?"

"Indeed."

"Oh, dear God. The very man who recruited my father into the army and whose life Wend saved at Bushy Run, so many years ago. Why—of all officers—should it fall to him to try kill the man to whom he owes his life?"

"Colonel Stirling offered to appoint another officer to take the command, but McDonald said he it was his turn to have the duty and that he was honor bound to carry it out whatever assignment was made."

The two friends sat in silence for a long time, Mary staring down at her now-cold tea, Kathryn staring at Mary. Then Mary wiped a tear from her cheek, looked up, and said simply, "It is all in God's hands now. And I shall pray to Him that He saves the one man I have ever loved, even if the hand of fate will never allow me to again hold him in my arms."

Late in the afternoon of the day after the partisan skirmish, Edward Childers checked the progress of Schreiber's squad who were sitting in a group making up replacement cartridges for the ones expended. Then he walked over to the front of the Wallen house where the wounded were being treated. Nell Porter was working with the local doctor, Kirby, as he looked to the men's injuries. She had a weary look on her face, but to Childers's eyes it did little to detract from her beauty.

She looked up as he approached, mustered a broad smile, and said, "What brings you here, Edward?"

"I just wanted to see how you were doing. And how Hoffman is faring." Hoffman was the single man of the Guides who had been seriously wounded in the skirmish. One of the partisans had slashed him across his chest with a long-bladed knife. Hoffman had initially paid little attention to the wound, but in the aftermath had found that it continued to ooze blood, so he had come to the hospital. Kirby had looked it over, taken some stitches, and kept the young private under his care to keep the wound clean and prevent mortification.

"Well, he's on the mend. It's good we're spending an extra day here at the farm. He should be able to ride when we leave."

Just then, Kirby called out, "Nell, we need some water. Could you fetch some?"

"Certainly, Doctor." She looked over at Edward. "How about helping me. There's four buckets, and if you carry two, I'll only have to make one trip."

Childers grinned. "Of course." He picked up two buckets. "Let's go to the well."

"No, we're going down to the creek. The water's clean, and it's easier to dip the buckets than to hoist it up from the well." She turned and headed for the stream, buckets in hand, with Childers following.

They walked through a small grove of trees, then Nell pointed to a spot where there was a gap in the underbrush that lined the creek bank. They passed through, and Childers found that it opened to a low spot where it was easy to dip the buckets into the water.

Nell put her buckets down. She smiled at Edward. "Will you fill all four? I want to just stand and rest. I've been bending and kneeling over the wounded men all day, and I need to ease my back."

"Of course!" He went to one knee and began dipping the buckets in the stream and shortly had them filled. Then he rose and turned around to find Nell standing close in front of him, a mischievous expression on her face and a gleam in her eye. She was tall for a girl, and her head was almost level with his. Their eyes met, and suddenly Nell reached up and enveloped him in her arms.

"Edward, you do want to kiss me, don't you?"

He took a deep breath, astonished at her forwardness. "God knows! Ever since the Queen Bess."

Without saying anything else, she kissed him, not a quick peck on the cheek, but with her lips pressed hard on his, and at the same time she pulled him close so that her body was tightly against him. He could feel her breasts on his chest, and the thrill of arousal coursed through him. He put his arms around her shoulders, and they stood that way, locked in embrace for a long time.

Then Nell pulled back a bit, but with her face still close to his and said, "I've wanted to do that ever since I looked down from the loft at the inn and saw you standing there beside Major Eckert. You looked so handsome and so gallant in your uniform." She grinned broadly. "Do you think I'm forward for ambushing you in this way?"

"I'll admit, I wasn't expecting it. But I welcome it."

"Tavern girls aren't afraid to move fast." She laughed. "I'll bet your southern women of the gentry, with their silken gowns, parasols, and milk white complexions don't behave like that."

Childers smiled, sighed deeply, and responded, "Regrettably, no." He looked at her for a long moment. "I admit I've never met a girl like you or had a kiss like that."

She kissed him again, this time more quickly, then pulled away and picked up two of the buckets. "We'd better get back, or Doctor Kirby will figure out what has been going on."

Edward said quickly, "Wait!"

She stopped and turned her head. "Yes?"

"We can't just leave it at that. Unless you just meant to tease me."

"I have no intention of leaving it at that. We're going to be here tonight and tomorrow night. There will be a chance to be together for longer than just a stolen kiss." She glanced at him with a provocative look, then turned and briskly walked off toward the Wallen house.

An excited and still-aroused Childers followed behind.

Barrett Northcutt sat before the hearth, staring into the flickering flames. He was in the common room of a small, rustic inn twenty-five miles north of Philadelphia. Outside, the evening dusk was rapidly turning into night. He had a cup of whiskey in his right hand and held his left hand to his forehead. A look of distress dominated his face.

Markwood, who had been outside with the escorting squad of dragoons that were making camp in the pasture at the rear of the inn, entered the room and joined the colonel in front of the fire and asked, "How are you feeling, sir?"

Barrett groaned and said, "Words are inadequate to describe it, Markwood."

"Well, sir, by my reckoning, after escorting Miss Fraser home, you could not have arrived at your quarters before 5 a.m. And we rode out just before the noon hour. Considering the time for preparations, you couldn't have had more than four hours' sleep."

Barrett took a pull on his rum. "Less than that. And I must admit that my head is still feeling the effect of the libation that flowed so freely at the banquet and ball."

"Well, sir, I will handle the details of taking care of the men and horses of our detachment. Why don't you retire now and make the most of the night."

Northcutt held up the cup and responded, "Yes, do that. Make sure the horses are well fed—we used them hard today. Let me finish this, and I'll be up to my room."

Markwood went to the counter and got some rum for himself and was just walking back to the table, drink in hand, when the common room's entrance door swung open to reveal a man who stood, hand on the door-knob, scanning the room. He wore a heavy overcoat against the night chill and a wide-brimmed hat pulled down nearly to his eyes. His visage was dark complexioned and tanned by frequent exposure to the sun. His face wore what looked like a two-day beard.

Then the stranger's eyes settled on Northcutt, and a tight smile showed on his lips. The man walked toward the colonel's table, meanwhile motioning toward the counter, and called out, "Barkeep, rum if you can, whiskey if that is all you have!"

On hearing the words, Northcutt's head snapped around to look at the stranger, and recognition spread across his face. He half rose from his chair. "By God, Harkness! The very man I most want to see!"

The man pulled off his greatcoat and took off the hat to reveal he was dressed in a well-tailored suit of clothes. His hair was dark, nearly black.

Markwood sat down at the table and said, "Harkness, how the hell did you find us? And what made you believe we would be traveling northward?"

"Two reasons. One, I was certain the news of the destruction of Tigh's partisans would elicit a response from Howe or Clinton, whichever one may now be in command."

Markwood said, "Howe, but Clinton takes over in two days."

"Regardless, I seem to have been right about the response. At least it got you on the road."

Northcutt, who was suddenly feeling much better, responded, "And a good piece of initiative that was. We rode, in fact, with the object of finding *you*." A puzzled look crossed his face. "How the devil did you manage to find *us*?"

"I thought this was the most likely road for you to use, and I started southward. When I got to the locale where you might have reached after getting my message, I started checking taverns and inns along the way. I suspected I'd found you when I saw that detail of dragoons outside."

Markwood asked, "But why did you feel it so urgent to find us? We would have been at your place in a day."

"Well, I have some most urgent and very beguiling word for you: new information of what Eckert and his party have been about."

Barrett, who had been slouching in his seat, straightened up and leaned forward. "Well, don't keep it a secret. Tell us what you know."

"The day after Eckert's troop arrived at Wallen Farm, and before the ambush of Tigh, he led a squad of dragoons on a fast ride up to Elizabeth Town."

"Why, that's right across the harbor from New York!"

"Yes, and they brazenly rode into town and went straight to an inn called the Good Queen Bess." Harkness looked in turn at each of the officers. "And then they took temporary possession of the inn and removed one of the borders, a young man, which person they took with them back to their camp."

Northcutt and Markwood shot quick looks at each other. Markwood's face lit up. "Colonel, you don't suppose that was Eckert's primary objective?"

"You are damned right that was their objective!" He slammed his cup down on the table. "It all fits together: a small detachment, all mounted, capable of moving fast. Washington sent them specifically to get that man!"

Markwood nodded. "And the skirmish with Captain Tigh was mere happenstance. Tigh just happened to be raiding in the vicinity and attacked the plantation where Eckert was encamped. He had no choice but to fight."

Harkness interjected, "Tigh's band attacked Wallen Farm the very night of the day Eckert snatched the man from the Queen Bess. They had been raiding other plantations in the area."

Barrett smiled. "Indeed, and if Tigh had not attempted to raid that farm, I vouch that Eckert, his Guides, and that man they took would have been on their way back to Valley Forge the next morning. The question is: What makes him so important that Washington sent a troop of his own Guides to take him into custody and then carry him off to Valley Forge?"

Markwood said, "Perhaps the son of an important man?" He shrugged. "We'll never guess it on our own. But it is *damned* important that we find out the man's identity and why Washington sought him.

"One other piece of information," said Harkness. "While at the inn, he sold off some of his clothing. It included the uniform of a Continental Army artillery officer. A captain."

"Yes, another important clue. But why on earth would a junior officer merit such attention?" queried Markwood. He paused and looked at Harkness. "Prithee, what is the name of the man they took out of the inn?"

"He never gave it to the innkeeper. But after he left, one of the serving maids was cleaning out his room and found a letter. It was addressed to one John Henry." He shrugged. "A common enough name."

Northcutt stared at the hearth for a long moment. "Henry? John Henry?"

Harkness nodded. "Indeed, Barrett."

Northcutt put his hand to his chin, frozen in deep thought. The other two men sat silent, watching Northcutt. Then suddenly the colonel straightened up in his chair and slammed his hand down on the table. "I've got it! Patrick Henry has a son named John! I saw the lad years ago in Williamsburg. I'll wager that's our man!"

Markwood exclaimed, "My God, the son of Virginia's governor. 'Liberty or Death' Henry himself! Of course Washington would want to get the lad to safety." A puzzled look came over his face. "But what was he doing in such a dangerous place, alone so close to New York?"

Barrett thought a moment then responded, "There is only one way we will find out: we must cut off and capture Eckert's column and take Henry into custody."

Markwood asked Harkness, "Do you know where Eckert's troop is now? Are they on the way back to the rebel encampment?"

"I know *exactly* where he is." Harkness stopped and then corrected himself, "Well, I know where he *was* when I left late this morning. He was still at Wallen Farm. He and his troops are taking care of the wounded and getting the dead buried."

Northcutt grinned broadly. "By God! That's a stroke of luck. That gives us time to get our troops in position to surround and capture him as he rides back to Valley Forge."

Now it was Harkness's turn to grin. "I thought that would be your objective." He reached into his pocket and pulled out a folded piece of parchment. "I brought a map of lower Jersey along, so we might plan for an entrapment." He unfolded the map and laid it out on the table.

Markwood got up and brought more candles from other tables to better illuminate the paper.

"This is pretty crude; I drew it myself. But it shows us what we need to make plans. Harkness put his finger down on the map. "This is Wallen Farm. I believe Eckert is still camped there." Then he traced his finger along a thin line. "This is the road he'll take southward."

Northcutt asked, "Is there not some other way he might go?"

"Not unless he wants to ride far out of his way. And remember, he has been away from the rebel army's quarters for several days. He assuredly is running low on provisions." The leader of spies held up his finger. "And there is another factor: Eckert has a wagon along, and this road is the only good one for wheeled traffic that goes in the right direction."

Northcutt nodded agreement. "You're right. He'll likely take the most direct route."

Harkness looked at the colonel. "Now, I've been thinking about all this as I rode. But I have a question. What force do you have afield? And where are they now?"

Markwood said, "We have sortied a troop of dragoons and two companies of light foot. They are on the road, encamped about five miles behind us. We passed them a couple of hours before we got here."

"Excellent! That force is most certainly adequate to the task, and if they march quickly in the morning, can be where they need to be for what I have thought out." Harkness moved his hand along the map. "And this is the place I propose to entrap him. Notice the natural barrier."

Markwood smiled. "Indeed! That will serve well."

"Now, I suggest that you position a blocking force at that point and have the remainder of the troops come up behind the Guides. The enemy will be surrounded and outnumbered five to one. I think Eckert will soon realize he has no choice but to surrender. I believe the job can all be executed with little or no bloodshed."

Northcutt studied the map and then looked up at Harkness. "Sir, you are not only a good spy; you are a tactician, as if you had been a soldier."

"I marched with Major Rogers in the French war."

Barrett smiled. "That explains it. And like him, you have stayed loyal to your king."

"I would have made no other choice."

Northcutt looked over at Markwood. "I say the dragoons will form the blocking force. If they leave their camp at dawn, they will have an easy ride to be in position. And then Major McDonald's Highlanders can march up to a spot where they can hide and lie in wait until Eckert passes them, and then come up on his rear at the appropriate time." He looked up from the map. "The distances, the time available—it all fits."

Markwood pulled out a notebook and tore out a page. "I'll get an order describing all this to McDonald and have it carried back to him posthaste by one of our dragoons."

Barrett nodded. "And tell him we'll join Hargate's troop of the Queen's Rangers as they pass here in the morning and will stay with them for the action."

Harkness stood up and reached for his greatcoat and hat.

Startled, Northcutt queried, "Will you not be staying the night after your hard ride of the day?"

"No, my dear Colonel. I'm going back to keep in touch with my watchers. I'll be sending the most recent information on Eckert's movements to you by courier as you ride."

Northcutt shook hands with the spy. "You have my admiration, sir. With good men like you, we cannot fail."

After Harkness had departed, Northcutt had another drink as Markwood wrote out the dispatch to McDonald. Then he carefully read it, to make sure it would be clear to the major.

When he had finished, Markwood asked, "All as you would desire, sir?"

"It is perfect, Markwood." He took a sip of the libation. "And my dear fellow, it seals the fate of Eckert. I have waited for this for nearly three years. Twice before I thought we had put finish to him, but this time we cannot fail. I say within forty-eight hours he will be in our hands or be in hell." A broad grin came over Barrett's face. "An outcome which will provide the greatest satisfaction to me."

The captain's face wrinkled up into a smile that matched Northcutt's. "I think it will do more than that, sir. If we prevail, we will deliver John Henry to our new general, and he will be in debt to you for a significant success at the very beginning of his command."

Northcutt put his hand to his chin and pondered the thought. "Indeed he will, Markwood. And it will give me an advantage in his esteem over that damned popinjay Andre—something I would relish nearly as much as the end of Wend Eckert."

"Major, we're ready to ride. Everyone is saddled, the wagon is loaded, fires are out, and we've cleaned up our camp."

Morning dusk was spreading over Wallen Farm, and Wend could see a glow on the eastern horizon that portended imminent sunrise. The smoke from the doused fires was wafting over the yard and tickling Wend's nose.

"Thank you, Mr. Childers. Go ahead and mount the detachment and lead out down the drive. I'll catch up with you after I talk to Wallen."

The young officer nodded and went to where the men were standing to their horses. Billy Wood approached, leading Wend's horse and handed him the reins. He thanked Billy and led the animal toward the front porch where Joseph Wallen stood. Rachel was beside him wearing a long cape over her night clothes, pulled tight around her against the May morning chill. Also with them was the militia lieutenant, Richard Dowling.

Wend stood at the bottom of the steps, looking up at the three. He was about to speak when Rachel reached down and extended her hand, which he took in his own. "Major Eckert, I want to apologize for the harsh words I spoke to you the other night, before the partisans attacked. I see now you made the correct decision. Our family can never repay you for what you did. You saved our lives and our farm from those desperate men. I shall always believe it was a miracle that you were able to prevail. And because you did, the people around Spanktown will have less to fear in the future." She looked up at the departing column and continued, "We will always remember the days that the Guides were here."

Wend replied, "Well, fortune was on our side. But it is I who must thank the Wallens. Your husband and his men were valiant as part of the defense. And you, Mrs. Wallen, did so much to help care for the wounded." Then he motioned over to Dowling. "And we are all in debt to the men of the county militia, who arrived just in time to assist and stood in line with the Guides."

Dowling acknowledged the compliment with a nod of his head, then said, "We'll be taking the prisoners up to Spanktown today. The major of our militia battalion is putting together an escort to take them to a camp in the northern part of Jersey."

Wend looked around. "I guess things are pretty well wrapped up here. I was glad to hear that Reverend Banbury had found a place to bury the dead partisans. It seems fitting that they will rest in a back field of the Graham farm, after they did so much damage there."

Joseph said, "Fitting indeed. And Banbury has vowed it will be an unmarked mass grave." Then he pointed toward the drive. "Let me walk with you before you mount. I have something to speak to you about."

Wend nodded, then touched his hat to Rachel and turned to lead his horse back toward the drive.

Rachel called out, "Godspeed, Wend Eckert!"

Wallen came down the steps and walked beside Wend. When they were twenty or so feet from the porch, he said in a low tone, "I wanted to warn you about Reverend Banbury." He paused a moment to gather his thoughts. "His anger has not cooled. He is determined to report you to Congress for not marching to save the Grahams. He will demand that you be cashiered. You must be prepared to defend yourself."

Wend thought a moment. Then speaking with more confidence than he felt, he replied, "Thank you for confiding that to me, Joseph. But I go with a clear conscience. If some report does make it to Washington, I believe I can justify my actions to his satisfaction. And if for some reason I am relieved of my duties, I shall most *happily* ride home to my good wife and children and resume my firelock trade. With either outcome I shall be quite happy. In any case, my biggest worry at the present is getting my men back to Valley Forge safely, and I will not let anything distract me from that."

Wallen extended his hand, and Wend shook it, then swung up into the saddle. He touched his spurs to the horse and was off down the drive at the gallop.

—ᵚ—

After leaving Wallen Farm, Wend had led the column at a steady pace that ate up the miles while preserving the horses' strength. He had ordered the men to dismount and lead their mounts frequently and allowed time out for coffee when the sun was at its zenith. But he had kept them at it well past the normal time to stop and make camp. Now he looked at the sky and the growing dusk as night approached. He turned in his saddle and called out, "Sergeant Quinn to the fore!"

The dragoon sergeant rode up from where the dragoons were riding just behind the wagon. He pulled up beside Wend and said, "I damn well hope you are calling me to say it's time to bivouac for the night. We need food and sleep, and supper's goin' to be very late if we don't stop soon."

"Sergeant, you are a master of the obvious. But I would suggest this is not the first time you've missed your regular mealtime." Wend waved at the road ahead. "By my estimate, we should be within a mile of the Millstone River. I intend to camp beside it for the night, where we will have good water for the horses and for cooking, and we'll ford it in the morning." He pointed ahead. "There's some smoke rising ahead, just visible in the evening light. I suspect it means there's a party of travelers already at the river." He looked over at Quinn. "Ride ahead and scout things out and locate the most advantageous campsite. We'll be up with you in a few minutes."

"Aye, Major!" The sergeant spurred his horse forward and momentarily disappeared over a small rise.

Wend signaled for the column to increase the pace as they headed for the river. They had gone another half mile and were just topping a rise, with the river visible in the distance, when Quinn came into sight around a curve in the road, his horse galloping as if chased by demons. Wend held up his hand to stop the column.

Momentarily Quinn arrived and pulled up his horse. "Major, there's dragoons at the ford! Camped out and waiting for us! Looks like Queen's American Rangers!"

Shocked, Wend asked, "How many?"

"At least a full troop. From the glimpse I got, they outnumber us!"

"Damn! Damn!"

"But that ain't the worst of it! They spotted me! There was pickets hiding in the woods on either side of the road! I pulled up to look at their camp, and they came out of the woods on foot, two of them, trying to grab the bridle of my horse. I beat them off with my saber and was able to gallop off." He looked back toward the river. "But it's sure they know we're here!"

Childers had ridden up from the rear of the column. "What are we going to do Major Eckert? They may be saddling up to come after us."

Wend thought hard. "Probably, but it will take them a few minutes." He looked at Quinn and Childers. "Our best move is to turn around. I saw a wagon track headed north a couple of miles back. Maybe we can take that and make our way around them and find another ford."

Quinn scowled. "I say we form into a column of threes and put flankers on either side of the wagon. Then we charge! Charge *immediately* and push through them before they realize what's toward, and then ford the river. That's our best choice!"

"We've only got ten dragoons trained to fight from horseback, Quinn. There's probably thirty or forty dragoons in that troop."

Quinn turned in his saddle and pointed toward the river. "But the bastards won't be expecting it, Eckert. They'll think we're retreating, like you want to do. We'll take them by surprise and push through them to the river. And in that situation, I'll put my ten dragoons up against thirty of the Queen's Rangers any day of the week!"

Wend was about to respond when he heard Billy Wood's voice call from the wagon, "Major, there's a rider coming in from behind us. Riding like the devil is after him!"

All eyes turned to look at the stranger. Wend saw that Billy had been right: the rider's horse was at full gallop, a plume of dust trailing behind. Then he looked at the man himself, and realized there was something familiar about him. In a few seconds he had it—it was Crowder! Crowder the spymaster!

In a few seconds the spy reached the detachment and pulled up, horse and rider breathless.

Puzzled, Wend asked, "Mr. Crowder, what are you doing here?"

"Heard that Miss Porter was traveling with you. I came to take her back to her home, now that she's fulfilled her mission." He looked back, then at Wend. "But now there's danger at hand! Major Eckert, you better get across the Millstone posthaste! There are Highlanders coming up behind you! Lots of them!"

Wend sat frozen. "Highlanders? Behind us on the road? Where did they come from?"

Crowder replied, "It appears they were hiding in a grove of trees well off the road. They emerged just after I passed them! Called for me to halt in the king's name, but I ignored them and was out of musket range before they could react."

Wend turned to Quinn. "Sergeant, get back there and take a look. *Fast.* Tell me how many they are and how rapidly they are coming."

Quinn didn't reply, merely spurring his horse to the gallop back up the road.

Crowder repeated, "Sir, you *are* mounted. You must push forward and get across the river, and march hard to escape the soldiers! Or at least you can stand them off from the other bank of the stream."

"No, Mr. Crowder, I can't do that."

"You can't? For God's sake, why? I don't understand."

"I can't do that because there is a troop of the Queen's Rangers blocking the way. I'd have to fight my way through, and they outnumber us."

A look of dismay came over Crowder. "Why, it must be a trap! Somebody planned this!"

"You are damned right somebody planned this. They were lying in wait for us. I have feared something like this since we got Mr. Henry out of Elizabeth Town, and now it has happened."

Childers was staring at him, and Eckert saw the touch of fear in his eyes. "Major, what are your orders?"

Wend forced himself to think. Looking around, he saw that the road crested at another small ridge just a couple of hundred yards ahead of them. He thought, *The wagon track probably descends from that rise to the river.* He shouted, "Everything forward! Forward to the top of that rise!." He called to Edward, "Mr. Childers, get the troop up there and have them dismount and take defensive positions around the wagon! Make a perimeter large enough to cover all the horses and the wagon! Do it now!"

As the column rushed up the hill, Wend sat his horse, watching for Quinn's return. He didn't have long to wait. The sergeant soon came into sight, his horse flying over the ground. He pulled up directly in front of Wend.

"Crowder is right! There's at least a hundred Highlanders coming fast. I make it light Bobs, at least two companies. One company is wearing the colors of the Black Watch." He swept his arm around to take in both sides of the road. "They're coming in open skirmish order, formed in a wide front. They are fixin' to cover our rear and flanks!"

Wend swore in frustration and said, "And the dragoons of the Queen's

Rangers will cover our front. It's a perfect encirclement." He motioned back to the ridge. "We're taking defensive positions up there. Go check to make sure the men are in the best positions."

"Best positions? Hell, there be none. We ain't got a chance."

"Just do it sergeant. Now!"

Wend sat on the slope, watching the road. Darkness was rapidly closing in, but in the last light he saw what he was looking for: the approaching enemy. First a small advance guard came into sight, cautiously scouting the road and the bush. In the failing light, they were shadowy figures. Then the main skirmish line appeared, a few moving on the road, and others slipping through the trees that bounded both sides of the track. Quinn had been right: they were in a wide front, ready to envelop the Guides detachment when they encountered it. Behind the line rode an officer, a tall sergeant, and a piper walking beside him. Behind the officer was a reserve force, which Wend estimated to be a half company. Wend sighed. There would be no chance of his detachment evading the Highlanders.

Wend felt rising desperation. They were wedged between dragoons at the river and light foot coming up from behind. Soon the trap would be closed. He desperately searched his mind for a way out of the cordon closing on his detachment but found none. Realization flowed over him that he and his men were doomed to capture or death, and his mission to keep John Henry out of British hands had ended in failure.

Eckert sat there in desolation, watching the approach of the foot soldiers. Then suddenly, out of nowhere, an idea sprang into his mind. It would be a desperate measure indeed, disastrous to him and his men, but he realized it was the only way that offered a way to fulfill his orders from Washington. And it must be done immediately if there was to be any chance of success. With a heavy heart, he turned his horse and raced for the crest to join his men.

—m—

Northcutt relaxed in his camp chair, warming himself before a fire close by the banks of the Millstone River. Darkness was rapidly gathering, and he was quite comfortable with a cup of rum in his left hand and a freshly lit cigar of Virginia tobacco in his right. Markwood sat on the ground on the opposite side of the fire, his face lit by the flickering light of the flames. Nearby were the fires of Hargate's troop of the Queen's Rangers, most of whom were finishing up the evening meal.

The captain said, "As late as it is, I guess Eckert's troop is not coming today. Maybe we'll see them sometime tomorrow."

Barrett didn't immediately answer. Instead he took a pull on the cigar and savored the smoke, then exhaled. Then he responded, "Indeed. It appears that he has lingered longer than we expected at that farm near Spanktown. Perhaps he has some wounded who must recover enough to travel. That would not be unexpected from a stiff fight."

As he was speaking, Captain Joshua Hargate joined them after checking the camp guards and the horse picket line. "Well, Colonel, we're set for the night. I've got a pair of men standing picket in the bush beside the road, about a quarter mile to the northeast. They'll give us good warning if the Guides approach." He waved back up the road. "And that courier I sent to McDonald has returned. He says the light foot are encamped out of sight of the road about a mile away. The major says he won't allow any fires until later tonight just in case the enemy comes along in the next hour or so."

Northcutt nodded to Hargate. "Yes, George and I were just discussing that. Odds are that Eckert won't be here tonight, but I'm glad McDonald is taking the precaution."

Hargate smiled. "Well, whenever he comes, we'll be ready and crush him between us like closing a vice." He paused, then started to speak, "I look forward..." Then he suddenly stopped speaking and stiffened, looking across the river.

Markwood asked, "What is it, Joshua? You look like you see something."

Hargate relaxed. "No, I *thought* I saw something moving for just an instant on the far bank, but now all is quiet. Must have been a trick of the eye in this darkness."

Just then a voice called out from the road. "Captain! Captain Hargate!" Two men—a sergeant and a trooper came running toward them. In a moment they had arrived, and Northcutt could see that the trooper was out of breath, as if he had been running.

The sergeant said, "Captain, Trooper Pullen just came in from the picket on the road. He and McClellan had a scuffle with a dragoon! A dragoon of the Guides."

Hargate demanded, "Are you sure he's from the Guides?"

Pullen responded, "Well, sir, he wore a gray coat and a black helmet, sir!"

Markwood said, "Sure enough, that would be the Guides. That's what the troop from South Carolina wears."

Northcutt said, "Tell us what happened."

Still trying to get his breadth, Pullen gasped out, "Well, this dragoon was scouting, that's for sure. We let him get right beside us, then we jumped him, tryin' to get him off his horse. But he pulled his saber and laid about with it." He shrugged. "He smacked McClellan in the head and knocked him to the ground. Then he whipped his horse around, and I couldn't hold on. He rode off at the gallop back up the wagon track."

"Damn," said Hargate, "Eckert knows we're here."

Northcutt shrugged and smiled. "It doesn't matter, Captain. We've undoubtedly got Eckert between us and McDonald's light foot. Now all we have to do is close the trap."

Markwood nodded. "Yes, McDonald should be coming up behind the Guides now. We just need to take proper position to block them, and Eckert will have little choice but to surrender."

Northcutt left his chair and tossed away the cigar. "Joshua, let me talk to the men."

Hargate called for the troopers to assemble.

Northcutt strode over to stand before the gathered dragoons. "Men, hear me! You are all Virginians! You fought with me for Lord Dunmore. Remember this: in June of 1776, over a hundred of your compatriots in the King's Loyal Virginia Legion were killed or captured on the beach near Mobjack Bay. You escaped their fate only because you were not part of the detachment that went on that raid. Our friends were killed by a company led by Major Wend Eckert! And Eckert personally and intentionally shot Major Welford, who was leading the regiment at the time. It was a dishonorable execution, not war." Northcutt pointed up the road. "Now Eckert and his men are approaching us. And this time, it is we who have set a trap for them. Tonight we have the chance to obtain vengeance for what happened at Mobjack Bay! Have that in mind when you have the enemy in your sights and remember those who died on that black day two years ago!" He looked over at Hargate. "Now let us prepare!"

Hargate shouted, "Sergeant, get all the fires out! And have the men take the positions we picked out earlier."

The sergeant said, "Aye, sir." Then he shouted to the troop at large. "Carbines! Pistols! Take your place for dismounted action!" He pointed to a corporal. "Harley, take your squad and move up the road as skirmishers! If the enemy approaches, give them a shot and then fall back slowly to join the troop, keeping them in sight as you retreat! If they stop and take defensive positions, inform me so that we may prepare to attack!"

Immediately the men sprang up, kicking out the fires, and grabbing their firelocks, and they headed for the bushes surrounding the ford.

Northcutt walked over to his chair and reached down beside it where his horse pistols were in their holsters. He pulled out the pistols and stuffed them in his belt. Then he turned to Markwood, a broad grin on his face. "George, the moment I have been anticipating has finally arrived. In a short time, I will have Eckert exactly where I want him."

Markwood, who had also picked up his pistols, responded, "And a feather in your cap it will be indeed. You'll be known as the man who captured Eckert of the Guides."

Chapter Seven
Duel at the Ford

Wend arrived at the crest of the ridge and saw that the men had taken positions in a rough circle around the wagon and horses. A few were prone on the road, aiming their firelocks in the direction of the enemy. Others were on their knees in the bush on either side of the road, weapons at the ready. Wend glanced toward the river and could make out in the gloom a squad of loyalist dragoons advancing on foot along the road toward their position. He must act fast to put his plan into action, before the enemy fully encircled them.

He dismounted near the wagon and looked around for Crowder. He waved for the spymaster to join him, and they quickly walked to a spot behind the wagon where they could speak confidentially. Whispering, Wend said, "Crowder, I'm trying to think of a way to get Henry and a few other people out of here. By that I mean Nell, Melinda, you, and a couple of others. I believe escape of a small party may be possible by sneaking through the woods. Do you have any familiarity with the local terrain?"

"Indeed, I've spent some time in this area. I recall paths through the woods along the river, going northward toward a ford which gets you across the stream to a tiny village on the western side. It goes by the name of 'Rocky

Hill.'" He smiled. "But it will have to be done on foot. The locals call the entire area 'The Devil's Featherbed' because of all the rocks and boulders that spot the ground and make travel difficult." He raised a finger. "Near the village there's the large estate of a man named Berrien, who is actually an officer in the Continentals. Rockingham, it's called. If we could get there, I'm confident the Berrien family would provide succor and hide a party if the British began a search."

"That's what I wanted to hear." Wend motioned for Crowder to follow him around to the other side of the wagon. Meli, Nell, and John Henry were standing there. He gathered them together and said, "We're getting you out of this trap. He put his hand on Crowder's shoulder and explained, "He will guide you through the woods to a safe refuge." He waved to Meli. "Get a bit of provisions out of the wagon, just enough you can carry on your persons. And be quick about it." Then he called for Billy and Childers to join them.

The two men came from their positions, weapons in hand. He quickly explained the plan to them and told Billy to help his wife get supplies and bags to carry them. He finished by saying, "The rest of us will resist the British as a diversion to enable you to escape."

For his part, Childers stiffened, a look of defiance on his face. "Sir, I protest. I *will* not go. If the Guides are staying to fight, I must remain and do my duty. No one is going to accuse a Childers of seeking safety while my comrades are in danger. I will not be branded a coward!"

"I admire your *gallantry*, Edward," Wend responded, "but not your *thinking*. Now listen carefully: There has to be an officer with the party. I'm giving you the responsibility to get these people, and particularly Henry, safely through to Valley Forge. That is our mission, and it is to you to make sure it is finished. Second, I need someone of rank to report to Washington and tell him the story of our expedition." Wend waved his hand, taking in all the man at their defense positions. "Over the last few days, these men accomplished a remarkable service for our cause, and I want you to make sure that Washington understands what they did." He gave Childers a brotherly smack on the shoulder. "Now get these people together and get on your way. Crowder will guide you through the bush to a refuge, and then you must get the party onward to army headquarters."

Quinn, who had been both listening and also observing the movements of the dragoons coming from the river, called out, "If they're leaving, they must go now! The dragoons are coming up the slope in dismounted skirmish order! And they and the Highlanders will soon be in the woods on our flanks. Anybody getting out has got to go this minute!"

Wend looked down toward the river. At that moment, the moon came out from behind the clouds, and he could see that Quinn was right. Then he turned and looked in the other direction and saw that the Highlanders were also closing in.

Meli was still up in the wagon, throwing bags of food down to the ground. Wend said, "Meli, that's it! Jump down, the party must leave instantly."

Meli didn't answer. Instead, she froze where she was. Then she stood up straight in the wagon, hesitated a moment, then stepped to the front and braced herself by putting her hands on the back of the seat. Her body stiffened, and she cocked her head.

Billy called up to his wife, "Meli, what are you doin'? Come on down, like the major said!"

Mel waved her hand to quiet him. "Hush your mouth, Billy. Everyone be silent!" Then she put her hands up to her ears for a moment. "Listen! Listen! I knew I heard it!" She pointed toward the ford. "Someone is sounding a hunting horn! From down 'cross the river!"

Every man and women froze, straining their ears.

Then Wend heard it and his heart skipped a beat. In the distance, a horn was playing the chase call!

Suddenly Trumpeter Bloom was beside him, tugging on his sleeve. "Sir, sir! That's Hildreth blowing the horn. Hildreth! I'd know his tonging of the chase call anywhere! He plays it just a little different from anyone else!"

Hildreth was the trumpeter for Bradley's troop of Marylanders!

Wend jumped up into the wagon bed to get a better view and moved beside Meli. She pointed down to the river, plainly visible from the height of the wagon.

"Look at that, Major! Ain't that the most loveliest sight you ever did see?" Then she added, "And I declare, the sweetest music I ever heard!"

Then, with the bright light of the moon illuminating the river and the adjacent land, Wend saw it: the Guides Cavalry, both troops at the charge, sabers held high, horses splashing through the river while Hildreth constantly blew the horn. Then he heard shots ringing out from the near shore: the Queen's Rangers firing at the oncoming dragoons. He saw one man fall from his horse. But the shots were two few and too late to stop the onrushing horsemen. Momentarily they came up onto the near riverbank and laid into the enemy troops.

Quinn called out, "Major, the Rangers' skirmishers are pulling back! They're running to join the fight down by the river!"

Wend called back, "Quinn, you bastard, you are about to get your wish! We're going to charge for the river and join with our cavalry!" Every face of the Guides turned toward him, looking for orders. "Now listen, all of you! Everything has reversed! We were caught in a trap between the Queen's Rangers and the Highlanders. Now the Rangers are caught between us and our cavalry! We're going to charge into the enemy and then cross the river! Quinn, form your men in column of threes." He called to Schreiber, "Form your squad behind the wagon. Billy, get the women into the wagon. Henry, ride right behind the wagon. Mr. Childers, bring up the rear! Now everyone mount!"

Wend jumped down from the wagon and swung up into his horse. He called to Crowder, "Stay beside Henry if you can!"

Wend looked around and saw that everyone was ready, the soldiers mounted and in formation. Billy was at the reins of the wagon team, the two women were crouching behind the seat. Wend rode over beside Childers and whispered, "You'll be in the rear. Watch Henry and make sure he gets across the river. If he falls off his horse, get him up behind yourself. Or drag him if you have to. If he's dead, bring the body. But alive or dead, get him across!" He paused and said, "Edward, *now* is the time for that gallantry you were so concerned about."

"I won't let you down, sir!"

Wend rode forward and took his place at the front of the formation, Bloom beside him. He looked over at the trumpeter, "Bloom, when we charge, keep blowing that horn so that our cavalry down there know who we are and that we are coming!"

"You got it, sir! And it will be a pleasure!"

Wend stood up in his stirrups, pulled his sword from its sheath, pointed it toward the river, and called out at the top of his voice, "Forward at the gallop! *Everything* forward!"

And with that, the detachment rushed down the hill toward the Millstone to the pounding of hooves, the noise of the rapidly spinning wagon wheels banging over the ruts of the road, and the brassy, blaring sound of Bloom's trumpet piercing the night.

Northcutt and Markwood stood checking the priming on their pistols, and Hargate had walked over to where the road opened into the wide, cleared space beside the river. His own pistols at the ready, he was staring into the darkness, waiting for his skirmishers to return and to discern the advance of the Guides detachment. The Ranger dragoons were covering in the bush bordering the open area, carbines in hand, ready to take the Guides under fire when they approached.

Then suddenly Northcutt was startled to hear the sound of a hunting horn, blowing the well-known foxhunting chase call. It took him a second to realize it was coming from behind them, from across the Millstone. He and Markwood spun about as one and stared across the river. At first, nothing could be seen. Then, to their horror, a large body of cavalry emerged from the woods on the far bank, coming down the road in a column of fours. Without hesitating, the horsemen entered the water and, sabers held high, began crossing the river.

Markwood shouted, "What the devil? Who in God's name is that?"

It was Hargate who provided the answer. "Damn!" he shouted. "It's Continental cavalry! Looks like a couple of troops!"

Barrett stood frozen, his mind refusing to function, unable to put into cohesive thought what his eyes were presenting. Finally he found words. He shouted to Markwood, "God in Heaven, it's a disaster!"

Hargate was screaming to his men. "Face about! Carbine and pistol fire at the head of that column! Fire as rapidly as you can!"

Immediately a ragged volley came from the surprised loyalist dragoons. Northcutt saw a rider crumple and fall into the water. Near the head of the column, a horse went down, the dragoon jumping off into the stream, but coming on by foot.

Now the head of the column was almost at the near riverbank.

Then suddenly came the sound of a second hunting horn, playing the same call as the rebel cavalry. It was emanating from the road behind them. Markwood looked up the hill and he could see a column of horsemen approaching at the gallop, sabers flashing in the moonlight. "It's Eckert and his troop! They're charging down the hill! We're being attacked from behind!"

Hargate screamed, "We can't stand before attacks from both sides!" He waved a pistol toward the tree line. "Retreat into the bush! Hide and fire. Every man for himself!" Then the captain turned and ran for the woods, and all his men disappeared after him.

Northcutt stood staring, mesmerized, at the approaching cavalry, unable to move. Suddenly he felt a tug on his arm. It was Markwood. "Sir, we must run! We must run for the woods! Come instantly!"

Finally Barrett found himself able to move. He turned and followed the captain into the forest.

—ѡ—

Wend Eckert would never remember the details of the charge down from the ridge crest. It was a blur of trees rushing past, the fearsome shouts of Quinn and his dragoons, the skirmishers from the Queen's Dragoons firing a few wild shots and then scattering before the galloping horses. One memory was, however, vivid. As he approached the open area near the ford, he saw the Guides cavalry, still mounted, pistols out, firing into the tree line. In the center of it all was Warren Bradley, the Maryland patrician, calmly sitting his tall hunter in the manner of a man born to the saddle, left hand with the reins, right holding a pistol at the ready as he observed the actions of his men.

Wend raised his hand and called out "Halt" to the detachment. Then he rode over to Bradley. The captain grinned and shouted above the noise of firing, "Fancy meeting you here, Eckert! We seem to meet in the most unlikely places." Then he pointed at the tree line with his pistol and said, "I'm about to order dismounted action so we can pursue and finish off this troop of Queen's Rangers!"

Wend held up his hand. "No, Bradley! There's no time for it!"

"What do you mean? We've got them just where we want them! Broken, some hiding, some running. We can decisively put them out of action!"

Wend repeated, "No! There's no time." He pointed back up the road to the ridgetop. "There's two companies of light foot—Highlanders—coming fast behind us! At least a hundred."

Bradley stared up the road, and as he was doing so, both he and Wend heard it: the wailing of a bagpipe through the noise of battle. He said loudly, "Damn!"

Wend ordered, "Get everyone back over the river! *Posthaste.* You lead them, and once there, set up a defense line on the bank. The British may try an assault! And Highlanders are the hardest hitting troops in the British Army!"

"Right, sir!"

Wend continued, "I'll remain here with a small rearguard until everyone is across, in case the Highlanders get here while we're crossing, or the Queen's Rangers rally after you leave."

"Got, it, Wend!" Bradley turned his horse and was about to shout out the orders.

Then Wend spied the line of picketed horses of the Queen's Rangers. He grabbed Bradley's arm. "Warren—their horses! There's at least forty of them! Order a detail to take them off the picket line and lead them across the river!"

Bradley's face lit up. "Damn right! We'll get them all!"

Wend called out to Schreiber. "Sergeant! Dismount your men! Prepare to act as skirmishers! We're going to cover the retreat across the river!"

Schreiber's answer was to order the dismount of his squad, with two of the men acting as horse holders. Wend pointed up the hill. "Sergeant, position your men so they are under cover but can fire up the road. When the light foot advance guard comes down the hill, we can amuse them for a few minutes."

"Aye, sir!"

Then Wend called out to Childers. "Edward! Get the wagon and Henry and Crowder across! Go now! I want them all out of danger!"

The lieutenant touched his hat, then spun his horse around and called out for Billy Wood to get moving. Wood slapped the reins, and the team, fearful and snorting at all the noise, surged ahead. Wend looked on as the wagon and the others descended into the river and started toward the far bank.

Wend turned his horse and watched the withdrawal. He saw Fairfield and his South Carolina troop forming to follow the wagon. Bradley had sent a squad of his Marylanders to get the Rangers' horses, while the rest of the troop continued covering them with fire into the woods. Wend noted that there were scattering shots coming from the tree line. Obviously some of the Rangers had taken cover and were rallying instead of running.

At that moment Schreiber called out, "Major! Skirmishers coming down the road! Highlanders, sir!"

"Give them a few shots! Let them know we're down here and ready to fight. Slow them down!"

Wend looked around. Bradley's men had the Ranger horses off the picket line and were heading toward the ford. He thought, *Just a few more minutes, and Schreiber's squad will be able to mount and retire.* He looked up the road and saw that the Highland skirmishers were pushing hard, moving along and through the woods on either side.

Wend glanced back at the river and saw that the Marylanders and the horse herd were all in the stream. *It was time to go.*

Then Wend heard a sharp snap as a ball whizzed past his head. He looked over at the tree line and saw enemy dragoons visible now in the bush. Clearly they were rallying.

"Schreiber! Cease firing! Mount and retreat across the river!"

"Aye, sir!" the sergeant shouted back, and called for his men to take to their horses.

The Highlanders were closing in now, boldly rushing down the road. Wend turned his horse and retreated a few yards back toward the riverbank, then turned again and pulled a pistol from its saddle holster. He squeezed off a shot in the direction of the advancing light infantry, hoping to give them a moment's pause while Schreiber's men were mounting. It seemed to work, for most of them dodged back into the bush.

Meanwhile the sergeant's men had mounted and were urging their horses for the river, passing Wend in a rush. He pulled his other pistol and stood his horse, looking to see if any dragoon or Highlander appeared. He waited just a few seconds, then pulled his mount around and headed for the river.

And at that instant the horse screamed in pain and reared on its hind legs, then collapsed to the ground. Wend was thrown off and lay stunned beside the animal as it continued to shriek in agony.

Wend lay there for a time, disoriented, barely conscious; it could only have been seconds. Then he heard a vaguely familiar voice calling from a distance, "Markwood, I got him! I've got Eckert! He's down beside the horse. Come help me!"

Wend shook off the fog in his head and looked toward the speaker. Then realization washed over him. *Northcutt!* It was Barrett Northcutt who was standing about ten yards away, a smoking pistol in his hand. As he watched, Northcutt put the pistol into his belt and took a step toward where Eckert lay.

Suddenly Wend realized that, miraculously, the pistol he had drawn before the horse went down was still in the tight grip of his hand. He got his finger on the trigger and quickly swung it toward his assailant. He was still dizzy, but aimed as best he could and pulled the trigger.

Wend couldn't see where the ball struck, but Northcutt gasped, put both hands over his right chest, turned around, staggered one step, and then went down. The officer who had been standing near him quickly went to his side.

Wend dropped the pistol and closed his eyes, the mist settling back into his brain. He thought, *They'll take me prisoner, but at least I got a ball into Northcutt.*

He lay there, unable to move. The world seemed to be spinning around him. Then he heard the sound of horse hooves approaching.

An Irish voice, coming from above him, said, "Now, my darling Major, are you going to lie there all night and let the British make a prize of you?"

Wend opened his eyes and looked up to see Shay O'beirne, seated on his tall mount, staring down at him.

The Irishman leaned down and extended his arm down toward Wend. "Now pick yourself up and take my hand, and don't be slow about it!"

From nearby, someone was firing pistols. And then Wend was shocked to hear the voice of Simon Donegal call out, "I've fired both pistols, and they'll be coming for us now. We need to get out of here!"

Wend, somehow, found the strength to get to his knees. O'beirne grabbed his arm and jerked him to his feet. Then he kicked his foot out of the stirrup and said, "Now be a fine lad, and put your foot in the stirrup! And swing up behind!"

With great effort, Wend climbed up behind the Irishman.

"Good lad! Now hold onto me!"

Wend put his arms around Shay, who immediately spurred his horse. The animal leaped forward and smashed his way through two Highlanders who had come out of the trees and been running toward them. In an instant they plunged down the riverbank and were pushing through the water of the Millstone. Several shots snapped past them as they went. Wend looked back and saw Donegal riding close behind. With him was Quinn and three other dragoons.

The crossing seemed to take an eternity, but Wend realized it could have only been a couple of minutes the way O'beirne and Donegal were pushing their horses. When they arrived at the far bank, the Irishman pulled up his mount, and Wend slid to the ground.

Wend looked up at O'beirne and said, "You have my gratitude. You saved me from capture or worse."

The lieutenant laughed. "Now what would the Guides be without Eckert? That aristocrat Bradley would be in charge, and sure enough that would be no fun."

"Speaking of fun," Wend responded, "What are you doing here with the cavalry? I seem to recall that you are the first lieutenant of the Frederick County Light Foot."

"Now my darling Major, I made a heartfelt appeal to our dear Captain Bradley, on the grounds that he could use every experienced rider and swordsman on this little trip, seeing you had reduced the ranks of his horseman by taking ten dragoons with you. And after a brief moment of thought, he decided it made sense."

Meanwhile Donegal had dismounted and had come up beside them. "How are you feeling, Wend? Are you wounded?"

"No, Simon, just shaken up by the fall. And my head is clearing up fast." He looked at the sergeant. "Which reminds me, How is it that you came along?"

"Von Steuben released me from drill service. His work is finished, and the army's getting ready to move. So I rounded up a horse and came along."

While they were talking, Warren Bradley and Geoffrey Fairfield had come up. Bradley said, "We've set up a defense line. I put Schreiber's squad in the center, Fairfield's troop on the left, and mine on the right. We've got about sixty men available."

Wend asked, "What about casualties?"

"We took some. Four dragoons missing. One went down in the river in the beginning, and the other three didn't make it back. A couple of men have minor wounds." He paused a second and then said, "And that young lady who was traveling with you, Miss Porter, was hit by a shot while the wagon was crossing the river."

Wend felt a knot in his stomach. "How bad is it?"

Bradley shook his head. "I don't know. Meli Ward and Trumpeter Bloom and that fellow Crowder are looking after her."

Wend sighed. "All right. Let's keep alert. There's at least a hundred of the light foot over there, and the Queen's Rangers troop may be rallying, which would give them at least another thirty. They may feel strong enough to stage an assault."

O'beirne grinned. "And angry enough since we've got their horses."

Fairfield snorted. "They may outnumber us, but we're in a strong position here on a high bank. They'd lose a lot of men, even if they could cross successfully."

The Irishman looked at Fairfield. "They might give it a try. Especially since your South Carolina boys scooped up their young ensign."

Wend turned to Fairfield in surprise. "We've got one of their officers, Geoffrey?"

"He was hit by a ball on his leg and sitting on the ground when we charged into their camp. Seemed appropriate to scoop him up. McCrae stunned him by smacking a pistol on the side of his head and then dragged him back across the river."

Donegal said, "Aye, I'd bet the Rangers will be outraged. Lost their horses and a subaltern. And when they arrive back at Philadelphia on foot, I'm thinkin' they'll be the laughingstock of their regiment."

They all chuckled at the thought, and as they did, an important question occurred to Wend. He said, "Warren, you arrived at just the right moment. But I've been puzzled about it since I first heard the sound of your hunting horn, back when we were up on the ridge. How the devil did you and the cavalry happen to be here?"

"Washington called me to headquarters. The general was worried about how long you had been gone, and he had just gotten a message from one of his watchers that a column of cavalry and foot had left Philadelphia two days before and headed north. Washington put two and two together and thought they may have been sent to intercept your detachment. He dispatched us to find you."

Wend was about to respond when a call came from Schreiber. "Major! There's a rider coming across the river, and he's carrying a white flag!"

"Wave him in, Sergeant!"

Wend, accompanied by Bradley and Fairfield, walked toward the riverbank. As they arrived, the flag bearer emerged from the water and pulled up his horse. Wend saw it was a young officer of the 42nd. He said, "Well, sir, who are you and what can we do for you this evening?"

The officer responded, "I am Lieutenant McDougal of the 42nd, looking for Major Eckert of the Guides."

"I'm Eckert, sir."

The lieutenant stared at Wend for a long moment, seeming to size him up. Then he touched his bonnet and said, "Sir, Major McDonald, commanding our detachment, asks for a parley."

Wend stiffened. "McDonald? By any chance Charles McDonald? Formerly of the 77th Highlanders?"

"That is correct, sir."

Wend and Donegal, who was standing nearby, exchanged quick looks. Then Wend asked McDougal, "What concerns Major McDonald?"

"He wishes to discuss the disposition of the wounded and prisoners, sir."

Wend replied, "I'm amenable to that. Where will we meet?"

The Highland lieutenant waved behind himself. "Major McDonald proposes on horseback in the middle of the stream as soon as convenient for you."

"Tell him Major Eckert agrees and will meet him in a few minutes."

McDougal said, "I shall relate your answer to the major." Then he saluted, turned his horse, and recrossed the Millstone.

Wend looked at Donegal. "Sergeant Major, get some white cloth and put it on whatever kind of stick you can find. You'll accompany me to the parley."

Donegal grinned broadly. "And a very interesting meeting that will be." He hurried off to make a white flag.

The other officers were looking at Wend, and it was Warren Bradley who asked the question on everyone's lips. "Wend, how do you know this Major Charles McDonald?"

Wend smiled. "I marched with him during Bouquet's campaign to relieve Fort Pitt during the Pontiac War and fought with him at Bushy Run, fifteen years ago. As did Donegal."

Geoffrey Fairfield said, "A striking coincidence."

Wend glanced at Fairfield. "Geoffrey, you above all should know that fate works in strange ways."

The captain sighed and made a quick laugh. "Indeed I do. One can never predict when paths will cross." He paused and smiled. "Or recross."

Then Donegal, now mounted and carrying a white flag, joined the group. He was leading a horse for Wend. "Na we're ready to go meet with McDonald."

Wend took the reins and mounted. Together the two rode out into the Millstone to meet their old friend.

—ɱ—

Wend and Simon reached the midpoint of the river and pulled up to wait for their counterparts. They could make out several officers in a discussion on the far bank, and then one man broke off, mounted his horse, and entered the stream, followed by another rider carrying the flag of truce. As they approached, Wend soon recognized the figure of McDonald. Then, he realized that the man holding the flag looked familiar also but couldn't quite place him.

It was Donegal who got it. "By God, Wend, that's Tavish carrying the flag! Ian Tavish, the piper!"

Wend looked closer and realized that although older and heavier, it was definitely Tavish—known for strong lungs playing the pipes and loquaciousness in conversation.

The two men of the Black Watch pulled up in front of Wend and Donegal. McDonald momentarily stared at Eckert and said, "Well, Wend, the years have treated you well. And it's good to see an old comrade in arms, even if it happens in water up to our stirrups and as adversaries in an unfortunate war." He looked over at Simon and continued, "And of course Donegal is at your side. I would have expected nothing else."

Donegal interjected, "It would be perfect, Major, if Bob Kirkwood were here, but I've na heard from him since that day at Fort Pitt when the old 77th marched off, and he stayed with the 42nd."

Tavish laughed and spoke up. "Aye, your old partner in crime! You two were the best foragers in the regiment. Your fire always had the best food." He added, "And as luck would have it, we saw Bob Kirkwood back in '76. It happens he's a got a big coopering works, and he wrote a book about the old days with the 77th and 42nd during the French War." He laughed again. "And you're in it, Donegal, but under another name."

"Kirkwood went back to making barrels? The devil you say! He joined the army to get away from working in his father's coopering shop."

"Whatever changed his mind, he's making money at it." Tavish raised a finger. "And he's the one who helped get Mary..."

McDonald cut him off by saying, "Wend, I see you are still wearing the gorget I gave you for saving my life at Bushy Run."

"I always wear it in action—I believe it brings me good fortune."

"Indeed, I hope that proves correct." Then he said, "But although we could talk for hours about the old days, we must get to business."

Wend nodded. "Yes. You called for this meeting. Your lieutenant mentioned wounded and prisoners."

"Indeed, sir. We have three of your men—two wounded and one dead. And you have our Ensign Pulling, who I am led to believe has a significant injury.

I would propose an exchange. We have no medical people with us, save a surgeon's mate, and have our hands full treating our own wounded." He smiled at Wend and said, "I presume you would be most happy to have your men back and honor the dead soldier with a respectful burial. And we most desire to have Mr. Pulling returned to us. I believe that would be a fair exchange."

Wend considered McDonald's words for a moment, then a thought hit him. "Your proposal suggests you contemplate no further military action in this affair."

"That is quite accurate, Major Eckert. I am not such a fool as to order an assault across a river against a strongly held position. I've seen the marksman of the Guides at work and have no desire to sacrifice good men simply to drive you off the riverbank. And even if we were successful, I am in no position to pursue your mounted column, since you have dismounted our dragoons. Regardless of what I might desire, this mission is over save for getting my men and wounded back to Philadelphia."

Wend immediately said, "Then I agree to your proposal. I suggest we send a wagon with two men over. They will carry your ensign and will return with the three casualties. And I assume the men on the wagon will receive your guarantee of no interference."

"I accept your plan, and you have my word regarding the safety of your men."

"Thank you, Major. We will return to our lines and send over the wagon forthwith."

Wend turned his horse, as did Donegal. But McDonald spoke up. "I would have a word in private with you, Major Eckert."

Pulling up his horse, Wend said, "Donegal, get back to our lines and prepare the wagon and Ensign Pulling. Have Lieutenant O'beirne and Corporal Wood man the wagon."

Donegal looked back at McDonald, then nodded to Wend. "Aye, Major." And then he turned to the two Highland men and said, "And I hope the next time we see each other is at a snug tavern in time of peace!" And with that he was gone.

Tavish waved to Donegal and then withdrew a short distance toward the river-bank.

When the two officers were alone, McDonald spoke in a quiet tone, "Wend, I wanted to talk to you about Mary Fraser."

"I thought that might be what you had on your mind."

"You know she is back with the army? That she came over with the regiment?"

"Donegal and Baird found out about it from soldiers of the 42nd and 71st who were captives in Virginia."

McDonald laughed. "Baird? Is that old rascal still above ground?"

"He's doing quite well for a man over fifty with a bad leg. Gets around very well. He lives down on my farm—Eckert Ridge—near Winchester." Then Wend said, "They kept the information about Mary from me until recently. Didn't want me thinking about her while I was in command—they thought it would distract me. But it eventually slipped out." He shrugged. "But what is it you wanted to say about Mary?"

"With the support of the 42nd's proprietary colonel, General Murray, Mary has become the matron of our regimental hospital. However, at the moment, she is seconded to the army's general hospital in Philadelphia. You last saw her when she was sixteen. Now she is a mature woman: beautiful, intelligent, educated in letters, accomplished in the arts, and with social graces well above that expected of one of her birth and background. Consequently, she is pursued eagerly by numerous young and not-so-young men of substantial families and means. But she resists all advances, even those of senior officers. Right now she is being courted by a lieutenant colonel of a loyalist regiment on the staff of General Howe. He is a man of great means and influence here in America. You know I recruited her father into the army and watched out for her as if she were my own kin when she was orphaned. It tears my heart to see her consign herself to a life of spinsterhood. She is woman who should be well married and have the love of her own children instead of caring only for those of others."

"What is keeping her from marriage?"

"For God's sake, don't be obtuse, Wend. We both know it is her deep affection for you, an obsession which began when she was a child and which persists, against all reason, over all these years. Mary is now thirty. If she does not act soon, spinsterhood will indeed be her fate."

"Why are you telling me of this? How can I change her sentiments?"

"Because I want you to convey a message, through me, that will free her. Tell her the passion of your youth has faded. Give me words that encourage her to find the comfort of a life with someone else."

"You can tell her that I have found a life with a woman whom I do love, who has been a faithful wife, and who has been a good mother to our children. As long as she is alive, I will be faithful to her." Wend paused, choosing his words. "But I cannot, and will not, deny that my love for Mary is eternal and is part of the very fabric of my soul. If I were free, nothing would keep me from her. About that I cannot be false to her." He picked up the reins and made ready to leave. "You may tell all that to Mary, and nothing more."

McDonald stared at Wend for a long moment, then said, "That is not what I had hoped for, but I will convey that to the lady." And then he smiled and added, "And until we meet again, God be with you, Major Eckert."

Wend returned the smile and said, "And with you, Major McDonald."

And with that the two parted, riding back through the stream to rejoin their comrades.

—∞—

As Wend guided his horse up the riverbank, the wagon, driven by Billy Wood, was about to enter the water. O'beirne sat beside him on the seat, and Ensign Pulling sat in the bed, his back up against the seat. Wend held up his hand to stop them.

Wend dismounted and called for O'beirne to slip down from the wagon and come talk with him. The Irishman walked over to where Wend stood.

"Well, my good Major, what is it you want to discuss?"

"I have some confidential instructions for you."

"Oh, do you now?" He grinned conspiratorially. "And what might those be?"

"Now listen carefully: just after my horse was shot and I lay on the ground, I shot Colonel Northcutt."

"Indeed I saw that happen while Donegal and I were crossing the river to get you."

"I don't know how serious his wound is, or if he is dead. Keep your eyes and ears open to learn anything you can about his condition. It's important to me."

"Now that I can understand." He grinned broadly. "I know how much affection you feel for the august colonel."

"Your sarcasm is up to its usual standard, Shay. Just find out as much as you can."

"Consider it done." And with that he walked back to the wagon and climbed up into the seat. Momentarily Billy slapped the reins on the backs of the team, and they were on their way through the ford.

Wend was standing there watching them when Warren Bradley came up to him. "I had the sergeants take a muster. The men we are missing number a total of four: Harding of my troop—he was shot crossing the river, and his body floated off—and Small, also of my troop. Fairfield also is missing two of his Carolina men. The names are Cooper and Fawley."

"Well, we'll know their condition when the wagon brings them back." Wend sighed. "It would be better for them if we had a surgeon. We'll just have to do the best we can for them until we get back to Valley Forge."

"Ah, but we do have a physician. It turns out that fellow Crowder, who came in with your detachment, says he is one. He's with Miss Porter now."

"Crowder is a *doctor*?"

"He says so. And he produced medical instruments from his saddlebags."

Wend thought, *Suddenly a lot of things over the past few days make sense.* He asked, "How is she doing?"

An expression of distress came over the captain's face. "Crowder says her wound is mortal. He's doing the best he can to ease her pain now." He took a deep breath. "A shame, Wend. She's a lovely woman."

Wend sighed. "Indeed. I'll go see her. She has helped us greatly." Then Wend looked at the men in their defense positions and said, "Warren, release the men from their line. They can start squad fires and make coffee. See that rations are distributed."

The captain glanced across the river. "You think there is no danger of an attack after the exchange?"

"No, Major McDonald has given me his word he doesn't plan an assault, and no officer in the British Army is more honorable. There will be no more action here tonight."

Wend saw that a fire had been made some distance behind the lines, and the prostrate figure of Nell Porter lay beside it. Crowder was on his knees at her side. Meli and Bloom knelt on the other side. Childers was on one knee next to the doctor, looking down at her. Anguish was written all over his face.

Wend walked over to stand beside the lieutenant and in a whisper, asked, "Is there no hope?"

Edward turned to look at him, and Wend could see tears on his face. He silently shook his head to indicate *No*.

Wend looked down at the girl, who was lying on a blanket and partially covered by another. A bloody dressing was on her right side, and her clothing had been partially cut off. The rest was stained with blood. Nell's eyes were closed. She was groaning and gasping for air, and blood oozed from her lips. Wend didn't have to be a doctor to realize she was near the end.

As he watched, she opened her eyes and looked up at Crowder. "Oh, father, I can't feel anything! Everything is so cold."

Crowder leaned down and put his arms around her and pulled her close to him. He cried. "Oh, Alice, my little Alice! Please not yet."

Wend saw the girl's body shudder all over, and Crowder held her close to him for a long time as if trying to keep her warm with his body. Then he gently laid her back down. Her eyes were open, staring emptily up at the night sky. Blood had erupted from her mouth and covered her chin. The spy remained on his knees, hands clasped in front of him, obviously in prayer. Wend could see some of Nell's—or he realized—*Alice's* blood on his face.

After a moment, Crowder opened his eyes, stared down at his daughter for a long moment, then gently closed her eyes and pulled the blanket over her face.

Suddenly Childers reached down and pulled back the blanket. He gently kissed the girl on the cheek. Then he re-covered her and stood up.

Crowder stared at Childers for a moment, sensing what had occurred between the two young people, then pushed himself up from the ground. He looked around at the others, then said, "There was nothing I could do. There was no way to save her. The ball was in too deep and did too much damage." He sobbed, and Wend could see tears streaming down his face.

Wend took Crowder by the arm and gently walked him a little distance from the fire and the people around it. He reached into his pocket and pulled out a kerchief, and said gently, "Here, sir, you have blood on your face."

Crowder took the cloth and wiped his face all over, removing the blood and tears. Then he sighed deeply.

Wend said, "I am committed to the cause of this war, but I don't know that I could have asked my daughter to go into a place of danger."

The spy looked over at him and said, "Nor could I. Alice was my oldest child and the closest to me: she had been acting as my nurse since she was fourteen. And she was as enthusiastic as any man about winning independence for New Jersey. She knew that I was doing work for Major Tallmadge. She wanted to help, and she started watching the British for me, mainly going out and reporting troop movements. There was no real danger in that. But then when we got word that someone who might be Henry was staying at the Queen Bess, Alice volunteered to go there and find out his identity. It was an adventure for her. She was all excited about impersonating a tavern server. She found the right clothing and even changed the way she wore her hair. I dropped her off in Elizabeth Town, and she walked to the inn and asked for a job, like any young girl out of a situation. She told old Grimsby she was an orphan and had worked at a tavern that burned down and needed work. He didn't ask many questions and took her up on it right away. She wasted no time looking up the man we thought was Henry and identified him immediately. Then she got word to me and started watching over him." He sighed. "You know the rest."

Wend searched for words. After a moment he said, "I'm sorry for your loss, sir. She was a brave girl and helped us both at the inn and the fight at Wallen Farm."

Crowder took a deep breath. "She was so young and had so much more to experience in life: the love of a good man, womanhood, child bearing, all the rest. She was barely out of her childhood."

Wend said softly, "She experienced some of that in the last few days: the love of a good man and womanhood."

Crowder looked quickly over at Childers and then back at Wend. "Him? They were together?"

Wend nodded. "It happened fast, as many things do in war. They became infatuated with each other in the days after our raid to Elizabeth Town. My dragoon sergeant told me that they were seen sneaking off to a secluded pine grove next to a creek the night before we left Wallen Farm, and Lieutenant Childers was carrying a blanket. It was the first, intense passion of two young people."

Crowder replied, "Then I'm glad for her. At least she experienced that."

After a moment of silence between them, a thought came to Wend. "I wish I hadn't allowed her to come with us: I should have left her at Wallen Farm. She could have made her way home from there, and she would be alive today."

"You mustn't blame yourself, Eckert. We cannot second-guess fate." Crowder looked around, then said, "I must leave now, and ride to Rockingham. It is only a couple of miles hence. I know the Berriens, and they will loan me a wagon to come get Alice and take her home. We live in a town well to the northwest of Spanktown. I ask you the favor of not marching from here until I return. I would not like to see her lying unattended."

Wend shook his head. "No, I'll not need to make that promise. When our wagon returns from the British camp, I will have Billy Wood drive you and your daughter to Rockingham. And you will have an escort of an officer and dragoons to ensure there is no interference."

Relief spread over Crowder's face. "Thank you, Wend. That will make things much easier. I don't want to leave her alone."

Then the distraught father walked back over to the fire and sat down to keep his daughter company.

—m—

The soldiers were huddled around squad fires, finally able to cook their rations. The smell of coffee permeated the campsite. Wend was standing with Bradley and Fairfield in discussion about plans for the morrow. He had told them about his promise to transport Crowder's daughter to Rockingham in their wagon and had assigned Fairfield to provide an escort from his troop. He thought a second and then said, "Childers will be in charge of the escort. He became enamored of the girl while we were at the Wallen place, and I believe he will want the mission."

Bradley nodded. "Then we will plan to depart when the wagon and escort return from Rockingham?"

"Indeed. It should be in the early afternoon. We may need the wagon to carry our two wounded if they are as serious as McDonald implied."

Wend had just finished when a sentinel called out, "The wagon's on the way back across the river!"

Wend and Bradley walked to the edge of the river and watched as the wagon crossed, maneuvered carefully by Billy Wood. He drove it out of the stream, up onto the bank, and brought it to a stop in front of the two officers.

Warren looked up at O'beirne on the seat beside Wood. "What's the condition of the men, Shay?"

The Irishman swung his legs out and dropped to the ground. "Small and Fawley are seriously wounded. They need attention fast, but I don't think they're in danger. Cooper's body is in there, covered by a blanket. He took a ball in the head. Probably went down without feeling anything."

Wend nodded his understanding. "Billy, take them over to that fire in the rear. Meli and Bloom will look after them. And have Mr. Crowder look them over and do what he can." Then he pointed to the team. "Keep the animals in harness after you unload the casualties. I have another job for the wagon, a matter of some urgency."

"Aye, sir." Wood slapped the reins on the team and headed the wagon for the fire. Bradley called out to one of his sergeants. "Sawyer, detail some men to get the wounded and dead out of the wagon." Then he walked off to supervise.

O'beirne said, "Now, my dearest Major, I suspect you'll be wanting to know about that Colonel Northcutt, who we both know was the man that cooked up that raid on your farm two years ago."

"Were you able to find out anything?"

"Didn't take any effort at all." He grinned. "They as much as told me all on their own. A medical orderly was watching as a couple of men loaded our boys into the wagon. I was standin' by that Highland major, and the orderly says to him, 'Sir, Northcutt needs a surgeon. I've got a dressing on him, but he's drifting in and out of consciousness. The ball's in deep, and he needs more than I can do." The Irishman shrugged. "The major called out to a lieutenant to take a detail and find a nearby farm to requisition wagons for their wounded. By the way, they got at least a half dozen besides the colonel. And McDonald said the detail was to ask if the farmer knew where a physician could be found."

Wend considered a moment. "So Northcutt is alive but perhaps on the border between life and death."

"Seems logical, from what I heard,"

Wend stood silent, looking at the far side of the river. "As I recall, there were several farms just before we got to the river. But no sizable villages nearby that I know of. They may have to take all their wounded back to Philadelphia to get the services of a surgeon."

A glimmer appeared in O'beirne's eye. "That would be very hard on a badly wounded man, bumping along on rough roads for a day. Wouldn't surprise me at all if he didn't survive the trip."

"Shay, I was thinking just the same myself."

Wend walked over to the fire where Meli had a pot boiling. Childers and Henry sat looking into the flames. Wend smelled coffee. "Meli, is that stuff ready?"

"Sure 'nuff, Mr. Eckert. And I got some salt-beef boiling in the pot. You'll have to be satisfied with soldier food tonight, 'cause everything else is used up 'ceptin' some bread we got from the Wallens' kitchen."

"I need the coffee more than anything else. It doesn't seem like there will be any sleep for me tonight."

Meli poured a cup and handed it to him.

Wend looked at Childers. "Edward, I have promised that our wagon will take Alice's body to an estate named Rockingham. Crowder tells me it is only a few miles hence. Corporal Wood will drive, and the wagon will be escorted by an escort of four dragoons from Fairfield's troop. You will be in charge of the detail."

The lieutenant looked up. "Yes, sir."

"You'll leave at first light. I suggest you go talk to Fairfield and arrange for the men of the escort."

The young officer nodded but kept staring into the flames. Wend said, "*Now*, Edward. Get it set up so they're ready to go. Dawn isn't that far away."

Childers pushed himself up. "Aye, sir. I'll see to it immediately."

Meli looked up from her pot. "Mr. Eckert, he be mighty broke up about that girl. Ain't easy to fall in love with someone then lose them, all in a few days."

"Yes, I know." He looked at her. "That's why I'm giving him the detail. It will keep him busy and will be a way for him to say farewell."

Meli responded, "Yes, it's always good to keep busy when you are sad." She poured another cup of coffee and said, "I'll take this over to that Mr. Crowder." She turned and walked over to where the spy was maintaining his vigil.

Wend took a drink of the coffee. It was strong, as Meli's always was. But he knew he needed its stimulation. Then his thoughts were interrupted by the voice of John Henry.

"I doubt that escorting the remains of that girl will help Edward forget about her." He looked up from the fire. "*You* can't claim to be an expert on losing a woman."

Wend felt a surge of exasperation at Henry's self-pity and gave the young man a hard look. "And *you* are? Well, Mr. Henry, you are quite wrong about that. In fact you couldn't be any more wrong. Let me tell you a story." He rose and went over to the pot and poured himself another cup.

Henry was looking up at him. "John, in 1759 my family started a trip to Fort Pitt along Forbes Road. My father had been appointed armorer by Colonel Henry Bouquet, the military commander in Pennsylvania. The colonel requested that we travel in company with, and assist, the family of a lawyer from Philadelphia who was to become the first magistrate at the Forks of the Ohio. It happened that he was a widower but had a sixteen-year-old daughter who was traveling with him."

"So you are going to tell me that you fell in love with the girl?

"Of course I did. She was beautiful and sassy, with long gleaming blond hair. I had never met anyone like her. And strangely enough, it turned out she reciprocated my feelings. An odd combination: a girl from the wealthy elite of Philadelphia and the son of a gunsmith, serving as his father's apprentice." Wend looked into the fire for a moment, then continued, "One night we sneaked away from the camp of our families and made passionate love beside a stream called the Conoquochegue. Two days later her father found out about our romance and forbade me from having anything to do with her."

Henry was staring at Wend now, listening with rapt attention. "So that ended the affair? Things must have been quite awkward with the families traveling together for weeks."

"No, there wasn't much time for awkwardness. The next day our caravan was attacked by a Mingo war party."

"So she was killed in the attack?"

"No, worse than that. Everyone in our caravan was killed except myself and her. I was left unconscious on Forbes Road because the Mingo thought I was dead. They even took part of my scalp." He pulled back his hair at the rear of his head to show the circular scar. "She was taken hostage by the war party and forced to become the wife of the Mingo war captain."

"My God! So you never saw her again?"

"Actually, I did." Wend paused and looked at the lad. "I was saved by a company of Highlanders marching eastward along Forbes Road. With them was a scout named Joshua Baird who took me to his sister's place in a back-country village called Sherman Mill. It was a village of Ulster people."

Scorn came over Henry's face. "You mean you lived with the *Irish*?"

"John, a piece of advice. Don't ever let an Ulster person hear you calling them *Irish*. They are lowland Scots who simply happened to spend some time in Ireland. Do so, and you may find it necessary to defend yourself." Wend stared at him for a moment, then continued, "At any rate, I couldn't get over my feeling for the Philadelphia girl. So, years later, when Pontiac's War broke out, and I was eighteen, I volunteered to serve as a scout with Colonel Bouquet when he marched to relieve Fort Pitt from the siege by the Ohio Indians. It was a way to get to the west to try to find the girl."

"Yes, I've heard about that: Bouquet's men fought the warriors at a place called Bushy Run."

"That's right. At any rate, after we defeated the warriors and relieved the fort, Bouquet sent me as a scout for a company of Highlanders with a mission to offer peace terms to the Indians. And as luck would have it, I found the girl, Abigail, in a small Mingo village."

"So you brought her back? You were reunited?"

"No, John, the fact is she rejected me. Abigail decided to stay with the Mingo. She was serving as their doctor and had become dedicated to them. She felt she had a duty to help the village, and doing so provided a measure of satisfaction to her. And beyond that, she also realized that she would be treated with scorn by our society for living with an Indian and having his children."

John Henry stared at Wend for a long time, considering the story. Finally he said, "You must have been devastated."

"Yes, John, I was. But the point is, I got on with my life." He looked directly into Henry's eyes and continued, "Eventually I met another lady, different from Abigail, but beautiful and intelligent, whom I married." He shrugged. "I'll never forget Abigail, but I found love with a good woman and the joy of the children we produced together." Wend stared at Henry for a moment, then said, "Perhaps you might want to think on that."

John sat looking at Wend for a long time but said nothing. Then he turned back to the fire with a contemplative expression on his face.

Wend sat drinking the coffee.

After a few minutes Henry asked in a voice empty of emotion, "How long will it take to get to Valley Forge?"

Wend looked over at the youth. "I expect to get back late the day after tomorrow." Wend took another sip. "If we don't run into any more trouble with the British."

"What is going to happen to me when we get there? Am I going to be court martialed?"

"I don't know, John. Undoubtedly Washington will want to see you. He'll be the one who decides your case." Wend shrugged. "But from what he said to me, one way or another he's going to send you back to your father."

"What if I want nothing of the sort?"

Wend looked at Henry. "John, we've gone over that before." Wend waved his hand to take in the camp. "I don't suppose you have noticed that a lot of effort has been expended on your behalf. Troop movements at considerable expense, three skirmishes, lives lost."

"Don't try to shame me. I didn't ask for any of it."

"But it has been done. Done at the request of your father. Obviously he wants to work things out with you. And given that many men have done *their* duty to fetch you, I would say it's a matter of *your* duty to at least see what your father has to say about it all—about him and Dorothea, about his feeling toward you, about you and the entire Henry family." Wend grinned. "And of course, you will obviously have a chance to tell your father what *you* think of both him and Dorothea if you choose to do so. As a matter of fact, I wouldn't mind being there as a fly on the wall to hear that conversation. In any case, I rather suspect that one way or another General Washington is going to insist on it."

Chapter Eight
Washington's Order

It was coming on full night and pleasantly warm at Valley Forge as Wend Eckert sat at the mess table of the Guides. He was observing with critical eyes as Colleen McGraw checked the fitting of a uniform coat on John Henry. Edward Childers sat in a camp chair, also watching the proceedings.

The Guides cavalry had returned late the previous day. Wend had immediately reported verbally to Washington, who had set a meeting with Henry two days hence, giving him time to read Wend's written report before speaking with the lad. Wend had set about finding a way to get the young man suitably attired. He had immediately turned to his old friend, Mrs. McGraw, proprietress of the Red Vixen Sutler Company, who had extensive resources in her wagons.

Colleen stood back and looked at the erstwhile officer. "There, it fits as well as I can do without taking it apart and remaking the whole thing."

Wend looked up from his work and asked, "You've done a marvelous job, Colleen. Frankly, I am puzzled at how you managed to get some young artillery officer to part with his coat. Any presentable uniform is at a premium."

"The gentleman in question said he had two coats and was quite ready to part with one for the opportunity to spend a night with one of my girls." She turned and grinned at Wend. "I even gave him his choice of which one."

"That was very generous of a woman known principally for her dedication to the concept of profit."

"Generosity *hell*. You damn well know it goes on your account, which extends to several pages in my ledger."

"You know I don't have the money to pay what you consider I owe."

"And you damn well know it's not a question of money. There's not enough money in the world to pay for what you owe me. But you also know you could be paid in full any time you want and do it in just one night."

"And you know I can't do what you desire."

"Not *can't*, actually *won't do it*." She gave him a wicked smile. "But some day you'll weaken, and I *will* get my payment."

Henry, who had been standing silent, sullenly submitting to the fitting, looked at the two older people and spoke up, a puzzled expression on his face. "I don't understand what you are talking about. It doesn't make any sense."

Colleen gave the young man a knowing look. "It makes a lot of sense to me and Wend Eckert. All that matters is that he knows what I mean."

Wend sighed and turned to Henry. "A long time ago, Mrs. McGraw was a tavern maid and helped me escape from some men who wanted to kill me. That's what she's talking about."

Colleen laughed. "That's only part of it. The rest is what happened in a room at that tavern later that night." She grinned. "Or more to the fact, what didn't happen."

Wend felt his face reddening and turned to Mrs. McGraw and snapped, "Damn it, Coli, that's enough!"

Colleen stood grinning at Wend.

Henry raised his eyebrows as he gained some appreciation of what they were talking about. Then he shrugged and continued, "And I don't understand why all this is necessary simply for me to meet Washington. He has seen me before with father in Williamsburg."

Wend responded, "Well, Mr. Henry, much as you object, you are still considered a serving officer of the Continental Army. And General Washington has a well-known predilection toward formality. Things will likely go better if you look the part. And those clothes that you have been wearing since the Queen Bess simply do not fit the occasion."

Colleen made a face. "Not to mention the smell."

Wend grinned. "Yes, indeed there is that." He paused a moment, giving the young man a stern look. "And if Washington decides to send you before a court martial, you will definitely need a uniform."

Henry sighed. "So in essence you are making sure I am properly outfitted to go to my execution. But in any case, I told you I left a letter of resignation in my tent."

Wend laughed. "Don't be silly. I don't know whether you actually wrote that letter or not, but Washington didn't send out an expedition to find you for the purpose of ordering you to the gallows or the firing squad. The point is you will go before him with a dignified appearance, and we shall see how things turn out tomorrow." He turned to Childers. "Edward, take him to quarters. Have him ready to accompany me to the Potts House immediately after the noon hour tomorrow."

Once the two had departed, Colleen, who was collecting her sewing materials in a basket, looked over at Wend and commented, "There goes one very confused young man. His mind is in total disarray."

Wend sighed. "Well, he can't shake off the loss of that girl, with whom he was clearly besotted." Wend shrugged. "And even more to the point, he can't forget what, in my estimation, certainly appears to be a betrayal by his father."

Colleen gave Wend a knowing, cynical look. "A night with one of my girls would solve most of his problems. I've no doubt it would drive the memory of the high-born, genteel Dorothea Dandridge right out of his mind and give him a proper perspective on life and the opposite sex."

"Now, my dear, Colleen, not all problems besetting men can be solved by the tender attentions of your ladies. Washington will deal with young Henry, but personally Edward Childers is really the one I'm worried about."

"Lieutenant Childers? Why, pray tell?"

"He is morose because he fell in love with a young lady and lost her all in four days."

"What? I don't understand."

Wend explained Alice's role in recovering Henry and what had happened between Edward and Alice during the expedition into Jersey and finished by describing the young girl's end at the Millstone.

"Good Lord, how devastating that must have been for Edward. And of course, her father."

"Yes, and Edward is having a hard time getting over it. His duties are suffering. I'm looking for a way to take his mind off the girl." Wend pointed a finger at Colleen. "And don't tell me he needs a night with one of your girls."

She put her head back and laughed. "Maybe not, but in any case, it wouldn't hurt."

Wend put his hand to his chin. "He was courting a girl back at Williamsburg, a daughter of the gentry and thought he was in love with her. However, his life in the circle of elegant Virginia society did little to prepare him for a girl like Alice. I don't think he had ever encountered a female who was not only beautiful, but also tough, self-sufficient, and world wise. I'm afraid the memory of her, and the grief over her loss, has made him reconsider his love for the Virginia lass, Emma Wilbourne."

"Is that so bad? Maybe it's a good thing for him to broaden his outlook regarding women."

"The Wilbourne girl is very attached to him. She writes incessantly, and Edward used to live for her letters." Wend looked at Colleen. "The fact is, he is born to the gentry, and the way things work among the wealthy class of Virginia, his parents will be looking for him to marry suitably. His father has the largest and most prosperous land holdings in our county and expects Edward to wed a woman who matches or enhances the family's wealth and influence. I wish I could find a way to reignite his romantic feeling for Emma."

"I think you worry too much. Probably over time, he'll find he still has deep feeling for her. He'll look back on his time with Alice as a romantic diversion. Time heals things." She looked over at Wend. "Except for what's between you and me. I'll not forget that night in the tavern you made love to me and then sneaked away while I was sleeping, leaving me to wake up alone after expecting another bit of gratification in the morning. Your debt won't be paid until you make it up to me under the covers."

"How many times to do I have to tell you that I did that because I was afraid those men would come back in the morning? I wanted to make sure they didn't come after me while you were there and possibly harm you in the process."

Colleen grinned. "So you say. But I'll get my payment someday." She put her sewing basket on the table and sat down in a camp chair beside Wend. "Now, if you don't mind, I will take a measure of payment in the form of a cup—or maybe two—of Donegal's good whiskey." She looked up at him. "Could you fetch me some, my dear Wend?"

—m—

Mary Fraser was working in her room at the offices of the general hospital when she heard the sound of booted feet moving rapidly through the hall accompanied by the metal clinking sound of a saber and other military accouterments as the man walked. She glanced out the open door just in time to see a green-coated dragoon stride past. It piqued her curiosity, but she went back to work, for she still had numerous things to do before she could return to the 42nd.

But it was only a couple of minutes later when there was a tap at the door, and she looked up to see the hospital's director, Michael Morris, standing just inside the room, a piece of paper in his hand.

"Mary, we need to get ready to receive wounded men. There's been a serious skirmish in New Jersey."

A knot formed in Mary's stomach.

Morris continued, "I've got a dispatch from Major McDonald of the Black Watch that says he's got nine men who need attention." A look of distress came over his face. "Brace yourself, Mary. I regret to say one of them is Colonel Northcutt."

Mary rose to her feet. "Does it say how serious he is?"

"The colonel took a ball in the chest. McDonald says he's in grave condition and mostly unconscious. He thinks the ball must be removed if he is to survive. They're bringing him here in a wagon; they couldn't find a competent surgeon near the site of the skirmish."

"When will they be here?"

"The courier thought it would be no more than a couple of hours."

"What are your instructions for the disposition of the wounded?"

Morris thought a moment. "Send the soldiers down to one of the general wards, whichever has adequate room, and we'll put Northcutt in the Ridgley house."

Mary nodded. The Ridgley House, located next door to headquarters, was for officers. "I'll get the word out and have our people prepared to receive the wounded in both places."

Morris put his hand to his chin. "I'll send Dr. Stewart down to care for the soldiers, but I'm going to assign Dr. Grant to Northcutt. He's obviously going to be a complex case."

"Yes, Dr. Morris. I'll alert nurses to be available where they're needed."

"Excellent, Mary." The director raised an eyebrow and said in a gentle voice, "I know that Northcutt has been escorting you to various social functions, and I'm not blind—obviously he has affection for you." He paused and then continued, "So I'm assigning you to act as his personal nurse."

Mary felt her stomach tighten and blurted out, "Oh, sir, I'd rather not."

Morris shot her a bemused look. "I don't understand. Northcutt has been very kind to you. And I assumed you returned that sentiment to some degree."

She bit her lip and tried to think of an appropriate answer. "Yes, he has. And that's why I'm afraid it would be *too* personal."

Morris walked over and put a comforting hand on her shoulder. "I know it will be difficult to tend someone to whom you are so close and whose wound might well prove fatal. But I think your mere presence around the colonel may give him strength. He'll need all he can muster. And given Northcutt's importance on the staff, we need to have him treated by our best. I suspect that the attempt to extract the ball will be very challenging, requiring a most delicate touch. Alex Grant is our most accomplished surgeon, and you are our most experienced nurse."

Mary sighed deeply, "Yes, Director. I quite understand." She thought a second. "I'll get word to our nurses to organize for the enlisted wounded, then I'll go over to Ridgley House and prepare a room to treat Colonel Northcutt."

—∞—

Wend and John Henry ascended the front steps to the Potts House. Henry had been very quiet on the short walk from the Guides' camp. He looked over at the captain and saw that there was a worried, yet defiant, look on the lad's face. He thought, *Judgment day has arrived for the wayward son.*

They entered the hall, and Wend went right to the adjutant general's office. Colonel Scammell was looking down at papers on his desk. Wend said, "We're here to meet with the general, per instructions, sir."

Scammell looked up at John for a long time, his eyes appraising the young officer. Henry squirmed under the inspection. Finally he said, "Go right in; General Washington is expecting you."

Wend led Henry to the commander in chief's door and tapped gently, then opened it halfway.

Washington looked up, and Wend said, "Good afternoon, sir. I have Captain Henry with me."

The general nodded and motioned for them to enter. Without acknowledging Henry, he said, "Major Eckert, I have read your report. It is very thorough. Most importantly, you and your men are to be commended on accomplishment of a difficult mission. The skirmishes at Wallen Farm and later at the ford on the Millstone River were well executed. The fight at Wallen Farm eliminated a band of partisans that was causing many problems for our people in the area."

"Thank you, sir. Of course, we were most fortunate that our stratagem worked that night. And on the return journey, even more fortunate that you dispatched the Guides cavalry to reinforce my original detachment."

"Reports from our sources in Philadelphia made it obvious that the British intended action against you. We were aware within a few hours of its departure that an expedition had marched, and it seemed clear the purpose was to intercept your detachment. It was a necessary and easy decision." Washington paused and looked at the young captain. "Now, Major Eckert, I would like to speak confidentially with Mr. Henry. However, I request that you, sir, remain at headquarters. I will have more to say to you when the captain and I have finished our discussion." He pointed to the door. "And please close that on your way out."

Wend took one of several chairs in the hall, prepared for a lengthy wait. However, in about twenty minutes, the door opened, and John Henry emerged. He had a chastened, almost hang-dog look on his countenance. Wend stood up, and without saying anything, the young man took a seat next to where Wend had been and stared straight ahead.

From inside the office came Washington's voice. "Major Eckert, please come in."

Wend walked in, and the general motioned him to sit down in a chair in front of the desk.

"Major, I'm going to have a written reprimand and a discharge from the army prepared for Mr. Henry. Then I'm sending him home to work things out with his father and the rest of his family."

"Yes, sir."

Washington reached down to a drawer and pulled out a small leather purse. He handed it to Wend, who could feel the weight and shape of coins. "That will cover the cost of a suit of clothes for young Henry and traveling expenses to get back to Williamsburg."

Wend was slightly puzzled. "General, are you saying that you want me to take care of his travel arrangements?"

"That is *precisely* what I am asking of you. You have been in this from the beginning, Henry is in your camp, and thus you are the best man to handle it. Besides, you are a Virginian. Best to keep this all in the family, so to speak." Washington rose and walked over to the hearth. "I also want someone—an officer—to accompany him on the journey." He turned and looked directly at Wend. "Speaking frankly, the young man is so depressed by the situation that he is likely to lack the will to actually finish the trip on his own. I think that what you had to do to bring him down from Jersey speaks to that."

Wend nodded. "I agree, sir."

"So we need to find an appropriate, responsible officer to escort him."

Wend was struck by a thought. "Sir, I believe I have the very man. My adjutant, Lieutenant Edward Childers."

Washington cocked his head as if in thought. "Childers? Childers..." He raised a finger. "Is the lieutenant from Frederick County?"

"Indeed, sir."

"Back in the fifties—during the French War—I knew a man named Childers when I was colonel of the Virginia Regiment and headquartered at Fort Loudoun in Winchester. *Langston* Childers was his name. He was in a group of men I dined with at the Golden Buck one evening. Then he subsequently helped support a small outpost fort on his land near his residence. Is this officer related?"

"Indeed, sir. He is the son of the very man. Langston now has the largest holding in Frederick County. Greenfields is the main plantation, but there are several subsidiary farms attached to it."

"Well, then, your young lieutenant certainly has the appropriate lineage.

I take it he is a responsible officer, or you wouldn't have him as your adjutant or recommend him for this assignment."

"He was the first officer who joined my company back in '76. I was hesitant about him at first, for he was a new militia officer with no active experience, but he has proven intelligent and dedicated to his duties. He played a vital role in controlling the musketry in our fight at Wallen Farm and led the charge which forced the partisans to surrender." Wend added, "And of particular note, he was a friend of John and Dorothea in Williamsburg during his days at William and Mary. I am confident that would enable him to have more influence with John."

Washington's face lit up. "Ah, yes. I most certainly agree, Eckert. Make it so." He walked back over to his desk. "Make preparations for the two to travel, and I will soon have both Henry's discharge and a letter to Patrick ready." He thought a moment. "The letter will be personal and confidential, and I expect young Childers to carry it and hand it over only to Patrick Henry."

"Understood, sir. I'll get the two men ready for their journey."

Washington sat quietly, staring into the distance, obviously thinking things over. Then he looked over to Wend. "Major, thank you for your service in this matter. But the time has come for us to focus on things more central to the war. I have it from our watchers in Philadelphia that Clinton has now relieved Howe in command and that the British are actively making preparations to abandon the city. It is time for you to put your legion in condition for the campaign, for with the sad state of our cavalry, I must depend on you to provide the information that will shape the movement of the army."

Wend took that as his dismissal and stood up. "The Guides will be ready when the time comes, sir."

Washington said, "Yes, I trust they will."

Wend left the office and motioned to Henry where he sat. "Come along, John, we need to get you ready to go home."

—ꟽ—

Mary stood beside Dr. Alexander Grant as he made a first examination of the unconscious Barrett Northcutt. She had supervised orderlies as they gingerly removed the colonel from the farm wagon that had transported him to Philadelphia and then to the ground-floor room that had been prepared for his care. Now Grant was carefully removing the blood-soaked dressing that had been applied over the colonel's chest wound.

The surgeon inspected the injured area and then Northcutt's entire body. Grant said, "Look at his color; he's clearly lost a lot of blood. I was told by the 42nd orderly that he was hit by the small-caliber ball of a pistol. That's fortunate because, in my judgment, if he had taken the larger ball of a musket, he would not have survived a wound in this location." Then, having removed the dressing, he looked over at Mary. "Clean out the surface around the puncture. I can see very little with all the dried blood. Meanwhile, I'll get ready to attempt an extraction."

"Yes, sir," Mary responded. She took soap and water and cleaned around the wound, which was just in the middle of the right chest. Blood began to ooze out of the wound, but she was able to stop most of it by applying pressure directly on the puncture. Meanwhile, Grant, having taken off his jacket, rolled up his shirt sleeves, and donned an apron, was back beside the table.

Mary stepped back. "I think you'll be able to see more now." She pointed at a small table nearby. "I've laid out the probe and several extractors—including a long-necked one, since I believe the ball is lodged deeply."

"Excellent." Grant looked at Northcutt. "It's fortunate that he's unconscious. They said he's been mostly out since he was hit and delirious at other times. I can't imagine the pain he would have felt in that wagon as it bounced its way here."

The surgeon pulled the open hole as wide as he could with the fingers of his left hand and inserted the forefinger of his right hand into the wound. He moved it around, attempting to make contact with the ball. He sighed, withdrew the finger, and then looked over at Mary. "The ball is very deep. I can't touch it."

Mary bit her lip. "What about the ribs. Did it break anything?"

Grant shook his head. "No, he's a lucky bastard. It looks like the ball went between two ribs. The upper one appears to be slightly chipped; I felt a jagged edge. That will be painful enough if he survives." He thought a moment. "The wound needs to be flushed with clean water. There's bound to be bits of uniform material, bone particles, and plain dirt in there."

"I've got some water ready." Mary went to the table and got a pitcher of water and also got a wad of cotton cloth.

Grant stepped back. "Go ahead and flush it out."

Mary poured water into the hole, then set the pitcher down and rolled the cloth to make a tube. She inserted it into the wound, and gently moved it up and down. It absorbed most of the water, and when she removed it, she saw particles of cloth adhering to the cotton. Then she poured a bit more water into the wound and wrapped clean cloth around a forceps and used it to swab the hole using a circular motion. Then she put it down on the table and looked up at the doctor. "That's the best I can do." Then she examined the material on the forceps. "Doctor! I think I see a piece of bone here."

Grant came over to the table and examined the cotton. "Damn! You are right. It's a small piece. Hand me some tweezers." Mary did so and the surgeon carefully removed the bone chip. "There may be more in there, but we've done the best we can." He pointed to the table. "Hand me the longest probe."

Mary gave him the instrument, which was a straight metal rod with a slightly bulbous end. Grant took it and carefully inserted it into the hole. Then he slowly, methodically felt around the area.

As he did so, Mary picked up the long-nosed bullet forceps, or extractor, which had concave tips shaped to fit around a ball. She held it ready to hand to the doctor.

Grant made a tight smile and sighed. "There it is; it's under the rib, just peeping out. It's going to be a nasty job getting a hold on it."

He removed the probe and handed it to Mary, who in turn passed him the forceps.

Grant inserted the implement into the wound and gritted his teeth. "The damned thing's hiding under that rib." He felt around for a while. "No, I can't get a hold on it!" He removed the extractor and handed it to Mary. "Let me think about this a moment."

Mary said, "I once saw the surgeon of the Seventy-Seventh move a bullet with the tip of a Catlin blade."

"Indeed, I was just thinking of that. Hand me a thin-bladed, sharply pointed one."

She did so. Grant took it and inserted it down the wound. "I fear I'm going to have to widen the entry wound to get enough angle." He slightly widened the wound with the blade, then probed under the rib with the point. After a moment he said, "Yes! I've got it!" He delicately maneuvered the Catlin for several moments. "There, I think it has moved enough."

Mary gave him the long-necked forceps again.

Grant probed for a moment, then exclaimed, "There! By God, I've got a grip on the damned thing." He slowly, carefully retracted the forceps and held it up, the small pistol ball held tightly in the curved tips. Then he handed the forceps and ball to Mary. "There, save it. If the esteemed colonel ever regains consciousness—which is far from a sure thing—he may want to see the piece of lead which caused him all the pain."

Mary said, "I've got needles and thread ready to close the wound."

"Yes, it's small enough that should be fairly easy."

She handed him a needle and checked the thread length. "That should be enough."

The doctor looked at it and simply nodded. Then he went to work carefully stitching the wound. It took only a few minutes, then he handed the needle back to Mary and stepped back from the table.

As he removed the apron, he said, "All right, put a clean dressing on the wound and hold it in place with a bandage wrap around his chest. Then set up a continuous watch on him. If and when he regains consciousness, he's going to find himself in great pain." He made a final look over Northcutt. "Have me called when he is conscious."

Grant turned and opened the door to leave. Mary began preparing the dressing. Then she heard Grant talking to someone in the hall, and momentarily he came back into the room. Another officer, wearing the uniform of one of the loyalist regiments, was with him. The officer's uniform was wrinkled and dusty. Obviously he had just come from the field.

"Mary, this is Captain Markwood. He works with the colonel on the staff. He was with him at the skirmish and witnessed his wounding."

"Pleased to meet you, captain."

Markwood made a slight bow and responded, "I know who you are,

Miss Fraser. Colonel Northcutt often mentioned you fondly and spoke of escorting you to the Mischianza." He motioned toward the prostrate officer. "I'm glad that it is you who will be taking care of him."

Mary simply nodded.

Grant spoke up. "Mary, Captain Markwood will act as the liaison with the staff. Please keep him updated on the colonel's status."

Mary said, "Of course, sir."

Grant looked down at Northcutt and then turned to Markwood. "If I might ask, precisely how did he come to get this particular wound?"

Markwood took a deep sigh. "It was a most unfortunate situation. We had set up a trap for a detail of Washington's Guides, which had penetrated into New Jersey and ambushed a group of our partisans. We were waiting for them at a river crossing with a troop of dragoons. And there was a detachment of light foot waiting to come up behind the Guides column once we had stopped them." He stopped and sighed deeply. "But it was we who were surprised. A squadron of Continental dragoons burst upon us from across the river, and the Guides detachment attacked us from the other side."

Grant furrowed his eyebrows. "So you were in the trap instead of your quarry?"

"Precisely. We scattered and took shelter in nearby woods. But after the combined detachments of the Guides had crossed the river, except for a rearguard, Northcutt caught sight of the Guides commander, a certain Major Eckert. He was mounted and directing the rearguard."

On hearing his words, Mary felt her heart begin to pound.

Markwood continued, "Northcutt, who has a personal grudge against Eckert stemming from their days in Virginia, ran out of the woods and shot at him with a pistol. He missed, but hit his horse, and Eckert was thrown to the ground and lay stunned." He looked at Grant and then Mary. "Northcutt ran over to take him prisoner, but Eckert revived and, still lying on the ground, shot Northcutt with a pistol." He shrugged. "It was a desperate shot, quickly snapped off, but it hit the colonel."

Mary, fear wracking her body, controlled her voice and asked, "And what happened to Eckert? Did you capture him?"

Markwood said, "No, damn it! We should have had him, except for the damnedest piece of work I've ever seen." He gathered his thoughts. "In just a few seconds, a group of the Guides, who had seen Eckert go down, rode up out of the river. The best I can recall, it was an officer, a sergeant, and four dragoons. The dragoons fired at some of the Highlanders who were approaching and forced them to take cover. The sergeant, who was wearing—of all things—the bonnet of a Highland regiment, fired at me, and I scurried back to cover. Meanwhile the officer somehow got Eckert off the ground and mounted behind himself. Then the whole lot rode back across the river, carrying their major to safety."

Mary felt relief flow through her body. *Wend was safe!* Then, to hide her joy, she turned back to Northcutt and began attending to the dressing.

Grant said, "Well, Markwood, I'm sorry things went so bad for you. But we'll take good care of your colonel."

Markwood said, "For that we can be thankful. I'll be in touch with you, Miss Fraser."

Mary briefly turned her face toward the two men and nodded, then focused her attention on Northcutt.

Grant showed Markwood out and shut the door behind himself.

Mary stopped her work and stood shaking. She put her hands to her face and breathed deeply for a long minute to calm herself. As she was doing so, it occurred to her that the sergeant in a bonnet could only have been

Simon Donegal. That thought was comforting: Donegal looking out for Wend, just like the old days. Then, when the shaking subsided, she clasped her hands in front of herself and said a short prayer of thanks for Wend's survival. Afterward, she looked up toward heaven and said out loud, "Oh, Lord, why are you testing me like this? Why must it be my duty to save the life of the very man who tried to kill the one I love? And will do so again if he recovers?" She unclasped her hands, for she knew there would be no answer, and she could only ponder the strange turn of fate that had put her in this position.

Then she went to work to complete the dressing and bandages of the person whom she now despised above all others.

Colleen McGraw said, "Well, Captain Henry, Mr. Shepard is the best tailor I know. He'll make you a fine suite of clothes, and he'll do it with dispatch."

They were in the camp of the Red Vixen Sutler Company. John Henry was leaning back on the side of one of the four great Conestoga wagons that carried the goods of Colleen's business. Edward Childers also stood nearby, his arms crossed, watching the proceedings as he leaned up against the wagon.

Colleen continued, "We need to get you something that will stand up to the rigors of travel and still look presentable when you are reunited with your father, the governor."

Henry shrugged. "Mrs. McGraw, my father knows what I look like. He's seen me in every kind of clothing. He's seen me without any clothing at all. Let's just get it done."

Colleen gave Henry her most severe "*I mean business*" smile. "Now, *sir,*

General Washington said you were to be suitably dressed, and Major Eckert is relying on me to ensure it happens."

Shepard looked sharply at Colleen. "Mrs. McGraw, did you say his father was a *governor*?"

"Indeed, Mr. Shepard. He's the governor of Virginia, which I am told is our largest state." She laughed. "Or colony, whichever you prefer."

"Ah, that would make him *Patrick Henry*, wouldn't it now? The fellow who made that 'Liberty or Death' speech before the war started?"

Colleen nodded. "The very same. It happens Mr. Henry here has finished with his army service and is going home to see his father for the first time in years. And he must leave in a couple of days. Are you up to making him a suit of clothes in that time?" She put her hands on her hips. "Or do I have to find another tailor?"

"Of course, madam. But I shall have to make it my first priority." He smiled craftily. "Which, of course, will entail a *premium* cost. Indeed it will." He raised a finger. "And in hard money. None of that Continental scrip. Or some damned useless army promissory requisition."

Colleen held up a couple of coins. "We are prepared to pay you handsomely, and in hard money."

Shepard's face lit up. "Mrs. McGraw, it is indeed a pleasure to do business with you. That will do most nicely." He reached out to take the money.

Colleen closed her fingers around the coins. "You think I'm a fool? I didn't get where I am by paying in advance. You'll get your money when you deliver that suit. And you'll get less if it isn't here two days hence." She waved toward John. "Now get busy and take Mr. Henry's measurements. And when you are done, we'll take a look at fabrics. We need something of quality and of a color that will look good with that red hair of his."

As that moment, Corporal Billy Wood appeared. He looked around and then said to Childers, "Lieutenant, I got a message for you. The major wants to see you. Posthaste, sir."

"All right, Corporal. Tell him I'll be right there."

—∞—

"You asked me to report, sir?" Edward Childers stood in front of Wend's desk, which was under a canvas fly in front of his hut.

Wend responded, "Yes, Edward, sit down." Then he put aside the paper he had been reading. "I'm assigning you to a special duty. It will be an independent job away from the legion and will require a lot of responsibility on your part."

Childers, having taken his seat, sat up at the edge of his chair. His face reflected great excitement. "What is it, sir? A patrol to see what the British are up to?" He leaned forward. "I heard we were going to start doing that, now that the British are about to leave Philadelphia." He shrugged. "At least, that's the rumor." He smiled. "It will be great to get away from my adjutant's desk!"

"Well, indeed you are going to get away from your desk, but not for a patrol."

Childers's smile disappeared to be replaced with a look of puzzlement. "Not a patrol, sir? Then *what*? I don't understand."

"You are aware that Washington is sending John Henry back to Williamsburg?"

"Of course, sir. I was just over at Widow McGraw's place watching him getting measured for his new clothing."

"Well, Washington wants an officer to accompany him. I discussed it with the general and nominated you. He remembered that he knew your father and agreed you would be a good choice for the duty."

Edward stared straight ahead, a bemused, disappointed look on his face. Then a flash of anger crossed his countenance. "I'm supposed to make sure John goes home? Make sure he doesn't go on the run again? I'm to be his nursemaid? Almost like he's a prisoner?"

"Washington wants to make sure that he actually gets home. He's put a lot of effort into finding and retrieving John. He doesn't want it to be wasted."

Then he looked up at Wend. "But, sir! There's another thing: The summer campaign is about to begin. I would miss part of it!"

Wend sighed. He had expected some reticence by the young man. "You remember our conversation on that ridge above the Millstone River? When I ordered you to lead a small party to safety?"

The young officer nodded.

"Well, this is a similar situation. Hold your gallantry—there will plenty of campaigning for you in the future. And the truth is, *you* are the ideal man for this assignment."

Childers looked like he was about to argue the point, and Wend held up a hand to stop him. "Now listen: You are a longtime friend to John, and you know Dorothea. I'm counting on you to use that friendship—and a measure of tact—to help John accommodate himself to the situation that exists in his family. If there's to be some sort of reconciliation, John's attitude must change before he gets to Williamsburg."

Edward sighed deeply. "Yes, I'll admit there's still a lot of anger in him."

"Exactly. Look, it's going to be a ride of many days. You'll have time to help him come to terms with reality, and I'm counting on you to do that. There will be long evenings at inn common rooms or beside a campfire. That's when your friendship will count for a lot to help change his outlook."

The lad stared down at the ground for a long time. Then he looked up at Wend. "Yes, I can see what you mean." He sighed again. "And I do want John to get over his anger and move on with his life."

"Good lad! Now there's a couple of other things to discuss. First, you'll be carrying a letter from Washington to Patrick Henry—a private, personal letter. You are to ensure that it gets into the governor's hands."

"I understand, sir."

Wend reached into a pocket and pulled out Washington's purse. "And here are funds to pay for the trip to Williamsburg. They come from Washington himself—his personal funds. You are to use it to pay for the expenses of the trip—lodging and food along the way. Try to be as frugal as possible. You may want to spend some nights camping to save money. When you get to Williamsburg, give the remaining amount to John. He'll need it."

"Yes, sir."

There was a pause in the conversation as Wend figured out how to say the next part. Finally he put on as comradely a face as he could manage and leaned forward so as to speak in a confidential, personal manner "Edward, there's something else. It concerns you personally."

"Me, sir? I don't understand."

"Edward, you've been on constant service since we left Winchester. You were the first officer to join the company of light foot, back in early '76, right after the loyalist raid on Eckert Ridge." Wend raised a finger. "That's over two years. Two years, and you've not had any leave since then. Most of the other officers have had some time, usually over the winter encampments, to go home and see their families."

"Well, I'm single."

"Yes, but so is Shay O'beirne, yet he's taken some time off, even if it was to go carousing with tavern maids and unattached young ladies."

Childers brightened up and laughed. "And some not- so-unattached but *very* willing ladies."

Wend grinned knowingly. "Well, there is that." He paused a moment, then continued, "But as I recall, there is a most attractive young lady named Emma, who lives near Williamsburg, for whom you have for years had a measure of affection." He looked meaningfully at Childers. "And who regularly corresponds with you. This would be an opportunity to spend some time with her."

Edward bit his lip, and a thoughtful look took over his countenance. Finally he said, "Perhaps, sir."

Wend said in a stern tone, "Well in any case, I'm authorizing you a period of leave after you get to Williamsburg. And I'm ordering that you use it. How you do that is up to you. You can spend it carousing in taverns or seeing old friends or visiting with Miss Wilbourne, whichever suits your fancy." He paused and looked into Childers's eyes. "However, given the young lady's fidelity to you, I should advise that you perhaps owe her some companionship." He waved his finger at the youth. "In any case, there will be plenty of campaigning left when you do get back."

The lieutenant rose to his feet. "Yes, sir. I understand."

"So go to Captain Bradley and arrange for two strong horses. And then clean up any paperwork you've got on your desk and make a turnover with Ensign Berry—he'll be temporary adjutant during your absence. I expect you'll leave in two days' time."

Captain George Markwood tapped on Major John Andre's door to his office at British headquarters.

"Come," was the muffled answer from inside.

Markwood opened the door and walked inside. He saw Andre attending to papers on his desk, busily writing something on parchment.

Andre looked up, recognition on his face. "Ah, yes, Markwood. Do come in."

Markwood put a hand on a chair and asked, "May I sit down?"

"Oh, please do, George. I assume you have something of importance. You *must* be aware of how busy we are getting ready to march."

Markwood thought, *I've never come to Andre's office when he didn't protest how busy he was.* But he said, "Yes, of course. But what I need to discuss can't wait. It's about the recent expedition up to New Jersey."

"Well, I read your report and passed it on to the general." Andre made a tight smile. "I can't say he was happy about the outcome."

"No, I daresay not."

Andre held up a finger. "And I must say, I deeply regret what happened to poor Northcutt. How is our *dear* friend?"

Markwood laughed to himself. *Yes, I'm sure you are so sorry. And that you consider him a dear friend.* However, he said, "Yes, thank you for your concern. Northcutt is still unconscious after extraction of the ball. Only time will tell about his recovery."

"Indeed, indeed, Markwood." Then Andre put a questioning look on his face. "So what is it you wish to discuss?"

"Well, as you read in the report, we believe that the primary objective of Eckert's detachment was to recover Patrick Henry's son, John."

"Yes, I saw that statement. But I must say, Markwood, that idea seems *most* speculative to me. Northcutt was making a lot of assumptions on that, and in the end you were not able to verify it, given the disaster on the Millstone." Andre smirked. "And to be honest, when I told him, General Clinton found the whole idea quite preposterous."

Markwood stared at the major for a long moment while he controlled his rising irritation. Then said, "Well, my dear Andre, the general will have to suspend his doubt. I have newly received information that confirms the matter." He motioned to the door. "I have someone here I believe you will be glad to meet."

"Who might that be?"

Markwood called out, "Come in, sir!"

A tall, dark-complexioned man emerged from the hall. His overcoat was dusty as if he had been traveling hard by horse, and he wore a wide-brimmed hat pulled down over his forehead.

Andre stiffened. "And who might you be, sir?"

"You may call me by the name of Harkness."

The major stiffened, "Oh, I *may*? And it is *just* Harkness?"

"That's all you need to know."

Markwood noted Andre was staring at Harkness with a frown on his face. "John, Harkness is the leader of our web of watchers and agents in New Jersey and eastern Pennsylvania."

Harkness said, "Given my position, I don't much like appearing in public with officers of the army; I have put out that my political persuasion aligns with the rebels. But I had urgent information that couldn't wait for finding a good courier. So I came myself."

Andre continued to stare at him for a moment, appearing to size up the man, then said quietly, "I quite understand. And pray tell, what is this urgent information that you are bearing?"

Markwood interjected, "He can confirm that the man whom Eckert was after was indeed Governor Patrick Henry's son and that he is in Washington's camp at this moment."

Andre stiffened. "The deuce you say! And just *how* do we happen to know this?"

Harkness said, "I've got a man who has access to Valley Forge. He is a tailor in a small town outside of the city, who does much work for different regiments of Washington's army. He has free run of the camp. He has provided us much useful and reliable information."

Andre nodded. "Excellent. So how did he happen to find out about the man suspected to be Henry's son?"

Harkness looked around the room and, seeing a spare chair, pulled it up with the rear toward Andre. Then he straddled it and sat down. He took off his hat and dropped it on a nearby cabinet. He leaned forward, his hands grasping the chair back, so that he was quite close to Andre. "There's no more *suspecting*. He knows it is Henry's son with great certitude. It happens he was hired by a certain Mrs. McGraw to make a suit for him."

Markwood said, "Mrs. McGraw is a widow who runs a sutler company based on several Conestoga wagons. And she also maintains a bevy of tarts, considered to be the best in the army. And it happens she always camps near the Guides."

Harkness gave the two officers a knowing look. "From what I hear, she's a striking-looking woman of about thirty, with auburn hair. And she's close to Eckert. *Very* close. Visits with him all the time."

Andre raised his eyebrows and cocked his head. A sly grin came over his face. "Are you implying she's his *mistress*?"

Harkness replied, "Shepard says there's many in the camp who think so, considering the amount of time she spends in his bivouac. And Shepard says he's seen her sitting by Eckert's side at the campfire, very cozy like."

Andre asked, "How interesting. Is Eckert married?"

Markwood responded, "Indeed he is. Northcutt's seen his wife and says she's a raven-haired beauty. In fact, he says many consider her the most beautiful lady in the county surrounding Winchester."

A conspiratorial smile came over Andre's face. "Now this is all a bit of information about Eckert that we could find useful in the future."

Markwood said, "Indeed, it is a tantalizing insight into the man. But let us remember that at the moment we need to concentrate on the John Henry aspect. Harkness, tell him about Washington's plans for Henry."

Harkness was about to speak when Andre put his hand to his forehead and interrupted, "Wait a moment: As I recall from your report, Markwood, John Henry was found at an inn in Elizabeth Town, in his cups and selling his personal items to survive."

Harkness replied, "Ah, yes. That's quite correct. It seems that something disillusioned him, and he left the army abruptly." Harkness looked at the other two men. "At any rate, he had no presentable clothing. That's why Mrs. McGraw brought in Shepard to make up a suit for him. And as he was measuring the lad, he overheard talk from Mrs. McGraw and a friend of Henry's, a young lieutenant in the Guides. The gist of it was that Washington is sending him back to his father in Williamsburg." The spy stopped to gather his thoughts. "Then the tailor found out that Henry is to leave Valley Forge in a few days, escorted by one officer."

Markwood commented, "Obviously the officer is to make sure he gets home."

Andre shrugged. "All this is very interesting. And George, you have clearly proved the point that the lad in question is John Henry." He said in an almost mocking tone, "You have my congratulations." Then he raised his hands. "But damn, sir, what does it all matter? We lost the opportunity to seize young Mr. Henry at Millstone River. Why rehash it now?"

Markwood replied, in the tone and manner of a tutor instructing his student. "Because, my *dear* fellow, we now have another chance to snatch young Henry." He motioned to Harkness. "Tell him your idea."

Harkness leaned forward in his seat. "Shepard—the tailor—has learned that the escort for Henry will be the same lieutenant who was at the measuring. And when Shepard returned for the fitting of the suit, the two of them were discussing their travel plans. In short, we know the route they will be taking."

Markwood added, "And we also know when they will leave. At that fitting of the suit, Shepard faked having made a mistake and said he must take it back to his shop to correct it. Then he got word to me. He promised to have it back by tomorrow. So Henry can't leave until then."

Harkness gave a stern look at Andre. "And as Northcutt planned, we can make good use of young Henry if we take him into our possession. We can make it known that the son of one of the most virulent rebels has abandoned the cause. Think of the value of properly framed commentary in news journals, such as a piece entitled 'The Abject Disillusionment and Desertion of Patrick Henry's Son.' It will encourage loyalists and dishearten those of the patriot party."

Andre rose and started pacing back and forth, deep in concentration. Then he stopped and turned to face the other two. "So you are saying we capture the two of them somewhere on the road. But how do you propose doing it? We don't have any real control of the wagon roads south of Philadelphia." He raised his finger. "And a troop of horse would attract considerable attention and likely be intercepted by a rebel patrol or even cause Washington to dispatch his own cavalry to counter us."

Markwood said, "We don't need any damned dragoons. Myself, Harkness, and two of his men will be adequate to overpower Henry and his friend. And we'll travel in regular clothing so as not to attract attention."

Harkness added, "They won't be expecting any trouble. We'll scoop them up and have Henry back here in a couple of days." He leaned back in his chair and smiled for the first time since he had entered the room. "I say Clinton will love the idea. It will erase the embarrassment of the Millstone and turn the whole affair into a triumph for the crown."

Andre stood thinking for a long minute, arms crossed in front of him. Then he looked up. "All right, I will take it to the adjutant general and General Clinton immediately. In the meantime, make your preparations to ride."

Chapter Nine
Complications on the Road

Wend sat at a worktable beside Andrew Horner's wagon. Horner was his former apprentice, now a journeyman gunsmith who traveled with the army to service weapons. It was late afternoon, and the two were working together to make a new pair of pistols for Wend. Horner's wife, Emily, was tending a stew pot at the family fire.

Wend was carving the pistol stocks from blocks of wood while Horner had a metal tube in a vice as he cut it to form a barrel.

Horner looked up from his work and then said to Wend, "That real young colonel—Hamilton—is walking over this way."

Just at that moment Wend heard a voice say, "Well, here you are Eckert. I've been looking for you all over the Guides camp area."

Wend looked up to see Alex Hamilton standing nearby, watching. Without stopping his work he said, "Good day, Alex. To what do we owe the honor of your company?"

Hamilton held up a sheet of paper. "I have orders here. Your copy of orders to the entire army."

"What's up, Alex? We're not marching out for the campaign already?"

"Hardly, Eckert. The British are still firmly ensconced in Philadelphia.

In fact, it's the order for a grand review of the army. A delegation from Congress is coming, and Washington wants to show off how well trained the army has become from Von Steuben's work."

"Pray tell, when is all this to happen?"

"Three days hence. And your legion will be leading the parade." Hamilton grinned. "So you'd better be ready to put on a good show—everyone looking sharp and your drill up to snuff."

"The Guides will be ready." Wend pointed to the end of the table with his knife. "Drop the order there."

The aide-de-camp put the papers down, then asked, "By the way, what the devil are you up to, Eckert?"

Without looking at Hamilton, Wend replied, "Alex, what does it look like? I'm shaping the stocks for new pistols. I lost mine in that skirmish at the Millstone River. And I'm in a hurry precisely because we'll be going on campaign soon."

"You're making the new pistols *yourself*?"

"Alex, may I remind you I am a gunsmith by trade?"

"Actually, I hadn't known. But Wend, for God's sake, the army is full of horse pistols; I should think it would be a simple matter for the commanding officer of the Guides to obtain a pair."

"Indeed it would. However, I dislike horse pistols, at least for my personal use. I prefer lighter ones closer in size and weight to dueling weapons. They're easier to handle. Moreover, my father taught me a family secret about shaping the handles that makes for easier and more precise aim, particularly when you have to shoot in a hurry. It has saved my life more than once, the last time being at the Millstone." He thought a second, then added, "And it saved John Henry's life at the Good Queen Bess Inn."

Hamilton didn't respond at once. Instead he stood thinking, then a sly smile came over his face. "My dear Wend, are you aware that Washington has the idea that it is not proper for officers and gentlemen to engage in manual labor?"

"I don't claim to be a gentleman. I'm a simple mechanic who was foolishly made an officer by the Frederick County Committee of Safety."

The staff officer cleared his throat. "Wend, you should be aware that a couple of years ago—right after the army arrived in New York—Washington, while inspecting the camps, came across the colonel of a newly arrived Connecticut militia regiment with his coat off, cutting the hair of one of his privates." He paused for a moment.

Horner looked up from his work. "So are you saying the general told the colonel it wasn't appropriate?"

"No, much more drastic than that. In fact he ordered the entire regiment to go home. He banished them from the army, on the grounds that the colonel was not acting as a gentleman, and their discipline was inadequate."

Wend stopped his work momentarily and looked up at the young officer. "So you think he would be quite unhappy with me doing work like this? That I'm not behaving as expected by an officer and a gentleman?"

"Indeed! I should say he would think it *most* inappropriate."

Wend looked over at Horner and grinned broadly. Then he turned to Hamilton. "Alex, why don't you go tell the commanding general you saw me working with my hands—carving wood like a simple tradesman." Wend laughed. "And I'll immediately tell Captain Bradley he has command of the Guides, and I'll go to my quarters and pack my bags. Then I'll go home and most happily take up my trade, making muskets and pistols for the army and enjoying the comforts of my good wife and the pleasure of watching my children grow up." He pointed in the general direction of the Potts House. "Yes, go tell Washington immediately."

Hamilton chuckled to himself. "Eckert, you are incorrigible."

Wend wrinkled up his face in puzzlement. "*Incorrigible?* I'm afraid we common tradesmen are not familiar with long words like that. What does it mean?"

Hamilton looked at the heavens and shook his head. "It means you are beyond correction or reformation; you refuse to act in proper form."

Wend looked over at Horner. "Andrew, I *really* like that. I think it describes me perfectly."

Horner grinned and said, "Indeed, sir, it's a fair description, and I'm confident Mrs. Eckert would immediately agree."

Wend laughed. "Horner, you are definitely correct about that."

Hamilton sighed deeply. "We all know that I spoke in jest. Washington isn't going to sack you as commander of the Guides. He relies on you too much, not like some Connecticut militia colonel."

Wend couldn't resist. "Damn my bad luck. Looks like I shouldn't go pack my things after all."

Hamilton was about to speak when he was interrupted by the sound of a woman's voice calling out, "Wend! Wend! We must see you!"

Everyone turned to see Colleen McGraw hurrying toward them, almost at the run. Right behind her was Edna Farley, her main assistant, and Edna's son, Charlie, trailing behind.

Wend called out, "What's the hurry, Colly? You look like the devil is at your heels!"

Colleen responded, "He's not after me, but there are devils after your Mr. Henry and Lieutenant Childers!"

Puzzlement spread over Wend's face. "Devils? What kind of devils?"

"British, that kind of devil!"

Edna arrived, gasping for breath. She pointed to Charlie. "He heard them making plans to take your Mr. Henry on the road!"

Wend looked over at Hamilton, whose face showed distress. Then he asked Charlie, "How did you happen to hear this?"

It was Edna who answered. "Charlie drove me into that village east of the encampment. We was going to buy some supplies for the Red Vixen. And while I was dickering at the store, he went to a tavern nearby. That's where he heard it."

Charlie was nodding vigorously. "That's a fact, Major. I was at the counter, and I heard two men talkin'. At first I didn't listen too closely. There was lots of other people talkin', and they was hard to hear. But then I heard Mr. Henry's name mentioned. So I looked around, and I saw that tailor—Shepard—sittin' at a table with another man."

Wend dropped his carving work and knife on the table and stood up. "So what were they saying about Henry and Childers?"

"They was layin' plans to go after them on the road. Shepard was sayin' he'd gotten Henry's clothes back to him, so they knew he'd be leavin' Valley Forge right soon. Then this other man and some others was goin' to ride and hunt them down."

Hamilton interrupted. "And they didn't spot you?"

Edna replied, "Shepard ain't got no idea who Charlie is. They ain't never been introduced."

Charlie nodded. "That's the truth. I've seen Shepard from a distance, but he ain't seen me 'cept as someone around the camp. Fact is, he looked right at me in the tavern a couple of times but didn't recognize me. I'm sure on that!"

Wend said, "Charlie, tell me what this other man—the one talking with Shepard—looked like."

Young Farley shrugged. "I didn't see much. He was in a dark overcoat, and he had a wide-brimmed hat that he kept on the whole time. He had dark, shifty eyes that kept moving about the room as he talked. He looked at me once, but then just moved on. The look in his eyes didn't match the expression on his face."

Hamilton spoke up. "I've seen that before. I call them 'dead eyes.'"

"Yes, sir, I'd agree with that. They sure enough looked dead to me." Charlie stopped a moment, then smiled. "But I got somethin' else. I got his name. I heard Shepard call him Harkness."

Wend asked, "Did you hear his first name?"

"No, Shepard just called him 'Harkness.' He said it two or three times that I heard."

Wend had heard all he needed. He waved in the direction of his headquarters. "Charlie, run over to our camp and see Ensign Berry, the new adjutant. Tell him to find Captain Fairfield and have him report to me right now." Wend grinned. "Have Berry tell Fairfield I have a job only he can do."

Charlie nodded and took off at a run. Wend looked at Colleen and Mrs. Farley. "Thanks, Edna, you've done us a real service."

Hamilton's face showed his concern. "When did Childers and Henry leave?"

Wend responded, "Just after dawn this morning. They've got a good start, and we don't know where the British party are, or if they've already caught up with them." Then he turned to Hamilton. "Please go tell Washington about this. And also tell him I'll have Fairfield and a squad of his men riding out of here within the hour. Within the hour!"

Hamilton looked at Wend inquisitively. "You're not going yourself? I mean, to make sure Henry is safe? And there may be a tricky situation if the British already have taken them. I should think you would want to handle this personally, after all the trouble you went through up in Jersey."

Wend sat down and picked up his knife. "Alex, Fairfield is the perfect man for this job. Take my word for it: I assure you that before he was in the army, he and his sergeant, Quinn, had a lot of experience finding and stopping people on the road. He'll sniff out this Harkness and his men if it can be done—undoubtedly better than I could." Wend smiled. "And as Washington told me, I need to get my command ready for the campaign. I don't have time to be riding over the countryside." He reached down and picked up the partially carved stock. "And then there's these pistols that need to be finished."

—~—

Major Charles McDonald dismounted and tied the reins of his horse to a hitching post, then went up the steps of the Ridgley House and entered the center hall. A middle-aged nurse was sitting at a desk in what had been the parlor. McDonald told her who he was, then asked to see Mary.

The nurse stood up and said, "She's in with Colonel Northcutt. I'll tell her you are here, sir."

In just a minute, Mary appeared, and her face broke into a smile when she saw him. "Charles! It's so good to see you."

"Mary my Lass, you know I'm always happy to see you. Now is there somewhere we can talk? In private?"

Mary pointed to a door, and they entered an unused room. She turned to face him and motioned to a chair. "Please sit down." She pulled over another chair.

McDonald said, "And how is Northcutt doing?"

"Well, it's been nearly two days since Surgeon Grant extracted the ball from his chest, and he still has not recovered full consciousness. I and the other nurses take turns sitting with him. Once in a while one or both of his eyes open a small amount, just a sliver, and then close again. Then there are periods when he groans softly." She bit her lip. "It's still not clear that he'll fully recover. We keep cleaning the wound, but there is a good chance of mortification."

"It was unfortunate that we could not get a surgeon's attention for him in a more timely fashion."

There were a few moments of silence, then Mary asked, "But Charles, why have you happened by?" Then her face brightened, and she said, "Dare I anticipate you have some news about Wend?"

McDonald made a tight smile. "Indeed I do. But first let me tell you what happened at a ford on the Millstone River." He quickly told her about the skirmish at the river and Wend's survival.

Mary nodded as he spoke, then said, "Charles, I heard a good deal of that from Captain Markwood. But it was good to hear the rest from you."

"Well, Mary, did Markwood tell you I met with Wend and talked with him?"

Mary's face brightened. "No! Not a word! Oh, please tell me about it!"

"Well, before I do, I have something for you. It's from Wend, although a bit indirectly." He held out the box and opened the lid. "Mary, it's one of Wend's pistols. He lost it during the fight."

Mary took a deep breath. "Yes, I recognize it. I've seen it before—long ago at Fort Pitt, in 1763. He showed me his pistols and told me about how he had made them with his father."

"Well, he left both his pistols behind when he was saved by some of his men. And I recovered them later from beside his fallen horse." He smiled. "I've taken the liberty of keeping the other for myself."

Mary nodded. "Indeed, he used one of them to shoot that warrior at Bushy Run. Just as he was swinging his hatchet at your head."

McDonald nodded. "Yes, there's no way to tell which one he used at that moment." He passed the box over to Mary. "But we can each keep one as a memory of him and those days when we marched together."

Mary grinned. She picked up the pistol and carefully held it in her hands, looking at it from different angles. A thrill of emotion ran through her body; *this very firelock had been in Wend's hands jus a few days ago!* She took a deep breath to calm herself, then glanced up at McDonald and said, "Well, there are more scratches and small chips out of it than when I held it before."

"Yes, Mary, I dare say it has had some hard usage over the years. But I tried them out, and I can vouchsafe that they still shoot true."

She held the pistol up and looked at McDonald. "Charles, I shall always be indebted to you for this." Then she put the pistol back in the box and set it on a table beside her chair. "But you said you talked with Wend. Prithee tell me what he said."

McDonald stood up and began pacing the room. "We met on horseback for a parley in the middle of the river. It was for an exchange of wounded prisoners. I took Tavish with me to carry the white flag." He stopped and looked at Mary, a grin on his face. "And who do you think was with Wend?"

"Tell me!"

"None other than Donegal, the old rascal!"

"Simon? It's sure he is serving with Wend?"

"Indeed. Now, Donegal was dressed in one of those backcountry hunting shirts the Americans wear, but damned if he didn't have on his old blue bonnet from the 77th!"

Mary grinned. "Yes, I can picture that. And how was Wend? How did he look?"

"He was shaken up a little from being thrown from his horse but otherwise perfectly fine."

Mary said quietly, "Did you talk to him—aside from the military parley?"

McDonald nodded. "Yes, and that's what I wanted to tell you." He sighed deeply. "I brought up your name and told him what you were doing and that you were still unmarried."

"Oh, what did he say to that?"

"I must say, he was surprised. And then I took a liberty: I told him you were still in love with him."

Mary stiffened. "Charles! You didn't!"

"Yes, and I'm damned glad I did. I told him you were still a spinster because of your devotion to him. And you know it is true." McDonald looked into her eyes. "And here's what you should understand: He was quite bemused that you would still be single and keeping a flame burning for him. He straight out said I should tell you that he is most contentedly married and totally dedicated to his good wife and four children. He made it quite clear that he remembered you fondly, but his youthful passion of fifteen years ago has long ago subsided." He thought a moment, then said, "I vow those are his words so far as I can remember."

McDonald could see the shock in Mary's face. She sat quietly, staring into the distance for a few moments, and then he reached out and gently put his hand on her arm. "Mary, you *must* face reality. Wend has a life of his own, and now you must endeavor to seek the comfort of happiness with a good man and the warmth of your own children."

Mary sat there silent for a long minute. Then she stood up and said, "Charles, I thank you for this pistol and retelling the conversation you had with Wend. And I will think about your advice."

"You are most welcome, my dear. I'm sorry my words could not have conveyed more happiness. But they are the reality."

Mary nodded, then said, "I will be here only a few more days, then I will be returning to the regiment for the march to New York. It will be my pleasure to be reunited with so many close friends." Then she turned to the door. "I must get back to my duties, to relieve the nurse who took my watch."

McDonald bade her farewell, then walked out into the sunlight of the front steps. He stopped there, feelings of guilt overwhelming him. He sighed deeply, mentally castigating himself for the lie he had just told to the woman he cherished like his own daughter. He gritted his teeth and thought, *But damnation, it had to be done. Mary is in the fulsomeness of her womanhood and at the height of her beauty. She must move on from her devotion to Wend Eckert if she is to have the kind of life she has earned with all her determination and hard work. If she is able marry well and raise a family, I will be satisfied to live with having told a falsehood and will be willing to answer for it when I stand before the Lord for judgment.*

And with that Charles McDonald mounted and set off to return to the camp of the Black Watch.

Edward Childers pulled his horse up, and Henry did the same alongside him. Evening twilight was settling around them, and just ahead of them was a small village. He could see a couple of stores, a blacksmith shop, and most importantly, an inn.

"John, the horses are near finished for the day. That inn looks like a likely place to stay for the night, and it has a stable for the horses."

"You'll get no argument from me. We haven't seen anything as inviting along the way. And I hope they have a decent cook."

They rode to the inn's yard and, passing the front door, saw a sign that proclaimed it to be the Fountain Inn.

Henry looked around and said, "Deuced if I can see a fountain anywhere."

"If you're interested, I'm sure the proprietor can educate you. As for myself, a drink, a meal, and I'll be ready for bed."

A young stable boy came to take their horses and the two men, carrying their saddlebags and pistols, went into the inn. After engaging a room on the second floor and dropping their kit, they went back downstairs to the common room for supper.

The room was filled with patrons at the counter and tables. Some were travelers—two tables were occupied by couples and at least one family with children was present. Clearly the Fountain Inn also served as the local tavern, for a number of tradesmen and farmers were at the bar and tables.

The two found an open table and took seats. A young, attractive serving girl soon approached. Smiling broadly, she said, "My name is Deborah. Now what can I do for you gentlemen?" Edward looked her over. She had blond hair showing below her cap, and she wore a very low-cut gown, exposing an eye-catching bosom. She stood looking at them in a coquettish, provocative way, one hand on her hip.

Henry asked, "Do you have any rum?"

The girl threw back her head and laughed. "Where have you been, sir? We've not had any of that for over a year, what with the blockade. But we do have some good whiskey and plenty of ale."

"We'll have the whiskey," answered Childers, glancing over at his friend, who nodded agreement. He looked up at the girl and said, "We've quite gotten used to it."

Deborah put one hand on her hip and said, "Now, we have roasted goose, rump steak, and a stew made o' beef and vegetables tonight. Will you have something?"

Edward asked, "What vegetables?"

The girl gave them a conspiratorial look, glanced back at the cook room, and said in a low voice, "Tell the truth, sir, I never ask them that. They just throw in whatever they got, and I ain't interested in finding out what they be."

Henry shrugged. "Yes, I don't fancy a surprise either. I'll take the rump steak."

Childers said, "And I'll have the fowl." He paused, "And we'll have bread to go with it."

Deborah nodded. "I'll get the whiskey first, then have your food right behind." She turned and walked toward the counter.

The two young men watched her go. Edward said, "She's a neat little bit, isn't she, John?"

"Indeed." Henry thought a moment then continued, "You know, she reminds me of that girl Lilly at Hansen's Tavern, down by William and Mary."

Edward put his hand to his chin. "Now that I think on it, she does indeed." He looked over at his friend. "Wonder if she's still there?"

Henry smiled. "Well, we shall be in Williamsburg soon enough, and you'll have the opportunity to find out." Then a shadow passed over his countenance, and the smile faded away as he reflected on what arrival in Williamsburg would mean for him.

Deborah brought their cups, followed soon after by their plates. The two pitched into their meal with gusto after the long day in the saddle. They were well into their food when suddenly the front door of the inn swung open, and a man stood in just inside, his hand still on the knob and framed by the darkness behind him.

Childers saw that the newcomer was dressed in a long overcoat and wore a broad-brimmed hat. The man was tall and dark-complexioned and had piercing eyes, which darted around the room as if looking for something or someone. Edward felt a chill when the man's eyes stopped at him and lingered for a long moment, seeming to appraise his appearance. Then he shifted his gaze to Henry, and immediately the hint of a smile came over his lips. The stranger looked behind himself and said to someone outside, "George, this is the place we want. Have the horses stabled and come in with me."

The man entered the common room and walked over to the counter. Shortly, another man joined him. He also had on a heavy overcoat. They ordered whiskey and stood together talking quietly.

Edward felt unsettled by appearance of the two men, but he shook off the feeling and went back to his meal. Shortly the outside door opened again, and two more men, dressed for the road, came in and took a table at the far end of the counter.

Henry had also noticed. He looked over at Edward. "A busy place."

Childers shrugged, trying to ignore a sense of anxiety about the men. "It seems many travelers find this a convenient place to stop for the night."

Just after noon, on the second day after Northcutt had arrived at the hospital, Mary was in the reception room at the Ridgely House, talking with Nelly Forster, one of the nurses.

Suddenly Pauline Wells, who had been sitting with the colonel, hurried into the room. "Mary! Mary! He's waking up! Northcutt opened his eyes and looked around the room, then closed them again. But I thought you'd want to know, you being so close to him."

Nelly's face brightened up. "Indeed, Mary! I know you'll be so happy to see him recovering!"

Mary sighed and rose from her chair. "Yes, I'd better go look in on him."

A funny look came over Pauline's face. "Mary, I must say, you don't look very excited to see that the colonel is awakening! I thought you'd be overjoyed. I mean, after he was so near death."

Mary smiled at the other two. "I guess I'm just too weary to show excitement, after the vigil of the last few days. Of course I'm glad to see Barrett recover."

She walked to Northcutt's room and entered, standing at the door for a moment to observe. Barrett was indeed regaining consciousness. She could see him moving restlessly in the bed.

Mary walked over and stood beside the bed, and after a few moments, Northcutt's eyes opened wide. At first they seemed unfocused, but then he blinked several times and looked around the room. Soon they fixed on Mary. The eyes opened wide, and a smile formed on his face. He raised a hand as if to touch her and tried to speak, but only a dry croak issued from his mouth.

Mary quickly said, "Now Barrett, don't try to talk. Your throat is too dry!"

She got two additional pillows and propped Northcutt up. Then she poured him a cup of water from a pitcher on a side table. She made him sip it slowly, even though he was extremely thirsty and wanted to gulp the liquid down. Finally he had had enough and settled back down into the pillows.

Barrett took a deep breath and said just one word, "Mary." Then he closed his eyes and lay peacefully in bed and presently began breathing the deep, regular rhythm of sleep.

She sat with him until the late afternoon when Pauline was due at any time to relieve her to get something to eat and sleep for herself. It was then that Northcutt awakened. His eyes opened wide, and he looked around until he saw Mary. She rose and walked over to the bed. "Can you talk now, Barrett?"

Northcutt smiled, and then said in a slow, halting voice. "Y-e-s. I c-a-n." He reached out and took Mary's hand. "Where am I?"

"You are in the army general hospital in Philadelphia."

"How long have I been here?"

"You arrived in a wagon from New Jersey the day before last. Surgeon Grant and I removed the ball from your chest immediately. Then we could do nothing more but wait to see if you regained consciousness and strength." She forced a smile. "But obviously you are now on the road to recovery."

With great effort Northcutt reached out with his hand and grasped Mary's arm. "Mary, all this time I was dreaming—dreaming one thing over and over again. I was floating in an ethereal place, like being suspended between heaven and earth. It seemed time had stopped." He tightened his grip on her arm and looked directly into her eyes. "But you! *You* were there! I often saw you floating above me like an angel." He stopped and sighed deeply and smiled. "Like my guardian angel!" He stopped again and thought for a moment. "And at other times you were beside me, looking down at me, just as you are now."

"Yes, Barrett, indeed I have been watching over you most of the time. You sometimes opened your eyes a wee bit. Perhaps that is why I appeared in your dreams."

"No, no, Mary! You don't understand. You *are* an angel. I've known that since that night in Halifax when you helped Betsy Loring with her," he hesitated a moment, looking for the right words, "her *female* problem. You are always strong but also tender. And you minister to people in need, providing both physical care and, most importantly, solace for their soul. How could you not be in my mind as I wandered in the clouds?"

"Barrett, you so flatter me. And it is natural for you to feel affection and gratitude after such a terrible, frightening thing happening to you." She adjusted his blanket. "What you need now is sleep."

Northcutt was about to say more when there was a tap on the door, and Pauline peeped in. "Mary, there's a Colonel Stirling here to see you. Actually, to see both you and Colonel Northcutt. Is it all right for him to come in?"

Mary turned to Northcutt. "Do you feel up to seeing Colonel Stirling?"

"I'd rather be just with you, but it would be impolite not to see him." Then he grinned broadly. "And Thomas and I have indeed enjoyed some memorable evenings around the card table, back in New York in the early '60s."

Mary turned back to the door. "All right, Pauline, have him come in."

Colonel Thomas Stirling stepped into the room. He looked first at Mary, then at Northcutt. "Well, Barrett, you look a little banged up but in remarkable condition for a man who took a ball to the chest just a few days ago."

"Yes, I am lucky." He looked at Mary. "But with Miss Fraser's tender care and the good offices of the physicians, I should be in good form in due course."

"Well, unfortunately you will have to deal with some time in a wagon during your convalescence."

Northcutt looked puzzled. "I'm not sure what you mean."

"I've just come from Clinton's headquarters. The date for the move to New York City has been set. The army will begin leaving on June 18. The 42nd has been assigned to General Grey's brigade. We'll immediately begin moving from our billets here in the city to encamp on the northern outskirts in preparation for the march. Some other units of the army will go by ship, as will most of the loyalist civilians. Cornwallis will have the command of our division while marching to New York." He looked over at Mary. "I'm told the general hospital will travel overland."

Northcutt said, "Thank God for that. I have a terrible time on the ocean, and I'd rather take my chances in a wagon."

Mary responded, "We've been preparing for the march. And I've got to finish my preparations, so that I can rejoin the regiment, as was arranged between Surgeon Potts and Doctor Morris."

Stirling nodded. Then he and Northcutt exchanged pleasantries for a few more minutes. Finally, Stirling said, "Well, Barrett, I'll let you rest. I must get back to my headquarters to make plans for the move. But I shall see you in New York, and hopefully you will be far enough along in your convalescence to engage in games of chance!"

"Indeed, I have no doubt Thomas. Just make sure you have adequate funds ready."

"Always, Barrett." Stirling opened the door, then looked back at Mary and signaled for her to come with him into the hall.

She joined him and shut the door behind her. "Did you want to talk with me?"

"Indeed, Mary. It's about your return to the regiment."

"Yes, I'll be back in just a few days now."

"Well, I'm well aware of the arrangement between Surgeon Potts and Morris. What I wanted to say was that I also appreciate how close you have become to Barrett and how frequently he has escorted you to social occasions." He smiled and put his hand on her arm. "Much as we would miss you, I want you to know that you are free to remain with the general hospital for the journey to New York, so that you can administer to Barrett. Your decision to do that would be completely understandable."

Mary felt rising panic and stiffened. She had been living for the day she could return to the 42nd hospital. It had helped her get through the days beside Northcutt. Her mind raced as she tried to think of how to respond. "Colonel, I believe Barrett is showing that he is very strong. And there are many fine nurses here at the general hospital. I believe my services will be much more valuable at the regimental hospital, particularly if the rebel forces engage our column after we leave Philadelphia. And while I'm grateful to Colonel Northcutt for his kindness to me during the time here in the city, I consider my duty to my fellow Scots much more pressing." She thought a moment. "And of course, I'm expected to return to the general hospital after we reach New York, so I will be able to help Barrett finish his convalescence then."

Stirling smiled in a benevolent manner. "Mary, I'm proud of you. In my experience, you have always put the needs of the regiment over your own personal desires. We all look forward to having you with us again in just a few days."

Mary felt relief flow through her body. "As do I so look forward to being with close friends again."

Stirling nodded. "Well then, that's settled. Now I'm off to my headquarters, for there's much to do before we march."

Edward Childers finished up his roasted goose and looked over at John Henry. "Well, I propose we have another cup of the whiskey and then retire for the night. We need to push on right at dawn tomorrow."

Henry nodded. "I will second that motion. I'm quite ready for a peaceful night."

Edward looked around for Deborah and saw her at the end of the counter. He waved to her and held up his cup. The girl smiled her understanding.

She was just walking toward them with two new cups on a tray when the stranger in the broad-brimmed hat swiftly walked from the bar, followed by the man who had accompanied him into the inn. He took the two cups off the tray that Deborah was carrying and said to the girl, "We'll deliver these." Then he turned to face their table and said, "Gentlemen, we're going to join you for a little talk."

Childers responded, "I don't seem to remember inviting you to take a seat at our table." He thought, *Damn, I shouldn't have left my pistols in the room.*

The stranger laughed and retorted, "I'm certain you didn't invite us. Nevertheless, we *will* join you."

The two men sat down. Childers, stifling the feeling of fear rising inside, asked, "May we have your names?"

"My name is Harkness," replied the man in the broad hat." He looked over at his companion. "And this is George Markwood." He smiled slyly. "Actually, *Captain* Markwood of the Loyal Virginia Legion, seconded to the British general staff."

Edward said, "And do you have a first name, Mr. Harkness?"

"It's just Harkness."

Markwood spoke up. "Gentlemen, we are quite certain that we are in the company of Mr. John Henry, lately captain in the Continental Artillery, and a certain Lieutenant Childers of the Guides. Am I not correct?"

Childers felt a knot forming in his stomach. "Perhaps. Why does that matter?"

Markwood looked directly at John. "It matters because you have an appointment with General Clinton, who is particularly eager to have a friendly Tête-à-Tête with the son of Virginia's governor."

Edward said, "And what if neither my friend nor I have any interest in waiting upon the general?"

Harkness slowly opened the front of his greatcoat, to show the butts of two pistols. "We suspected you might have some reticence to coming with us. So, as you can see, we came prepared with instruments of persuasion."

As he spoke, Markwood opened his greatcoat, and Childers could see his uniform underneath. He also had a pair of pistols.

After he had opened his coat, Markwood waved his hand in the direction of the counter. "We also have additional persuasion in the form of some compatriots."

Childers and Henry turned to see the two other men, both now showing their own pistols.

Markwood cleared his throat. "So now we are all going to get up together, leave the inn, and take horse back to the city. It would be preferable if all this were done without any unpleasantness."

Henry sighed. "What about our things—they're in a room upstairs. Can we go up and get them?"

Harkness laughed. "Never say we'll deny you the comfort of your kit. But just tell me the room number, and we'll have them fetched for you."

Childers and Henry looked at each other. Edward said, "John, I'm sorry things turned out this way." Then he looked over at Harkness and said, "Our room number is—"

But before he could get the rest out, the common room door was flung open and banged loudly against the wall. Everyone in the room stopped talking and turned to look at the source of the disturbance.

Standing in the door was a dragoon officer. He wore a short gray jacket with green facings, white breeches, and black leather boots reaching up to just below his knees. A saber hung at his left side. On his head was a black leather helmet. Immediately after entering the room, he removed the helmet and dropped it carelessly on a nearby table.

Harkness and Markwood whipped out their pistols. Harkness pointed his pistol at the newcomer and said, "Stay where you are!"

The dragoon said in an even tone. "I shouldn't dream of moving."

Markwood said, "Who are you, sir?"

The dragoon officer didn't immediately answer. Instead, he pointed at the drawn pistols. "Gentlemen, I urge your caution. Those damn things can go off unexpectedly in the heat of a moment like this." Then he shrugged. "I am Captain Geoffrey Fairfield, of Wando River Farm in South Carolina, and I have the honor of commanding the 1st Troop of the Palmetto Light Horse." He smiled broadly. "Currently assigned to the Legion of Continental Guides." He nodded and touched his forehead in an informal and jaunty salutation.

Around the room, the patrons, who had been silent watching the scene progress, came alive. "By God, the Guides! Washington's Guides! What are they doing here?"

When the buzz quieted down, Fairfield said, "Now, I might ask the same question: Who might you gentlemen, perchance, be?"

Edward spoke up before either could answer. "Geoffrey, they're British!" He motioned toward the two. "One says his name is Captain George Markwood." Childers pointed directly at Harkness. "The other said his name is 'just' Harkness. And they're here to carry us off to Philadelphia as prisoners."

Fairfield smiled broadly. "Now, Mr. '*Just Harkness*,' that's *quite* an intriguing name. Very mysterious and all that."

Harkness said, “Damn it, Fairfield, let’s stop playing word games. It must have occurred to you that there are the pistols of four men aimed at you. And that you are our prisoner as well as these two.”

Fairfield raised his eyebrows, then said in a calm tone. “Yes, let’s discuss that question in a civil manner.” Then he went to reach into the breast of his jacket.

Markwood raised his pistol. “Keep your hand in view! I’ll shoot!”

Fairfield raised a hand dismissively. “Sir, that is *quite* unnecessary. As you can observe, I am carrying no pistols.” Then, calling Harkness’s bluff, he reached into the breast of his jacket and pulled out a long, thin cigar. “You see, I was only getting one of these. It’s of very fine Virginia tobacco, rolled by good ladies down in the Tidewater.” He motioned it toward the two British. “I have more. Would you gentlemen care to have one?”

Harkness said, “What the devil do you think you are doing?”

Fairfield grinned. “Why, it should be obvious. I’m going to smoke the cigar. I find tobacco is very soothing at tense moments like this.” Then he looked around and saw Deborah standing at the counter. “Miss, would you be so kind as to get me a lighted taper from over there at the hearth? I’d do it myself, but I prefer not to take my eyes off those men with all the firelocks pointed at me.”

Deborah said in a plucky voice, “Here, I can do better than that.” She picked up a lighted candle from a holder on the wall and walked over to Fairfield. He put the cigar in his mouth and leaned down slightly for her to light it.

But Deborah reached up and plucked the cigar from his mouth. “Please, sir. I find it much easier this way.” She put the cigar in her own mouth and touched it with the flame, drawing deeply until she had it going well, then quickly handed it back to Geoffrey.

Fairfield looked at her and remarked, "Now Miss, my complements. In addition to your beauty, you seem to be a lass of many talents."

She flashed him a provocative smile and answered, "I've been told that before, sir. For one reason or another. But never by a gentleman from Carolina." Then she walked back to her place at the bar.

Markwood had grown impatient. "Now, sir, we have had enough of this charade." He stood up and said, "We are going to leave with these two." He pointed toward Henry and Childers.

Harkness also rose and said to the two of them, "Gentlemen, get up."

Fairfield took a long drag on his cigar and then expelled the smoke. "I'm afraid I cannot permit that." He motioned to Childers with his cigar. "You and Henry stay exactly where you are."

Markwood brandished his pistol at Fairfield. "Sir, you are quite impudent for a man in your position, without pistols at hand."

"Well, I may not have a brace of pistols as you gentlemen each hold, but I have something better."

Harkness asked, "Better? What the devil are you talking about?"

"A brace of sergeants." He called out in the direction of the door that led to the interior of the inn and called out, "Quinn! Are you there?"

Upon cue, the door opened, and Sergeant Quinn appeared, holding a pistol in each hand. All eyes turned to look.

Then Fairfield turned toward the counter and called, "McCrae! Time for you to join us!"

McCrae stepped out into the common room from the doorway of the cook room. Everyone's head swiveled to see the new arrival. He was similarly armed as Quinn and took position where he could cover Harkness's compatriots.

"Now, gentlemen," said Fairfield waving toward his right, "Let me introduce you to Sergeant Quinn, late of His Majesty's 11th Dragoons." He shook his head. "Nasty-looking fellow, isn't he? What with that scar along his left cheek and then, of course, there is the ear with the lower half missing." Then he pointed to the left. "And this is Sergeant Freddie McCrae, who by no small coincidence is also a former member of that august fighting corps, the 11th Dragoons." He grinned. "The two were great friends in that regiment, and I assure you both are excellent shots with a horse pistol, particularly at this range."

Then Fairfield called out again. "Trumpeter Bloom! Now's the time for your grand entrance."

Bloom casually walked in through the open outside door, and after a moment he was followed by four more men. All were holding pistols.

"Now, gentlemen," said Fairfield to Harkness and Markwood, "*Now* would be the appropriate time for you to realize there is no way out of here for you alive, save dropping those pistols and becoming *my* prisoners." He waved his hand in a sweeping motion to take in the common room and all its occupants. "Besides, my experience is that exchanging fire in such a confined area is a nasty business and would almost guarantee that some of these good citizens suffer injury or worse. So I beg you, on your sense of gentlemanly honor, to take this opportunity to submit."

Suddenly Harkness grabbed Henry by the collar and jammed his pistol against the side of the young man's head. "You're wrong. There's one way out. That is for you to back off and allow all of us with the governor's son to leave unharmed. If you don't, I'll not hesitate to pull the trigger! Now I say move aside and let the five of us depart."

Fairfield shook his head. "Mr. '*Just* Harkness,' I'm most disappointed with you. Cold-blooded assassination of a governor's son? I must say that's quite ungentlemanly behavior."

Markwood dropped his pistol onto the floor. "Harkness! I quite agree. We have only one choice, and that is to surrender."

"Damn you, Markwood! To hell with gentlemanly behavior!" Harkness yanked on Henry's collar to get him moving. He called out to the other two compatriots, "Let's get out of here!"

But before he could take a step, a pistol shot rang out. Harkness's pistol fell out of his hand, and he sagged to the floor, hit in the side. Everyone looked in the direction from which the shot had come, to see McCrae's pistol smoking.

But Harkness wasn't finished. One firelock had dropped to the floor beside him, and he grabbed the weapon and pointed it at Henry. "Damn it, I'll shoot!" He began trying to push himself up with his other hand.

In the blink of an eye, Deborah sprang forward from the counter, tray in hand. She came up behind Harkness and swung it down hard, deftly hitting his gun hand and sending the pistol scooting along the floor. Fairfield stepped forward and grabbed it.

"Nicely done, Miss Deborah!" Fairfield looked over at McCrae. "Great shot, Sergeant!"

"Hell, sir, I was aiming to kill him, but the bastard moved just as I pulled the trigger."

Fairfield shrugged. "All the same, well done." Then he looked toward the counter. "Where is the proprietor of this fine establishment?"

A chubby, balding man in an apron stepped out from behind the bar. "That's me, Josiah Fountain, sir."

Fairfield said, "Ah, yes. Now do you happen to have a place where we could lock these four miscreants for the night?"

Fountain nodded vigorously. "Indeed I do. There's the cellar. It's got a bar on the door. I can show you the way."

"Not me—show Sergeant Quinn, who will shepherd our prisoners down there for a cozy evening."

Markwood motioned toward Harkness. "This man needs medical attention."

Fountain said, "There's an apothecary in the village who does doctoring. I'll send for him."

Fairfield beamed. "There you are, Markwood. Never say that the Guides don't take care of the wounded after the action." He turned to Quinn. "Now, Sergeant, get these four down to the cellar and post a guard at the door."

As Quinn led the British off, Childers came over to where Fairfield stood. "I don't understand how those men knew to come here for us. And more important, how did you know about those men?"

Fairfield put his hand on Childers's shoulder. "It seems you were spied on, in our very camp." He quickly explained about the tailor and how young Charlie Farley had discovered the plot.

Having finished, Fairfield said, "Now my young lad, it's time for you and John to retire for the night. You've had enough excitement for one day, and you need to be on the road tomorrow at first light." Then he looked over at the counter where Deborah stood. "And I must spend some time with Miss Deborah to make sure she understands my gratitude for her actions this evening." He thought a moment, winked at Childers, then added quietly, "And find out what other talents she possesses."

Chapter Ten
Decisions

Barrett Northcutt was propped up in his bed at Ridgely House, bored stiff at being forced to remain bedridden. Grant, the surgeon, had come in to take a look at him earlier in the morning. He and the nurse Pauline had removed the dressing from his wound, inspected the progress, and then applied a new dressing and bandage. The doctor had proclaimed that the healing was going well, with no mortification visible. But of course, recovery would be a matter of weeks.

Now Northcutt was alone and dealing with the constant aching in his chest. He had to remain still, for any movement of his upper body aggravated the chipped and bruised rib and sent a wave of pain through his body.

Then there was a knock on the door, and Pauline looked in. "Colonel, you have a visitor. It's Major Andre. Do you feel up to seeing him?"

Northcutt sighed. He hadn't seen Andre since before the mission to capture Henry. Undoubtedly the major was coming to gloat over the failure. But he vowed he wouldn't give the staff officer the pleasure of seeing him frustrated. "Of course, nurse, send him in."

The dandy major strode into the room. "Ah, my *dear* Barrett. So *glad* to see you. And the nurse tells me the good news that you are doing well. Very well indeed." He smiled and continued, "All of us at the staff have been so worried about you."

"Ah, yes, John. I'm sure they are, and you can't know how comforted I am by your words."

"Indeed, sir, I knew you would be." Andre walked over to the window and looked out at the traffic in the street. "Of course, to be honest, there was much disappointment at the outcome of your mission." He shrugged. "It seemed so promising when we discussed it that night at the Mischianza. A pity how things turned out."

"I understand. But in war, one must always be aware that the outcome is never certain."

"Of course, Barrett, of course," Andre said in a soothing voice. Then he turned from the window and looked at Northcutt. "But this may surprise you: it happens that we may still succeed in laying our hands on young Mr. Henry."

"What? How can that be?" In his astonishment, Northcutt took a deep breath and moved in the bed. He was immediately stabbed by a sharp pain. His face registered the agony.

Andre stepped forward. "Are you all right, my dear Barrett? Should I call the nurse?"

Northcutt held himself perfectly still for a moment, and the pain passed. "No, no, I'm fine. But how is it that you think Henry can yet be captured?"

"Well, it happens that your assistant—Captain Markwood—came to me in the company of a devilishly sinister man, called simply by the surname Harkness."

"Yes, he works for me. He leads a wide net of spies and watchers. You may consider him sinister, but he is very good at what he does. And of course, his name isn't actually Harkness."

"Indeed. I'm sure it all goes with the business. In any case, by a stroke of luck, one of his men, a tailor named Shepard who works out of a village near Valley Forge, was called on by the rebels to make up a wardrobe for Henry. And, as it happens, he overheard the plans for Henry's travel back to Virginia along with the expected day of departure. Harkness proposed intercepting him on the road south." He looked down and smiled at Northcutt. "I was pleased to take the plan to Clinton, who immediately approved it, as a neat way of reversing the unfortunate outcome of your mission." He paused to let that sink in, then said, "Markwood, Harkness, and some of their cohorts rode out a couple of days ago to intercept Henry and another officer accompanying him."

Northcutt asked, "And have they captured him?"

"They're not back yet, although I expect them any time now. Henry couldn't have gotten far."

"Well, I'm sure the general will be delighted to see young Henry in our possession."

"Yes, I look forward to seeing Clinton's face when I escort the young man into his presence." He glanced at Northcutt. "I'm so sorry you can't be there to witness it."

Barrett took a deep breath, which hurt, then said as pleasantly as he could manage, "Yes, I'm *quite* sure you are, John."

There was a prolonged silence in the room, and Andre was about to respond when there was a tap on the door, and it swung open to reveal Mary Fraser standing in the hall. She was dressed in a traveling bonnet, a blue gown, and a black cloak. She looked first at Andre, then at Northcutt. "Am I interrupting? Should I return later?"

It was Andre who answered. "Please come in, Miss Fraser. I know how much Barrett would like to see you."

Northcutt smiled and said, "By all means, do come in, Mary."

Andre made a small bow to her. "Miss Fraser, you do look lovely, as you always do. And since I never got the chance to say so, let me complement you on how stunning you were in your gown at the Mischianza." He looked over at Northcutt. "Don't you agree, Barrett?"

"Of course. Naturally, I made that clear to Mary that evening."

Mary smiled at Northcutt. "Indeed you did, Barrett."

Andre looked back at Mary. "And I'm not the only one who felt that way. I saw the eyes of many young officers stealing glances at her, and then at you, Barrett, with envy in their eyes."

Mary said, "I'm most flattered by your compliments, Major."

Andre nodded and then looked over at Northcutt. "And at least one officer went beyond simply glancing at Miss Fraser. While you lingered behind after our meeting with Howe and Clinton, making your plans for the expedition with Markwood, it seems Captain Tarleton took the opportunity to ask for a dance with Miss Fraser. And I must say, there were many eyes on them when they were out on the floor. They made such a lovely couple."

Mary looked over at Northcutt. "I met Captain Tarleton last year in New York. It seemed only polite to accept his invitation while you were busy, Barrett."

Barrett smiled. "Of course, Mary. How could I object while I was leaving you alone so long in the ballroom?"

Andre said, "Well, I should leave you two alone to visit." He picked up his hat, then bowed to Mary again. "My deepest respects to you, Miss Fraser." He went to the door, but then turned back to Northcutt. "Barrett, I'll let you know about developments in the matter we were discussing." With that he left the room.

Northcutt looked at Mary. "I'm so glad to see you, Mary. You have not been about as much as previously."

"Well, I had to finish up my preparations for the general hospital to travel. I've done that, Barrett, and that's why I'm here. I must say goodbye. I'm going back to the regiment."

"Must you depart so soon? It's damned boring, just lying here, and I so enjoyed you sitting with me."

Mary moved close to his bedside and said, as cordially as she could manage, "I must get back in time to help them prepare for the campaign. And besides, you know I'll be coming back to the general hospital after we arrive in New York. So this is just goodbye for now."

Northcutt looked up at her and nodded. "I understand. Well, at least you can spend some time with me today. The days will be long until I see you again."

Mary shook her head. "I'm afraid not, Barrett. I must go see Betsy Loring off. She is taking ship this afternoon, and I have promised her I would ride down to the quay with her."

Northcutt was silent for a long moment. "What about Howe? Won't he be there to see her off?"

"No, Barrett, he sailed for New York, and thence to England yesterday. They had already made their farewells. And Betsy now is abandoned by virtually everyone who used to say they were her friend. I feel it my duty to be with her in these last hours before she leaves America, perhaps never to return."

Northcutt sighed deeply. "Then I shall reconcile myself to solitude until New York. In the meanwhile, Mary Fraser, take care. I worry about your safety so near the scene of action."

Mary looked off into the distance. "I have lived in a marching regiment most of my life. You must realize I know how to take care of myself and trust in the Lord's provenance. So may He be willing, I will see you in New York." She reached down and touched his hand, and then she was gone.

Barrett listened as her footsteps faded down the hall, and then there was the sound of the house's front door closing as she stepped outside. He shuddered as he contemplated the possibility that she might be leaving his life.

He lay there, recalling Mary's recent behavior. He reflected, *There's been a definite coolness toward me since I arrived in hospital. Clearly she knows it was Eckert who shot me—undoubtedly McDonald told her what happened and that I attempted to kill him. It probably disgusts her to be with me, although it has been her duty as a nurse.* Northcutt lay there, thinking hard. Reality hit him like a thrown rock: as things stood presently, his continued pursuit of Mary was probably futile. In frustration he pounded the mattress with his hand, and instantly pain wracked his entire upper body. When it had subsided, he was able to think again. Then it came to him: There was only one way for him to again find favor with Mary. Eckert must be taken out of the picture permanently. Would that Eckert died in the coming campaign—it was always a possibility, for Eckert and the Guides were usually in the forefront of action. But he couldn't leave that outcome to chance—the Virginian was nothing if not a survivor. No, he, Barrett Northcutt, would have to *make* it happen. The question was *how*. He thought, *I have always been able to manage events in my favor. I did it with business when I first arrived in the colonies, I did it while in the service of Lord Dunmore, and now I will do it in the course of this war. Sooner or later, I will find a way to achieve the finish of Wend Eckert and ensure that it is done in a way that doesn't indicate my hand in it. Then I will be there to console Mary and make her realize that her best life lies in marriage to me.*

Northcutt was still contemplating all that when weariness overcame him, and he dropped off into deep sleep.

—ꟿ—

The morning dusk was coming on rapidly at the Fountain Inn as Sergeant Freddie McCrae stood holding the horses while Childers and Henry secured their saddlebags and other kit to the saddles of the two animals. McCrae had sent Bloom up to fetch Geoffrey Fairfield, who wanted to see the two men off.

The sergeant smirked and said to Childers, "It may take Bloom a while to get our captain down here, for there's na doubt he's had a busy night with that young tart."

At that moment, Childers heard the door of the inn open and looked around to see the dragoon captain emerge. He was in his shirtsleeves, the white of his shirt standing out in the semidarkness, and his hair was astray. Clearly he had come directly from bed. Then behind Fairfield he saw Deborah, a cloak over her night clothes against the morning chill, her blond locks down around her shoulders. She stayed in the doorway, leaning up against the sill, arms crossed in front of her, watching the proceedings. A wry smile was on her face.

Fairfield asked McCrae, "Are they ready to ride?"

"Ready as we can make them, Cap'n."

Fairfield walked over to where Childers stood. "Now listen, lad, I want to give you some advice. I've had a bit of experience in traveling the roads without exposing myself to unwanted eyes."

McCrae laughed out loud. "I can vouch for that!"

Fairfield shot the sergeant an irritated glance, then looked back at

Childers. "Now take my advice, Edward. Don't stay at inns or taverns until you get out of Pennsylvania. Ride around towns and villages when you can. Camp in secluded areas off the road and shield your fire from view as much as possible. And keep your pistols close at hand."

Edward asked, "Are you saying there may be more British after us?"

"I don't have any direct knowledge of that, but it's possible. And there may be bands of partisans or local militia suspicious of two men traveling alone who might give you unwanted attention."

McCrae interjected, "Not to mention the chance of highwaymen, which our fine captain knows much about."

Fairfield snapped at the sergeant, "McCrae, that's enough."

At that moment Bloom emerged from the inn, carrying two canvas bags.

Fairfield pointed to the bags and said, "I've arranged for provisions enough to keep you going for a few days."

Bloom helped the two young men strap the bags to their saddles.

When they were done, Fairfield put his hand on Henry's shoulder. "Now lad, I'm going to offer you a bit of counsel. It's sure you're going to have a hard moment with your father when you get to Williamsburg. But don't be cowed or apologetic, for if anyone owes an apology, it is Patrick Henry. You are a grown man, and you need to deal with him as one. Beyond that, he's got the woman, and nothing you can do will ever change that. So put all that behind you and work things out with your father so you can both go ahead. And then find a woman who knows how to please you and make a life for yourself."

John Henry looked at Fairfield for a long moment, then said in a determined tone, "I hear you, sir. And thank you for your advice."

Fairfield gave Henry a pat on his arm, then turned to Childers. "Now,

Edward, no more delay. You need to do many miles before the day is through. And when you get to Williamsburg, go see that girl who has been writing you all the letters. And I'll see you back with the Guides in a few weeks."

Childers nodded and smiled. "Indeed, Geoffrey!" Then he and Henry mounted, brought their horses up to a cantor, and rode off with a wave.

Fairfield looked over at his two sergeants. "Ah, youth. Would I were that young again. I vow, I'd make some different choices."

Quinn gave him a knowing look. "No, you wouldn't. You'd be just what you've always been. A rogue and a highwayman."

"I'll second that," said McCrae.

Fairfield shrugged and grinned. "Perhaps there is some truth in what you say."

The two sergeants and Bloom watched the two riders for a moment longer, then the three walked back to their billet in the inn's yard.

Fairfield went to the door and wrapped his arm around Deborah's waist, pulling her close and looking into her eyes. "Now, my beautiful lass, let's get back upstairs and finish what we were about."

Deborah ran her hand through her hair and laughed. "Sir, you'll have to be quick about it, for I'm due in the kitchen soon, and if I'm not there, Mr. Fountain will be after me with a stick."

"Then let us not waste a second."

—m—

As Mary Fraser approached the house on Walnut Street, she saw a wagon parked at the front. Two men were loading it with chests and trunks, talking and joking as they worked. They stopped and touched their hats to her as she arrived. She acknowledged their greeting and went up the steps and tapped on the door, which was immediately opened by Betsy Loring's maid, who showed her to the drawing room.

Betsy sat in a cushioned chair, a wine glass in her hand. When she saw Mary, she put the glass down and rose to embrace her and held her close for a long moment. "Dear Mary, I'm so glad we could be together one last time. And that you could make time to see me down to the waterfront."

"Don't be silly, Betsy! How could I not come today after how close we have become over the last two years?"

"Yes, I'm glad you came for that reason, Mary. But there's another reason I wanted to be with you this one final time." She paused, settled herself in her chair, and took a deep sip of her wine.

Mary saw that her eyes were red and detected a tear in one eye. "Why, Betsy, you've been crying!"

"Why shouldn't I cry? I'm leaving the colonies, where I've spent my entire life, and taking my children to England—what to all of us is a strange land. And who knows when, if ever, I shall return? Who knows the outcome of this cursed war?"

"I think you'll feel better once you are aboard ship and on your way. It's always difficult at the beginning of a journey; so much is uncertain." Mary thought a moment. "And of course, you have just said goodbye to General Howe, your friend and benefactor for so long."

Betsy made a thin smile. "How diplomatic of you, Mary, to put it that way. 'Friend and benefactor.' You always put such a delicate touch on things." She took a very deep breath. "But that is what I want to talk to you about, before we depart. I want to explain why I became the general's consort; I want you to understand why I did such a thing."

Mary shook her head. "Betsy! I've *never* questioned your motives. I've seen too much of the world and the army to do that. You don't have to explain to me."

"No, I don't have to, but I feel I must. And in any case, we have time until my carriage arrives. I want to sail knowing you understand how I became the general's—she paused for a long time staring into the distance—how I became the general's whore."

"Betsy!"

"That's what they call me, isn't it? I've seen the journal articles, the broadsides. I've overheard people talking. They say I am *Cleopatra* to his *Antony*. I'm the general's *little filly*. I'm the *doxy* who keeps him entertained. *Mistress* is by far the nicest word they use." She took more wine. "Some even say I am the reason William has hasn't struck the rebel army harder when they were in confusion or retreat. They say he's too busy with me at the card table or taking the comfort of my bed to attend to his duty to extinguish this rebellion."

Mary stared down at her hands while Betsy spoke, then looked up. "Nobody in the army thinks that the general has not prosecuted the war to his utmost. Look at the affection the officers showed Sir William at the Mischianza."

"Yes, yes, those close to him know the truth: that he has persisted in believing that he should treat the rebels with forbearance so as to make the ultimate reconciliation easier. And he has told me in private that he often hesitated to order direct assaults because of what happened at Bunker Hill, back at the siege of Boston. The slaughter of our soldiers that occurred there hangs heavy on his mind. He's confided to me that the rebel army lacks discipline and the knowledge of proper tactics and are easily driven away in the open field. But put them behind a stone wall or in trenches at the crest of a hill or in deep forest cover, and they will stand firm and serve our men with a fearsome fusillade of fire. He dreads sending his men against such mortal danger. England does not have enough soldiers to waste them in costly assaults. Look at how many German soldiers we have had to pay to assist us. He prefers to confound the enemy by tactical maneuvers that defeat them while conserving the lives of our soldiers." She shook her head. "But those who criticize William don't understand that or intentionally ignore it in order to bring him down. And instead, I am targeted as the cause of it all."

"Betsy, you must put this all behind you. A new life lies before you and your children. Try to shake off all this gossip."

Betsy looked at Mary. "Shake it off? How? Word of my relationship with Howe has spread to England. I have heard that even King George—the king himself—knows my name and my reputation! Where can I go where people will not look askance at me?" She took another sip of the wine, then said, "I beg you listen. Here is how all it began and why I have done it all."

Mary leaned close to her and put a hand on her arm. "Of course I will listen if you feel it will help."

"Yes, yes, it will. It will help my soul. Now listen: It began in the spring of 1775. Joshua and I were secure in our fortune; we stood to inherit a share of my family's shipping business, and Joshua had been appointed both the high sheriff of Massachusetts and also the deputy surveyor of the forest in New Hampshire." She sighed. "Both appointments conferred power and a very comfortable amount of compensation." She smiled thoughtfully. "We had just built a new house in the country, about five miles outside Boston." She bit her lip, and a frown crossed her face. "Then, in mid-April, Joshua, who was in Boston carrying out his duties, called for me to join him. He wanted to give me information about the restlessness among the country folk and how I should act to try to avoid trouble. So I took to my carriage and brought my oldest child, Liza, who was five, with me. I left my twin boys, Wentworth and Joshua, who were not yet two years old, in the care of the governess at the house."

Tears appeared in Betsy's eyes. "But that led to a great misfortune. I was in Boston when our soldiers marched out to look for the weapons that the colonists were hoarding at Concord. After the battles at that town and Lexington, the rebels laid siege on the city. I was trapped and cut off from my sons!"

"How terrible for you!"

"That was far from the worst. The rebels, because of Joshua's position as sheriff, took the twins into custody and burned our house." She put her hand to her eyes, then said, "So in one fell swoop I lost my dear boys and our home."

"You must have been desolate."

"That is far too mild a word. I was insane—literally insane—with worry over the boys. Joshua put me in touch with a cousin of his, a young lady of intelligence and courage, who was able to get through the lines disguised as a country woman. In a few days, she was back but brought terrible news. The boys had been put in the care of a kindly couple. But both had somehow contracted a fever." Betsy took a deep breath and wiped her eyes again. "And little Joseph had succumbed to it." She stared into the distance for a long moment. "Poor Joseph! My precious little boy had gone to eternity without even the comfort of his mother holding him as he breathed his last."

Mary shook her head. "Betsy, I should have been beside myself. How did you bear it?"

Betsy sipped her wine, then said, "I went into melancholia, eating little, staying in the apartment that was our city residence. My only consolation was that Liza was with us. Joshua went about his duties as well as he could considering the siege. But after weeks like this, our luck changed. General William Howe arrived, sent from England with other generals and troops to reinforce the commander, General Thomas Gage."

"How did that change things for you?"

"Joshua had served in the army during the French War, and as chance would have it, he was a lieutenant in the Seventeenth Foot. The commandant of the battalion at that time was none other than Lieutenant Colonel William Howe."

Mary stiffened in her chair. "I'm beginning to see how things"—she searched for the discrete word—"evolved."

"Yes, General Gage put on a reception for the new officers who had arrived with the reinforcement. As loyalists of some stature, we were invited to attend, and Joshua coaxed me out of my languor to accompany him. Howe greeted my husband as a long-lost comrade, and I was introduced to him at the same time. He spent a good deal of time with us that evening and was very solicitous of me. In the course of conversation, Joshua mentioned the situation with baby Wentworth. Howe was very sympathetic."

"A few days later, Joshua came home in great excitement. He said that Howe had spoken to Gage, and the commanding general had agreed to include the subject of my baby in the periodic negotiations that were conducted with the rebels."

"Oh, Betsy, you must have been very excited."

"I was at first, but matters dragged on for weeks without any developments. I sank back into depression. But then things changed. Strangely, it was because of matters on the other side: Washington arrived to take command of the rebel army." Betsy smiled. "He had a different attitude than the New Englanders who had been running the colonist force. When the subject of Wentworth was brought up, I understand he was immediately sympathetic and arranged for the return of my child. I believe he thought it might be a gentlemanly goodwill gesture to help smooth the negotiating atmosphere." She looked over at Mary, her eyes brighter than at any other time in their conversation. "And so it was that Wentworth was returned to my arms."

Mary looked at her friend. "And I'm sure you were very grateful to a certain William Howe."

"Indeed. And the general continued his support of us. We were invited to many social events over the next three weeks, always at the sponsorship of Howe. But our personal lives were a mess, for we had not only lost our house, but all our lands, business property, and financial resources. All were confiscated by the rebels. We were in fact in a state of destitution, living only on Joshua's earnings as sheriff, not that he did much, because the king's holdings in Massachusetts were now only the city of Boston itself."

Betsy poured herself another glass of wine and refreshed Mary's glass. She drank deeply, then continued her narrative. "That situation persisted throughout the summer. Then the battle at Bunker Hill and Breed's Hill took place. We saw William soon afterward, and he was visibly shaken by the massive losses of our troops. He confided to Joshua that England could not sustain such a heavy price. But the important thing was that the battle finished Thomas Gage. In September of 1775, an order came from England recalling him and putting Howe in command of all our forces in America."

"I see. And that put Howe in an even better position to help you."

"Indeed. Shortly after taking command, William called in Joshua to his headquarters and offered him the position of commissioner of the prisoners, with a most significant annual remuneration." She looked at Mary with a knowing glance. "And of course, you understand there were other ways that a man in an office such as that could realize financial gain." She shrugged. "It would mean that we had a chance to recover from our losses to the rebels and regain some measure of security."

Mary looked down at her glass and said in a low tone, "But the general wanted something in return."

"Yes, that soon became clear to me. He found ways to keep Joshua busy and meanwhile invited me to evenings with him and other senior officers at the Faro table and other social events. I don't deny I enjoyed the game and the excitement of wagering. I have always had a weakness for games of chance." She looked at Mary and sighed. "And the attention I received from being the general's companion was very flattering." She thought for a moment, then said, "You can guess that, after a while, he made clear exactly how I could repay him for the kindness to our family." Betsy shrugged. "He became insistent in a most diplomatic way, and soon I realized I must surrender to his desires. I felt I had no other choice, for it was the only way my children would have a measure of security in the uncertain, turbulent world into which we had suddenly been thrust."

Betsy held up her glass before her face and stared into it, as if it were a crystal ball that had information to impart to her. Then she shrugged. "So it began. And William, knowing that he must present at least a patina of respectability, began arranging for other officers to accompany me to events. Frequently it was Barrett Northcutt's brother, who was a major in Howe's regiment. Then, when events drove us out of Boston, William arranged for me to travel on his ship—the sixty-four-gun ship of the line *HMS Chatham*—to Halifax. He said it would be more comfortable for me. He found an excuse to keep Joshua involved on official business so that he left on one of the last ships to depart from the city." She looked over at Mary. "And you know the rest: of my 'female' problem that brought us together in Halifax, and you've been with me through it all since then."

There was a long silence, then Mary said, "You don't have to answer, but there's something we have never discussed: How all this has affected things between you and Joshua? How have you dealt with it?"

"Joshua sensed from the beginning what Howe wanted. But he was desperate to repair our financial situation, as was I. So it became—how shall I describe it—an unspoken understanding between us. Howe made sure that Joshua was kept traveling almost constantly on the business of managing the prisoners. And on those occasions when Joshua was at our residence, in New York or here, we had a tacit agreement to act as if all was normal." She again stared into the distance and the two women sat for a long time quietly. Finally Betsy broke the silence. "It has shown me to what length you can go and to what extent you can compromise yourself to survive and achieve a measure of comfort." She turned to Mary. "You must understand this: My greatest hope is that when this war is over and Joshua rejoins us on a permanent basis, whether here or in England, we can put all this behind us and resume some semblance of a normal life. I pray that we can regain the affection we had in the first days of our marriage, and if not, at least we can maintain a cordiality that will benefit the children and allow them to have a normal upbringing."

Mary felt a surge of sympathy for her friend and, rising from her chair, walked over to Betsy and put an arm around her shoulders. "And I hope that your prayer will be answered. But know that I completely understand your motives, and that I will keep you in my thoughts, and share your hope that all this can be put behind you. And above all, that you can find peace with yourself and Joshua as you go forward."

Betsy took Mary's hand in hers. "Thank you, I don't know how I should have gotten through all this without an understanding friend such as you."

At that moment, the maid entered. "Ma'am, the carriage has arrived. The coachman is at the door. Shall I fetch the children down so that you may depart?"

Betsy Loring put down her glass, stood up, and squared her shoulders. "Yes, it is indeed time to go to the ship."

George Washington, astride his stunning gray horse Blueskin, sat in front of his staff, surveying the Grand Parade ground at Valley Forge. Next to him, also mounted, was Von Steuben, who had organized and directly supervised the entire proceedings. The parade ground itself was for the moment a vast ocean of emptiness, illuminated by the morning sun. Next to Washington's staff stood a gaggle of about fifteen men in civilian dress, a delegation from the Continental Congress who had traveled from the current meeting place, York, Pennsylvania, and for whose edification the review was intended. Alex Hamilton was with the august men of Congress to shepherd them and explain events as they occurred. Behind the general and his staff was arrayed the Life Guard, both the mounted and foot segments. Also standing in formation was the Marechaussee company—the army's newly formed provost unit.

At the far western end of the parade ground, a battery of twelve pounders was in position. Behind the battery were gathered the women, children, and other people of the camp, all excited to watch the performance. The captain of the battery stood behind the guns, looking down at the watch in his hand. When it registered exactly 9:00 a.m., he raised and lowered his hand, and two of the cannon fired, one after the other.

Immediately afterward, all present heard the sound of fifes, accompanied by drums beating a military cadence. The congressmen turned to look in the direction of the music and were immediately rewarded by the sight of a column of light foot, in column of fours, emerging from the main part of the camp. The men were uniformly dressed in linen hunting shirts, brown breeches and leggings, and black hats with a flat brim turned up at the rear of the crown. One of the congressmen said in an audible voice, "That's the Guides! Look at their shirts and black hats." There was a buzzing of talk among the men as they stared at the approaching company. Once the foot unit had come fully into view, the two troops of Guides dragoons followed, riding in column of threes.

Eckert rode at the head of the Guides column and raised his sword in salute as he passed Washington. Then he wheeled his men to pass around behind the Life Guard formation and that of the Marechaussee, to a point where he formed the Guides on the left of the other household troops.

Marching close behind the Guides came the rest of the army in brigade formation. A few battalions were well uniformed. But most of the men's uniforms, where they had them, were often tattered and mismatched. Some wore only civilian clothing. However, virtually all were shod, which was a great improvement from when they had straggled into the encampment in the autumn of the previous year. And most importantly, all carried well-maintained muskets and proper accouterments. But most striking was that, despite their ragged clothing, all the men marched in step with the measured tread of trained soldiers, all presented military posture, all carried their firelocks at the proper angle, and all maintained the prescribed interval. As he watched the parade, Wend reflected that he had never seen British regulars drill with more precision.

Each brigade passed in review before Washington and the group of congressmen and then, maintaining perfect formation, wheeled left and marched into their prearranged positions on the parade ground. As they approached their designated place, in sequence each battalion redeployed from column of fours to form a two-rank battle line. This continued until the entire army—above ten thousand men—stood arrayed across the Grand Parade in two long, two-rank battle lines, one behind the other.

The army stood that way for a few seconds, then a single shot from the artillery battery sounded. Upon that signal, the army began a *feu de joie*—a sequential firing of muskets as both a demonstration of precision and a salute to the men of Congress. It began with the first two man file on the right flank of the first battle line firing their muskets into the air. Immediately the next two men fired, and then the next two, until the firing had rippled all the way to the leftmost flank of the front battle line. Then the instant the front battle line had finished, the rear battle line picked it up from their left flank, and now the shots proceeded from left to right, ending when the last two man file on the right flank discharged their firelocks. The powder smoke from the muskets formed a low cloud above the heads of the soldiers that slowly floated away, propelled by the light breeze. In the aftermath of the firing, there was a few seconds of silence followed by an outburst of clapping and cheering from the congressmen and the spectators behind the artillery battery.

When the applause had subsided, the army presented arms. Washington took the salute, then dismissed the parade. Upon a signal from Von Steuben, the brigades from left to right began marching back to their quarters.

As the soldiers marched off, Hamilton started herding the congressmen toward the Potts House. An aide walked over to where Wend sat his horse. "Major Eckert, General Washington will be conducting a briefing of the congressional delegation at headquarters shortly. He wants the generals of division and the commanding officers of all his household units to attend. Please repair to the Potts House at your earliest convenience."

Wend signaled for Bradley to take charge and lead the Guides back to their campground, then rode to headquarters. He had just tied his mount to a hitching rail and was standing by the front steps as Hamilton led the delegation into the house. He was surprised when one of the congressmen, dressed in a somber black suit, stared at him for a long moment, in a glaring manner, as he climbed the steps. He racked his memory to think if he knew the man but drew a blank. Puzzled, he followed the delegation into the house.

Chapter Eleven
Difficult Transitions

The carriage that Betsy Loring had hired was sitting at the curb in front of the house, along with the wagon carrying the family's baggage. It had the leather top down in view of the warm day.

Mary exclaimed, "Why, what a beautiful coach. And that team of blacks are quite handsome."

Betsy looked over at Mary with a twinkle in her eye. "Well, as long as so many people in the army and Philadelphia will be glad to see me leave, I thought I might as well depart in style!"

The coachman opened the door, and Mary helped to shepherd little Liza and Wentworth into the vehicle. Then he assisted both women up to their seats. In a moment they were off down Walnut Street toward the waterfront, followed by the wagon.

Betsy said, "It would have been nice if Joshua could have been here to see us off, but he left two days ago for New York to attend to business. He has much to do to get ready for the arrival of the army in the city." She winked at Mary. "We said our goodbyes before he left."

Mary looked at her friend. "The war disrupts everything." Then she had a thought. "Where will you stay in England?"

"Joshua's parents—the old commodore and his wife—are taking us in at their place in Highgate, which is on the northeastern edge of London. They tell me it is very pleasant. We shall stay there until I can find a suitable place in the country."

The carriage stopped rather abruptly. Mary looked around to see that the quay was in sight, but there was a cluster of carriages, wagons, horses, hand carts, and people on foot carrying bags. "My God, Betsy, look at all the people hurrying toward the waterfront! All taking ship to leave Philadelphia!"

Betsy sat taking in the vista. "Yes, so many afraid of what will happen when the rebels march into the town. There will be a reckoning for those who have cooperated with the army."

Mary said, "Yes, and I am told that the city's rebel sympathizers are already becoming restive and more assertive."

The coachman worked his way through the bustling crowd until they had arrived at the quay wall. Mary asked, "Which is your ship?"

"The *Enchantress*. I'm told she is quite large and well found."

At that moment the driver pulled up. He looked back from his seat. "There's your vessel, ma'am: the one with three masts anchored in the stream."

Mary looked at the ship. "Oh, it's very pretty looking. And indeed very large!"

Betsy was staring at the merchantman. "Yes, thank goodness. Hopefully we will have a comfortable voyage." Then she turned to the driver. "They said they would have a boat ready at this time to take us out. Can you find it?"

"Aye, ma'am. I'll see to it."

After the driver left, Betsy turned to Mary. "Now listen. I know you are returning to your regiment at its encampment after we take ship. She swept her hand to take in the carriage and team. "I have engaged the rig and driver for the full day. The coachman is to take you to your quarters to pick up your baggage and then onward to the camp." She grinned mischievously. "I'm leaving in style; you shall arrive in style!"

"Betsy, I couldn't!"

"But you must. It is my farewell present to you."

Mary was about to continue her protest when a male voice interrupted. "Good afternoon, ladies."

Mary looked around to see Captain Banastre Tarleton of the 16th Light Dragoons sitting his horse close by the carriage. She exclaimed, "Captain Tarleton! Sir, I must admit my surprise at seeing you here. Do you know someone who is taking ship?"

The dragoon smiled at both ladies. "Only Mrs. Loring." He touched his hat to both ladies. "But I was exercising my horse and happened to ride by the headquarters of the general hospital. So on a whim, I inquired after you, Miss Fraser. They told me you were seeing Mrs. Loring off and then going on to the 42nd. Hearing that, I thought to be so bold as to make my farewells to you both at the same time." He grinned. "Alas, for an unknown length of time to Mrs. Loring, but hopefully just a brief time for you, Miss Fraser, for we shall both shortly be in New York City."

Betsy shot Mary a mischievous glance, then looked over at Tarleton. "So the truth is you came down to see Miss Fraser. Am I not correct?"

Tarleton touched his hat again to Betsy and grinned. "You have me, Mrs. Loring. I plead guilty as charged." Then he recovered quickly. Bowing slightly in the saddle, he said, "But it is my good fortune that I could spend some time with two beautiful ladies, not just one."

The two women looked at each other and laughed. Betsy said, "Well said, Captain. We are pleased to entertain your compliments."

Meanwhile, the coachman had returned with another man, who was in nautical dress. He said, "Ma'am, this be the second mate of the *Enchantress*. He's got a boat waiting for you and will arrange for your things from the wagon to be transported out to the ship."

The mate touched his cap to Betsy. "Aye, ma'am. We're ready for you to take the boat out to the ship, Mrs. Loring. And your cabin is prepared for you." He turned and motioned toward the vessel. "We must move expeditiously. The master is in a hurry to sail while this good wind prevails, ma'am. It's a long trip down the river to get into the open waters of Delaware Bay and then the ocean."

Betsy turned to Mary and threw her arms around her in embrace. "Oh, dear Mary, this is goodbye. I shall so miss you. You have been with me through the best and the worst of times. I shall remember you with friendship and gratitude."

Mary responded, "And I will always keep you in my heart, Betsy."

Tarleton slipped off his horse and stood ready to hand Betsy down from the carriage. "Mrs. Loring, may I assist you?"

Betsy descended, and with Mary's help, the two children followed. The mate escorted them to the waiting boat.

Mary and Tarleton stood watching. The captain said, "Well, that's the end of the Howe chapter of this war. And now things are in Clinton's hands."

Mary looked over at Tarleton, who was not much taller than her. He was very lean and lightweight, which befitted a cavalryman. She had to admit he looked very dashing in the red coat with blue facings, white breeches, and red-crested black helmet of the 16th. She asked, "Are you familiar with the general?"

"Not particularly, but Harcourt, the lieutenant colonel commandant of my regiment, is quite cordial with him—enough to know that some important reorganizations are coming to the army."

"I've heard some of it. Colonel Stirling told me the 42nd has been brigaded under Major General Grey."

"Yes, Clinton is shuffling the foot battalions among brigades for better balance of the army." He turned to Mary with a gleam in his eye. "And he also intends to reorganize the cavalry, and I am told, confidentially, there is a plan to raise a new provincial regiment of light dragoons." He paused momentarily and then continued, "Actually, I should say a legion of mixed dragoons and foot. He grinned. "Which will provide new opportunities for advancement of certain officers."

"From the way you speak, can I take it that you expect to have some role in it?"

"Ah, you are a quick one, Mary Fraser. There is considerable competition for billets in this forthcoming legion, and I am honored that there has been frequent mention of my name." He looked at her with a knowing grin. "In the meantime, I have just been promoted to brigade major of Erskine's brigade of horse."

"Indeed, sir? Then I must extend congratulations, Captain Tarleton. That is a signal advancement for one so young and so recently of the army."

"Well, my dear Mary, things do happen *rapidly* in wartime. Particularly if one is so bold as to seize the opportunities that present themselves."

Mary didn't have to be told that Tarleton was referring to his central role in the capture of the rebel general, Charles Lee, two years previously, which had led to the then cornet's rapid promotion to captain. And indeed he was young, at least five years younger than she. She said, "Well, we may hope things come to happen as you desire." She looked out into the harbor, where the boat carrying the Lorings was nearly to the *Enchantress*. "Well, I must get back to the hospital to collect my things and then hurry to the encampment of the 42nd."

"Indeed, Mary. And I intend to escort you."

"Why, Banastre, that is a most thoughtful offer. But that will not be necessary. And it would take so much of your time."

"Oh, but I *insist.* The streets are literally clogged with traffic as so many people are trying to leave the city, either by road or sea. And then there are rebel sympathizers who are becoming more militant all the time as the date for the army's departure approaches. There have been some confrontations with our troops." He extended his hand to help her up into the carriage. "So you see, it is manifestly the gentlemanly thing for me to do."

Mary stepped up into the carriage and took her seat. She had no polite way decline his offer. "Banastre, you are so gallant. How can I refuse?"

The dining room of the Potts House served as the headquarters meeting room. It was not particularly large and now was quite crowded indeed. The men of the congressional delegation were seated in chairs around the moderately sized table and in other chairs that had been brought in for the occasion and placed wherever room could be found. The major generals of the army—Nathaniel Green and Lord Stirling—stood together against the far wall. The commanders of Washington's household troops, Wend, Gibbs of the Life Guard, and Von Heer of the Provosts, stood with their backs to the window that looked out the front of the house. Officers of Washington's staff were packed tightly along the wall and in the wide entranceway to the room, where they could hear and see the proceedings.

The room was filled with the conversation as the assembled men waited for Washington to appear.

They didn't have long to wait. In just a few minutes, the adjutant general,

Alexander Scammell, called the room to order and, and those seated came to their feet while Washington strode in, accompanied by Major General Lee and Baron Von Steuben. He quickly indicated for the congressmen to take their seats.

Washington took his place at the front of the room, where maps of Pennsylvania and New Jersey had been pinned to the wall. He looked around the room with that serious gaze of his that inevitably gained the attention of everyone in his sight. "Gentlemen, our purpose here is to preview what we expect to be the opening of this summer's campaign. But first, I have a couple of announcements. He turned and motioned toward Lee. "As you are aware, General Lee has been returned from British captivity by means of exchange and, after some time in York consulting with Congress, has resumed his duties with the army. He will, of course, be my second in command."

Lee nodded and said, "It is my pleasure to be back and to rejoin our forces."

Washington turned to Von Steuben and held up a sheet of parchment. "As you may be aware, the former inspector general, General Conway, has resigned from the army. Subsequently, Congress has seen fit to appoint our compatriot, Von Steuben, who has served us so long and so well as a private volunteer, to the office of inspector general with the rank of major general."

There was clapping from the officers and congressmen at the announcement. Wend watched Lee and noticed that his enthusiasm was quite reserved at the announcement.

Washington resumed speaking. "Those of us who have seen what General Von Steuben has achieved since he began the training and reorganization of the army can do nothing but agree with his appointment." He looked around the room. "Clearly, today's evolutions on the parade ground bear testimony to his success. And we look to see the results of his training in action as we take to the field."

There was another round of applause, which was particularly enthusiastic from the military officers.

Washington allowed the applause to continue until it died down of its own accord, then said, "Now it is time for us to discuss the coming operations." He looked over at Colonel Scammell. "The adjutant general will explain what we believe will soon be toward."

Scammell walked over to the maps. "As you are aware, Clinton has succeeded Howe in command of the British Army. We have been appraised by our web of spies that the new general is planning to abandon Philadelphia and consolidate his forces around New York City." He paused and looked around the room. "Our watchers in Philadelphia say that the British are even now preparing to leave. Many battalions that have been billeted in houses, warehouses, and such are being moved into tented camps on the outskirts of the city and undergoing intensive drilling in preparation to take the field. A portion of their soldiers and many loyalist refugees are boarding ships to be transported to New York by sea."

Washington interjected. "So you see, when the British march, we will not be facing their full strength. Moreover, Clinton's intention is simply to travel from Philadelphia to New York rather than to actively seek combat. They will have a large number of wagons in train, which they must protect. Put another way, the deployment of their troops will be for defense, not offense against us. Given that condition, I believe we may well find an opening to strike a significant blow." He paused and looked at the congressmen silently for a long moment, then turned back to Scammell and motioned for him to continue.

Scammell resumed his narrative. "When we get word the British are departing, we will send out light forces to determine their precise route of march and their disposition of units for the journey. Those light units will be Major Eckert's Legion of Continental Guides, a mixed horse and foot force, and Colonel Morgan's corps of light foot."

McKean of Delaware, the leader of the congressional group, displayed a puzzled look, then cleared his throat and said, "What about your cavalry? Won't they go into the field to watch the British? Isn't that their function?"

Washington rose and stood silently looking at the delegation for long seconds as he gathered his thoughts. Then he clasped his hands behind his back and said in a serious tone, "You are quite correct, sir; that that is the cavalry's function. And you have hit upon an important problem facing us. The truth is, our brigade of light horse is not ready to take the field. Most of the animals that we possess fared poorly during the winter for lack of forage and feed. Many died. We have enough left to mount only a fraction of the men. We have procured some horses from the local farms, but they must be trained to a level that will make them serviceable for army use before the brigade can take the field, and that cannot be accomplished before the British move." He paused again. "Fortunately, the British are having similar problems, and a goodly number of their dragoons have been dismounted and are serving as foot soldiers." He motioned toward Wend and said, "However, we have maintained two troops of well-mounted horse in Major Eckert's command, and they can be augmented to some degree by the mounted troop of my Life Guard. Until we can bring the cavalry brigade up to a serviceable strength, Eckert's and Morgan's troops will have to perform our scouting. Fortunately, gentlemen, they are mostly composed of border country men who are experienced in just that kind of work and have proven themselves in previous campaigns." He nodded to Scammell to continue.

Scammell turned back to the maps. "I will conclude by showing you the dispositions of the British around Philadelphia." He did so by pointing to the locations of various formations and defensive positions that had been marked on the maps. Then he wrapped things up by saying, "Once we are informed that the British are marching out, we will have troops ready to immediately reoccupy the city, so as to ensure that order can be maintained." He smiled at the congressmen. "And to ensure the city is safe for Congress to return from York."

Scammell stepped back from the map and looked over the audience. "Now, gentlemen, we are prepared for any comments you wish to make or answer any questions which you might have."

McKean simply stated his thanks for the briefing, then looked to his compatriots. "Are there any inquiries you would make?"

A congressman stood up. Wend felt a touch of anxiety when he saw that it was the man who had stared at him on the steps.

McKean said, "Ah, yes, Reverend Long of New Jersey. Please go ahead."

"I have a very serious matter to address. I have received a written correspondence from a certain Reverend Banbury in New Jersey—who is from near the town of Spanktown and whom I know very well." He turned and motioned toward Wend. "He relates that a detachment of soldiers from this army, a detachment under the command of Major Wend Eckert of the Guides, while encamped on the farm of Mr. Joseph Wallen, refused to march to the aide of the people on two adjacent farms who were under attack by a scurrilous band of renegade partisans. Those farms were owned by stalwart supporters of our cause, Mr. Edward Dawson and Mr. William Graham, and were less than a mile from where Eckert was camped. Both farms were burned, the owners were hanged, and several other people were killed because of Eckert's refusal to march or do anything to provide succor. Reverend Banbury is supported by written attestations from some people of those two farms who—miraculously—survived."

It became very quiet in the room, and Wend felt the eyes of everyone on him. He sensed his face redden.

Long had resumed speaking, addressing Washington directly. "I must demand that the commanding general open a court of inquiry to investigate Major Eckert's behavior. I am confident, based on the reports I have received, that he will be found guilty of malfeasance. And upon that verdict, I demand that appropriate action be taken to discipline him. I personally believe he should be removed from command of troops and cashiered!"

In the heavy silence that fell over the room in the wake of Long's words, Wend felt all eyes suddenly on him; he stared straight ahead to avoid meeting anyone's gaze. Scammell looked over at Washington, as if tacitly questioning how he should deal with Long's assertion. Washington stared at Long for a very long moment. The silence in the room persisted, and if possible, deepened. Then he clasped his hands behind his back and walked over next to where Scammell stood. Scammell vacated his place and discretely moved over to one side of the room.

Washington, in a grave tone, began to speak. "Gentlemen of Congress, I'm going to answer Reverend Long's assertion. I am quite familiar with the event of which the congressman speaks, for Major Eckert reported on it in extensive detail in his written report to me. Moreover, our spies have separately corroborated it. Now, bear with me, for I'm going to start by recalling an incident of the last war—the war against the French. An event that, as a matter of fact, took place in 1754, more than twenty years ago."

The general stood, hands clasped behind his back, gathering his thoughts. He stared into the distance for a long time. There were upwards of thirty men in the room, and every eye was on him. Then, finally, he began to speak.

"Gentlemen, on that occasion, I was a young major myself, an officer of the Virginia militia. I had been sent, with a small number of men, to report on the activities of the French in the area of the Forks of the Ohio, particularly their construction of fortifications there at what is now called Pittsburgh. We were not at that time at war, but tensions were high. I was camped with my force some forty or fifty miles from the Forks, at a place called Great Meadows. A party of friendly Indian warriors came to us, very excited. They reported that a small party of the French were nearby and that they were planning hostile action against us. The leader of the Indians strongly urged that we make a surprise attack on the French party, as a way of ensuring the safety of my men. After brief thought—regrettably too brief—I acceded to his idea, and we stealthily approached the French and then assaulted their position. Our attack was successful, killing many of the French. Unfortunately, the Indian war captain assassinated their leader, a young man named Jumonville, after the remnants of the French had surrendered. I was appalled by his action. I was further appalled to find after we had interrogated the survivors, that the French party had not been sent to attack us, but instead to present us with a letter from their commander at the Forks: a letter suggesting that we meet and conduct negotiations."

Washington took deep breath. "In that situation I acted with impetuosity, without fully considering the matter. I did not analyze all the alternatives or the potential results of my action. In this case, our attack on that French party led to the beginning of hostilities and eventually a full-blown war with the French." He paused to let that sink in, then looked at all the faces of the congressmen. "Now the facts of the case about Major Eckert's action are quite different, but the essence is that he, like I, was confronted with a serious situation and had to weigh all the potential outcomes and decide how to proceed."

The commander in chief paused and fixed his eyes on Long. Then he continued, "Major Eckert was faced with an impassioned demand to provide assistance to people in extreme distress. Any man would have felt the strong, almost irresistible humanitarian impulse to instantly march to their rescue. But in the heat of that moment, he had the forbearance to correctly assess the dangers of that course of action. He knew he was far outnumbered. He understood that he was unfamiliar with the lay of the land. And he knew that if he marched under those conditions, he faced the possibility of himself being ambushed by a much superior force. And he understood the grim reality that most of the people on those farms had already met their fate, one way or another. Most importantly, he also correctly assessed that the partisan band was likely to continue on to the farm where he was encamped. With that in mind, he prepared his own ambush for the partisans. And he did so brilliantly. The result was that the partisan band, which amounted to one hundred men and had been ravishing the countryside, was annihilated. Destroyed—never to harm the people of New Jersey again. It is clear that Major Eckert saved many more lives and property than if he had attempted to help farms that were, in large measure, already destroyed and where the partisans had worked their will on the inhabitants."

"Now, Reverend Long, those are the facts—I repeat what I said earlier—both from Major Eckert's report and the reports of our watchers in New Jersey." Washington stopped for a long moment, then said, "Sir, mark this: in war commanders have to make grim, hard decisions. There is no doubt in my mind that Major Eckert made the correct decision. So, Reverend Long, let me be clear: I will initiate no further inquiry of his actions or motivations."

Washington stepped back, clearly finished.

Long sat wordless. A long moment of silence hung over the room.

Finally, Scammell cleared his throat. "Well, gentlemen, if there are no further questions, we retire to the tent adjacent to this house, where a midday repast will be served."

He looked around, and no one had anything else to say. Wend noted that Long was looking down at the floor. In a moment, all the group, military and congressional, began to file out of the room.

Wend stood where he was, not wanting to be thrown in with any of the congressmen, let alone Long.

Then one of Washington's aides, Lieutenant Colonel Richard Meade, pushed through the crowd and came up to Wend. He said curtly, "Eckert, General Washington wishes to speak with you. In his office, immediately."

Wend felt a knot in his stomach. *What did the general want to see him about? Was Long or McKean still pressing for an inquiry despite Washington's statement at the meeting?* With some trepidation, Wend followed the crowd out of the room and went across the hall to the doorway of Washington's office. He could see both the general and Scammell were in the room. Washington was seated at his desk, reading some papers, and Scammell was beside him, also looking down at the papers.

Scammell looked up and saw him standing there and said, "Come in, Eckert. The general has some things to discuss with you."

Wend did so and spoke up before Washington could say anything. "General, I greatly appreciate your words of support in the meeting."

The general looked up at him, eyebrows furrowed in mild puzzlement. Then he responded, "Eckert, do you suppose that I have called you here about Congressman Long's accusations?"

"I thought there might be more ramifications."

"Disabuse yourself of that idea. I supported you because you did the right thing, and there will be no more about it. We don't have time for any courts of inquiry that would simply find exactly what I told the congressmen in the meeting." He tapped the papers on his desk. "What I wanted to see you about is what's in this report." He leaned back. "It appears that the British departure from Philadelphia is nigh. All their battalions are in camps outside the city, drilling and exercising. Some cavalry formations are already patrolling out in the countryside. Many ships have departed carrying loyalist sympathizers to New York or England. Their stocks of ammunition, provisions, and other supplies are being loaded into wagons."

Scammell spoke up. "The point is, your legion and Morgan's riflemen must be ready to take the field. Specifically, do you have any needs which we can help with?"

Washington nodded. "Indeed, we'll be sending you and Morgan an order to have your men ready to depart on short notice."

Wend stiffened. "General, ever since you warned me a few days ago, we have been making preparations. We are as ready as possible except for one matter."

Washington leaned forward, concern spreading across his countenance. "And what is that?"

"The matter of horses. Some of ours have been used hard during the foraging and the expedition into Jersey. They need dedicated time in pasture. Some are just worn out or old. It will limit our ability to scout." Wend looked first at Scammell, then Washington. "We captured over forty horses from the Queen's American Rangers at Millstone River. I'm told you are planning to send them to the Cavalry Brigade at Trenton. I know they are woefully short of mounts, but I respectfully request that at least twenty of them be diverted to the Guides."

The general looked up at Scammell. "Make it so." He stopped a minute, then said, "And add several more mounts to what the major has requested, as replacements to go along with the Guides when they march. There will be casualties during the campaign." He shook his head. "If the cavalry brigade can't support our scouting needs, we must make sure the Guides dragoons are well mounted." Washington sat back in his chair, his jaw set. Then Washington scowled and turned to his adjutant general. "Scammell, when I die, I tell you they shall find this want of good cavalry written on my heart."

Wend said, "Thank you for your assistance with the horses, sir. I'll also draw necessary provisions immediately, to have them ready when the call comes."

Scammell nodded. "I'll send a note to Greene to give you first priority with rations."

Wend came to attention. "Thank you. If that's all, I'll get back to my camp."

Washington held up a finger. "One other thing. What's the last information you have on young Henry's travel back to Virginia? I know you sent a patrol out to make sure the British didn't intercept him."

"Captain Fairfield arrived back in camp yesterday, sir. In fact, he apprehended some men who were attempting to capture Henry and Lieutenant Childers. He brought them back and turned them over to the provost. I think it unlikely that Mr. Henry and Lieutenant Childers will have further trouble with the British."

Washington was looking down at the papers again. Without looking up at Wend, he said, "Good, good. Thank you."

Wend walked to the door to leave. Suddenly Washington called, "Oh, Major Eckert!"

Wend turned and stood in the doorway. "Yes, sir?"

Washington was sitting back in his chair, his right hand on his chin, as if he were contemplating something important. "One other thing: Colonel Hamilton mentioned at dinner several nights ago that you lost a brace of pistols in that skirmish at the Millstone River. And he said you were making a pair with your own hands to replace them. He saw you carving their stocks. Am I to believe that report is correct?"

Wend bit his lips in trepidation, unsure of what Washington intended. "Yes, sir, that's true."

Washington grinned. "Well, Major, you had better hurry to get them finished. We can't have you riding around in the campaign without appropriate sidearms."

Wend smiled back. "Aye, sir. That will be done!" And with that he departed.

—m—

The gentle sunlight of early June warmed the two riders' shoulders as they guided their mounts at the trot along Williamsburg's Gloucester Street. There was considerable traffic in the roadway—carts, wagons, and men on horseback, as well as numerous pedestrians. Edward Childers felt pleasant memories stirring within himself as they passed familiar shops, taverns, and inns. Many were places where he and John Henry and other men of the young social crowd of a few years back had spent their time when not pursuing studies at William and Mary, or reading for the law, or clerking at counting houses. He was about to remark on it to his companion, when he looked over and realized that John was in no mood for fond reminisces. His mouth was set, the muscles of his face tight, his eyes staring straight ahead. Edward thought, *He's steeling himself for the meeting with his father, which will likely be within the hour.* So Childers remained silent, keeping his thoughts to himself, and presently they came to the Palace Green and turned up the drive toward the great brick mansion.

Neither was a stranger to the Governor's Palace, for they had attended a number of events there in the years just before the war, when Lord Dunmore had held forth at the head of the capital's society and entertained the Tidewater gentry in glittering banquets and balls. Suddenly Edward recalled one such evening in the grand ballroom when he had been introduced to, and first danced with, Miss Emma Wilbourne, the high-cheekboned, doe-eyed, golden-haired, slim-waisted daughter of one Howard Forthright Wilbourne, whose elegant plantation house and surrounding farms lay along the York River.

The two pulled up at the front of the mansion, dismounted, and hitched their horses. Edward looked over at John Henry, whose eyes were staring at the mansion. He said, "John, are you ready?"

Henry looked over and took a deep breath. "How can I be ready for this? But let's get through it."

They walked up the short walkway to the main doors and entered the reception area. There were numerous men standing around, some talking together in groups, all apparently waiting to conduct business with the governor or other functionaries. A young man was seated at a desk to one side and appeared to be the receptionist or secretary. A very well-fed, well-dressed man of middling age was standing there talking to him.

Edward and John stood in front of the desk, and the young man turned and stared at Childers's uniform. Then he asked, "Yes, Lieutenant, do you have some business here?" The portly man stood looking at the two of them with a critical eye, as if to assess their importance.

Childers withdrew Washington's letter from his coat pocket. "I am

Lieutenant Childers of the Legion of Continental Guides. I have just come from Valley Forge with a communication for Governor Henry from General Washington."

The secretary reached out. "I will receive that and deliver it to him."

"Sir, I have orders from the general that I am to hand it to the governor myself. It is of a personal nature." Then he motioned toward John. "And in any case, this is Mr. John Henry, the governor's son, whom I am confident the governor will immediately want to see."

The young man looked perplexed, and his eyes swiveled to look up at John. "I fear I don't understand."

John spoke up. "Mr. Childers is quite correct. I've just left Gates's army in New York. Please take me to my father forthwith."

The secretary still looked uncertain and sat staring at the two men for a long moment. Then he said, "I will announce your presence when the governor has finished his current…"

His words were interrupted by a young female voice crying out, "Johnny! You're home! Home to Virginia! Father will be so happy!"

Everyone in the room turned to see three young children, two girls and a boy, accompanied by a middle-aged woman, standing in a door that opened to the garden. Edward looked at John and, for the first time since the Queen Bess Inn, saw him break into a genuine smile.

"Annie! Betsy! Neddy!" He leaned over to accept their hugs as they wrapped their arms around him. "I'm so glad to see you all!"

The woman accompanying them stood with a smile on her face until the hugs were over. Then she said, "John, it's nice to finally meet you. I'm Miss Barron, the governess." She looked down at the secretary. "Mr. Prout, I'll take them upstairs to the family quarters."

John said, "And Lieutenant Childers will accompany us."

Miss Barron pointed in the direction of the staircase and led off, with the young children skipping ahead.

The two men followed up the stairs just behind. Edward glanced around the lobby and could see that the eyes of all the men in the room were following them. At the top of the stairs was a landing with several doors. Another secretary sat at a desk in front of one door, clearly the entrance to the governor's office.

Miss Barron went to another door. "We'll go in here until the governor is free of his present appointment."

The children hurried into the room, followed by the governess and the two men. And there, ensconced in a wing chair in front of a large window, with a book in her lap, sat Dorothea Dandridge Henry. She looked as lovely as Edward had remembered, having seen her for the last time at the Independence Ball right there in the palace back in July of 1776. She had been perhaps eighteen then. Now, at twenty, she had a more mature beauty. Her raven hair was perfectly coiffed under a lace cap. She wore a blue gown that well matched the color of her eyes. Her high-cheekboned, narrow face bore an expression of warmth.

The oldest girl, Annie, who Childers guessed was ten or eleven, called out to her, "Look, Mother Dorothea, look! Johnny has come back to us!"

The three children huddled around Dorothea, in obvious closeness and fondness to their stepmother. She smiled down at the girl. "Yes, I see."

Then Childers saw something else. Under the blue gown, which was loosely fitting, it was blatantly evident that Dorothea was with child. With child—and quite far along. He looked over at John and saw him staring at the greatness of her waist and abdomen. Shock registered all over his face. It suddenly occurred to Edward that this changed everything—Dorothea's condition had brought reality home to John.

Dorothea saw Henry's expression and said, "Yes, John, I am with child. *Patrick's* child. I'm going to present you with a brother or sister about August. Just a few weeks from now." Then she quickly turned to the governess. "Miss Barron, will you take the children to lessons now? John and Edward and I have much to discuss."

When the children had left, Dorothea turned back to the two of them. Her face had turned serious. "John, your father has been in indescribable anguish since we found that you had left the army, and your location was unknown. Nothing is more important to him than reconciling matters between the two of you. I'll take you in to him shortly, but first I want to tell you some things—about how our marriage came about and what it has come to mean."

Henry shrugged and stared down at the floor. In a quiet, resigned voice he said, "What can you say that will change anything? What's done is done."

"It won't change things, but give me the consideration of listening to what I have to say."

Childers said, "I will wait outside in the hall while you talk." He turned to go.

Dorothea stretched out her hand to him. "There is no need, Edward. We were all friends here in Williamsburg. We have spent much time together. I want you to hear what I have to say so you will also understand." She carefully put a marker in her book, closed it, and placed it on a table next to her chair. Childers thought he could literally feel the silence in the room hanging over them.

After a moment, Dorothea looked up at John. "I want you to know that my father and Patrick arranged the marriage before I was even aware that your father had any intention of matrimony."

A look of puzzlement came over John's face. "And you let it go at that?"

"John, it was not the first time my father had made a decision about my relationship with a man. A few months before I met you, there was a handsome and dashing sea captain who wanted to court me, and I was most willing to accept his attentions. But Father decided he was not suitable, not a man of the kind of substance—and station—that he wanted for me. I was disappointed, but I felt I had no choice but to accept my father's judgment and obey. Then, months later, when father told me he wanted me to marry Patrick, I will admit that I was upset for a while. But it was only for a brief time. I thought things through and soon realized that fate was presenting me with an important opportunity." She reflected a moment, then said, "No, not an *opportunity*, a *duty*. The duty of helping your father establish the government of a new state and of a new nation—a kind of government not seen before in this world. I realized that he would be at a disadvantage if he didn't have a lady to help with the society of the capital and the state. And it came to me that my upbringing and the stature of my family had suited me for just that role."

Henry said, "So you decided to let your head guide you instead of your heart."

Dorothea took a deep breath and closed her eyes for a second, then opened them and said, "There is some truth to that. But let's be honest. Marriage should be about both of those things. Sometimes one outweighs the other." She looked between the two men. "And in the beginning, my thoughts of duty and being part of the momentous events that are occurring in Virginia outweighed the feelings of my heart. But John, you must understand that I soon developed a deep admiration for Patrick and, yes, a strong affection for him. I would not now be happy to be married to anyone else, and I ask that you understand that."

John was staring beyond her, looking out the window into the garden, and didn't say anything, although she looked at him as if expecting him to do so.

Again silence settled on the room. After a long minute, Dorothea cleared her throat and said quietly, "And there is something else that has occurred, something important. After Patrick and I were married, I realized that Patrick's three youngest children needed someone to look after them. And so I took up that responsibility also. It's a duty in which I have found much fulfillment. I will never be able to take the place of their birth mother, of Sarah, but I try to be like an older sister to them, and John, they have accepted that role." She smiled. "Actually, as you heard, they call me *Mother Dorothea*; it is not a title I requested from them, they got together and decided upon on it themselves. But I am proud of it."

She made as if to rise from the chair and seemed to have some difficulty. Edward ran to assist and gently took her arm. That was all she needed, and she was quickly on her feet.

She smiled at him. "The baby often makes it difficult for me." Then she sighed. "And I fear losing forever my thin waist."

Childers said, "Dorothea, you look lovely even in your present condition."

She grinned even more broadly. "That's a very gallant lie, Edward Childers!"

Miss Barron leaned in through the door. "Excuse me, Mrs. Henry. The governor has finished his appointment."

Then Dorothea turned back to Henry and said in a serious voice, the voice of a woman accustomed to having her way with things. "Now, John, I'm going to take you in to see your father. And before we go, I want you to promise me three things: First, that you will accept that I am content with my life as it is now. I would not have things any other way." She paused, then said, "Second, that you will make every effort to reconcile with your father, for otherwise his heart will be broken. And third, that you will work in good faith with Patrick and me to cement the amity and strength of our family, the Henry-Dandridge family, going forward."

John Henry stood frozen, now staring at her. Then he took a deep breath, nodded, and said in a quiet, resigned voice. "Dorothea, you are asking a lot of me. But, yes, you have my word. My word on all of that. I will do it for *you*."

"Good." Then she looked over at Childers. "Please stay here, Edward. I shall be back very shortly."

Edward thought of something. "Oh, Dorothea. I have a letter here from General Washington for Governor Henry. I was ordered to deliver it to him personally." He handed her the folded correspondence. "But I am certain giving it to you will be the same thing."

"Of course. I will see that Patrick gets it immediately." She took it from Edward's hand and went through a connecting door to the governor's office. She was back in a brief moment. She took John by the arm and said, "Come along—let's go show your father that his son has returned." She walked, leading him through the door to the next room. Childers watched as they disappeared inside, and the door shut behind them.

Edward walked over to the large window, which looked out on a garden in the rear of the mansion. It was located between the ballroom, which had been added on to the original part of the mansion, and the boundary wall. Two gardeners were at work, tending the spring plants and clipping the green shrubbery hedges. After watching them for a while, he found a comfortable chair across from where Dorothea had been sitting. He thought about what might be happening with the army: Had the British actually left Philadelphia already? Were the Guides in the field? He felt a flash of anguish at being away when there was work to be done.

Then his thoughts went to Dorothea herself. It was incredible how she had changed. In his mind he had remembered the eighteen-year-old girl who had chatted and giggled with Emma and the others at various balls and parties. She was still as beautiful as ever, but now she had become far more mature, beyond her true age—undoubtedly brought on by the responsibilities of being the governor's lady and the need to manage the Henry children.

Then he heard the door open, and Dorothea emerged and shut the door behind her. He stood up and walked toward her.

She gave him a small smile and sighed deeply, as if in relief. "It's going to be all right, Edward. I was so worried about what would happen when they met. They both have such fiery tempers! And the first few minutes were quite tense. But now they are in there sitting side by side on a settee, both of them with tears running down their cheeks. I knew it was time to leave and let them talk things out."

Edward thought a moment, then asked, "What do you think will become of John? Where does he go from here, even if amicability with his father is restored?"

"A good question, Edward, and something Patrick and I have been discussing. It happens that Patrick is buying a large plot of land—ten thousand acres—along Leatherwood Creek, in the open country well to the west of Richmond. Once the legal matters are settled, he's going to give John a large portion of the land to start his own plantation. It will give him something with which to occupy himself. I'm confident that eventually he will find a good woman and be content to start his own family."

"Indeed, but I think it will take some time." Dorothea nodded but said nothing. In the silence, Childers thought the polite thing would be to take his leave and let the family to their devices. "I'll be on my way, Dorothea. It was good to see you again."

She pointed to a chair and said in a mock peremptory tone, "Oh no you don't, Edward Childers! You've just come from the army. You must sit down and spend some time telling me what is going on in the war, or I shall never forgive you. And I particularly want to hear how you found John."

So Edward related to her the whole story about finding young Henry, about the fights at Wallen Farm and the Millstone River, and the incident at Fountain Inn. Then he told her about the long winter at Valley Forge: of the desperate days of November and December, the near starvation of the soldiers amid the freezing temperatures, and the snow and ice. He also explained how Washington had put Nathaniel Greene in charge of finding provisions and the way the Guides and other units of the army had swept the countryside for food until the supply lines had started to function properly. He also explained how Von Steuben had arrived in January and transformed the army, reorganizing the brigades and battalions and training the officers and men to perform evolutions in the field. He explained with pride how Von Steuben had taken one look at the Guides and said he would not spend a moment with them, for they were the one corps that already knew their business. He finished by saying with pride in his voice, "And this year, Dorothea, when the army leaves Valley Forge, I am certain we will give the redcoats a hard surprise!"

She smiled and said, "Yes, pray that you will. We need good news of the war."

Then Edward said, "Yes, and I want to be there to see it, and to be part of it. That's why I'm leaving as soon as possible to get back to the Guides."

Dorothea gave him a sharp look. "Edward! What about Emma Wilbourne? You *are* going to see her, aren't you?"

Edward bit his lip and started to respond. "Well..."

But she interrupted him. "You must! I've been in correspondence with her. She mentions you all the time. And I just got a letter from her. She said she hadn't received anything from you for a long time. She's worried to death about your well-being—she thought perhaps you had been wounded, or gotten sick, or worse."

"Well, I obviously I have been busy."

"Edward, you *must* go see her! She is so fond of you. Don't disappoint her." Then she added, "The family left their house here in Williamsburg a fortnight ago. They are down at the plantation on the York for the summer. You know you will be welcome there." She laughed and flashed her eyes and an ingratiating smile at him. "That is the *counsel* of the governor's lady! And a true Virginia gentleman would not displease her, would he?"

In the same spirit, Edward stood up and bowed. "I would never do anything to disappoint you, Mrs. Henry."

Then a serious look came over Dorothea's face. "Edward! One more thing before you go: when you do return to the Guides, please express my gratitude and that of Patrick to Major Eckert for his service to the Henry family in returning John to us." A thoughtful look came over her face. "Two years ago, Patrick and I watched your company—the Frederick County Light Foot—march out of Williamsburg on their way to Yorktown to take ship and sail to join Washington's army. On that morning, Patrick told me how much he admired Eckert, and how he thought he might be useful to Virginia and himself in the future. He could not have known how *soon* that would happen or that the service would be of such a personal nature. So I urge you to explain that to Major Eckert."

"Yes, Dorothea, indeed I will."

She moved close to him, and put her hands on his shoulders. "Then Godspeed, Edward. And may he protect you in battle."

Chapter Twelve
A Time for Campaigning

Edward Childers sat in the common room of Hansen's Tavern, a mug of ale before him. The establishment had long been a frequent hangout of students at William and Mary, and, looking around the room and observing the number of young men present, he concluded that was still the case. The place resounded with loud conversation and laughter. When he had come in, Childers had been surprised to find that Lilly Barton, a serving maid he had known in his college days, still worked at the tavern.

She had grinned broadly as she recognized him and immediately came over to his table. "Why look at you, Edward Childers! Or must I now call you *Lieutenant* Childers, in that pretty uniform of yours?"

"Just Edward, as usual, Lilly. Formality is the last thing I want at Hansen's."

A thoughtful look came over her face. "It's almost three years since I last saw you. And when did you join the army?"

"Not long after I went home from college. Now I'm in the Legion of Continental Guides, with Washington's army."

She frowned. "Oh, I heard stories about how awful the winter was at that place the army is now—that Valley Forge."

"It was only really bad the first couple of months. But then we started getting enough food and other supplies. Everyone is in good shape now, and we're ready to start the summer campaign."

Now she looked puzzled. "So what are you doing down here? You on leave of absence or something?"

He thought about how to answer and immediately decided to leave any mention of John Henry out of it. "I'm acting as a courier from General Washington. I brought a dispatch for Governor Henry. I'll be returning to the army posthaste." He grinned. "So treat me nice today, Lill, for I have a long journey ahead, and I'll be traveling fast."

"I *always* treat you nice. Always have. You ain't had no complaint, *ever.*" She put a finger to her chin. "Say, it's about the noon hour. How 'bouts I bring you some nice roasted beef and potatoes. I recollect you always used to like the way they do that here."

"Sounds perfect, Lily."

"Good. You just sit here and enjoy that ale, and I'll have it right out for you."

Childers lounged back in his chair and looked around the room. He thought, *God, how young these college lads seem.* He mentally shook his head. *And I'm only three years from being one of them.* Then he realized how being in the army and in the midst of a war had aged him. *I probably would think their banter to be silly now, even though I was undoubtedly saying the same kind of things not long ago.*

Soon Lilly was back with his food and put the plate down before him. She put her hands on her hips and said, "There, you just relax and enjoy that. I'll bet you don't get no food like that in the army."

Edward grinned and replied, "You are absolutely right about that. Boiled salt pork or beef, and we're lucky if there's any kind of vegetable."

She made a face. "That sounds terrible." Then she stood there for a few seconds and said, "Hey, you said you had to hurry back to the army. But ain't you stayin' long enough to see that girl you was so sweet on and always talkin' about with your friends—that John Henry and that Frenchman, Dohickey Arundel?" She laughed. "The one who got himself killed up at Gwynn's Island?" She put her hand to her chin. "Yeah, now I remember her name. It was *Emma*. Emma Wilbourne. Of that rich Wilbourne family that has a big house here in town and a plantation down on the York. Sure and you are goin' to see her, ain't you? You wouldn't travel all this way and not do that, would you? Ain't nobody gonna question you takin' a day or two for that!" Then, without waiting for an answer, she was off to wait on a long table of lads across the room.

Childers took a long time at his meal, savoring the food and the atmosphere of the common room. And at the same time, his thoughts were heavy on his mind about two young women: the pretty dark-haired daughter of a Jersey physician who had gone to her grave for the cause of liberty and the golden-haired girl of the Tidewater gentry, very much alive and only a few miles away.

When he had finished the food, he lifted his mug and finished the dregs of his ale. Then he went up to the counter and paid Josh Hansen and waved to Lilly, who smiled and waved back. She called out across the room, "God be with you, Edward!"

Childers walked out to where his horse was waiting, sleepy eyed, at the hitching post. He stood there for a long time, staring out at the busy street, but not seeing it, for his mind was racing as he tried to make a decision. Then he set his jaw, turned to the horse, tightened the girth, took the reins in his hand, and quickly mounted. He swung the horse around and came up to the trot, heading not for the road that led north, but toward the one that led eastward to the York River.

—∾—

It was early evening when Edward Childers turned his horse into the drive at the Wilbournes' estate, known as River Pines Manor, and momentarily reined in the animal. He had been there several times before the war and now, looking over the grounds, perceived that little had changed. He looked up at the great house: it was red brick of similar hew to those used for the Governor's Palace, and the original, center section was three stories—the third right up under the roof with dormer windows. It was a center hall design, with a double front doorway above a set of steps. That part dated from the early 1700s, when Howard Wilbourne's father had founded the plantation. Sometime in the 1750s, matching two-story wings had been added on either side. There was a slight, but noticeable, difference in the shade of brick visible. But all in all, it was an impressive mansion.

Off to the north, nearly shielded from view by a line of thick pines, were the quarters of the African field laborers and those who practiced the various crafts necessary to operate the estate. To the south was the wooden cook house, connected to the nearby wing by a flyway. Beyond the cook house, separated by another row of pines were the cabins of the enslaved Africans who worked in the house.

Behind the mansion was the wide York River and a view of forestland on the far bank. Taken together, the house and grounds were an estate that befitted one of the most wealthy and influential families of the Tidewater.

Childers urged the horse forward along the drive. Then, a hundred feet from the house, he pulled up again, for he had noticed that a number of carriages, chaises, and saddled horses were gathered off to the south. Several liveried black drivers and coachmen stood in a gaggle, talking and laughing with each other. He thought, *Something's going on here—some sort of social gathering.*

Edward sat his horse, pondering the situation. As he pondered, he heard music emanating from behind the house. He was hesitant to intrude on the Wilbournes, who were obviously entertaining a party of invited guests. He was just about to turn around and ride back to town when he heard a voice call, "Mr. Childers! Mr. Childers, sir!"

He looked to see the Wilbournes' African butler, known as Mr. Isaac, standing at the front door. The black man grinned broadly and called out, "Mr. Childers, I saw you out the window! You come right in! I know Miss Emma be so very glad to see you! She'll be real excited when I tell her you're here!"

Edward rode up to the front steps and dismounted. A stable boy came running up from where the carriages were parked and took the reins.

Childers looked up at Isaac. "Is there some sort of party going on?"

"Oh, yes, sir. The family is havin' a barbecue for all the neighbors up and down the river. Just to celebrate their arrivin' from Williamsburg for the summer season." He grinned. "You come right in, and I'll fetch Miss Emma right fast." Isaac led Edward into the front hall, then hurried away, exiting through the rear doors.

Childers put his hat down on a table that already held at least a score of others and smoothed his uniform coat. Suddenly the rear door swung open, and Emma swept into the hall, hands holding her skirts off the floor so she could move faster.

"Edward! You're here!" She rushed up to him and took his hands in hers. "I've been so worried! There hasn't been a letter for nearly a month! And that was so very delayed from when you wrote it. I feared that something had happened to you. That you were sick or wounded in hospital." She took a deep breath. "Or worse!" Not satisfied with holding his hands, she put her head on his chest, which was easy for her to do given her diminutive height.

Edward gently put one hand on Emma's golden hair and the other on her shoulder and looked down at her, reflecting that she was even more beautiful than his two-year-old memories. Then as he did so, he heard a discrete cough from the rear of the hall and looked up to see Mr. Howard Forthright Wilbourne standing there, accompanied by Isaac. Wilbourne had his hands clasped behind his back and with a very serious, and Edward thought, slightly disapproving look on his face.

Emma called out, "Father! Look who's here! It's Edward!"

"Ah, yes. Indeed, I quite see. Mr. Childers, welcome to River Pines. I'm glad to see that you are in good health." Then he raised his eyebrows. "I must say, this is quite a surprise."

The tone of his voice did not reflect any degree of enthusiasm.

Childers took his hands from Emma and walked down the hall, extending his hand to Wilbourne. The plantation master took the hand and shook it. Edward said, "I hope my presence is not interrupting anything, sir. I see you have guests."

Wilbourne looked at his daughter and said, "Of course you are *quite* welcome. In fact, I should be most gratified if you will join us and give us all the news of the war and the army." He looked at his daughter, who had now joined them at the rear door. "And I am quite certain that if Emma had found out that you had been in Williamsburg and not waited upon her, there would have been the devil to pay around here for the rest of the summer." He made a slight smile, then turned to the door and waved to the outside. "Let us join the guests."

They stepped outside into a garden area framed by immaculately trimmed hedges. To one side a string ensemble was playing. Emma's mother, Patricia, left the couple she was conversing with and walked toward them.

Edward made a small bow and said, "It's a pleasure to see you again, Mrs. Wilbourne."

"Edward, the pleasure is mine. And we are so glad to see you back safe and sound. She cocked her head. "What has brought you back to Virginia?"

Childers repeated the story of being a courier to the governor, deciding not to mention John, at least for the present.

Then Howard Wilbourne signaled the musicians to stop playing and clapped his hands together to attract the attention of his guests. "Ladies and gentlemen, we have an interesting development. Our new arrival, Lieutenant Childers, has just come down from Washington's army. I've prevailed upon him to give us all the latest news from the war."

The guests—Edward estimated there were over forty—gathered around and gave him their attention. He essentially repeated what he had told Dorothea. He emphasized the training of Von Steuben and told of how Greene, as quartermaster general, had gotten the supply lines working for the army. He also explained how the British were expected to leave Philadelphia—perhaps they already had—and march to New York, whereupon Washington intended to strike a hard blow. As he spoke, they assemblage listened with rapt attention.

When he had exhausted the news, Emma captured him and, taking him by the arm, said, "Now we're going to get you something to eat. Some good Wilbourne food! You look so much thinner than before the army. We can't have you wasting away! And after you've eaten, we're going to sit down together and catch up with ourselves." She smiled and led him off to the long table laden with all sorts of meat and vegetables and sweets that Edward hadn't seen for years. As they walked, she whispered in his ear, "And you must stay here with us. I've already gotten Mother to agree."

He looked down at her. "What about your father? How will he feel?"

"Don't worry about him. He'll do what Mother says!" She frowned for a brief moment and bit her lip. "At least in *this* matter. So I shall have you to myself for the next few days."

—⁂—

By the time the last of the Wilbournes' guests departed, night had descended, and Emma led Edward to a settee located at one end of the portico, which stretched across the rear of the mansion. The two sat close together, talking and watching the moon as its light illuminated and reflected off of the flowing waters of the York River. There was a small boat sailing in the moonlight, its stern lantern casting light on the water. Childers thought, all in all, it was one of the most beautiful sights he had ever seen.

After a while, Emma put her arm around Edward's arm and leaned up against him. She said, in a soft but serious voice, "There's something I need to talk to you about."

He looked down at her. "What is it?"

"Father was very cordial to you this evening, but that was out of politeness. The truth is, he's not very happy that you are here."

"I sensed something like that—from looking at his face when I arrived. Why is he unhappy about my visit?"

"Father thinks I should marry someone who has roots and influence here in the Tidewater." She paused and gathered her thoughts. "Someone with wealth and family connections throughout the gentry."

"He doesn't consider that my family is part of the gentry? He'd better hope my father doesn't hear he's said that." Childers thought for a moment. "Has he got anyone in mind? Or is it just a general predilection on his part?"

"He definitely has a specific person and family in mind. In fact, he's already talked to the father. At least once that that I know."

Edward took a deep breath. "Who is this august lad he has fixed on? Do I know him?"

Emma looked up at him with her blue eyes. He thought they had never been more alluring. "Yes: it's Percival Arden Stonebridge."

"What!? What! *Percy Stonebridge*? Of course I know him! He was in the class ahead of me at William and Mary. But he spent more time in the taverns and at gambling tables than at his books. Not that he is very good at wagering. Everyone knows he passed out of college simply because of his family name. And he is insufferably full of himself."

"Well, his father was in the Burgesses and sat on the Royal Governor's Council, and now he is in the legislature. And their land holdings are large and very productive." She paused and looked at Childers. "Father is determined to see me married into a family he considers our equal."

Edward stiffened; a flash of anger shot through his body. But he controlled himself and the tone of his voice when he said, "And I suppose he doesn't consider the Childers of Frederick County of the proper stature?"

Emma bit her lip for a second, then replied, "Well, he thinks only a man from the Tidewater can have proper lineage for his daughters."

He looked at Emma. "And does his eldest daughter share that sentiment?"

She wrapped both her arms around him and pressed herself against his side. "His eldest daughter knows what she wants, and it's most certainly not Percy Stonebridge." Then she moved back a little bit and continued, "But you know it is tradition that a daughter, particularly the oldest daughter, follow the father's guidance—for the sake of the family's influence and place in society. Father is set on an alliance with the Stonebridges." She looked up at Edward. "Look what happened between John Henry and Dorothea. Her father jumped at the chance to have her be the governor's lady, and she felt compelled to obey and marry Patrick."

"And so you too would accept your father's choice, even if you felt nothing for the man he selected?" He looked at her sharply and pulled back slightly. "Or am I misguided? Do you see something in Percy?"

"Percy spent some time with me at a ball last month. And he's been here to see me. He is reading law in Williamsburg. Most families would consider him a proper match."

"I would not ever let that ass represent me in a matter of the law. But you haven't answered me directly about Percy. Are you going to follow your father's decision?"

She stared at him with a determined look in her eyes. Then she said, "Not if you want to formally court me and marry me. Not if you are willing to fight father to have me. Dorothea dutifully obeyed her father, but I'm *not* Dorothea. I want above all to marry the man I love, and who loves me. I guess that's what I really wanted to tell you tonight."

Childers looked at the beautiful woman beside him. He felt his heart beating and thought, *So here, tonight, has come the time to make a decision.* And in an instant he knew what the answer must be. It was no longer simply a matter of his feelings; he must uphold the family honor.

He took a deep breath. "I will talk to your father and tell him I desire to marry you—to marry when my service in the war is finished." He paused and shot her a questioning look. "That is, if you are willing to wait for me?"

She threw her arms around him and kissed him, not on the cheek, but right on the lips. Then she said, "Of course I will wait! You are the only one I have ever wanted."

"But when the time comes, you will have to come live with me in Frederick County. It is in many ways different from here in the Tidewater."

"It will be an adventure. And being with you will be the best part of the adventure!"

"Then I will indeed speak to your father tomorrow."

Emma sat up and stared out at the river for a time, then turned to him with a stern look in her eyes. "Now listen, Edward: You will have to be strong with him. When he decides on something, he can be quite stubborn. And I must confide, he has strong prejudice against me living in the Shenandoah Valley—so far away." She turned to him and smiled conspiratorially. "But I shall go to Mother's room tonight and tell her about your," she paused, grinned, and said, "about *our* decision. And I *know* she will support me. Father will have to hear her out, at least to consider what she wants." She put her hand on his shoulder. "But in the end, it will be up to *you*. You will have to convince him that the merger of our families will be advantageous." She looked up into his eyes. "But I have faith in you, Edward. I know you can do it."

Major Charles McDonald sat in the headquarters tent of the 42nd, going over a map of the country between Philadelphia and New York City. With him was the regimental adjutant, Lieutenant Owen McDougal. The two were making themselves familiar with the possible routes the army would take on their march northward. The regimental commandant, Colonel Thomas Stirling, was at a meeting with their brigade commander, who had just received marching orders from Clinton's headquarters and would soon be back with the plan for the journey.

McDougal, standing at McDonald's shoulder, traced a path from Philadelphia up to Sandy Hook. "Major, that's the most advantageous route if the plan is to cross the harbor from Sandy Hook and ferry the troops over from that point. Note that there are two good routes up to the crossroads town of Monmouth Court House, but only one out of that town to the Hook."

"Yes, but we're not sure that Sandy Hook is where Clinton intends to have the navy ferry us across—it could be up at Perth Amboy."

"Yes, sir. But that's a bit of a longer march than to Sandy Hook. There are two good ways to go to Amboy—there's a road northward from Monmouth." McDougal pointed to a point on the map. "But it's a bit shorter to go up through Allentown, then northeast to Amboy." He shrugged. "We should know the plan when the colonel gets back."

"Yes, Owen, you're correct about the distances. I've been looking at the map. But my worry is less about the route than what the *rebels* plan. Either way we go, the column will be stretched out over a great distance, what with wagon convoys, women and children, and loyalist conveyances. And they shall all have to be escorted, which will be a drain on our strength. I fear that Washington won't be able to resist the temptation to strike as we march—he'll see it as a great opportunity. We may find ourselves fighting a rearguard action all the way to either Sandy Hook or Amboy."

Just as he finished talking, Sergeant Tim McGregor, the sergeant major, came to the tent flap. "Na beggin' your pardon, Major McDonald. Miss Fraser has arrived."

The two officers looked around to see a broad smile on McGregor's face. "And she's arrived in style, if I do say so, sir! She's ridin' in a bloody great carriage!"

McDonald shot McDougal a puzzled look and walked out of the tent. And immediately had to admit McGregor was not exaggerating in any way.

Mary was ensconced in a very elegant, black-painted open carriage, with a sleek team of blacks, driven by a liveried coachman, which was coming toward them. Then he noticed something else. She was accompanied by a young cavalryman in the uniform of the 16th Light Dragoons. A spirited, saddled riding horse was tied to the rear of the carriage and pranced in impatience at being restrained.

McDonald felt a surge of concern registering within, for he recognized the dragoon.

McDougal, standing beside him, whispered a question. "Do you know that man, sir?

"Damned well I know him. He's Banastre Tarleton."

The lieutenant raised his eyebrows. "You mean the one who captured rebel general Lee back in '76?"

"The very same."

"I understand he was promoted directly to captain from coronet as a result."

"Yes, and he's been glorying in it ever since." McDonald looked over at the younger man. "Owen, the man is a dissolute rake. He got lucky by chance and Lee's carelessness, and now he's been the darling of New York and Philadelphia society ever since he snatched the general. And cutting quite a swath with the women."

"What's Mary doing with him? He's the type I would have thought she would avoid."

"Yes, and I intend to find out what is going on." He motioned to the adjutant. "Come with me."

McDonald walked out to where the carriage had pulled up.

Mary called out, a broad grin on her face, "Major McDonald! I have come back to the regiment."

The major smiled at her. "Indeed you have. And that's quite a conveyance you have there. Did you perhaps inherit a fortune without my knowing?"

Mary laughed. "You know better than that. It's a hired carriage that was loaned to me by Mrs. Loring. She arranged for it to transport me and my baggage to the camp. It was most gracious of her."

"Indeed. And I see you have an escort from the 16th."

"Yes, Captain Tarleton offered to keep me company."

Tarleton spoke up. "Good day, Major. Yes, I ran into Mrs. Loring and Miss Fraser at the harbor, and I thought it would be providential for me to accompany Miss Fraser to your camp. The rebel sympathizers are becoming restive in Philadelphia, and my perception is that it is not safe for unaccompanied British women—particularly those attached to the army—to be moving about the city."

"On behalf of the 42nd, I thank you, Captain. Now we can take care of Miss Fraser from here."

Tarleton recognized McDonald's peremptory and disapproving tone but took the cue and stepped down from the carriage. He touched the visor of his helmet and made a small bow to Mary. "Well, Miss Fraser, it has been my pleasure. It will be even more pleasure to see you in New York."

Mary responded, "Thank you for your company, Captain. I'm sure our paths will cross in that city. Until then!"

"Indeed, Ma'am." Tarleton smiled, then went to the rear of the carriage to retrieve his mount.

McDonald turned to the adjutant. "Mary, Lieutenant McDougal will join you to show the way to the hospital area. And to help you get settled."

"Why, thank you, Charles." She turned to McDougal. "It's good to see you again, Owen! Won't you join me in the carriage?"

"It will be my pleasure." The lieutenant stepped up into the conveyance to sit beside Mary and called out, "Driver, go straight ahead. The hospital is just a short distance."

McDonald watched the carriage drive away and then turned to Tarleton, who was standing by his horse, also starring after the carriage. He said, "Well, Captain, she's a lovely lady, is she not?"

Still looking at the carriage, Tarleton responded, "You will get no argument from me. I must say, I have long found myself enamored of auburn-maned women, and I vouch she is the most attractive I've ever seen. A beautiful, lustrous shade of hair, and I find her sun-darkened complexion well complements her." He turned to McDonald. "I don't particularly favor the pure-white complexion many women strive to attain. It seems so artificial."

"I quite agree. So, Captain, if I may be so bold, is it your intent to pursue her favors?"

Tarleton, who had turned back to the carriage, slowly faced McDonald. A smile came over his face, and he looked over him as if making an appraisal. "Now that's an interesting question for *you* to ask, Major. Do you fancy yourself her protector? Is she in some way related to you?"

"In a manner of speaking, Tarleton. I recruited her father to the army more than twenty years ago. Mary was only a child then, a tiny lass at her mother's skirts. I began watching over her when her father died in battle and her mother succumbed to the fever during the West Indies campaign. She has been raised by the regiment, and in all practicality it is her home, if she can be said to have any at all. She is beloved by the veterans—the corporals and sergeants—and worshiped by the subalterns." McDonald paused for effect, fixed his eyes directly on Tarleton's, then continued, "So be careful how you tread, Captain. Ensure your actions are honorable in regard to her."

Tarleton raised his eyebrows and twisted his mouth into a sneering smile. "Ah, so you *do* fancy yourself her *protector.*" He shook his head. "Now, Major, let me point this out: Miss Fraser is a full-grown, mature woman. In fact, although she doesn't show it, I'm aware she is a few years older than myself. And, I must point out, a rather remarkable lady who combines the *practicality and worldliness* of one bred in the camps with the *grace of a gentlewoman* in the ballroom. Given that, I say she is quite able to take care of her own affairs. And heed this, *sir*: I *will* act with regard to her as I choose. And I *choose* to be in her company as much as possible. Particularly after the army arrives in New York." He touched his hand to his helmet in casual salute and mounted his horse. Then, looking down at McDonald, he said dismissively, "I trust I have made my intent clear. Good day, Major." He touched his spurs to the animal and was off at a trot toward the entrance of the camp.

McDonald was staring after him, fuming inside, when he heard a voice ask, "Charles, is that young Tarleton of the 16th just riding off?"

McDonald turned to see Stirling standing in front of the tent. "Indeed, Thomas."

"What the *devil* is he doing here?"

"He escorted Mary Fraser to the camp."

The colonel turned and stared after the rider. "Damn! I don't fancy that young peacock becoming involved with her. He's an impudent ass. And a wastrel to boot. I knew his father, a fine man who died too early. Young Tarleton got a £5,000 inheritance, and the fool went through it in a year at the gambling tables and in the brothels of London. Then his mother bought him a commission to give him a final chance to make something of himself."

"Well, he just made it clear to me that that becoming involved with Mary is precisely his intention."

Stirling's face muscles tightened into a stern expression as he looked after the departing dragoon. "We shall have to see about that." Then he looked over at McDonald. "Well, Charles, we have our marching orders. Let's go to the map, and I'll show you what Clinton has planned."

—ɱ—

Edward Childers paused before the door to Howard Wilbourne's study. He felt both weary and tense. *Weary* because he had spent a sleepless night. The room that Wilbourne gave Childers was cramped, poorly furnished, and as far away from Emma's as could be managed in the mansion—an obvious indication of the elder Wilbourne's feelings toward him. But the reason for his weariness was not the discomfort of the room but the fact that he had spent the night marshaling his arguments in favor of the union of his family with that of Wilbourne's. The *tenseness* came because he realized the next hour would be the most important of his life to date. After hesitating a few moments, he gathered his courage and knocked on the door.

Wilbourne's voice answered, "Come in."

Childers opened the door. He saw the plantation master sitting before his desk, still dressed in riding clothes after his forenoon turn around the fields. A small fire crackled in the hearth against the morning chill. Wilbourne had a pair of spectacles over his nose as he reviewed papers before him. He looked up and removed his glasses. A door behind the desk apparently led to another room, and Childers wondered what that might be. "Yes, Edward?"

"May I come in, sir? There's a matter of some importance I should like to discuss with you."

A look of resignation came over Wilbourne's face. Clearly he knew what Edward wanted and had no appetite for the impending discussion.

But regardless of how he felt, Wilbourne responded politely enough. "Certainly, Mr. Childers. Please come in and have a seat." He motioned to a straight-backed chair near the front of his desk. As Edward did so, he rose from his own chair, walking in knee-length boots, and poured himself a glass of liquor from a decanter. Almost as an afterthought, he turned and asked, "Will you have one?"

"No, thank you, sir."

Wilbourne resumed his seat, took a sip of the libation, and then stared at Childers for a long moment. His face was that of someone resigned to dealing with a distasteful matter. Finally he said, "Well, young man, what is it you wish to discuss?"

His body stiff, Edward leaned slightly forward. "I've come to gain your permission to marry Emma."

Wilbourne took another sip, then stared down at his glass. Silence hung heavy in the room. Finally he asked, "Can I assume you have discussed this with Emma?"

"Of course."

"And she is sympathetic?"

"No, sir. Not sympathetic. *Enthusiastic.*" He met Wilbourne's eyes. "We have a mutual and very deep affection for each other."

Wilbourne considered that for a moment, then said, "I am surprised, young man. Surprised you did not profess that the two of you are in love. *Deep, passionate love,* as they write about in those European romances, the ones they call..." he looked at the ceiling for the moment, searching for a word. "Ah, yes—the ones they call *novels.*"

"Sir, I would not, at this moment, say *love.* I believe affection grows into true love only after a man and women are together for a sustained period and come to fully understand each other. I would say the concept of love is a combination of affection and mutual respect."

Wilbourne looked up from his glass, his eyebrows raised in apparent surprise. "An interesting way of putting it, although I might say rather mature and sensible." Then he rose, took his drink in hand, and stood staring into the hearth. After a moment he reached over to a small table, opened the wooden humidor that rested there, and took out a cigar. He put the glass down on the mantel, picked up a taper from a basket nearby, and used it to light the tobacco. He took a deep puff, then turned to Childers.

"Now, young man, I appreciate the fact that strong attraction exists between you and Emma. I would have to be blind not to see that. However, attraction, affection, or love, however you cast it, is not the only factor in a good marriage—in fact, perhaps not even the most necessary. We are discussing the union of two families and all that entails."

"I quite understand that, Mr. Wilbourne. I should like to explain why an alliance of the Wilbournes and Childers would benefit both families."

Wilbourne exhaled smoke and quickly said, "Frankly, sir, I think that would be superfluous. You should understand that I am already in preliminary discussions with another party regarding matrimony for Emma: a family of significant influence and property here in the Tidewater which will nicely complement ours."

"I believe you mean the Stonebridges of York Landing Manor, which abuts your estate. And the man you are considering as husband for Emma is Percival, the oldest son. Am I not correct?"

Wilbourne took a strong draw on his cigar, then exhaled the smoke in a long stream. "Well, Mr. Childers, you seem to have good information. And knowing that, you should understand why a marriage of Percy to Emma would be extraordinarily beneficial to both families." He looked over his cigar and added, "Beyond that, you must understand that I have no intention of allowing my daughter to live in the wilds of the Shenandoah Valley, surrounded by uncouth Irish and German migrants and where houses must be fortified against the raids of the native tribal warriors." He shrugged. "Why, I have heard that it is not uncommon to have stockades around residences and that many manor houses there have escape tunnels in case of attack by the Red Indian war parties."

Childers had an urge to laugh in Wilbourne's face. But he was able to control himself and said in a calm voice, "Sir, with all respect, your information is quite outdated. The tribes have long ago left the Shenandoah, most moving to the Ohio Valley. There has been no war party raid since the French War. During that war, Washington, then colonel of the Virginia Regiment, did indeed build a small fort on our property, but it has now been razed, and a house for one of our overseers exists in its place. And I can say with pride that our manor house at Greenfields Plantation is quite comparable—in size and comfort—to yours." Edward gathered his thoughts for a moment, then continued, "And I respectfully take exception to your characterization of the people who have settled in the valley. Although years ago there was friction between the ethnic factions, in the last decade the inhabitants of the valley have become mostly amicable neighbors who live together in substantial harmony." He raised a finger. "And let me make this point: the Guides are made up of men from several colonies, including many Germans and Ulster men in addition to those of English origin. We depend on each other, with little regard for which country from which we came originally. And our commandant, Major Eckert, is a gunsmith of German heritage who is married to an Ulster woman."

"You say your commander is a simple *mechanic*? Not a *gentleman*?"

"Sir, such things are not uncommon in our military. We are building a new kind of army for a new nation, the like of which is unknown anywhere else in civilization. The head of our artillery was a bookseller in Boston. Our quartermaster general owned a foundry for making ship's anchors. And I must say, I am very proud to serve under Major Eckert, for Washington considers him to be among the ablest officers in the army. I have personally seen him lead in action for over two years, and I have the utmost confidence in his ability."

Wilbourne stood staring at Edward over his cigar, smoke swirling in front of his face, obviously not able to find words to counter what had been said.

Edward seized the moment and pressed ahead with his planned arguments. "Sir, you should be aware that the Childers' holdings are the largest in Frederick County, and in fact spill over into much of the next county to the south. They consist of our main farm and five others. I don't intend a direct comparison to your plantation, but I have checked, and our total acreage under cultivation exceeds that of your holdings. Beyond that, we have considerable land yet to be cleared and put into crops."

Wilbourne raised his eyebrows, then returned to his seat behind the desk. He waved his cigar at Edward. "Continue, young man. I admit that you have said some intriguing things. In any case, since you are determined to persevere, I will hear you out."

"Thank you, sir. I will be quick about it, for my case speaks for itself." He rose and put his hands behind his back. "I am the second son of the family. My eldest brother, William, is married and will of course inherit the main part of our holdings. Incidentally, he is planning to stand for the legislative seat representing Frederick County—the one formerly held by James Wood before he took command of his regiment. There is little doubt that William will be successful." He paused and looked at Wilbourne. "I'm sure you are acquainted with Colonel Wood. He is great friends with my father."

The plantation master nodded. "Certainly. We have worked together in the legislature and other matters here in Williamsburg."

"Now, Father has promised me that when I marry, he will give me title to our Rocky Brook Farm. It is four thousand acres and mostly under cultivation. Beyond that, it is adjacent to considerable uncleared acreage that will provide for expansion."

Wilbourne shrugged. "An admirable holding, Childers. But Percy Stonebridge is the oldest son of the family, and as you are aware, I have no sons. Emma will eventually inherit most of this plantation, which of course her husband will control. So in all practicality, the two plantations will merge into a vast landholding here along the York. The production of tobacco will be prodigious, and sited along the river, transportation to market will be quite easy."

"Indeed, sir, if you want to limit the plantation to growing and selling tobacco."

"Limit it? What other cash crop *would* you produce? Virginia tobacco is known and desired for its quality. For pipes and," he held up his cigar, "for these. They are in rapidly growing demand."

"I would of course, grow tobacco to some degree. But I have another type of crop in mind for most of my land. One which could in the end prove far more lucrative."

"*More* lucrative than tobacco? And pray tell, what do you suppose that to be?"

Edward said one word. "Grain."

Howard Wilbourne threw his head back and laughed explosively. He looked at the ceiling as if seeking patience from the heavens. "Sir, there is *no* money in grain. Every dirt farmer grows grain for his own use. We grow some for our bread and flour. But grain as a cash-producing crop? Hardly, sir!"

"You are quite correct, if the plan were to sell it. But growing grain—wheat, rye, barley, corn—would be the means to an end—a very specific end. Quite simply, I intend to build a distillery and produce whiskey from the grain, sir. There is great demand for whiskey since the blockade ended the importation of rum in any significant amount."

The plantation master made a face. "But see here, Childers. What you say may be true for the present. But when the war is over—whatever the result may be—rum will again begin to flow into the colonies. Then there will be little interest in your whiskey. It is a frontier country libation."

"To the contrary, sir, I do not think that will be the case. The country is developing a taste for good whiskey. My experience is that the men of the army prefer it. And you see the same in taverns throughout the land. And if produced here, it will be cheaper than rum distilled in the West Indies, or even rum distilled here from molasses produced in the West Indies which must be shipped here at considerable expense and undoubtedly taxed by government."

Wilbourne stared into the distance for a long time, then looked over at Edward. "I concede there might be some merit to what you say."

"I'm confident about it, sir. And there are other factors to consider. Growing grain requires much less field labor than tobacco. You yourself, I am sure, know tobacco must be cultivated intensely to get good quality. And then there is the drying and curing. It is a long process. With grain, far fewer African slaves are required. And I, like you, know that acquiring and maintaining in good health substantial numbers of Africans is the largest single cost of producing tobacco. Growing grain for whiskey is much cheaper and the profit is thus far more substantial than tobacco."

"No one knows better than I the cost of maintaining Africans." He shrugged. "But I'm not sure there is as much profit in spirits as you seem to think."

Edward reached into a pocket and pulled out a piece of paper. "I thought it might be necessary to show you some actual figures to convince you." He walked over to the desk and laid the paper in front of Wilbourne. "So I spent some time last night putting these on paper. You'll see that it is a comparison of tobacco production costs against those of whiskey." He smiled, "I was always good in mathematics in college, and I have been working out the figures while in the army. My commandant, Major Eckert, and the sergeant major, Simon Donegal, are in the whiskey business together and helped me with the numbers."

Wilbourne laid his cigar down, put on his reading glasses, and ran his fingers over the lines on the paper. After a few minutes he looked up at Edward. "I will allow that these seem to make sense." He bit his lip. "But they don't cover the cost of building a distillery and hiring a man who actually knows how to distill the liquor."

"I have assurances from my father that the capital for that will be forthcoming when I am ready to proceed, which obviously will be after I leave the army, whenever that might be." He looked down at Wilbourne, who had turned back to the paper of calculations. "There's another point I would like to make."

Without looking up the elder man said, "Go ahead, sir."

"You talked earlier of the fact that this this plantation would be merged with that of the Stonebridges at the time Emma inherits it. I ask that you consider instead the implications of an alliance by marriage between River Pines and our Greenfields Plantation. I would ask you to recall that tobacco crops are very hard on the land, depleting the richness of the soil. Were this estate to come under my control in Emma's name, I would use resources earned from Greenfields to plant crops that would help replenish the soil, thus ensuring the continued viability of the plantation into the future." Edward resumed his seat in the straight-backed chair and said, "I should think that the assurance of maintaining this manor as a productive unit and a fitting legacy of your ownership would provide comfort to you."

Howard Wilbourne picked up his glass and downed a large sip of the whiskey. He said nothing and simply stared over at the fireplace.

Edward gave him a few moments to consider what had been said, then began making his final argument. "Now I should like to mention a delicate matter. I have no desire to cast aspersions on anyone, but you should be aware that I was at William and Mary at the same time as Percy."

Wilbourne looked up. "Indeed?"

"Yes, sir. And if I may speak confidentially between one gentleman and another, there are some things you may not be aware of about him."

The planter's face tightened. "If you are about to denigrate young Mr. Stonebridge before me, I shall not entertain your comments, sir!"

Childers ignored his words and pressed on. "I will just mention one attribute of him. I beg you listen. You may or may not think it relevant to your decision."

There was a moment of silence. "Well, sir, if you *must*. What is it you wish to say?"

"Just this, sir. Percy was quite involved in games of chance and always in need of money. He was not known as being particularly skilled at the table, a situation aggravated by his heavy consumption of libation when he played. I know for a fact that several times he had to ride down to Stonebridge Plantation to obtain large sums of money from his father to resolve debt."

Edward was sure that concern showed in Wilbourne's eyes.

But Wilbourne asked, "What is your point? How is this relative to our discussion?"

"Simply this, Mr. Wilbourne. I have just pledged to maintain the integrity of this plantation and do all in my power to keep it flourishing. Considering his wagering habits, can you trust Percy Stonebridge to do the same?"

Wilbourne bit his lip. Childers sensed that he had hit home with the remarks about Percy. Edward looked directly into Wilbourne's eyes. "That's all I have to say. I hope you decide that you see in me someone who will both cherish your daughter and create an alliance that both the Wilbournes and Childers can be proud of."

The master of River Pines Manor crushed out his cigar and then quickly downed the last dregs in his glass. Then he said, "Well, Mr. Childers, I will profess that you have given me something to think about. And I must take the time to do that. I will give you my answer on the morrow. Until then, spend the day relaxing in the hospitality of my home."

Childers rose. "Thank you, Mr. Wilbourne, for listening to my proposition. Certainly I will abide by your decision, whatever it may be."

Wilbourne looked up at him and nodded. Edward turned and left the study, closing the door after himself.

He walked a few steps down the hall, and suddenly a door swung open, and Emma stood there. She put her finger to her mouth to keep him from speaking and, taking his arm, drew him into the room. Edward realized it was a sewing room. She said breathlessly, "You did wonderfully!"

Childers looked at her in puzzlement. "How do you know?"

Emma pointed to a door in the wall. "That connects to Father's study. I shamelessly had my ear to the door frame—there's a rather wide gap—and I heard much of what you said, although I missed some when you spoke in soft tones or moved farther from the door. But from what I did hear, you were very convincing. And I know Father—from the tone of his voice, he really is considering what you said."

"Well, my beautiful little spy, then you know he said he would give me an answer tomorrow."

"Yes! I was afraid he had his mind hardened and would simply tell you no right away. Now I shall go to Mother and insist she press him to accept you as my betrothed. She is already inclined to our side. She has never had any affinity for Percy or for any of the Stonebridges." She pointed to a chair. "Now sit down and go over exactly what you said again so that I can use it to fully convince her and give her the ammunition to use tonight." She grinned broadly, then said with a conspiratorial expression on her face, "Father likes to think he makes all the important decisions, but he also understands that he will have no peace if he goes against Mother."

Chapter Thirteen
On the Move

The familiar sights and sounds of a regiment breaking camp and preparing to march surrounded Mary Fraser as she stood in front of her tent. It was just past dawn three days after she had returned to the 42nd, and she was happy to be back in her role as the matron of the battalion hospital. The months in Philadelphia had been enjoyable, but it was good to be surrounded by people who constituted her army family—in reality, the only true family she had. There *had* been the eight years when she served as the governess at Bonniecrest Manor in the Highlands, and she had come to think of that as her home. But that had all come to an abrupt end one terrible night when the new master, in drunken lust, had tried to have his way with her, and she had been forced to dispatch him with her dagger. She shuddered at the thought of it.

But she didn't have much time for the memories of her last days in Scotland, for suddenly she saw Tim McGregor, the sergeant major, coming toward her.

"Good day now, Mary! Have you got yourself all together for the march?"

Mary smiled at Tim. There was always a measure of tension between them, for thirteen years before, at Fort Pitt, Tim, having just been made corporal, had courted her and finally asked her to marry him. She had been tempted by the offer, for Tim was handsome, and she had developed real affection for him, but she had ultimately chosen to pursue the role of governess for which she had been studying and preparing all her life. So she had left him and eventually the army behind, thinking she would never see him again. But then the lust-driven actions of Bonniecrest's master had brought her back to the regiment. McGregor was now married and the father of two children, who all marched with the regiment. She said, "Yes, I'm all packed, Tim, and ready to go."

He nodded. "All right. Tavish is bringing up wagons and a work party to load the hospital. We've got one for you to ride in and carry your things." He looked around and pointed down the row of tents. "Here they come now."

Mary looked to see Piper Sergeant Tavish and several privates walking beside the wagons as teamsters maneuvered them through the camp. Tavish waved at her, a wide grin on his face.

McGregor touched his bonnet and said, "Na lass, I've got to get along and check on the companies. We'll be marchin' soon enough. Colonel Stirling wants to make sure we're ready to take our place in the column. If any battalion is going to cause a delay, it'll na be the Black Watch." And with that he was off down the company street.

Mary turned and called out to the piper, "Ian! Where have you been? I've been back three days, and I haven't seen you till now."

"Ah, now, my sweet lass, it's busy I've been, getting' ready to march. And we've been drillin' the lads hard. They've been all livin' in little groups in houses all over the city, these many months, and forgettin' their training. But I told Tim I'd help you get loaded up."

Mary motioned toward her tent. "I'm all packed. My bags are all in there. And Surgeon Potts wants me to keep all the apothecary supplies with me in my wagon." She pointed to another tent. "They're over there."

"Aye, na don't you worry, Mary, well get them all safely loaded." He pointed to a covered wagon. "And that's where you'll be ridin' on the march, in great style."

The wagons had now pulled up in the hospital area. Tavish called out to the men of the detail, "All right now, you two lads, get Miss Fraser's bags out of this tent and load them into the small wagon. And careful how you handle her things." He motioned to the rest of the men. "You others, get the medical supplies out of that tent. And step lively, we haven't got all morning!"

The sergeant put his hands on his hips, watching as the men worked. Mary looked up at the tall piper. "Tavish, were you along on the expedition where the skirmish occurred at the Millstone River?"

"Ah, Lass, indeed I was. Piping for Major McDonald. And let me tell ya, that was a sharp little fight. Short, but very sharp indeed! Some good men went down."

She leaned close and asked in a low voice, "Did you see what happened to Wend Eckert?"

Tavish winked at her. "Why am I na surprised that you would ask me. But indeed I did see everything." He leaned over, whispering conspiratorially, and gave her an account of Wend having his horse shot out from under him and then being rescued by his men. "Now don't you worry, Mary. He's well. He was a little shaken up by bein' thrown off his horse, but I saw him later at the parley with Major McDonald in the middle of the river, and he was as good as ever."

Mary said, "That's comforting, Ian."

"And I heard what he said about you to the major." He grinned at her.

"The major sent me a distance away 'cause he wanted to talk in private, but words carry over the water, particularly in a still night like that. Here's the thing: sure and the major tried to get Wend to say he wasn't in love with you anymore, but Wend said he would always love you, even though he's happy with his wife and family."

Mary felt a shock run through her body. But she recovered quickly and responded, "Ian, thank you so much for telling me that. It makes me feel much better."

"I knew you'd want to hear that from me, even if Major McDonald hasn't already told you." He thought a moment. "By the way, Donegal's still his old self. He was wearing his bonnet from the old 77th. And one thing's sure: He's learned to ride a horse a lot better than back when we marched with Colonel Bouquet. When they came to rescue Eckert, he was handling a horse and firing pistols like a King's Dragoon." He shook his head. "You remember how he could barely stay on when they first gave him and Bob Kirkwood horses so they could act as scouts?"

Mary laughed. "Yes, I remember that. It was quite comical!"

"Well, lass, it's sure he's been doing a lot more riding this last fifteen years." Tavish called out to one of the work detail, "Hey there, laddie! Now you be careful with those boxes. They got surgeon's stores in them!" He turned to Mary. "Lass, we'll talk more later. Maybe in camp tonight. But na I've got to see to these lads' work."

"I'll welcome a visit from you, Tavish. Anytime!"

The piper walked off toward where the men were carrying things from the surgeon's tent and stopped to talk with Mr. Potts, who was watching the progress of the loading.

Mary smiled to herself. *So Charles McDonald lied to me about Wend.* She knew she should feel angry and betrayed by the major's false words but immediately realized what he had been about. *He's still trying to get me to forget Wend so he can get me married off to one of the young officers of the regiment. That's been his hope all along. Still playing the role of my stepfather.* Rather than anger, she felt a surge of fondness for the man who had felt responsible for looking out for her well-being for so many years. She thought, *I'll act like I'm taking his advice and be receptive to the attentions of the subalterns. It will make him feel good. And in truth, I will welcome the company. Then when the war is over, I'll resume my dream of working as a governess. There will be a lot of opportunity here in America, however the war ends.*

Presently Surgeon Potts approached her. "We're all loaded and ready to move. Let me assist you into your seat. We must get to our place in the wagon convoy."

Mary smiled at the doctor and said, "Thank you, Mr. Potts; that's very kind of you," as he handed her up to her seat.

Potts said, "Stirling talked to all the officers in the mess this morning. He said General Clinton thinks it will be an easy march up to New York. But the colonel is not so sanguine. He believes the rebels will attack us." He shrugged. "If he's right, we may have a busy time of it in the hospital."

Mary looked down at the surgeon. "Well, Doctor Potts, that's the very reason I came back to the regiment."

Potts looked up at her and smiled. "And we are all heartily glad you are here." Then he turned and walked to his horse.

Just then Mary heard the sound of drums and looked up to where the regiment was formed in time to see the lead company step off. Almost immediately came the sound of bagpipes, and the entire regiment began to march. Stirling and McDonald were on their mounts to one side of the column, watching the movement. The driver seated next to Mary said, "Here we go, ma'am. Hold on." He slapped the reins down on the back of the horses, and they and the other wagons followed in the wake of the column.

—ᴥ—

Edward and Emma were sitting on the veranda, talking and watching the York River. It was late in the morning the day after Edward's session with Howard Wilbourne. The plantation master had left very early in the morning to make his rounds of one of the outlying farms, and he had not seen either Emma or Edward before leaving.

Emma said, "I'm worried. Mother has remained in her room all morning. Her maid says she is tired from being up late last night talking with Father and doesn't plan to come down until later in the day."

Childers sighed. "Are you saying that's a bad sign?"

"I don't know. But I'm worried."

"We'll just have to wait until your father returns. Then I'll wait upon him and ask for his decision."

They sat together quietly for a while, and presently there was the sound of a horse trotting up the drive.

Emma looked at Edward, anxiety in her eyes. "That will be father. He almost always returns in time for dinner."

Childers felt a knot in his stomach. The time of decision was approaching.

Suddenly Emma turned and threw her arms around him. "Oh, Edward, I am so worried!" She looked at him with her large eyes and exclaimed. "I will not be like Dorothea! I'll not marry a man I don't desire. I will marry the man I love. And you are that man. I vow, if father says no, I will run away and join you in the army. I'll become a camp follower, if that is what it takes to be with you!"

He put his arms around her. "I want to be with you also. But let's be patient and see what your father says." He hugged her close and held her in a long embrace.

Almost immediately they heard the sound of booted steps coming along the hall toward them. Edward released Emma and stood up just in time to see the master of River Pines Manor emerge from the rear door of the hall.

Wilbourne was dressed in his riding clothing. He looked at the two young people with a serious expression on his face that betrayed nothing about what he was thinking. Then he cleared his throat and said, "Good morning, Emma. Morning, Mr. Childers." He paused a moment. "Emma, if you will excuse us for a time, I have something to discuss with the young man. It will not take long." He motioned to Edward. "Sir, let us repair to my study."

Childers looked over at Emma to see her lips puckered in worry and dread in her eyes. She quickly put her hand to her mouth. He smiled at her with a confidence he did not feel, then turned and followed Wilbourne back into the mansion.

Upon entering the study, Wilbourne went over to the side table and poured himself a drink and downed it in one gulp. Then he stood staring at the glass in his hand as if trying to decide what to say. The silence hung over the room, and Edward decided to break the ice. "How was your ride around the property, sir?"

Wilbourne turned around. "I didn't make rounds today. I had other business today. In fact, I rode directly over to the Stonebridge place to have a talk with him."

Edward's heart sank. *Had Wilbourne gone over to finalize marriage arrangements regarding Percy?*

"I went there to tell Stonebridge that I had made a decision about Emma marrying Percy." Wilbourne, drink in hand, walked over to a window and stared out at the river for a few seconds. Then he turned to Edward and said, "As cordially and tactfully as I possible I informed him that I was discontinuing negotiations on the matter."

Edward, hardly believing what he had heard, said, "Sir?"

"I told him Emma was to become betrothed to you, sir. That your nuptials would occur soon after you returned from your time in the army." He smiled and continued, "Last night I discussed the idea with Mrs. Wilbourne, who I must say had some strong feelings on the matter, and then I spent some time thinking things over further. Finally I decided that your proposition made sense and was in the best interest of Emma and our family."

Edward felt a rush of emotion, of almost giddiness. "Sir, I will never give you cause to regret your decision."

"Yes, well you damn well better not." He turned back and filled another glass with liquor and then refilled his own. "But congratulations, Edward. You are getting a marvelous young lady, and I sincerely hope you both may be happy in the marriage. He handed the glass to Edward and held up his own. "Here's to the union of our families, to the alliance of the Tidewater and the Shenandoah. May it always be cordial and," he smiled, "beneficial for us all."

The two raised glasses and sipped the libation.

Then Childers thought of something. "Sir, you will be hearing from my father, Langston. He will write to open a discussion of dower matters."

Wilbourne raised his eyebrows as if that surprised him. Then he shrugged and said, "Ah, yes. I hadn't thought of that. But quite proper, of course. Although we shall have a goodly amount of time to negotiate the matter, given your likely significant amount of time still in the army."

"Indeed, sir. But I should like to have it arranged in good time so that nothing will hold up the wedding when the moment comes."

Wilbourne smiled to himself. "Of course, of course. And you—and your father—will find that I *value* my daughter greatly." Then he put down his empty glass and said cheerfully, "Well, Edward, shall we go tell the rest of the family the good news?"

—~—

At the Ridgley House, the nurses and orderlies had been bustling around all day, getting ready to move and loading everything into the wagons. Northcutt thought the place was buzzing like a beehive as medical supplies had been crated up, linens packed away in boxes, and empty beds and mattresses taken out to wagons. Just after noon Nurse Pauline entered Northcutt's room and said, "Well, Colonel, we're almost ready to leave. The wagons are outside and being loaded. Orderlies will be transferring you to a litter in just a few minutes. They've got a good solid wagon ready to carry you and another officer. But meanwhile, you've got a visitor—a captain, who says he's got some important news for you."

Northcutt was puzzled. Then he realized it must be Markwood, finally back from his mission to catch John Henry. Enthusiastically he said, "Ah, yes! Show him in."

The nurse opened the door wide, and in walked, *not* Markwood, but young Banastre Tarleton, in a dusty uniform, looking as if he had just come in from the field.

Tarleton nodded and said, "Morning, Colonel." Then he unstrapped his helmet and removed it.

Northcutt, pondering what his presence could mean, responded, "To what do I owe this pleasure, Tarleton?"

"I've just come from headquarters. Andre wanted me to provide you some information."

"About what? I don't understand."

"About your compatriot, Captain Markwood." He walked over to the window and stared at the activity in the street, then turned back to Barrett. "Two days ago my commandant, Colonel Harcourt, acting on orders from headquarters, sent me with my troop to find out what had happened to Markwood and some other men who had been sent to intercept a couple of rebel officers traveling on the road southward from the city. I understand one of the officers was the son of the governor of Virginia."

Barrett said, "Tarleton, I'm familiar with their mission."

The dragoon shrugged. "At any rate, Andre was worried because they were overdue getting back."

Fear welling up inside, Northcutt asked, "So what did you find?"

Not answering directly, Tarleton said, "We tracked Markwood and his compatriots down to an inn at a small village a day's journey to the west. The Fountain Inn, it was called. A loyal sympathizer in the village told us there had been some sort of altercation in the inn and that Continental Dragoons had been seen bivouacked there for a night a few days ago." He grinned. "At first, no one in the inn wanted to talk to us. But after a little friendly persuasion, they gave us the story."

Northcutt could imagine what Tarleton meant by *friendly persuasion.* "All right, Tarleton, don't keep me in suspense. What happened?"

"In a word, Markwood and his men entered the inn, found young Henry and his companion there enjoying food and drink, and attempted to take them into custody."

"Attempted? What stopped them?"

"A squad of the Guides Dragoons arrived a few moments after Markwood." Tarleton raised his eyebrows and shook his head. "Somehow, they must have known about Markwood's mission." He shrugged. "In any case, they turned the tables on Markwood and his men. Shots were fired, a man named Harkness was wounded, and all of them were captured and taken back to Valley Forge by the dragoons. Henry and his friend traveled onward the next morning."

Northcutt settled back in his bed, shocked at the outcome. He had known Markwood since the days of Dunmore's fight against the rebels back in Virginia. He had been a faithful and efficient assistant and, more importantly, had developed considerable knowledge of the loyalist web in New Jersey and New York. And the loss of Harkness, the key man in his spy web, was a disaster. After a few moments he looked up at the young dragoon. "Thank you for relating that information, Mr. Tarleton."

"Ah, yes, Northcutt, you are quite welcome. As I said, Andre thought you would like to know."

Northcutt thought, *Yes, he wanted me to know but didn't have the courage to tell me himself that the mission he was so confident about had failed. Failed just like our ambush at the Millstone.*

Tarleton remained standing by the bed, a small smile on his face. "Now, if I may, Colonel, there is something else I should like to make you aware of, something rather more personal."

"More personal? What do you mean?"

"It's about Miss Fraser."

"Mary?"

"Indeed. I'm aware that you have," he paused to choose his words, "been escorting her to numerous events."

"That is no secret."

"Yes, well, it is my impression that although you have been giving her much attention, your advances, if I may call them that, have not, shall we say, settled on fertile ground."

"I'm not sure why that is your business, Captain. It would seem that is between the lady and myself."

"Well, I'm making it my business."

Northcutt stared at the insolent young peacock. It was obvious where this was going, and he felt anger rising within. "Stop beating around the bush, Tarleton. What specifically are you trying to say?"

"Just this, my *dear* Colonel. I'm giving you notice that I intend to give Miss Fraser considerable attention once we reach New York. I find her most attractive and highly engaging. And given your condition, it is unlikely that you will be able to entertain her socially for quite some time."

Barrett stared at the young officer for a long moment. "Are you aware that Mary is at least five years older than yourself? She is due to celebrate her thirtieth birthday."

"My dear sir, that does not daunt me in the least. We both know the lady appears much younger." He grinned broadly. "And there is much to say about a woman with," he hesitated a moment searching for the precise word, "shall we say *experience*. I like my ladies to be both beautiful *and* schooled in the ways of the world. And we both know that Mary is both of those things. After all, she came to maturity in a marching regiment and has long been the confidant of Mrs. Loring." He gave Northcutt a knowing look. "In truth, I have little time for young coquettes who are adept at flirtation but little else."

Throttling his anger, Northcutt said, "You may find that you misjudge Miss Fraser. However, I can't prevent you from directing your attentions to her. But let me warn you, better men than you have pursued her with the intent of matrimony and have been frustrated in their desires."

Tarleton raised an eyebrow and smiled again. "Matrimony? Now Colonel, I don't recall saying anything about *matrimony.* A relationship of that *permanence* is not on my agenda. I freely admit to having much more, shall we say, *informal* and *temporary* intentions."

"Whatever you plan, Tarleton, you may find Mary's ability to resist your charms stronger than you expect."

"Well, we shall just have to see, won't we now, Northcutt? Perhaps I shall succeed where others"—he looked at Northcutt meaningfully—"have failed. As a matter of fact, I have already begun my pursuit of the lady. You might be interested to know that I escorted Mary on her return to the camp of the 42nd three days ago, and I must say we had a most engaging and delightful afternoon."

Barrett didn't respond with words, simply glaring at the young officer.

Tarleton picked up his helmet. "Now, delightful as our conversation has been, I regret that I must leave you, Colonel, and rejoin my troop. We ride instantly to take up the advance for the army's journey northward. I bid you good day."

Northcutt watched as the dragoon strode out of the room. He settled back on the pillow with his mind in turmoil, thoughts swirling in his head about Mary and about Markwood's fate and the implications of the failure to capture John Henry. He set his jaw. Tarleton's pursuit of Mary was a complication he could not have anticipated in his fight to regain her favors. But there was nothing he could do about it in the short term, so he set that aside for the moment and turned his thoughts to the loss of Markwood. Then a thought occurred to him: Andre had been positioning himself to claim credit for the capture of young Henry, but in the end that had gone awry. He imagined the dandy officer having to stand before Clinton and explain the failure to the general. He smiled to himself. It was the most satisfactory thought he had had in many days.

His reflections were interrupted when Pauline swung open the door. "All right, Colonel Northcutt, it's time to move you. The orderlies are here, and we'll soon have you out in the wagon."

Barrett looked at the narrow canvas litter the two soldiers were carrying and knew that the next few minutes, as they transferred him first to the litter, then into the wagon, would be painful. He steeled himself for the discomfort as the men began the process of moving him. Northcutt comforted himself that at least they weren't taking him to a ship and the torture and chronic sickness he experienced when traveling by sea.

—⁂—

In the late-afternoon sun, Wend Eckert walked from his hut in the camp of the Guides to the nearby location where Andrew Horner's camp and tool wagon lay.

"You called for me Andrew? Does this mean the pistols are finished?"

"I've been rushing them, because of all the rumors that the army is about to move. They are ready for you to test fire, sir." Andrew pointed to his worktable. "Look them over. I just finished the final oiling of the wood."

Wend stood beside the table and examined the firelocks. "They look perfect, Andrew. The oil has brought out the grain. You selected a handsome piece of wood."

"I thought it would look nice." He motioned toward the weapons. "But the test will be how they shoot." He pointed toward a target about thirty feet away. "The target's set up, and the pistols are loaded."

Wend took the pistols in his hands and hefted them. "They feel good." He walked over to face the target. Andrew came over to stand beside him. Wend handed him one pistol and took the other in his right hand. He cocked the hammer and fixed his eyes on the center of the target, extended his arm, and pulled the trigger. The pistol fired immediately.

Horner stared at the target. "Looks like it's in the center, sir."

Suddenly a new voice spoke up. "Now that was intriguing, Eckert. You didn't really seem to aim. A nice trick."

Wend looked around to see that Hamilton had come up quietly behind them. He replied, "Alex, that's the design of the pistol. A family secret. If you hold it correctly, the curve of the handle puts you right on target if you keep your eyes where you want the ball to go."

Horner spoke up. "Sir, you want to fire the other one?"

Wend exchanged pistols with Andrew and quickly fired the second pistol at the target.

Hamilton exclaimed, "Damn, the ball hit right next to the other one."

Wend turned around. "The Eckert family have been gunsmiths for generations. We know our trade, Alex." He grinned and looked at the staff officer. "But I see some papers in your hand. What's your business with me?"

"I've got orders for you."

"Does this mean the British are moving?"

"A courier came in with the word that the lead units of Clinton's army have left their camps in the environs of Philadelphia and are marching for the Delaware River. The 16th Light Dragoons are leading the way. The advance units of the army should be crossing in the morning." He paused, then continued, "Washington called a council of war with all the generals and some of the senior staff. It lasted for hours. Lots of controversy. Washington was advocating to march posthaste and get into position to strike the British. Many of the generals agreed with him. But Lee was advocating caution, suggesting we simply observe the movements of the enemy and let them move up to New York unhindered. And several generals agreed with him."

"For God's sake, Alex! Let the British go without attacking? We've been waiting for a chance to hit them ever since we got to Valley Forge."

"General Lee thinks the army doesn't have the skill and discipline to face the British in the open. He believes it would result in disaster. He thinks we should save the army for raids upon the British outposts once they are in New York."

Wend thought a moment. "Lee hasn't been with the army for two years. His memory is of the defeat at New York and the disastrous retreat across Jersey. He was captured before we surprised the Hessians at Trenton. He's been sitting in New York socializing with the British and loyalists while he was on parole. I say he is unaware of what the army has become, and most particularly with all the work done by Von Steuben."

Hamilton stared at Wend for several seconds, then he nodded and said, "Bravo, Eckert. It happens that your thinking about Lee is very much along the line of Washington's." He said in a low voice, "In any case, Washington was able to convince the majority of the generals of his point of view. By voice vote, they decided the army will strike and strike hard. Lee was not happy, but of course had to accede to the decision."

"Frankly, Alex, the men of the army would be sorely disappointed—nay, angry—if the British were allowed to easily march to New York."

"Yes, Eckert. And it's going to be up to you to find the best place to attack." He held up one of the papers. "Here are your orders. You march at first light tomorrow, to get a feel for the composition of the British column and recommend where an attack will have the most effect." He paused and said, "The rest of the army will march by divisions throughout the day. You are to keep Washington constantly informed of your movements and that of the enemy by courier."

Wend took the order. "We'll be ready. I'll talk to my officers within the hour."

Hamilton nodded. "I've got to distribute other orders. Morgan and his riflemen are going out right after you." He reached out and touched Wend on the arm. "Good luck, Wend! Washington's counting on you." And then he strode off.

A half hour later, Wend stood before a gathering of all his officers. "Well, gentlemen, the moment we've been waiting for is here. The British are leaving Philadelphia, and we march at first light tomorrow as the eyes of the army."

There was a stir around the group. Wend quieted them and gave them some details of preparations. Then he looked over at Bradley. "Are all the horses from the Cavalry Brigade here?"

"Indeed, sir. McCrae and his detachment arrived with them this afternoon."

Newkirk spoke up. "The men have spent the last two days making up cartridges for the muskets. We've got all that we can carry, and we have extra to be stowed in the wagons. And all the provisions from General Green have been distributed to the men and the cook wagon, sir."

Wend nodded. "All right, get back to your companies and inform the men. Meli Wood will have a good, hot meal ready for the officer's mess tonight." He smiled. "It may be the last we have for a long time." He smiled. "All right, gentlemen, I'll see you for supper."

The officers hurried off to see to their final preparations. Wend sat down at his desk and started to write a letter to Peggy. He hadn't had much time and wanted to get something off before they departed. He had just written, "My Dearest," when he heard a female voice.

"So it starts tomorrow?"

Wend looked up to see Colleen McGraw standing by the cook fire, her arms crossed in front of her.

"Well, word gets around fast. But yes, Colly we depart at first light tomorrow. I expect you'll be following the army closely."

"No, you're wrong. I won't be following. I'll be *ahead* of the army. At least for the first few days. We'll leave with you tomorrow, then split off and find a good position to camp and watch how things develop and how—and where—the army moves."

"Colleen, you know that could be dangerous."

"I want to be in a good place to sell my goods to the troops if the army advances slowly or camps for a few days. We need to travel parallel with, but a little west of the army. Edna's son Charlie is a good scout, and he'll keep us informed of what's going on." She smiled. "I can't make money if I'm sitting somewhere behind the column where there aren't troops. And the men are used to having us close at hand."

"Well, you always seem to turn up in just the right place. But be careful, Colly."

"I'm always careful, but always profitable because I'm ready to take chances." She moved up close to him, looked into his eyes, then leaned over and kissed him on the cheek. "You're the one who needs to be careful. I always worry when you are in action." She stood up, looked down at the paper on his desk, and said cheerfully, "Now you be a dutiful husband and write a nice, sweet letter to your wife."

And with that, she was off, headed back to her collection of wagons.

—∞—

The June morning was sunny and warm with a gentle breeze wafting in from the river. The entire Wilbourne family—Howard, Patricia, Emma, and the two younger girls—had assembled on the drive before the front steps of the mansion. Willie, one of the grooms, had saddled Childers's horse and brought it from the stables and was standing nearby holding the reins.

Shortly, Edward came out of the front door. He had donned his hunting shirt. Over one shoulder he had slung his saddlebags, and over the other were the holstered pistols.

Howard Wilbourne's brows furrowed. "You are not wearing your officer's uniform?"

"Sir, the hunting shirt is much more comfortable for traveling. And I plan to ride hard during daylight and spend most nights camping beside the road. I don't want to soil the uniform coat."

"Ah, yes. I see. I'm just not accustomed to gentlemen wearing such attire."

Emma grinned. "Father, when the Guides are in the field, all the soldiers wear hunting shirts. And so do the officers—that's so enemy marksmen won't be able to identify them."

Edward glanced at Emma.

She added, "Yes, Edward told me that soldiers of the British light foot and Hessian Jaegers like to target officers with their rifle guns."

Edward replied, "So wearing the shirt will help ensure that I return to Emma after the war—something that is of the highest importance to me."

Patricia Wilbourne nodded. "And of great importance to all of us."

Edward went to the horse and laced the pistols and bags onto the saddle. Then he turned and said, "Much as I should like to, I must not dally. I fear the new campaign is already toward, and I must spare no time in returning to the Guides."

Childers shook Wilbourne's hand. "Sir, once again I pledge to you that from this day forward, your daughter's well-being will be foremost in my mind." He turned, touched his hat to Patricia and the girls. Then Emma quickly came into his arms. She was smiling, but tears were evident in her eyes.

"Edward, take care and come back to me safe and sound." She embraced him for a long moment.

Childers sighed deeply and said, "Returning to you, my dear Emma, will be my most important endeavor."

Then he turned and mounted the horse. Giving it the spur, Edward took the animal up the drive at the trot. Once out on the road, he pulled on the reins until the horse reared up on its hind legs, the forelegs poised high, flailing in the air. He held him there for a moment with one hand on the reins and with the other doffed his hat and waved it toward the Wilbournes. Then he eased off on the reins until the animal was back on all fours, spurred him, and was off at the gallop. Horse and rider immediately disappeared from view behind the pines that lined the roadway.

"Well," said Wilbourne, "One thing's sure: the lad knows how to handle a horse. I should like to see how he rides to the hunt."

Patricia said, "I'm sure you'll get the chance, Howard." She turned to her daughter. "Emma, will you take the girls to see Miss Thornton? It's time for them to take their lessons."

Emma gathered up her sisters and led them into the house.

Patrica said to her husband, "Howard, I know you had your doubts, but in the end you certainly made the right decision in the case of that young man."

"Thank you, my dear. After the lad talked to me, it became clear he has a sound mind, and his thoughts are focused on the future." He shrugged. "I must say, Stonebridge was not amused when I told him the arrangement with his son was off, but he'll get over it." A thoughtful look came over his face, then he looked to his wife. "My dear, did you happen to notice that Emma seemed flushed this morning? Do you think she may have a fever?"

"I should think she *would* have a glow, the morning after she became a woman."

Wilbourne's head snapped around. "What do you mean?"

"I heard a noise in the night which seemed to be coming from the young girls' room and rose to check on them. On the way I looked in on Emma's room—to find her bed empty."

"What?!"

"Oh, Howard, don't be so shocked. The boy's future in the war is uncertain at best. I'll not fault Emma for taking this opportunity for gratification. If nothing more, it will give her a memory to savor all her life."

"Well, I hope she doesn't find that the result is more substantial than a memory. That would be awkward."

"One night? Don't be silly, husband. How long did it take for us to conceive Emma?"

Wilbourne's face turned red.

Patricia grinned. "That's my point, Howard." She took his arm. "And think on this: we're blessed. Those two young people are going to give us some very handsome grandchildren. Now let's go out to the portico and watch the river for a while and enjoy this fine morning."

—ᨓ—

Private Johnny Blane shivered in the Valley Forge night, more from the chilly westerly breeze than the actual temperature. He looked over to the east and was cheered by the thought that maybe—just maybe—he could perceive a slight lessening of the darkness. It was only his second time on sentry duty since he had joined the 7th Pennsylvania Regiment two weeks previously. On the whole, he thought the idea of standing sentinel in the middle of a large encampment was rather silly and resented missing hours of sleep. He pulled his coat more snugly around himself, moved his musket to a more comfortable position, and hoped the time would pass rapidly until the hour of his relief.

Then suddenly he became aware of a muffled noise. Puzzled, after a few seconds he discerned that it came from a campsite some distance to the north, close by army headquarters. He strained hard to make out what was happening. Listening sharply, he began hearing the sound of men calling out to each other and the clinking of metal implements and other noises. Presently he heard a horse whinnying loudly, soon answered by others. Now it was becoming less dark and, looking closely, he found he could make out the shadowy forms of men moving around in the darkness. It occurred to him that whatever unit was in the camp area was getting ready to leave. Johnny wasn't sure what he should do, but he had been told if anything unusual occurred to call the sergeant of the guard. Well, he figured, this *was* unusual. He shrugged and turned in the direction of the hut that housed the duty men. "Sergeant of the guard! Sergeant of the guard! Post three! Post three!"

There was no immediate response. He wondered if anyone had heard him and was trying to decide whether to call out again or just let it go when he saw Sergeant Harwood come around the side of the hut and stride toward his position. He was buttoning up his coat as he walked. Then he was surprised to see another figure walking behind the sergeant. He squinted, and realized it was the officer of the guard, Captain Tolley. The officer quickly caught up with Harwood just before they arrived at where Blane stood.

The sergeant said in a gruff voice, "Now Blane, why the devil are you calling us out just before dawn, right here in the middle of Valley Forge?" He laughed and said mockingly, "Are the redcoats suddenly upon us?"

Johnny bit his lip. Had he been mistaken to call for the sergeant? Was he about to get dressed down? But he pointed up to the camp where all the movement was taking place. "Look over there sergeant. Something's goin' on. I thought you might want to know."

Both the sergeant and the captain, now standing right beside the young sentry, turned and stared.

After a few moments, Harwood said, "Damn, Cap'n. He's right. They're pulling out."

Tolley nodded "Indeed. Looks like it's everybody. They're hitching up all the wagons."

"Shit, sir!" exclaimed the sergeant. "Look at that—even Mrs. McGraw's teamsters are getting her wagons ready to move!"

Now it was definitely getting on toward morning twilight and Johnny could see things more clearly. He made out a line of dragoons standing to their mounts and a formation of foot soldiers all dressed in hunting shirts, with black caps turned up in the back. They were all wearing their packs and other accouterments. As he watched, a sergeant called the shirt men to attention and then ordered them to shoulder their firelocks. Immediately after came the order to march. They wheeled into a column of threes and turned onto the road heading eastward through Valley Forge, all of the men silent, only the tramping sound of their marching feet audible. In just a few moments the column was passing no more than thirty yards from where the three men stood. An officer, dressed in hunting shirt and black hat like the others, rode on a tall, long-legged horse at the front.

Following the foot soldiers came several wagons, and behind those walked a gaggle of women and children. They were followed by what Johnny realized were two troops of dragoons. Then there was a gap, and another group of wagons began passing. He saw that they were four great Conestogas with six-horse teams, led by two smaller wagons. Both of the leading wagons carried several women as passengers.

Harwood commented, "Well, Captain, wonder when we'll be seeing Colleen and her girls again?"

Tolley smiled. "No telling, Sergeant. In any case, it's sure we'll not have much time for them anytime soon."

Johnny was puzzled by the talk of the two older men. Screwing up his courage, he asked the captain, "Sir, what does all this mean?"

Tolley looked over at Blane and then winked at the sergeant. "Lad, it means that when you get off of guard, you should make haste to write your mother a letter."

"Sir? Write my ma a letter? I don't understand. Why?"

"How long have you been in the army?"

"Just been here for a fortnight, sir."

"Well, you might not get a chance to write your ma again anytime soon." He raised his eyebrows and looked at Blane ominously. "Maybe *never.* And she might just like to have something to remember you by."

The sergeant put his left hand on Blane's shoulder and pointed to the marching column with the other. "Them soldiers are Washington's Guides. Mostly border country men from Virginia, Maryland, and South Carolina. And if they're leaving—lock, stock, and barrel—it can't mean but one thing: the redcoats are out of Philadelphia."

Tolley nodded. "Lad, the Guides are Washington's own scouts. They wouldn't be leaving unless the campaign is beginning, and they're going out to track the British. And that means our time here in the Forge is over; we'll be getting our orders to march soon, maybe today."

Harwood stared out after the column, which was well past them now. "Aye, Blane, the Captain's telling it to you straight: when the Guides march, the army follows."

The End of
Fetching Captain Henry

Author's Historical Notes

Readers of the Forbes Road and Rebellion Road Series will perceive that this installment is something of a departure from previous practice for the two series. While this book is the fourth novel of the Rebellion Road Series published, it skips over two critical years of the Revolution since the events of the previous one, *Freedom at Gwynn's Island.* The normal practice has been to tell the story in sequential order. In fact, the original intent was for the two-year period of the Revolution from late 1776 to 1778 to be covered by two novels. However, in the course of researching and drafting *Freedom at Gwynn's Island,* I became intrigued with story of Patrick Henry's wayward son, John, and decided to skip ahead and spin a tale woven around the events of his recovery. Readers of the series can anticipate that I will fill in the gap in forthcoming books.

As has been the practice in the preceding novels of the series, below are some notes to provide historical background behind the storyline of the book and confess where fictional departures from events and the actual timeline have been taken to facilitate the telling of the tale. The reader may well have discerned that there are five main strains in this novel, specifically, (1) the Henry family triangle, (2) marriage among the gentry, (3) the partisan war in New Jersey, and (4) the Continental Army at Valley Forge in the spring of 1778 and the action to recover John Henry, and (5) the British situation in Philadelphia and Mary's relationship with Barrett Northcutt and Howe's mistress, Elizabeth Loring. Below is historical amplification of each of those strains.

Historical Background on the Henry Family Relationships, the Recovery of John Henry, and Marriage among the Gentry in Eighteenth-Century Virginia

The Henry Family. For reasons that should be obvious, most biographies of Patrick Henry have little if anything to say about the triangle between Patrick, Dorothea, and John. Not only that, those which do mention John's relationship with Dorothea and his departure from the army are contradictory. Here are the facts and some suppositions about the relationships.

(1) Dorothea was born in either 1757 or 1755, with the former date the most frequently reported. The only known portrait of her was made when she was elderly. However, there is a painting of her eldest daughter as a young lady, who is understood to have born a striking resemblance to her mother. If that is accurate, Dorothea was indeed a raven-haired beauty.

(2) Several articles about Dorothea's life mention her involvement with John Paul Jones while he was in Virginia before the war, and it is a major subplot in the 1959 movie *John Paul Jones*, which starred Robert Stack as Jones and Erin O'Brien as Dorothea. It is easy to understand such a situation, for although Jones never married, he was as effective with women as he was in naval warfare. However, at least one reference is skeptical that the relationship actually took place.

(3) Before Patrick took an interest in Dorothea, she had some relationship with Henry's oldest son, John, who was deeply infatuated with

her. Whether it was a matter of formal courtship or merely social involvement is uncertain. Then John joined the army, initially serving as a cavalry officer, but then transferring to serve as an artillery officer. It is supposed that he left expecting to return and resume his relationship and perhaps ask for Dorothea's hand.

(4) Patrick had lost his first wife and John's mother, Sarah Sheldon, in early 1775. Then Sometime in late 1776 or early 1777, the elder Henry met and became enamored of the raven-haired beauty Dorothea and negotiated the betrothal with her father, Nathaniel Dandridge, who obviously considered that marrying his daughter to a governor was more advantageous than to an artillery captain. From Patrick's point of view, it was essential that he, as governor, had an appropriate and genteel first lady. Given that the Dandridges were among the premier families of Virginia society, it also enhanced his status and influence, as a man who had come up from something of a hardscrabble background. The betrothal to Patrick was announced in early 1777. The marriage ceremony occurred October 8, 1777, shortly after Dorothea's (probable) twentieth birthday. Patrick was thirty-nine at the time.

(5) The extent to which Patrick knew about his son's involvement with Dorothea is not clear.

(6) Young John was informed of the marriage sometime just after the Battle of Saratoga (ended October 8, 1777). Shocked, he sank into deep despair and disappeared after carrying out his duty in the battle. Some reports say the reason he left was that after two years of fighting, the bloodiness of the war had deeply affected him, particularly after walking the field at Saratoga and being shocked at

the number of dead. One essay postulates that he had developed a case of what we now call PTSD. I don't see any conflict here; it could easily be a combination of emotions—frustration in love and disillusionment with war—which built up into a climax that sent John into a tailspin.

(7) Patrick, in a confidential and emotional letter to George Washington, appealed to the general to use his good offices and military assets to locate John. As indicated in the narrative, Washington destroyed the letter. In spring 1778, Washington by some means located young Henry at an inn in Elizabeth, New Jersey, close to British-occupied New York City, despondent and financially broke. Then the general, whether through his espionage network or some other channel, provided resources and transportation to John to enable him to return home.

(8) As indicated in the story, Dorothea was indeed pregnant with Patrick's first child by her by the time that John would have arrived in Williamsburg. Ultimately there was some form of reconciliation between father and son, and Patrick gifted John one thousand acres of land to build his own plantation and start a new life.

(9) Even though the marriage of Patrick and Dorothea was an arranged affair, it appears there was considerable passion between the two. The alliance produced eleven (!) children, a prodigious number even in an age of large families. Reportedly Dorothea was a loving mother not only to her own children, but to the youngest three of Henry's six children by his previous marriage. By all reports—and despite her youth—Dorothea, beautiful, smart, and endowed with the polite manners of the gentry, carried off her duties as first lady of Virginia in a capable and gracious manor. She was held in much esteem throughout the state.

So much for the historical part of the story. Now, obviously Wend Eckert's mission to rescue John Henry as portrayed in the narrative is fictional—the fights, the spies, the role of Northcutt and his henchmen. The timing of the fictional action to locate and return John is somewhat later than the actual date, which was in late 1777 or early 1778, not late spring 1778. But the reader will have observed that our narrative does take into account as much of the real story as is known.

Marriage and Dowry Matters among the Gentry. In the mid-eighteenth-century Tidewater Virginia, matrimonial arrangements within the landed upper class were quite structured and formal. The practical purpose of marriage was the solidification or enhancement of influence, wealth, and reproduction through the merger of families. Usually unions were between families of similar rank, but occasionally had the effect of elevating one member in social status. That was the case between Patrick Henry and Dorothea Dandridge. Dorothea came from a wealthy and land-rich family recognized as one of the most influential in Virginia. Patrick had risen from the lower class by means of his self-taught status as a lawyer, election to the Burgesses, his prowess as an orator, and accumulation of political power as the Revolution advanced. But before he achieved influential status as a politician, he had worked as a village storekeeper and tavern manager. His elevation to governor was the ticket to marry into an old established family such as the Spotswood/Dandridges, and the marriage essentially cemented Henry's status as part of the gentry.

Dowries were an important part of the marriage arrangement. The dowry represented the bride's family's valuation of the young lady, and could be made up of money, physical property, land, or enslaved individuals. It remained the bride's property through the marriage, although the husband took control of it. If something happened to end the marriage—death of the husband or in rare case divorce or other legal separation—the dower share went back to control of the woman. As discussed in the first chapter, Martha Washington's first husband died after a few years of marriage, and she then had control of both her dower share of his estate as well as the inheritance that would go to the children on their maturity. When she and George married, the dower amount and children's share passed to the control of Washington. Interestingly, the tradition that the bride's family arranges and pays for the wedding is a holdover from the dowry customs of the gentry.

The Partisan War in New Jersey

Partisan Bands. "Partisans" was the name given to unofficial militias and bands of renegades on both sides during the Revolution. They were the forerunners of what we call "guerrillas" in modern warfare. The British called *all* rebel militias partisans because they considered that militia organized by the states had no legal standing, the only legitimate militias being those loyalist forces formed by the British. From the time of the battle of New York City in 1776 through much of the northern war, New Jersey was contested territory, with certain areas loyalist and others with substantial patriotic sentiment. The roads and geographic corridor between New York City and Philadelphia had heavy British presence, for it constituted the line of communication between the two occupied cities. In this disjointed environment, numerous loyalist partisan bands, often of mixed ethnicity, thrived and received logistical and weapons support from the British military. Many plantations were ransacked, and former enslaved men took their revenge on the masters. The following reference is a summary of military action in New Jersey: Norman Desmanais, *The Guide to the American Revolutionary War in New Jersey: Battles, Raids, and Skirmishes* (Busca, 2011).

Derivation of Captain Tigh. The fictional Captain Tigh depicted in this narrative has his origins in a historical individual, one Titus Cornelius, an African slave owned by a certain John Corlies, a Quaker who possessed a farm near Shrewsbury, Monmouth County, New Jersey. In 1775, at age twenty-one, Titus escaped from the farm. While on the run, he heard about Virginia governor Lord Dunmore's November 1775 proclamation freeing slaves if they joined the loyalist cause (see the preceding novel, *Freedom at Gwynn's Island*). The young African, now going simply by the name of "Tye," made his way to Virginia and joined Dunmore's Ethiopian Regiment of African Americans, where because of his intelligence, initiative, and imposing size (he was over six feet in height), he was soon made a sergeant and became one of the mainstays of the unit. When Dunmore was driven out of Virginia at Gwynn's Island in the summer of 1776, the remnants of the Ethiopian Regiment were transported by ship to New York, where they were converted into a unit of Pioneers (engineers and laborers) used to construct fortifications. From this and other sources, Tye recruited a partisan company of Africans, supported by the British with weapons and other military accouterments, which became known as the Black Brigade. Titus was now known by the honorary title of "Colonel Tye," and his unit, probably the most effective of the partisan bands, raided rebel farms and plantations, gathering foodstuffs, livestock, and other supplies that were provided to the British Army. Tye's campaign lasted until 1780, when he was wounded in the hand during a skirmish. Within two days the wound became infected, and Tye developed tetanus and gangrene and died.

Valley Forge and the Continental Army

Foraging for the Valley Forge Encampment. Most people have heard about the privations of the winter at Valley Forge: near starvation, disease, bitter weather. What is not so well known is that the worst period was rather short, from November to December 1777, and that the situation got steadily better starting in January 1778. The lack of provisions was not because food and other supplies weren't available; in fact Valley Forge was surrounded by highly productive farms. Rather, as an economist might say, the local farmers were intent on maximizing their own utility. That meant that they were much more eager to take their goods to Philadelphia and sell them to the British, who paid in hard coin. They wanted nothing to do with the Continental Congress's worthless paper money. Moreover, the army's logistic system established by Congress, riddled with inefficiency and corruption, couldn't provide sufficient provisions from other parts of the country. Washington, not about to sit by and let his army starve, changed the game plan. He appointed his "go to" general, Nathaniel Greene, to the position of quartermaster and told him to get provisions by whatever method necessary. Greene's first step was to organize foraging expeditions in the areas around Valley Forge. Some of these featured brigade-sized formations of troops seizing chickens, cattle, grain, flour, and other edibles. Confiscated farm products were ostensibly paid for with vouchers to the Continental government. At the same time, Greene, who had been a successful businessman before the war, worked to make the army's supply system functional, improving the organization and arranging for provisions to be shipped in from more distant areas so as to eventually make the foraging sweeps unnecessary. In the narrative, Wend and his Guides had logically formed the tip of the spear in Greene's forage operations. A definitive reference for Greene's activities is Ricardo A. Herrera, *Feeding Washington's Army: Surviving the Valley Forge Winter of 1778* (University of North Carolina Press, 2022).

Women at Valley Forge. There were numerous women of the camp (and their children) present. Senior officers' wives, most of whom rarely marched with the army on campaign, journeyed from their homes for winter encampments throughout the war. Once the provision of supplies had improved, there was a very active social season among officers and their ladies, with parties and balls as alluded to in the scene with Caty Greene in the opening chapter. At the same time, recognizing the hardships the enlisted men were facing, many of the officers' wives spent their time knitting warm garments and stockings for the men. Martha Washington made a point of traveling to be with George in winter encampments and did visit with the different officers' messes at Valley Forge. Thus her fictional visit to Wend would not be out of line, particularly given the subject she wished to discuss.

Von Steuben's Contribution. High school textbooks touch on Baron Von Steuben with a line or two that simply says he taught the army to drill or march. Indeed, he's known as the "Drillmaster of Valley Forge." But the truth is he did much more than that; in fact, he taught the army to fight using the European tactics necessary to defeat the British in the open field. Moreover, he reorganized the entire army for more effective field operations. Before Von Steuben, officers and sergeants often got their units in formation for battle by pulling or pushing the soldiers into the proper position. After Valley Forge, the units could deploy, form battle line, and perform drill like a professional force. But Von Steuben also reformed the army's units into effective tactical formations. The regiments/battalions of the army were of irregular sizes, depending on status of enlistments or battle losses over time. A regiment might be a hundred men, or it might be five hundred. Von Steuben dictated that no formation of mainstream infantry should go into action with less than 180 files in its battle line. A "file" was two men, one behind the other in the battle line. Thus he was saying that the minimum size for an infantry battalion should be 360 rank and file, exclusive of officers and sergeants. To achieve this, he formed what could be called composite battalions for tactical purposes. He would combine two or more small or skeleton units into one for battlefield action, under the senior commander. Administratively, each unit would retain its independence, unit designation, and colors, but they would march and operate in the field and in battle as a single tactical battalion. He also reformed the army's brigade structure, making them more uniform in size and organization. Thus, due to Von Steuben's work, and with Washington's avid support, a new army marched out of Valley Forge into the Monmouth campaign. The British spy system largely missed what was happening. There is a story, which I will summarize for brevity, that Lord Cornwallis, commanding a division of the British Army as it marched northward from Philadelphia toward New York, was appraised by a dragoon troop commander that a rebel formation was approaching from behind a hill. As the general and the cavalry officer watched, a brigade of troops emerged into view on top of the ridge, marching in column. Then with great precision they deployed from column into battle line. Since they were at some distance, it was not immediately clear that they were rebels. Cornwallis responded to the dragoon officer, saying that he must be mistaken. He motioned toward the brigade and, to paraphrase, said, "Sir, look how they display (meaning how they marched and deployed). Sir, those are regulars (i.e., British troops)!" Then a gust of wind blew the unit's flag out, showing that it was clearly American. Cornwallis, stunned, reportedly said something to the effect of, "Well, it seems the rebels have been attending to their business over the winter." Von Steuben's activities in the Revolution and afterward are covered in the following book: Paul Lockhart, *The Drillmaster of Valley Forge: The Baron De Steuben and the Making of the American Army* (Smithsonian Books, Harper Collins, 2008).

The Legion in the Revolutionary War. In this narrative, Wend Eckert leads a mixed horse/foot unit called the Legion of Continental Guides. While the Guides is a fictional outfit, similar legions were quite popular in the war. As in Eckert's command, they were what we would in modern terms describe as a *combined arms unit*. The typical organization called for three companies of cavalry and three of infantry. Moreover, often a small battery of mobile artillery was appended. But in reality, the mix varied based on the availability of dragoons versus foot. At least in part, the legion came into being because of the shortage of suitable and trained horses for dragoon regiments. For example, early in the war the British 16th and 17th Light Dragoons had trouble mounting all of their men, so foot companies of dismounted troopers were formed to support the cavalry element. Whatever its origin, the legion was soon found to be an extremely useful unit, particularly in the Southern Campaign in the latter years of the war. There they were often used to operate independently for reconnaissance, raiding, and as a nucleus of regulars to support and stiffen formations of local militia raised to meet a contingency situation. Wend's detachment acted that way in the fictional skirmish at Wallen Farm, when it interacted with militia and farm hands to defeat the band of partisans. Many of the most famous outfits of the war were legions, including the loyalist Queen's American Rangers and Tarleton's British Legion. On the colonial side were Armand's Legion (formally First Partisan Corps), Lee's (Second Partisan Corps), and Pulaski's. Pulaski's Legion was unique, in that it was to consist of two troops of dragoons, one troop of lancers, a company of riflemen, and two companies of musket-armed light infantry. Then, making virtue of necessity, in the final years of the war, all four of the Continental Light Dragoon Regiments were also redesignated "Legionary Corps." Ostensibly each consisted of four mounted and two infantry troops. For further reading, the reference below discusses the organization and history of units in the Continental Army: Robert K. Wright, Jr., *The Continental Army: The Army Lineage Series* (Washington, DC: Center of Military History, 1983).

The Legion of Continental Guides. The fictional unit that Wend Eckert commands in this novel actually has a historical basis. In the army that Washington took to the battle of New York in 1776 was an outfit called Knowlton's Rangers. Washington formed it in August 1776 as a scouting, skirmishing, and spying organization under Lieutenant Colonel Thomas Knowlton. It consisted of 150 picked officers and men recruited from Rhode Island, Massachusetts, and Connecticut regiments. Perhaps its most well-known member was Nathan Hale, who was captured in the course of an espionage mission and hanged by the British, uttering the famous words, "I regret that I have but one life to give to my country." Knowlton himself was killed in battle on Long Island in September 1776. Under its new commander, Captain Steven Bolton, the unit served through the rest of the New York campaign but was captured as part of the Fort Washington garrison that surrendered on November 16, 1776, at the conclusion of the campaign. Thus, from a storytelling angle, it was logical to have Washington form a new unit to succeed Knowlton's command. In our narrative, in November 1776 he promoted Wend to major and combined three independent companies—the Frederick County Light Foot, the First Troop Palmetto Light Horse (both introduced in *Freedom at Gwynn's Island*), and the Ann Arundel Light Horse (from *Pursuit Through Chaos*)—into the

Legion of Continental Guides. This would have been done in time for the new unit to lead Washington's defeated army through New Jersey to the crossing of the Delaware River into Pennsylvania, which cut off Howe's pursuit and saved the army.

Cavalry Readiness in the Revolutionary War. Cavalry was important to both sides in the Revolution, but proved hard to maintain in the field, mainly because of lack of suitable and trained horses. On the American side, problems also extended to obtaining proper arms, accouterments, and horse tack. As stated earlier in the notes, the British sent only two regiments (16th and 17th Light Dragoons), but had trouble keeping them mounted and depended on loyalist units to supplement them, such as the British Legion and the Queen's American Rangers. Of the four Continental Army Light Dragoon regiments, it was rare to find one that was able to properly mount and equip more than 100 men while the organization authorization was for around 260. As described in the narrative, the cavalry brigade of Washington's main army was in such bad shape that it could not participate in the Monmouth Courthouse Campaign of 1778, which followed the Valley Forge winter Encampment. Washington's statement in the eleventh chapter, "Scammell, when I die, I tell you they shall find this want of good cavalry written on my heart," is something that he might well have said. I must admit that putting those words in the general's mouth reflects a bit of mild plagiarism, for they are a paraphrase of something the great British admiral, Lord Nelson uttered. In the aftermath of the Battle of the Nile (August, 1798), he is quoted as saying, "Were I to die at this moment, the words 'Want of frigates would be found stamped on my heart.'" Nelson was complaining that he was unable to locate the fleeing French fleet for he was short of frigates, which were the primary units used for reconnaissance in naval warfare, as the cavalry was in armies. However, it turns out that Nelson may have himself been borrowing from the Tudor Queen Mary I, who in 1558, famously said at hearing that the last English stronghold in France had been lost, "When I die, they shall find Calais written on my heart."

British Occupation of Philadelphia and Elizabeth Loring

The British in Philadelphia. While Washington's troops faced primitive conditions at Valley Forge, living in wooden huts in often inclement weather and facing food shortages, Howe's army was relatively snug in the city. Most of the men were comfortably billeted in private homes, many of which had been deserted by residents who favored the patriot cause and left the city when it became clear that the British would occupy it. Other vacant houses were broken up to provide firewood for the troops. However, numerous upper-class families, including those who ostensibly had sympathy for the cause of independence, socialized with the English officers. It was a matter of hedging their bets, since the outcome of the war was uncertain at that time, with the British seeming to have the upper hand. Thus we have daughters of the influential Shippen and Chew families involved with officers such as John Andre and Banastre Tarleton. Interestingly, daughters from each would in the end eventually marry American officers. As is well known, Peggy Shippen became the wife of Benedict Arnold (and was influential in turning him to betray the patriot cause), while Peggy Chew subsequently married Continental Army colonel John Eager Howard, who led the Maryland Line at the Battle of Cowpens and eventually became governor of Maryland. The Mischianza that Mary Fraser attended was probably the most extravagant—and most expensive—social event that had occurred in the colonies up to that time. As discussed in the narrative, it cost upwards of 3,300 British pounds, contributed by the army's officers. It was a tribute to their respect and loyalty to Howe, even though in England he was being criticized for not prosecuting the war aggressively and would, upon returning home, have to defend himself to Parliament.

The Intriguing Situation of Elizabeth Loring. There are three differing views regarding Betsy Loring's motivation and the actual type of relationship she had with William Howe.

(1) The relationship was not sexual, and as a young woman in her early twenties, Betsy simply enjoyed the glitter and excitement of social association with Howe and happened to be as avid a gambler as the general. Thus they spent much time together at social events and at the gambling tables. As one might expect, this is the position of the Howe family, as enumerated by biographer Julie Flavell in her book, *The Howe Dynasty*. Otherwise, few believe this to be the case. See Julie Flavell, *The Howe Dynasty: The Untold Story of a Military Family and the Women behind Britain's Wars for America* (New York: Liveright, 2021).

(2) Betsy was actually a patriot and was acting as a spy for the Americans, a *honey pot* in modern lingo, whose function was to distract Howe from aggressive action on the battlefield and pass information to the Continental commanders. There have been several essays/articles that advocate or touch on this idea. However, they are highly speculative, and no real evidence has ever been presented that would give this view credence. See Becky Lower, "Elizabeth Loring—Patriot or Loyalist?," July 19, 2019 (an article on the internet blog History Imagined: For Readers, Writers, & Lovers of Historical Fiction).

(3) She was indeed Howe's mistress, and she went into the relationship with the tacit or explicit approval of her husband as a means of reconstructing/recovering the wealth they lost in Massachusetts during the early days of the Revolution. Thus Elizabeth provided favors to Howe, and her husband was given the lucrative post of commissioner of prisoners as quid pro quo. This is the most frequent hypothesis and the position best supported by known facts about Elizabeth and the situation in which she found herself. It is certainly what most contemporary observers on both sides believed during the Revolution. In a time of arranged marriages and long, multiyear deployments by military officers and government officials, mistresses were frequent and had a certain level of acceptance in the society of the day. I have used this explanation of events in describing Elizabeth's actions in both this book and the preceding *Freedom at Gwynn's Island,* and it's essentially the story that she confesses to Mary Fraser in the tenth chapter. Probably the most exhaustive and well-documented discussion of Betsy Loring's background and relationship with Howe is an essay by Sean M. Heuvel in the book *Women Waging War in the American Revolution,* edited by Holly A. Mayer (Charlottesville: University of Virginia Press, 2022). Moreover, I think this explanation of her actions is supported by the fact that Elizabeth and her two early children were joined by her husband Joshua in England after the war, where they took up residence for the rest of their lives and produced three more children together.

Other Relevant Topics

Alcohol Consumption and the role of Whiskey in the Colonial/ Revolutionary America. Consumption of alcoholic beverages, including beer, ale, wine, and the harder varieties, was a major factor in life at the time—water was distrusted and liquor was considered healthful. In fact, most medicines contained a portion of alcohol. Soldiers were entitled to a daily rum ration and sailors were issued rum or watered down rum called grog. It's not wrong to say that the population in America of the 1700's contained a significant proportion of what we would now call functioning alcoholics. Before the Revolution, rum was the most popular "hard" liquor in the colonies. There were numerous refineries, particularly in the northern area, which distilled it from molasses shipped in from the Caribbean. Following the start of hostilities, the Royal Navy slapped a blockade on the American coastline and developing a substitute for rum became necessary. Small scale whiskey production had started in the colonies as early as the 1630's, but it rapidly came into its own on a large scale once the blockade became effective. The variety in the eastern settled areas of the colonies approximated what we now call rye whiskey, based on a predominance of rye grain, with smaller proportions of corn and barley. In the western backcountry, a variety based on a large portion of corn was distilled and over the years this would evolve into what we now call bourbon. After the war, whiskey continued its popularity and became a very profitable industry, with rum falling to second place. Thus with historical hindsight, it was easy to make our fictional characters Wend Eckert, Simon Donegal, and Edward Childers prescient enough to become early producers of whiskey. One historical figure who capitalized on the popularity of whiskey was George Washington. Interestingly, Washington had converted most of his agricultural production from tobacco to grain in the period between the French and Indian War and the beginning of the rebellion, mainly because he recognized the high costs of growing tobacco and its toll on the land. Then, in the late 1790's he hired a Scots farm manager named James Anderson, who understood whiskey production and convinced Washington to build a distillery. Anderson's son John became the chief distiller. After some experimentation, the Andersons settled on a formula of 60% rye grain, 35% corn, and 5% malted barley. The distillery soon became the most profitable endeavor of Mount Vernon and at the time of Washington's death, was the largest whiskey production facility in Virginia. In that year, the distillery produced 11,000 gallons resulting in a profit of $7,500, a fortune at that time. Some background on whiskey production in revolutionary America can be found in an article by Mary Miley Theobald entitled *When Whiskey Was the King of Drink* (Colonial Williamsburg Journal, Summer 2008, Available online at the Colonial Williamsburg website.) An interesting source about Washington's business and agricultural endeavors is Edward G. Lengel, *First Entrepreneur: How George Washington Built His and the Nation's Prosperity,* (Da Capo Press, 2016).

Washington's Crush. During the discussion between Washington and Wend in the first chapter regarding John Henry's response to his father's marriage, Washington admits that he once had a youthful obsession with a young lady who was beyond his reach. That woman was Sarah Cary, known to all as Sally, a beautiful lady who married George William Fairfax, and thus became part of one of the wealthiest and most prominent families in the colonies. Sally Fairfax and her husband resided at an estate named Belvoir (Much of it is now Fort Belvoir of the US Army), which was adjacent to Mount Vernon. Washington's brother Lawrence was a close friend of George William and often took his younger brother on visits. George quickly became enamored of lovely and vivacious Sally, who was three years younger than himself, and took every opportunity to be in her company. In 1756, Washington came home sick from duty in the French and Indian

War and Sally came over to Mount Vernon and stayed for a lengthy time to nurse him back to health. Her husband was in England at the time. There has been some speculation, unsupported by any evidence, that their relationship may have gone beyond friendship during this period. Later, during the Forbes Campaign to take Fort Duquesne at the Forks of the Ohio in 1758, then Colonel Washington wrote several letters to Sally, at least one of which some researchers consider was a circumspect, carefully worded profession of his love. Sally's response was to brush it off with a routine letter in return. The friendship continued even after Washington's marriage to Martha, with the two couples often visiting each other at their neighboring plantations. It ended when the Fairfaxes left on a visit to England in 1773 and never returned due to the outbreak of the rebellion. A quick read reference on the subject is David S. and Jeanne T. Heidler, *Sally's Secret: He Destroyed Her Letters, She Saved His,* (Blog article at "heidlers", www.djheidler.com). A detailed investigation of Washington's early life, including his relationship with Sally Fairfax can be found in a biography by Peter Stark, *Young Washington: How Wilderness And War Forged America's Founding Father* (Harper Collins, New York, NY, 2018).

Acknowledgments

I'm very grateful to many individuals for their assistance in producing this installment of the Rebellion Road Series. Pamela Patrick White extended permission for the use of her painting, *First Honors:Order of the Purple Heart* for use on the cover and promotional activity. We had six "beta" readers for this manuscript, including my son Michael, cousin Francis Tananis, and friends Dick Batiste, Spencer DeJarnet, Carolyn Hays, and Winona Pitts, all of whom provided sincere and useful feedback. This is the fourth book for which Elite Authors publishing organization performed the design work for the cover and interior and the copy editing of the draft and digitally formatted the finished product for upload to the online booksellers. The professionalism and production values of their members are superb. Above all, I want to thank the loyal readers of the Forbes Road/Rebellion Road Series, many of whom have contacted us on the Rebellion Road Facebook page or the Forbesroadbook.com website to express their appreciation, support, and suggestions for the content of the novels.

Robert J. Shade
Sunshine Hill Farm
Reva, Virginia
February 2024

www.ingramcontent.com/pod-product-compliance
Lightning Source LLC
Chambersburg PA
CBHW051952060726
47506CB00011B/83

* 9 7 9 8 2 1 8 3 6 4 1 8 2 *